OF FLAME AND FURY

FAE OF TÍRIA, BOOK 3

K. A. RILEY

CERTIFIED 100%
A.I. FREE!

Cover Design:

https://thebookbrander.com/

For the summer readers who occasionally seek shade and solitude.

PREFACE

A brief caution for my readers—more particularly, my readers' *parents:*

I have written quite a few books by now, most of which are suitable for younger readers. I try to keep my language light, though there are occasional acts of violence on the pages—and occasionally, a beloved character meets their untimely end.

I've had messages asking if certain books are "spicy," and in this case, the answer is yes.

So I leave it to you, the parents, to determine what level of "reader discretion" you wish to exercise when it comes to this book and series.

For those of you delving into this world, thank you for coming on this journey, and I hope you enjoy!

KARiley

SUMMARY

WHEN LETA'S sister Lyrinn disappeared after the Blood Trials, there was only one thing for Leta to do: seek solace in the arms of Prince Corym, the most powerful mortal in Kalemnar.

For months, she's been living in the palace and reveling in a life of wealth and luxury. The prince wants to marry Leta. The king approves.

On the surface, life is almost perfect.

So why, all of a sudden, does Leta want more than anything to flee the palace?

Overcome by vivid memories that are not her own—confusing visions of some other woman's life and love—Leta gets herself as far from Corym and the palace as she can. She may not yet know what the visions mean, but it's clear that her fate is far more complicated than she'd ever imagined.

As she flees, little does she know she's being tracked by a Fae—a sell-blade with a past of his own and a wall of ice around his heart.

The force that brought them together will prove powerful, relentless, and devastating. But will their attraction heal them... or shatter them both?

MAP OF KALEMNAR

To Tíria

The Rise

Dúngar

Castelle

River Dún

Belleau

The Lake of Blood

Domignon

Marqueyssau

THE MORTAL REALMS OF KALEMNAR

CHAPTER ONE

DOMIGNON
   Two Weeks Earlier

A sea of stars twinkled throughout the sky as evening rose over the palace's beautifully groomed gardens.

Prince Corym's features, illuminated by the full moon glowing high above us, were as handsome as ever. The deep scars torn into his cheeks did little to detract from his perfection. If anything, he now appeared more warrior-like than he had before the accursed Blood Trials had fallen upon the realms —and before a certain High Fae had tried to tear him to shreds.

He looked, I told myself as I stared up at his sculpted jawline and elegant cheekbones, like a leader of men.

"How long has it been, Leta?" he asked, seeming to read my mind as he slipped his fingers under my chin, drawing my eyes to his. "How long have I had the privilege of calling you my own?"

My own.

I let out a bashful laugh. "I'm not sure, your Highness. Many days, I think...yet too few. If I had my wish, we would spend a thousand evenings doing just this, then a thousand more."

"What a sweet sentiment," he cooed. "You really are perfect, aren't you?"

My cheeks heated, and I pulled my chin down, my gaze veering to the ground.

Back home in Dúnbar, no one would ever have accused me of shyness or modesty. I had always been confident to a fault—at least, that was what my sister Lyrinn had always said. She had never missed an opportunity to mention how skilled I was in the fine art of manipulation, of using my feminine wiles on every unsuspecting fool who came my way.

And who was I to argue? I had always had a strong instinct for taking advantage of men and boys, for using my looks to turn them into blithering dolts.

Not that I was arrogant enough to think myself the most beautiful girl in Kalemnar, or even in our small hometown of Dúnbar. The truth was, *any* young woman could seduce a man if she convinced him she had something to offer him.

Men were gluttons for the promise of a touch, a kiss. And if they thought they might receive even more, it was easy to get them to do absolutely anything.

They were not exactly hard to read.

But for some reason, I found myself a self-conscious thing in Corym's company. Over time, I had devolved into an insecure, blushing version of myself. I had never thought to question why, after all the weeks and months I'd spent with him, I still found myself timid and awe-struck in his presence.

When I'd first met him, I hadn't been nearly so tongue-tied as I was now. I had seen him as a prince, and a handsome one. But in those days, he hadn't intimidated me as I might have expected. Then again, I'd been under the impression that he and Lyrinn would live happily ever after.

All of Kalemnar had thought so, for that matter.

The plan had been simple.

Step one: He—and she—would win the Blood Trials together, defeating every Champion in their path and claiming victory for the realm of Domignon.

Step two: They would marry, and they would be granted all the Gifts of those who had fallen—which meant they would both be imbued with extraordinary powers, which they would eventually pass on to their children.

But the plan had crumbled to dust when my sister had fled Kalemnar along with the High Lord Mithraan...

The very Fae who had left the deep slashes that now marred Corym's cheeks.

I had not witnessed the moment when my sister had vanished along with the Fae—the moment when the Trials had ended abruptly with no winner named.

I had never imagined I would end up in Corym's arms at the end of it all. Nor had I ever pictured my sister rejecting a prince in favor of a Fae.

"Take a guess," Corym said, drawing me away from my thoughts and urging me to answer the question still hanging in the air between us. "How long do you think you've been living here in the palace?"

"Several moons," I told him, my brow furrowing with confusion. Why did it matter so much to him how long I'd been here? Was he weary of me already? "Eight or nine moons, maybe. I've lost track of time, truth be told." I offered up a beaming smile when I added, "All I know is I've never been so...so..."

Happy.

That was the word I had intended to utter.

Yet now as it came to the tip of my tongue, I froze.

Why, all of a sudden, did I feel as if I was forcing out a lie? After all, I *had* felt genuinely happy these last weeks, settled in as I was. I'd been accepted by King Caedmon and Queen Malleen as a member of the royal family. Surely it wasn't a stretch to say I was *content*, if not downright blissful.

But as I gazed into Corym's eyes and tried to force the word from my lips, it came again—a hint of some nagging reluctance, a flash of doubt, as though I were slowly coming to some long-brewing realization.

"Oh—I see what this is." Corym clicked his tongue and moved closer, pressing a gentle kiss to my forehead. "After all this time, you're still upset about your sister's betrayal." He said it lightly, as though he were talking about a little spilled milk. "Leta, Lyrinn never deserved you. She proved as much when she ran off with that bastard Fae. You're better off without her—as are we all."

The words were a blade twisting in my side. More than a few times over the weeks I had told myself the same thing— that I was better off without Lyrinn, that she had turned her back on me. After all, she hadn't so much as sent a letter to explain why she'd chosen to leave me so abruptly.

She had never sent me word of her whereabouts.

It was like she'd forgotten me entirely.

"She abandoned you, my love," Corym added, as if to plunge the blade in just a little deeper. "You know it as well as I do."

The prince and his father had told me repeatedly that throughout the Blood Trials, Lyrinn's behavior had grown more and more erratic. That she had turned unpredictable, violent, hostile. She was, they insisted, no longer the sister I had once known and loved.

Heartbroken, I had simply nodded and accepted King Caedmon's and Prince Corym's word as a brutal truth.

In the palace, I wasn't allowed to watch the Trials. The king had insisted that seeing my sister do battle for her life could prove traumatic. "You're such a lovely creature," he'd insisted. "I would hate to see that pretty face marred by tears."

At the time, I had taken his words as a kindness. The king was only being protective, I'd told myself. And ever since the day the Trials had ended, I had reveled in his son's protective nature, too.

But now, as I inhaled the night air, some long-dormant part of my mind was waking, pushing back against Corym's words.

A voice came to me from somewhere far off—yet so close that it seemed to echo inside me.

He's been lying all along.

Lyrinn would never *abandon you willingly.*

What in the hell was happening to me? Why was my faith in Corym faltering? This was the prince who had held me so often as I wept into his shoulder, the one who had reassured me with promises that he would look after me and keep me close for the rest of our lives...

Why did his words now ring so false?

I'm just tired, I told myself. *Once I've had some rest, it will all make sense again.*

My lip quivered slightly when I finally replied, "I suppose I'm still stunned that Lyrinn would simply leave without a word. It's not like her. She and I were so close. We—"

"We all do strange things for love," Corym interrupted sharply with an arrogance that implied he spoke from a wealth of experience. "You must accept that she is lost to that horrid Fae now. Forget her, Leta. Our future is here, yours and mine—and we will start our own family soon. You're of age now, after all."

A shock collided with my mind, like icy water on a hot day. "I'm...*what*?" I stammered. "What do you mean, of age?"

Corym laughed. "Why do you think I was asking how long you'd been with me? Did you not even notice your eighteenth birth-date passed by some weeks ago?"

My jaw dropped open, and I simply stared at him. "I..."

There had been a time not so long ago when I had thought my birth-date a distant point on the horizon. But as it turned out, our father had lied to Lyrinn and me all our lives about the timeline of our coming into this world. It was his attempt to protect us both from ever having to compete in the Blood Trials. All my life, I had thought myself younger than I was, and so had my sister.

Still, no one had actually told me what my true birth-date *was*. I had no way of knowing when I'd turn eighteen.

As it turned out, Corym and King Caedmon knew my age better than I did.

"I know, I know," the prince said. "I should have let you in on the secret. I suppose I wanted to keep it a surprise. I thought perhaps we could celebrate two special dates at once."

"Two?" I asked, overcome with sudden nervousness.

"Yes. My parents and I have decided it's time you and I married." The prince was beaming now, his gleaming teeth impossibly white in the moonlight. "War is coming, love. The Fae are roaming our lands, threatening mortals in every corner of Kalemnar. The people need some good news to allay their fear."

"I see. Yes...of course." My head was spinning, though with pleasure or pain, I wasn't entirely sure.

I would soon become wife to the heir to the throne of Domignon.

I would one day be queen.

It *should* have been the most wonderful news in the world. I should have been ecstatic.

But as I pulled my eyes up to Corym's once again, a sudden, horrifying desire to flee overtook me. I wanted nothing more than to be far from him. Far from Domignon.

I need to get myself to a place where I can breathe again.

With that thought, as if some distant god were answering my prayers, a force took hold of my mind, clenching reality tight in its grip. The world around me—the prince, the gardens, everything...vanished.

I found myself standing in a beautiful field of long, swaying grass, the sun shining high in the sky. A swell of pleasure permeated my every inch as I inhaled the air, taking in the distinct, lovely scent of wildflowers.

Instantly, I was filled with nostalgia for the land surrounding me, though it was a place I was certain I had never been.

In the distance, a figure appeared. A man, I thought, though his features were blurred and impossible to make out. He began to walk toward me, picking up his pace as he approached.

I reached for him, desire consuming me as if I knew exactly who he was and why he was important to me.

"Faster," I commanded aloud, the word strained with need. "Come to me, my love."

Except the voice that spoke the words—it wasn't my own. It was smoother, lighter, more carefree than my voice had ever been. It was like music on the wind.

This moment in time—this place, this memory, for I knew by now that it *was* a memory—none of it was mine.

I looked down at my body—the curve of my waist and breasts. Suntanned hands, one of which had what looked like a ring drawn onto one of its fingers.

This...wasn't me.

Who was this person—and how in the hell had I found my way inside her body, her mind?

I strained to get a better look at the man, to make out his features. But when he drew closer, just as his face began to clear...

The memory ceased.

Once again, I was standing in the darkness of the palace gardens, my head swimming with disorientation.

I looked down to see that my hand was on Corym's arm, my fingers digging in tightly.

"Leta?" he said softly. "What is it? Are you all right?"

"Did you...did you see that?" My voice was quiet, frantic. "Did you see him?"

"Him? Who are you talking about?"

My eyes widened. Gods, it must have been a waking dream. "I...I..." I stammered, looking for a way to explain my madness. "I think it was just a bit of dizziness. It's passed now."

As much as I wanted to deny it, though, the truth was far more complicated than a mere dizzy spell. More complicated than any dream that had ever unfolded in my mind. Some force had torn me from the time and place where I stood with Corym, and inserted me into someone else's body, into another realm entirely.

I had seen the world from some stranger's vantage point. I had experienced her senses, her memories. Her *life*. For a moment, I had become her. But who she was or where, I couldn't say.

"Dizziness," Corym repeated, almost giddy. "Gods be good, it's happening."

He was grinning like a child about to receive a gift.

"I'm so glad my discomfort amuses you," I snapped, a jolt of annoyance quickly canceling out my confusion and fear.

I couldn't remember a time when I'd ever been annoyed with Corym, not once since the Trials' end when he had offered me shelter and comfort in the wake of Lyrinn's disappearance.

But now, he felt like an irritating stranger rather than the young man I knew and cared for so deeply. His chiseled features had lost their allure, and the scars torn into his flesh seemed to glisten as if freshly opened by a wild animal's talons.

Whatever had just happened to me, whatever spell had been cast, I could now see the prince for what he really was.

You're laughing at me, I thought, glaring at him. *Taking pleasure from my pain and fear.*

"You misunderstand me," he said with a chuckle at seeing the icy expression in my eyes. "That is to say, I *am* pleased. But only because dizziness is a symptom of the Coming of Age. You, Leta, are about to come into your powers."

"No. That can't be right." I shook my head, pulling away from him. "My sister came of age at *nineteen*—that's when they say the Gifted come into their powers. If I'm only eighteen, then it's impossible."

"Leta..." Corym said, reaching out to touch my cheek. But I found myself drawing back, repulsed by his touch.

A voice twisted through my mind then, the same strange, distant, feminine lilt that had emerged from my mouth during the dreamlike vision.

~Corym is not to be trusted. He has lied to you for many moons, Leta. He has manipulated you, just as all mind-benders do. Free yourself of him, and you will begin at last to see the truth.

I shook my head, wanting to deny it. But even now, I could feel him pushing his way into my thoughts.

A gasp escaped my throat and I reeled backwards, reaching for something—anything—to support me.

~You can feel it now, can't you? You can feel him bending your will to his, taking hold of you.

"Leta?" Corym half-whispered, easing toward me. "Are you all right?"

Had I really been so blind that I had let him violate my mind daily since my arrival in Domignon? Had Lyrinn known what he was? Was that why she had left...

"I...I don't..." I muttered. "I don't understand what's happening to me."

Taking my arm, he guided me over to sit on a nearby stone bench. I inhaled a deep breath, fighting against the voice that had infiltrated my mind.

Perhaps I really was going mad. Or maybe it was some unforeseen fear of commitment that was warning me off the man I was convinced I had grown to love. Was this what they called *cold feet*?

But I knew in my heart that the truth was far darker than a case of simple doubt. As though a mask had been yanked from his face, I could see Corym clearly.

He was not all goodness and light. He was not kind. And under a superficial layer of near-perfection, I could feel a malevolence radiating, something ugly and cruel.

He had charmed me, convinced me for weeks on end that I cared for him and he for me. But I could feel the truth between us now, rising cold and rigid like a stone barrier between us.

~You must leave this place—and do not look back, whatever the cost. You cannot let him take hold of the powers when they come to you.

"Powers," I breathed in a half-whisper.

"Leta!" Corym snapped. His tone lacked the false sweetness I'd grown accustomed to. In an instant, the prince had turned into an open book, a vile collection of lies scrawled on its pages.

And all this time, I had failed to see him for what he was.

"I'm sorry," I said, forcing myself into the role of vulnerable, naive young woman once again. The woman he had carefully crafted over the course of several moons—one who submitted to him, who laughed at his jokes and blushed at his compliments. A woman who did his bidding every single time he commanded her, without even realizing she had become nothing more than a subservient plaything.

"I suppose you're right," I said with a meekness that nauseated me. "It's just the Coming of Age playing with my mind."

He looked skeptical for a moment, then smiled, relaxing his shoulders. "You know," he said with a sly grin, "a chambermaid here in the palace once told me the Coming of Age can hit early if a Gifted is close to finding their true mate. Which would explain what's happening to you. You and I are meant to be, Leta, and what's happening to you now—it's proof of our bond. This is fate."

~*True mate?* the hostile voice in my mind laughed. *He is no one's true mate but his own. That fool is incapable of love.*

"It's late," I blurted out, wincing as I forced the voice away, telling myself it was a fabrication of my exhausted mind. "Perhaps we should get some sleep."

Corym contemplated the proposal for a moment, then nodded. "Yes," he said. "Perhaps you're right." He offered me his hand, which I took, and helped me up from the bench. "To think that soon, you and I will share a bed. We will marry within a fortnight. We mustn't waste any time. Like I said—war is coming, my love."

I managed another smile, though it felt like a brutal strain of unwilling muscles. "You...really think a wedding would make our people happy?"

Corym looked taken aback by the question. "Of course it would," he said. "Royal weddings always bring the people together, and we need the support of Kalemnar's mortals if we're to conquer the invading Fae. You and I must present a united front—one that will strengthen our people's resolve. The Fae mustn't win this war. I won't allow it."

"Of course not, your Highness," I said.

The truth, I was too addled to think about war, weddings, or anything else. All I wanted was to get away from him—away from those conniving eyes I had once found so handsome, from the voice that now grated on my nerves.

Exhaling, I took Corym's arm and accompanied him back to the palace's eastern wing, listening as intently as I could while he told me of his plans for our future. The children we would have. The guests we would invite to the palace, and the balls we would throw for all of Kalemnar's noble families.

"If war really is on our doorstep," I said, "is it prudent to plan a wedding—not to mention a *family*? Shouldn't we wait a little for things to settle down?"

Corym laughed, unfazed by my hesitation. "Don't be silly—my father and I have already begun planning the festivities. And don't worry—when our armies venture out to do battle, you will be safe from harm here in the palace. I won't let anything happen to you."

My throat tightened when I asked, "And if I should wish to leave Domignon?"

Corym gripped my hand with a violent possessiveness that set off a chorus of alarm bells in my gut.

"Leave?" He let out a derisive snort. "Why would you ever wish to leave this place?"

"If I should wish to find my sister..."

Corym squeezed my hand still tighter and turned to me, anger clear on his features in spite of the night's darkness.

He pulled my palm forcefully to his chest, looked me in the eye, and said, "You will never seek her out, Leta. Do you hear me? Never. She is the enemy now, and you need to get that through your thick, obstinate skull."

And with those words, I knew I had no choice.

I would flee Domignon in the night, and never look back.

CHAPTER TWO

A veil of darkness fell over the woods.

Shapes shifted and moved in my periphery, and skeletal outlines of gnarled trees snatched at my cloak. Their limbs seemed to draw nearer with each gust of cold wind, threatening to imprison me and hold on like grim death until the King's Guard came to drag me back to the prince.

For two weeks I had hiked east, trying to put as much distance as possible between Domignon and myself. I had stayed off the roads, knowing full well that Corym and the king would send search parties to seek me out.

On my last night in the palace, after Prince Corym had escorted me to my chamber, he had whispered into my ear that he couldn't wait until our wedding night.

"I'll tear the dress from your body and taste every inch of you," he'd said—or rather, threatened. "You've never known the pleasures I will inflict on you."

Only a day earlier, his words would have sent a shock of pleasure pulsing through my body. I would have lain in bed that night, fantasizing about his lips, his eyes, his voice...

But the change that had come over me on the night of my departure had rendered him repellant. My former anticipation of a beautiful life had clashed with bitter disappointment, as if I'd taken a sip of wine only to realize it had long since turned to vinegar.

That night, after I'd bid him goodnight and sealed my door, I had packed a rucksack full of the most inconspicuous clothing in my possession, donned a long dark cloak over a white blouse and leather trousers, and, after swiping a little food from the kitchens, I had left the palace through one of the underground tunnels that led to a trail in the woods east of the city.

Lyrinn and I had spent much of our childhood roaming the lands around Dúnbar, the forests, the riverlands. We knew that territory as well as we knew one another's faces. But I had never been freed from the shackles of Domignon to explore the surrounding forests, thick and dark as they were, and teeming with vein-like, narrow paths and roads used by brigands, outlaws, and traders alike. I had no idea where I was going.

But at least I was free.

I was a fugitive—a young woman fleeing a young man most girls in Kalemnar would have slain to call their own.

For days on end, I stumbled down trails, forded ice-cold rivers and creeks. My mind was plagued daily with swelling oceans of memories, most of which belonged to someone else. I spent hours each day assaulted by clouded visions of a lover I had come to know intimately…and yet I still didn't know his name, nor had I ever seen his face with any clarity.

His scent, his touch, on the other hand—those were as familiar to me as my own features reflected in a mirror.

Admittedly, there was some small part of me that enjoyed those brief moments of madness—some hidden compartment in my mind that anticipated them eagerly, breathlessly. They were an escape from my hunger, my thirst. A respite from all I had left behind.

It was exactly two weeks and a day after my departure from Domignon that I found myself stumbling into a decrepit stone hunter's cottage set deep in the woods. My head swam as the sky darkened outside, my thoughts a chaotic jumble.

I dropped to the floor, my back to the cold wall. Exhausted by the mere thought of the coming dawn, I let my head droop down. But even as I willed myself to sleep, my body was met with fierce resistance from my mind.

A flash of light overtook the dark space around me, and then I found myself once again stepping into a life that had never been mine.

I surrendered to the sensation, memories flooding my mind of a life I had never lived, a love I had never known…lands I had never seen. In an instant, I was somewhere beautiful, in a strange, distant place far from anywhere familiar.

I was in the stranger's body, lying in the same field I'd often seen in my visions, laughing joyfully as the sun beat down in delicious golden rays. My fingers twisted in the grass, reveling in the cool of its blades against my skin. Glancing down at my torso, I saw that I wore a long, white dress of cotton, a few buttons open at the chest.

A familiar, masculine voice came to me on the air, and my lips turned up in a delighted grin.

"There you are," he said, deep and smooth, a smile stroking the syllables.

When I replied, the other woman's voice emerged from my throat once again. I had realized some time ago that the timbre of it was very much like mine—but not entirely the same. Perhaps, I thought, it was only the accent that differentiated us. Hers was like music, lilting and melodic. Mine was the accent of a northerner, the daughter of a blacksmith in a small town.

"What are you going to do," I asked in that foreign lilt, "now that you've found me?"

"Wouldn't you like to know?"

A moment later he was over me, his hands pressed to the ground on either side of my face.

He was silhouetted by the brilliant sunlight, his hair a random mess of dark brown waves as he pressed down and kissed me, his lips soft, warm. It was unlike any kiss from Corym or anyone else I'd known. There was something deeper in it, something desperate, as though we were both quenching a cruel thirst.

When he slipped away and rose to his feet, I moaned at the painful sensation of loss. I craved more. Needed more.

"Don't leave," I pleaded in the mystery woman's voice. "Just stay a little longer. Be with me."

He laughed gently, shaking his head. "You know perfectly well that I have no choice," he told me. "He's got a job for me, and you know the consequences if I don't oblige. Soon, you, too, will be working for him—and you'll understand."

"Don't remind me," I laughed. "I'm not looking forward to it."

He leaned down, cupped my cheek in his hand, and kissed me. "You'll be brilliant," he said. "Just as long as you don't give in to his more...violent...demands."

With that, the memory ceased and I fell into a deep, dreamless sleep at long last.

I woke as the sun rose.

I pushed myself to my feet, another bout of disorientation overtaking me. This time it was brief, and I wondered bitterly how much truth there was to what Corym had said about the Coming of Age hitting early when one's true mate was close.

"There is no way in all the hells that bastard is my true mate," I muttered, an acrid laugh working its way up my throat. If he was, then I may as well find a nice sharp branch and stab myself through the skull with it.

To think that in the blink of an eye, I had gone from believing I loved him to despising him. Somehow, I had turned into a version of my older sister—jaded, cynical, untrusting of anyone and everything.

For the first time, I was beginning to understand why she had spent so much of her life hidden in the shadows of a cloak.

People are horrid, and I want nothing to do with them.

Still, as I left the ruined house behind me, I reminded myself that there was something now roaming the lands of Kalemnar that was far worse, even, than people.

Fae.

Those deceitful beings were far more powerful than mortals. Crueler. Stronger in every conceivable way.

It was one thing to evade the king's men. But eventually I would need to make my way north toward the realm of Castelle —days and days of trudging through thick woods—while *also* avoiding the Immortals who now roamed the southern realms.

When I first laid eyes on Mithraan, the High Fae who took

Lyrinn from me, I had admittedly found him beautiful. And though Lyrinn had pretended not to trust him, or for that matter even to *like* him, I had seen her eyes when she looked at him. From the start, I knew the power he held over her.

Perhaps he loved her—if indeed Fae were capable of it. But he tore apart what remained of my family, and for that, I wasn't sure I could ever forgive him.

Pushing thoughts of his odious kind away, I hiked for an hour or so before I came to a fork in the narrow dirt path I'd been following, and had to choose whether to head right or left.

Without thinking too long and hard, I chose right—east. It would lead me toward the still-low sun and the realm of Marqueyssal. A land that I had seen only once, and only briefly, before the Blood Trials had begun. Some of King Caedmon's men had brought me there to a small chateau, ostensibly to keep me away from Lyrinn. They had told me it was for our protection, though I had never fully understood the necessity of separating us.

Still, I looked forward to seeing the realm again. Its landscape was beautiful, dotted with ancient fortified towns and cities built on picturesque, rolling green hilltops.

As I trudged along, the sun rising higher in the sky and the temperature along with it, I warned myself of the need to find a spring or a lake soon. My flask was nearly empty, and I wouldn't get far without water.

It wasn't long before the sound of a trickling brook met my ears. I tore off the trail, pulling my sack from my shoulder and grabbing my flask. I drank down its contents, and once I reached the stream, replenished it and did the same three times over to fill my empty stomach.

It was only when I took a fourth refill that I noticed a set of fresh footprints in the mud on the other side of the narrow creek—then, rising to my feet, spotted two more sets.

"*Balls,*" I muttered under my breath, sealing the flask and stuffing it back into the bag. I leapt across the creek, staring at the tracks, trying to sort out where they'd come from and where they were headed. Perhaps, if I were lucky, they would guide me to the nearest town.

I followed as long as I could—they meandered east, as I'd hoped, but did not rejoin the trail I'd been walking on. Instead, whoever had made them seemed to have forged their own crude path, snapping branches as they went, only leaving the odd intact print in the earth. The prints were large enough to tell me they belonged to men, and I cautioned myself. *Don't be too eager to find them. Men who creep through the woods generally aren't the friendly kind.*

When I came to a small clearing, I stopped, crouching at the base of a broad tree, and assessed my surroundings. A small pile of blackened rocks and charred wood lay at the clearing's center, a plume of smoke rising from fresh embers.

Someone had recently made camp in this place, and by all appearances, they hadn't left too long ago.

After pondering my options, I chose to circumvent the clearing to the western side then turn north in hopes of staying out of sight. But even as I rose to my full height and took my first step, the snap of a nearby branch cut through the stillness behind me.

I ducked down again, my eyes hunting around for the source of the sound.

Another crack came—this time from somewhere directly in front of me.

Another, to my left. This one was even closer.

My eyes darted this way and that in search of a fallen branch or large stick, or anything else I could use as a weapon. But when another snapping twig met my ears, I leapt into the clearing, hoping with everything in me that my legs could carry me fast enough to evade them—whoever *they* were.

"If you don't want a knife flung into your back, darlin'," a voice cried out, "you'll stop right there!"

No King's Guardsman would refer to me as "darlin'".

That, at least, was something to be grateful for.

Determined to call his bluff, I kept running, hoping to conceal myself among the thick wood on the clearing's far side. I'd lose the men then find a cave, a fallen trunk—anything. Once they realized I wasn't worth sweating over, maybe they'd leave me alone.

But just as I hit the clearing's edge, a large, broad-shouldered figure stepped out from behind a tree trunk and grabbed me by both shoulders, squeezing so hard that I shrieked in pain.

I looked up to see a vile face, all stubble, warts, and yellow-brown teeth as his lip curled up into a gruesome snarl.

He wasn't a Fae, at least—but he was hardly appealing. He smelled foul, like he spent his days flaying animals' flesh from bone then slept in the festering remains. It was impossible to force away the expression of disgust etched on my features.

"Good job, Grimm," a voice bellowed from behind me—the same one that had threatened me earlier.

A hand grabbed at my hood and yanked it down, which elicited a chuckle from deep within the speaker's chest.

"Let's have a look at her, shall we? Let's see what we've snagged."

The large man who had snatched me turned me to face his friend. Though the second man was admittedly much smaller, he still felt menacing. His greasy, matted hair was in dire need of a wash, so filthy that I could not tell if it was blond or brown.

Then again, I didn't much care.

"Pretty thing," he said with a grimace and a repugnant lick of his dry lips. "Ain't she?"

With the question, he looked over his shoulder, and I could see that a third man was now stalking across the clearing. This one was tall and rail-thin, his shoulders stooped as if he were perpetually making his way under a too-low doorway. "What do you think, Bale?"

"Very pretty, yes," the tall man said, scratching at his dirt-coated neck. "What we gonna do with her?"

"What the hell do you think?" the leader asked, grabbing at my shirt to yank it upwards, revealing far too much of my abdomen for my liking.

"Don't you touch me!" I snarled, throwing myself backwards—which only resulted in planting myself firmly in the large oaf called Grimm's chest.

The leader let out another laugh.

"I don't recall offering you a choice, Missy," he said, reaching out once again. This time, he peeled my blouse up slowly as the oaf held my arms against my torso, and I winced, tears burning my eyes as I felt my skin being exposed inch by inch to the cool air.

"Please," I moaned, my voice withering. "Stop."

The leader, smiling to reveal a set of jagged, blackened teeth, shook his head. "Nah," he said. "I don't think I will."

I sealed my eyes tight, willing them away—as if denying the sight of the three men meant this wasn't really happening to me.

It will be over soon, I told myself. *Whatever this is—eventually it will end, and they will move on.*

My heart hammered, blood thudding in my ears. I opened my eyes and watched as the leader drew the knife at his belt and pressed it to the place between my breasts, a cruel smile on his cracked lips.

Streaked with something brown and foul, the blade was

caked with animal hair. If he sliced into me and the wound didn't kill me, the ensuing infection surely would.

"Please," I said again, my voice a pitiful whimper. "Let me go."

"Oh, I don't think so," he replied. "You have something my boys and I want, and we plan to take it from you—and then take it again and again until you die with a smile on your face."

As tears burned my eyes and my heartbeat raced, I barely heard the deep voice that cut through the surrounding woods, swirling around my captors and me like a twisting net.

"If you three bastards don't wish to die slowly as I peel your flesh from your bones, you'll release her right now."

CHAPTER THREE

THE LEADER LET GO of my shirt and spun around.

"Show yourself, stranger!" he called, thrusting the dagger into the air before him. "Come forward so I can slit your throat quickly."

"From the looks of your weapon, it will take you a week at least to make a dent," the voice replied.

Across the clearing, a hooded figure in a dark green cloak stepped out from among the trees, his face masked in shadow. He had broad shoulders, muscular legs, a pair of worn leather boots.

"The prick doesn't even have a weapon, Boss," the tall, narrow man called Bale said, chuckling. "Look! No hilt, no quiver!"

I looked over, my heart sinking as I realized how right he was. My would-be savior had not so much as a dagger on him under that cloak; I could see his belt now, and unless some secret knife was cleverly concealed under his tunic, there was not much hope for me.

The "boss" pressed his dull blade to my neck. The fact that it wasn't sharp enough to immediately penetrate my flesh rendered the sensation all the more horrifying. It would take some effort to slice into me—not to mention a large dose of malice.

"You really think I am without weapons?" the solitary cloaked figure asked, his voice a feral growl. "Are you three miscreants quite certain of that?"

My captor dropped his knife to his side and laughed, doubling over as the shadowy figure moved slowly toward us.

"Listen," the greasy leader managed to say between exaggerated chortles of amusement when he'd straightened up and grabbed me once again, his foul breath meeting my nose in hideous puffs. "Piss off back into the woods, and I'll spare you. If you want to stick around to play with our spoils, fine. But I get a go at her first. She's fresh meat, she is. I can *smell* the purity on her."

With that, he made a show of groping for my breast. I yanked myself away, snarling a warning at him.

I peered over at the cloaked stranger, who raised his chin so that I could just make out the glow of two bright blue eyes under the shadows of his hood. He stopped when our eyes met, his entire body tightening as if he had just suffered a blow.

At seeing his face, I too tightened as a violent jolt of lightning passed through my bloodstream.

Those eyes...they were otherworldly and beautiful. I knew at once that he was an Immortal from the Fae-lands.

But there was something more—something that set my mind spinning in a vicious torrent of confusion.

Before I could stop to think what it was in his features that called out to me so forcefully, the self-proclaimed "boss" grabbed me and pulled me closer, drawing my eyes back to him.

"Now, let's get started, shall we?" he asked, tearing at my shirt as I let out a cry and struggled again to free myself.

The man's violation was the final straw for the bright-eyed

infiltrator. A look of wild rage set itself on his face and he shot a hand forward, fingers splayed. No physical weapon was unleashed from his grip, but I could feel a surge of unseen power, violent and terrifying, careen through the air toward where we stood.

My assailant dropped to his knees, grabbing at his throat and gasping for breath, strangled by an invisible set of hands.

His large companion pulled a short sword from a sheath at his waist. But instead of threatening me with it— it seemed he'd forgotten I even existed—he stepped forward to stand protectively between his leader and their foe.

Each of us stood frozen in our own world of fear as an enormous set of glowing blue wings sprang from the intruder's shoulders. Beautiful and terrifying at once, they looked like an intricate web of glass and lace combined—except that they seemed crafted entirely from light itself.

"Hells!" Grimm stammered. "You're...you're a fekkin' *Fae*!"

"Of course he is, you dolt," the lanky man sneered. "Didn't you see those eyes? He's the devil himself."

The Fae lowered his hood, revealing the entirety of his face for the first time, as well as a pair of tipped, shapely ears.

But it was his eyes that still drew me in—a piercing blue the color of the sky on the most cloudless of days. So exquisite, set as they were against dark brows and lashes. His cheekbones and jaw were as defined as sculpted marble. I gawked at him, convinced that I knew him intimately...yet I knew it to be impossible. I had only seen a few Fae in my life. Mithraan, his fellow Champion from Tíria, and an assortment of white-haired Lightbloods.

As for this one, I was beginning to think I'd conjured him into existence. Manifested him from the deepest fantasies of my addled mind.

No, I told myself. *He is not some pleasant dream. He's a nightmare, and I need to get myself away from him—now.*

"Are you hurt..." he asked, his eyes fixed on me, seemingly unconcerned with the others. "Leta?"

My legs almost gave out under me.

Leta.

How does he know...

My cheeks heated with shame, sudden horror ravaging me to think that he...*whoever* he was...was seeing me like this. He was so beautiful, so powerful.

He was perfect.

Meanwhile, my shirt was torn and filthy. I was so weak, so vulnerable, a pathetic victim of some half-drunk mortals. A damsel in distress—the very thing I despised.

I should have fought the bastards off when they'd first come at me. Taken the leader's blade and stabbed him with it.

Anything.

But as my cheeks heated and I stared into the stranger's eyes, the shame I felt was quickly replaced with a combination of anger and resentment.

Who are you, a Fae, to make me feel this way? I should despise you, not revere you. You may be beautiful, but you're also deceitful and cruel, just like the rest of your kind.

One of you stole my sister away, and I will not soon forgive that transgression.

The greasy man was still writhing on the ground as he struggled for breath, and the other two were too distracted to grab hold of me.

I should have fled then and there.

But try as I might, I couldn't bring myself to tear my eyes from the Fae's. It was impossible to convince myself he was odious when all I wanted was to move toward him, to touch his face...to ask if he was real.

I was frozen, desire taking hold of me against my will, against every fiber of my being.

Those eyes. Where had I seen them...

And then it came to me.

He's the memory.

The lover I've seen so many times in my mind's eye.

But how...?

A violent moment of disorientation overtook me then, and the clearing began to spin wildly in my periphery. But even as the world twisted and gyrated, the Fae's face never distorted. He was the only clarity in a landscape that was altering violently—one that had grown unstable, unpredictable. He was a beacon in a torrent of madness.

Who are you to me? I cried inside my mind as I pressed my palms into my temples. *Why is this happening?*

"Are you all right?" he asked, taking another step closer. "Did they do anything to you?"

The spinning world stopped. I shook my head, bowing my chin slightly, my shame growing unbearable. Against my will, the urge deepened inside me to run to him, to plant my face in his chest, to ask him to hold onto me.

He felt like comfort—like someone I had known long ago. Someone who had sheltered me from many a storm.

No. I don't know you. You belong to someone else.

Gods, what is happening to me?

Was he another mind-bender like Corym? Was he stalking me, toying with me for his pleasure?

Had the visions that had assaulted my mind come from *him*?

"I'm fine," I growled.

"Good," the Fae said, turning to the others. "Now, do any of you have anything to say for yourselves?"

"*I've* got something to say," the boss rasped in a strangled voice, wiping his forehead with the dirty sleeve of his shirt as he pushed himself to his feet. It seemed he had already forgotten how easily the Fae had subdued him. "We're going to slay you then dine on your flesh, Bàrrish."

"Bàrrish," the Fae echoed. "A term I have not heard in many years. It's good to see you mortals have not forgotten your old prejudices."

I had heard the same slur over the course of my life, in public places, spoken by men with foul mouths. When Lyrinn asked our father once what it meant, he'd told her it was an insult in the old tongue that meant "Outsider"...only in terms that were far less charitable. The insinuation was that Fae were lower than dirt—that they were death itself, festering, rotting corpses preserved for eternity.

"If the Fae still frequented these lands," our father had told us, "no mortal would dare say it to their faces. Not even the king himself. It's a swift way to beg for a death sentence."

And yet, the foolish leader had spoken it to the cloaked Fae as if it was nothing.

I watched as the men, newly energized by the insult their leader had hurled, advanced on the Fae, striding across the space between them as if they had entirely forgotten what he had done to one of them only moments ago.

When they were mere inches from where he stood, the Fae raised his hand, and with a mild gesture of his fingers, he stopped all three of them in their tracks.

Cries of agony rang out as a twisting series of barbed vines sprang from the earth, braiding together to grab at the men's legs and hold them fast. I watched in horror as blood seeped from wounds in their thighs, the vines' long thorns tearing into their flesh.

"Now, tell me again," the Fae said, stepping toward the leader, "what you were planning to do to the young lady."

The leader let out a forced laugh then said conspiratorially, "You know perfectly well. Come now, look at her. You're a red-blooded male, and she's a sexy little thing. There's plenty of her to go around, don't you think? Admit it—you'd pay a pretty penny to shove your dick into her tight little—"

Before he could finish the vile sentence, the Fae moved on him like a gust of wind, so fast that my eyes couldn't take him in.

The leader was on the ground again, the Fae standing over him. The dull blade was now clenched in the Immortal's hand, pressed so hard into the man's throat that he began to choke all over again.

When the Fae's eyes met mine, the dagger lost its dull patina and turned bright silver, its edge sharp as any blade I'd ever seen in my father's smithy. In the Fae's expression I saw pure hatred when he turned back to the men—a malevolence more frightening than anything on the mortals' faces.

He is going to kill them all.

And then, he'll kill me.

Without another thought, I spun around and sprinted into the woods.

Behind me, I heard the screams of a man in agonizing pain —sharp, horrifying cries of someone who knew death was coming for him. Then, when it ceased, another strangled cry, and another. The wails of animals being taken out one by one for slaughter.

Finally, with a sudden harrowing halt, the sound cut off and the woods fell silent.

Terrified that the Fae would catch up to me, I raced as fast as my legs would carry me, branches slicing at my face as I went, my eyes blurry with tears.

A flash of blinding light disoriented me again, and I stumbled, falling to the ground. Reaching a hand out desperately until my palm met the trunk of a nearby tree, I twisted around and sank against its supportive girth.

After a few seconds, I tried to rise to my feet, telling myself I needed to keep running. But each time I attempted to push myself up, I simply fell back down, my body devoid of strength.

A flash of memory came, and another, and another, all layered atop one another. His face, his body, his mouth on mine. The taste of him, the feel of him...all at once.

Gods.

The scent of him.

I tried to push him away, to rid myself of the scourge of the cruel attraction eating at my mind. But the harder I tried, the more vivid the memories became, as though they were pushing back against me, fighting against my very will.

I saw my hand on his chest, my fingers scrambling to undo his shirt. The feeling when he reached out and—

Stop! I cried inside my mind. *Stop. No more.*

But still my head swirled, and I was helpless, alone, confused and unable to tell reality from the dreamscape that had ensnared me.

The woods darkened as a wave of dark clouds gathered overhead, and rain began to fall hard and fast. Though it was not yet mid-day, it felt like the depths of night when someone reached down and picked me up, one impossibly strong arm locked behind my back, the other behind my legs.

And then he was carrying me, cradling me to his chest.

"No," I murmured. I was too weak to yell, to cry out, my mind and body overtaken by whatever sickness was destroying me from within. "Put me down. Leave me alone...please..."

The words came in a whisper, nothing more, and my captor ignored them.

He moved rapidly. I could feel the rain beating against my

cheeks as I tried to refocus my vision. Trees whipped by, green shadows in my periphery, dream-like and surreal.

After a time, we entered a shelter of some sort. A house, or perhaps a cabin. I couldn't tell anything about its features, other than that it had walls and a roof. My head was still swimming, my mind a bizarre jumble of dreams and reality.

None of it made sense.

Then, for a moment, my vision cleared and I saw him—the blue-eyed Fae, his face so near mine that I could have reached out and touched his cheek, had I been brave enough.

My lips parted. Then I spoke in that voice that wasn't my own. *Words* that weren't my own.

"I thought I would never see you again. I thought—"

"Yet here I am," he replied, touching my cheek. His lips were curled into a rueful smile. "I knew it was you. I knew..."

His eyes were such a piercing blue, intoxicating and dangerous. Cold and warm at once, and impossible to read.

I shook my head, pushing away the entity who had invaded my mind.

"What do you mean, you knew it was me?" I cried, retaking control over my own voice. I pulled away from him, recoiling in fear. "I don't even *know* you. Please—leave me be. I don't want you near me. You—you frighten me."

"Forgive me," he said softly. He straightened up and backed away, pain etched on his features. "Yes, of course. You're right to be frightened. I don't deserve—" He closed his mouth, then, shaking his head, turned to leave.

"Wait," I said, stopping him before he could reach the door. "Tell me how you know my name."

The Fae shook his head, then disappeared into the darkness beyond.

CHAPTER FOUR

I WAS STANDING in a sunlit field of wildflowers. Only, it wasn't me.

Again.

The vision, like the others, was peaceful and dream-like. Bliss filled me as I breathed in the air, my mind overflowing with pleasant thoughts.

I began to walk, my fingers grazing long blades of grass, my face raised to the sun. I could feel its rays warming every part of me, strengthening me with each step.

This place—wherever it was—really did seem like some form of paradise.

"There you are," a deep voice called out.

I pulled my chin down and looked ahead to see a figure moving toward me. He was tall, with dark brown hair. At first, his face was a blur as usual, his features indecipherable. I couldn't quite find the strength to conjure him entirely; I could only tell that he wore a shirt of white linen and a pair of brown leather trousers.

"Yes. Here I am," I replied. *Whoever I am.*

"I'm so glad I found you, love."

With those words, his features finally came clear. He stepped closer, his smile immediately addictive. It was strange to see those lips curled up at the corner—lips I had examined thoroughly in the clearing—searching for any sign of friendliness.

It really is you, I thought, inhaling his scent. *The Fae who protected me. The one who brought me to the shelter in the woods.*

But who are *you?*

I opened my mouth to ask the question, but found my lips twitching into a reflection of his grin.

It's not your body, Leta. Not your memory. You don't get to control what happens here.

When the Fae was close, he pulled me to him, lifting me easily off my feet and spinning me around as he pressed his lips to my neck. My heart filled with a sense of delight, of wonder, at the feeling of his mouth, his arms. His touch, which was as real as any I'd ever felt.

Yet how could this be? If this wasn't my own memory, how did I feel it so acutely?

Without another word between us, his lips crashed into my own and I almost melted to the ground with the power and perfection of it.

The kiss was intense, filled with need, with desire.

But there was something else, too. A brutal, nagging fear that it could be our last.

It felt like I had tumbled off a cliff, and my hands were grasping for its edge to keep myself from falling into a fate from which I would never recover.

What's going to happen to him? To me? Or rather...to her?

Desperate to hold onto this moment, I inhaled deep as he slipped his fingers down my neck, then lower, pulling at the buttons on the blouse I was wearing.

My heart raced with a realization:

We were going to make love in this field.

I wanted it. Every part of me ached fiercely. My need was painful, destructive, almost cruel.

He sank to his knees before me, taking a nipple between his lips, and I raised my face to the sun once again as he lashed at it with his tongue, a hand slipping over my other breast, a moan escaping his throat.

He moved down, down, his lips on my stomach, then down farther until he had yanked my skirt up, his hand slipping between my legs to discover I was wearing no undergarments.

"Gods," he breathed, tucking his head under my skirt and taking in a deep breath. "I am going to devour you—and then, I'm going to—"

The sound of a high-pitched horn cut through the air. He leapt to his feet, his face turning sharply to the right, then he pulled away, a look of torment in his eyes.

"It's time," he growled, his voice clipped, and then he twisted away and ran. And all I could do was reach out for him, pleading for him to stop.

"You can't go!" I cried. "I need to know who you are—who *I* am. Please..."

But the words never exploded from my mouth. The vision ceased and once again, I found myself alone in the present. Damp, cold, and miserable.

Through a half-shattered window, I could see that the dark clouds had disappeared. Sunlight poured into the small cottage where I was now sitting, working its way through dancing dust motes that looked like tiny flakes of pure white snow.

In spite of the chill on the air, sweat coated my brow, my chest. My breath came in hard, desperate gasps as if I had just run ten miles.

I shoved myself up against the cool stone wall as I struggled to hold onto the memory and the emotions that had just assaulted me. They were more sensual, more powerful than anything I'd ever felt—and ironically, more real.

Were these vivid moments really just a symptom of my Coming of Age? Had this same thing happened to Lyrinn—strange, twisted bursts of pleasure mixed with agonizing pain? Had she seen Mithraan in her mind's eye, making love to someone else?

These memories—they can't possibly be real, I thought. *Maybe he really is twisting my mind just as Corym did. A sadistic trick for the Fae's own amusement.*

Prick.

Famished and determined to forget how his mouth had felt on my flesh, I reached into my rucksack--which had somehow managed to accompany me to this place—and took a few bites of stale bread and a swig of water, then, when I was convinced I had regained full control of my mind for the time being, forced myself to get up.

It wouldn't do to stay here. The Fae knew where to find me, which meant every minute that I lingered here put me deeper in danger. Though why he hadn't already killed me, I couldn't say.

No matter.

I would head for the nearest town. If I played my cards right, perhaps I could find my way into a warm, comfortable bed tonight. It was not difficult, after all, for a young woman to persuade a drunken man to offer her shelter—though after the debacle in the woods, I would need to proceed with caution on that front.

As I left the cottage behind and began what would undoubtedly turn into a long, arduous hike, I puzzled over the visions that had been haunting me. Pushing my way through the dense forest, I worked to convince myself they were nothing more than a vivid series of pleasant dreams.

But each time I tried to reassure myself, my doubt grew just a little stronger.

I had *felt* the cool air on my skin, smelled the scent of wildflowers, felt the cotton blouse against my chest. I could still recall the sensation of his fingers and his lips on my skin, leaving frissons of pleasure in their wake.

Even the most vivid, pleasant dream had never felt that good. Which meant the memories *were* real. I had stolen them... or else they had been gifted to me.

But who would ever grant me such a privilege and curse at once?

Over the next several hours as I slogged my way through the woods, the visions returned to me in the usual brief spells, but no answers accompanied them. Now and again, I had to grab hold of a tree trunk to steady myself while flashes assaulted me of the lover whose name I didn't know, of his voice, his caress... his lips on mine.

Occasionally, I found myself slipping my fingers over my neck where he had kissed me—or her—whichever of us it really was. I moaned softly as I recalled the sensation of his tongue tasting my own.

Was he my enemy? Or was he something else entirely?

Never had I been so desperate for answers—yet so terrified of finding them.

Never had I been so desperate to see someone again...yet so afraid of what might happen if I did.

CHAPTER FIVE

I HIKED FOR SOME TIME, stopping occasionally to take a drink from an ice-cold creek or to rest.

Here and there, I leapt at the distant snapping of a twig or the sound of leaves rustling with sudden, flittering motion, but whenever I spun around to peer into the depths of the woods, all I spotted was a bird or a squirrel going about their docile lives.

Over time, the visions subsided, giving way to vague doubts that they had ever occurred. Hunger, thirst, and fear had been wreaking havoc on my thoughts for far too long, and I told myself the so-called memories were merely a result of my addled mind.

Still, something inside me seemed...*altered* since I'd met the Fae in the clearing. I felt awakened, like a part of my mind had revealed itself—one that had been hidden from me all my life. The world seemed clearer, brighter, more dangerous...all at once.

"Stop it," I chastised, muttering to myself. "You're not having some incredible breakthrough. Nothing has changed except that you're definitely going mad. Chances are the lack of food and drink is playing with your mind even more than Corym ever did."

It was nearly sunset when I finally caught sight of several plumes of white smoke billowing up above the treetops.

A town.

I picked up my pace, tidying my long waves of red hair as best I could as I drew closer to what appeared to be an uneven stone wall in the distance. All I had to do was get past it, and I had a real chance at finding a welcoming place to rest for the night.

A bath would have been nice, a chance to wash my hair, to clean myself up a little before encountering people. But the best I could do for now was hide myself in the foliage and change into a long blue dress I'd stolen from the palace before I'd left— one not so elegant as to make me appear wealthy, but pretty enough to bring out the blue in my eyes and draw the gaze of any curious onlookers.

I pulled my robe back on over the dress, unwilling to reveal too much of myself too soon, in case I should be met by the wrong eyes.

The town, it turned out, was little more than a village, and it had seen better days. Its surrounding wall had decayed enough that I could step over it easily in a few places where it had crumbled virtually to dust.

Its stone houses, too, looked in desperate need of renovation. Thatched roofs sagged, half the windows were cracked or broken.

Still, as I made my way toward what appeared to be the main thoroughfare, I could see that the place was substantial enough to contain a small temple, a quaint stone inn, and a pub called the Gander and Buck.

Desperate for something to eat and drink, I headed straight for the pub, which was surprisingly warm and cozy on the inside. Wood beams accented the ceiling and walls, and a fire roared in a hearth at the pub's center.

Once my eyes had adjusted to the interior darkness, I slipped over to the barkeep to ask for a pint of ale. I left a solitary copper piece—one of the few I'd managed to swipe from the palace—before pulling my hood around my face and tucking myself into a table in a dark corner.

Like every pub I'd ever frequented, the place was occupied by sweaty, surly-looking men, some of whom lacked the majority of their teeth. Most were old and grizzled, their skin creased by years spent laboring under the hot southern sun.

Eyes shifted curiously to me as I seated myself and set my rucksack on the floor, peering out from beneath my hood to study the room's occupants. I scrutinized the lot of them one by one, trying to work out if there was a single candidate here worthy of my attention.

I chuckled under my breath as it hit me: I felt like my old self for the first time since Corym had taken hold of me with his mind control. He had turned me into someone I didn't know— someone submissive, unthinking. A malleable creature he could manipulate any way he wished.

But now, I was free at last...and it was my turn to do the manipulating.

All I needed was someone I could persuade—with a glowing smile—to offer me a little food, a bath, a night spent in their stable, even. At this point, I would happily have shared sleeping quarters with an angry donkey.

The best candidates tended to be shy, insecure young men —the kind who felt unworthy of any woman's company.

Unfortunately, the gathered crowd looked altogether too confident for my liking.

I spotted two young men sitting at a distant table, their eyes fixed on me as I pulled my hood tighter around my face, hiding myself in shadow while I assessed them. They were inoffensive-looking enough, I supposed, though their eyes definitely betrayed the transparent look of overly optimistic males.

One of them—the taller of the two, with a head of curly, dark hair—seemed intent on staring me down. Clearly, he was the leader of their two-person clique. He raised his chin when my eyes met his and sat back, crossing his arms in silent challenge.

Or perhaps I should have taken it as a warning.

As his gaze burned into me, the scars that lined my neck flared with a sudden shot of pain and I winced, pulling my chin down and taking a long drink in hopes that the pain would subside.

My hand reached for the sensitive flesh, my fingertips stinging with a shot of impossible heat.

It's not enough that I've lost my mind—now my body is wreaking havoc on me.

I sometimes forgot about the scars that had adorned my ears, my neck, and my shoulders since my youth—marks left behind by a fire that had nearly killed Lyrinn and me when I was only a baby and she was a toddler. But now, they seemed intent on reminding me of their existence.

As I touched my fingertips to my neck, my skin cooled down. I sighed with quiet relief, grateful for this one small mercy.

The shorter of the young men—a ginger-headed thing whose face looked like it had been pelted with freckles—elbowed the other, apparently taking the gesture as a flirtatious one. The tall one rose to his feet and strode toward me, a smile expanding over a set of dry lips.

All I needed now was to convince him to drink until he couldn't form words then take me home with him and pass out on the floor while I claimed his bed.

A gust of cool wind blew into the pub as the door opened, then closed again. Another customer escaping his mundane life. Another man seeking quick inebriation. I didn't bother raising my eyes to see who it was.

I had already located my prey.

When the young man reached my table, he stopped and stared down at me, drawing my eyes up to his. I had already decided to play the shy country lass—the "Oh, my goodness, sir, I'm lost in the wilderness and I have no bed for the night," role that had always driven Lyrinn mad when I used it on the visiting young men who occasionally ventured to Dúnbar.

"You *live* here," she would chastise with a laugh. "Several doors down from the pub. You really expect them to believe you're some vulnerable young thing who can't find her way home?"

"Whether they believe it or not, it gets me a *lot* of free ale," I would retort. For that, she never had a snappy comeback. She couldn't deny that my methods were effective.

Lyrinn and I were different in many ways, but perhaps most stark was my willingness to speak to strangers. For her, the very thought of it was torture. There was a time when I had suspected her dream life was one where she lived in a house in the woods filled with books...and perhaps a cat or two.

Neither her life nor mine had turned out as either of us had expected, had they?

"Who might you be?" the young man asked, his smile expanding over his lips.

"My name is...*Leonora*," I replied, the pseudonym slipping over my tongue as if I'd used it a thousand times over the years —which I probably had.

"Leonora," he repeated. "And what might you be doing in Daggut...Leonora?"

Daggut. So, that's the name of this forsaken place.

Figures.

"Just passing through," I told him, chin down, eyes peering up at his like a hesitant puppy's.

By now, the latest arrival to the pub had taken a seat at a table in the far corner. I was suddenly aware of him—too aware, as if his presence were larger and more forbidding than anyone else's. I glanced briefly over to see that his features were concealed in the shadows of a black hood, his chin down—but that was all I could establish without outright staring at him.

Fear assaulted me. Was this a scout for the King's Guard, seeking me out for the prince? Was he planning to drag me back to Domignon in shackles?

If so, I needed to get out of here, and quickly.

"Won't you have a seat?" I asked the young man, gesturing to the chair next to me. He took it, pressing his elbows to the table, and leaned in close.

"It's getting late," he said. "I suspect you're in need of a bed for the night. If that's the case, I might be able to help you out."

The good news was that his insinuation was clear as polished crystal.

The bad news? His speech, too, was clear...which meant he was irritatingly sober.

"I suppose I'll just stay at the inn," I said softly, my voice deliberately high and meek. "Though I don't have much money."

"You don't need money," he said with a chuckle. "Not if you come home with me. My friend over there..." He nodded over his shoulder to his red-haired companion. "We would very much like to offer you accommodation for the night. All we ask in return is a little...*appreciation* for our generosity."

He leaned in even closer, pressing his palms to the table and grinning, and for the first time I could see how stained his teeth were despite his relatively young age.

Lovely.

I found myself tightening defensively, wishing for a blade of the sort Lyrinn had always carried on her.

The stranger in the corner no longer felt like the most dangerous man in the room.

"I see," I finally replied, my voice lowering to a near-whisper. "And how, exactly, would I be expected to show my appreciation?"

The young man reached over and took the edge of my cloak in his fingers, pulling it aside to eye the dress underneath. Suddenly, I wished I'd worn something less form-fitting. The blue garment was too low-cut, revealing just enough cleavage that his eyes went wide as he ran his tongue over his chapped upper lip.

"Oh, I'm only proposing a taste," he replied. "Of you—and you of us both, of course. Beds don't come cheap in these parts, so needless to say, we'd want to dip our wicks as well."

With that, my act was over.

I was not here to sell my body. Only to pretend I might *consider* it.

It may have seemed like a small distinction, but it was an important one.

"No, thank you," I said sharply, pulling back and raising my chin. "I have no interest in your rancid *wick.*"

With a grunt and an animalistic baring of his teeth, he slammed his fists down on the table between us. I could smell sweat on him now—and something else, too. Something vindictive and retch-inducing.

"I don't think you're hearing me," he said, straightening up and gesturing, arms spread, to the pub's interior. "I run this town. Don't I, boys?"

A chorus of, "Teryns! Teryns!" rose up around us. The prick's name reverberated through the air like clanging bells.

"While you're within Daggut's boundaries," he snarled, "you'll do as I say. Or I will grant every man in this town a chance to take you twice, even if it kills you. Understand?"

As I stared daggers at the bastard, my scars flared again with a sharp, piercing pain—but this time it ran deep, as though my veins had caught fire inside me.

My flesh burned with rage, my body growing feverishly hot.

"No man commands me to offer up my body," I snarled, pushing myself to my feet, my chest heaving. "I am not your property, nor am I anyone's. Lay one finger on me, and you will *burn* for it."

I slammed my mouth shut, and my eyes went wide.

The words had certainly come from my lips, from my own throat...yet neither they nor the voice that had spoken them was my own.

They were...*hers.*

The voice from the visions.

Why would I say they'll burn for it?

What did that even mean?

Was I really intending to set the place on fire?

It was insanity. And yet, I knew in my blood and bones that it was exactly what I intended to do. I would burn this entire town to the ground, if that was what it took to keep Teryns and his vile friends away from me.

The distant voice came to me again as I struggled to catch my breath, to regain control of my rage-filled mind.

~You won't even need a torch to do it, Leta. That's the beauty of it. You have no idea what you're capable of.

I gasped in horror. Feminine and commanding, she was a devil tempting me to sin.

And the truth was, I *wanted* to. I wanted to hurt this man and any others who thought they could threaten young women without consequence.

I wanted them all to suffer.

As I stared Teryns down, my fists clenched so tight that my knuckles ached. He recoiled, pulling back with such a violence that he tripped over a rickety wooden chair and went crashing to the floor. He scrambled to his feet, pointing at me.

In my life, I had seen frightened men speak of murderous Grimpers and poisonous mist, of dead bodies, ghouls, demons.

But I had never seen the face of a man so terrified as he was, looking into my eyes as he did now.

"What the hell is wrong with you, girl?" one of the older men asked, leaping to his feet at a nearby table.

"She's possessed!" another man shouted, backing toward the pub's front door.

I glanced toward the grimy window beyond him only to see myself in a vague, misty reflection. I looked warped, misshapen —but I could see now that the scars lining my neck were glowing with light so intense that the pub's lanterns paled in comparison.

As my eyes moved down my body, I saw that my fists, too, were glowing bright.

"A Witch!" someone shouted.

"There's no such thing as Witches, you knob," a drunken man drawled with a dismissive wave of his hand. "She's probably just one of *them*."

"She ain't! Look at her! You ever seen one of them do *that?*"

Them? What did he mean by that?

"Grab her!" someone cried. "Take her to the town square! We'll tear her apart!"

With those words, every man in the place began to move toward me—including the hooded figure who had seated himself in the far corner.

He was taller than most of the others by at least half a head, and when he moved into the light, I took a step backwards, pressing myself against the wall.

There was no mistaking that jawline, those lips.

It was the Fae I'd seen in a hundred visions since I had left Domignon.

The Fae who had kissed me, touched me, filled me with desire...but only in my waking dreams.

Damn him for following me here.

He moved slowly, his chin low, eyes locked on mine. But he stopped at the room's center and watched as two men lunged at me.

The Fae crossed his arms over his chest and grinned, waiting to see what would transpire.

With an angry snarl, I yanked myself away and shot my hands forward, my fingers splayed. My arms shook, my breath tight in my chest.

I need to leave. I need to get out.

With those words tearing at my mind, a flash of white light illuminated the space so brightly that the tables and chairs vanished, as well as the men who had been calling for my death only moments ago.

The only silhouette I could see—the only clarity in the blinding scene before me—was the Fae, a set of glowing blue wings spreading out behind him.

"Go," he said calmly. "It's not safe for you here. These men will not be satisfied until you're lying dead before them."

CHAPTER SIX

I RACED toward the door and out, fleeing into the street beyond.

Shouts erupted behind me, but I didn't turn around to look. There was no need to confirm the angry mob that was now pursuing us both, thirsting for my blood.

Cries echoed off the façades of stone houses, spurring me on. People had begun to emerge from the town's homes—women, men, children, even. Shouts of "Kill her!" erupted from behind me, and one or two men leapt forward from their homes' doorsteps, trying to grab hold of me.

I had just swerved out of one large man's reach, stumbling forward with frightened tears staining my cheeks, when a set of muscular arms grabbed me from behind and lifted me off the ground.

We shot into the air with impossible speed, soaring first above the rooftops, then over the thick woods beyond. A moment of shock passed quickly as I realized what had happened, and I kicked my legs out, struggling against the Fae's grip.

"Let me down!" I cried. "I'd rather deal with those mortal asses than with the likes of you!"

"I suspect you don't *actually* mean that," he replied, his voice unemotional—though I was certain I detected a smile in it.

Cocky prick.

"I do mean it!" I shouted. "Land, and set me free. I want nothing to do with you or the mind games you've been playing."

His lips grazed my ear when he said, "Why would I set you free, Leta? You would only run off again, and you've already proven you're terrible at evasion and remarkably skilled at getting yourself into dangerous positions. Besides, you know as well as I do that mortal men are insatiable fiends. Setting you down around here would be like setting a wounded rabbit free before a dozen famished wolves and hoping they wouldn't feast on it."

"You're calling me a wounded rabbit?"

"Yes, I am. Except that a rabbit has more common sense than you do."

I could feel the heat of his chest against my back as his powerful arms tightened around me. Growling in frustration, I looked down at the world now far below, knowing I should be terrified.

Yet by some miracle, I found myself calmed by the sight.

I told myself he was doing this to me—soothing my mind with some sort of twisted magic, just as I was convinced he'd subjected me to those—admittedly enticing—visions for weeks on end. He was trying to seduce me into thinking he wasn't a threat. But I knew better.

"Stop it," I sniped, irritated that anyone could hold such sway over my mind.

"Stop what? Flying? Holding you?"

"Stop toying with me! You're bending my mind, trying to

make me feel safe, even though I know it's the furthest thing from the truth."

He let out a chuckle. "On the contrary. You're *perfectly* safe—for now, at least. I have no intention of hurting you. And I am not bending your mind, whatever you may think."

"Then why have you been stalking me? What do you intend to do with me?"

"I intend to keep you from harm," he told me, a gust of wind cutting through his deep voice. "For now, we will head toward Marqueyssal and spend the night there. I am not yet accustomed to my wings, and I'm afraid I can't fly you a great distance, or I would take you all the way to your home near the Onyx Rise."

"My home," I replied. "How do you know..."

I stopped myself. He knew my name. Of course he knew where I had lived all my life. He was a Fae, and they had powers the likes of which I couldn't begin to comprehend.

"I know many things, Leta," he said softly. "Too many for my liking."

I had no idea what he meant by that, nor did I want to. So instead of asking, I muttered, "I thought Fae didn't have wings."

"You're not entirely wrong. They were stolen long ago from all High Fae. A punishment from a cruel creature, one who couldn't stand to see some among us holding power. But thanks to someone extremely resourceful, we recently found ourselves graced with the Gift once again."

"Lucky you."

I fell silent for a time, trying to convince myself that I wasn't enjoying the sensation of being held against the body I had touched so often in my visions—so close to the lips I'd kissed with a longing I had never felt for anyone before.

The truth was, all I could think of was how much I desired him, this Fae whose name I didn't even know. How I had secretly wished to see him again, hoped that somehow our paths would cross—hoped I could inhale his scent again in the real world, and not only in stolen memories.

Attempting to conceal my shame, I blurted out, "Are you going to make the same demands of me as that prick back in the pub did?"

My question was met with a stony silence, which I took as a yes.

"I see," I said.

"You see very little, actually," the Fae replied. "You make a great number of assumptions, but so far, none of them has been even close to correct."

"Fine, then. Here's another assumption: You're a High Lord."

He laughed. "I was at one time, yes. I suppose I still am, by blood. I do not call myself lord. I am a Valdfae. Some call us sell-blades, but I prefer to think of myself as a wanderer."

"Fine. You're a High Lord who pretends he's not. Assumption two: you're going to bring me somewhere, then kill me with some hideous spell or other, after you've had your way with me."

"I would sooner die than harm you."

I tightened in his arms. Without understanding why, I was certain that he meant those words.

He would die before seeing me harmed.

But...why? Why should he care? He didn't even know me.

"Tell me," he added when I fell silent again, "are your scars hurting you still?"

My tight form relaxed slightly as I realized the searing pain that had assaulted me earlier was entirely gone now.

"No," I replied. "I'm fine. How...how do you know they were hurting?"

"Because I could feel your pain."

A shudder ripped through me, and I struggled to conceal it.

The tone of his voice had altered into the same one I had heard in my visions. One filled with a deep, unmistakable affection and an intimacy like none I had ever known.

But I promptly reminded myself that in my visions, he had not been speaking to *me* at all. Whatever affection I heard was merely imagined, wishful thinking on my part.

"Look toward the horizon," the Fae said, cutting through the awkward silence. "That's where I'm bringing you."

I lifted my chin. In the distance beyond a thick cover of trees, I could see a large, walled city of light yellow-brown stone. Marqueyssal—the capital city in the realm of the same name, watched over by Lord Dubois. A city of wine drinkers, a domain of wealth and leisure. I had heard people speak of it over the years as one of the most desirable places to live in all the realms.

"Did Corym hire you to bring me to him?" I asked. "Will you hand me over when we land?"

"Prince Corym did not hire me, no. Neither did any mortal lord."

Perhaps I was a fool, but once again, I believed him.

Still, dread filled me as the Fae began his descent toward the city. I half expected a small army of lord's Guardsmen to greet us, to take me captive, pay the Fae his wages, then escort me to dungeons beneath the palace.

But instead of flying toward the impressive castle that rose up at the city's highest point, the Fae flew down to land in a small courtyard flanked by modest stone houses. We set down with remarkable gentleness on a surface of uneven cobblestones, my feet touching down as if alighting on a feather bed.

"You need some proper rest," my captor said as he finally released me. I stumbled forward, distancing myself from him as my eyes searched for an escape route.

"Flee if you like," he added with a half smile that I saw only when I turned to glower at him. "I will find you each time you leave me, even if you should sail across the sea."

"Will you?" I asked snidely. "How impressive of you. Is it my scent that you follow like a dog, or are you stalking me through some other sense entirely?"

"Though I will admit I find your scent quite pleasing," he said with a single, quick stride that brought him to within inches of where I stood, "it is not what draws me to you, *Lahnan*."

"That's not my name, and you know it," I snapped.

He cocked his head to the side. "I'm well aware. I was using a word in the old tongue."

"Which means what, exactly?"

I tried to inject venom into my tone, but instead, the question came out meekly, my voice trembling slightly.

His smile faded. "One day, perhaps I will tell you. But until then, it will remain a secret."

I found myself suddenly tongue-tied, forcing my eyes to lock on his own but quivering under his gaze. "How do you know about the...the memories? You did this to me, didn't you? You've been..."

Torturing me.

"No," he said. "If it were up to me, you would never have seen her mind. Never felt her emotions. You would think of me as a stranger, someone devoid of feeling. A husk. Because that's what I have become over the years."

The way he spoke the words tore at my heart. I could feel the pain in them, the loss. I wondered with a lump in my throat how long ago the events I'd seen in my visions had taken place —and what had happened since then to wipe the smile from his face?

"Who is she?" I asked quietly. "Who are *you*?"

He ran a hand through his thick hair and let out a deep sigh. "My name is Thalanir," he replied. "And *she* is someone with whom I once shared a fraction of a life. She has a connection to you—though not by blood. That's as much as you need to know for the time being. Now, come." He turned to guide me down a narrow alleyway, the only route out of the courtyard. I considered standing my ground and refusing, like an obstinate child, to follow in his footsteps even if I had to spend the night in the damned courtyard.

But I had no money, no connections in this city. And if I tried to charm another man into looking after me, I would no doubt be met with the same kind of lecherous behavior that had plagued me in Duggat.

I was at Thalanir's mercy, as much as I despised the thought.

So I trudged after him, wary but admittedly curious. I wanted more answers, and he was the only one who could possibly give them to me.

"Who hired you?" I asked. "You said you're a sell-blade. Someone *must* be paying you to—"

He stopped, his back to me, and held up a hand, commanding me to be silent. Annoyed, I attempted to step around him, but his arm reached out and pulled me against him. I could feel the drumbeat of his heart, the rise and fall of his broad chest with each passing breath.

"What are we—"

"Shh!" he hissed.

When I heard the sound of marching feet in hard-soled boots, I found myself sinking into him, suddenly grateful that he'd held me back.

The Fae stood stock-still, his arms locked around my waist, while two guardsmen in full uniform marched by.

"Lord's Guard," he breathed when they'd passed, his lips

caressing my ear. "Those were swordsmen, hunting a criminal and ready for a fight."

"A criminal? What kind?"

With his arms still tight around me, he whispered, "Probably a Valdfae. One with dark hair and blue eyes."

CHAPTER SEVEN

"You?" I asked when Thalanir began walking again. "Why would Guardsmen be hunting *you*?"

I didn't really expect an answer. But as we emerged from the alley to turn right on a broad street lit by a long series of hanging lanterns, he replied, "I'm sure you've noticed by now that mortals are not so fond of my kind. And now, they're convinced we're infiltrators, here to steal their land, their money, and probably their livestock. Battles have already begun raging between Fae and human in the North, near where you once lived."

"Yes, but why you, specifically?" I asked.

Something told me he was keeping some crucial detail to himself. Perhaps he'd done something to spur his own personal manhunt. Or *Fae-hunt*, or whatever the proper term was.

"Have they figured out that you kill mortals or something?" I added, chuckling as if I were half-joking. But something in his expression told me I wasn't going to like the answer.

He stopped walking and rounded on me, staring down with those impossibly blue eyes that felt like they could tear my soul from my body.

There was a coldness in his expression, an absolute lack of remorse when he said, "Yes. They know I've killed many mortals. And others, as well." As he watched the blood drain from my face, he softened his voice. "I will not hurt you, Lahnan. My word is good, whether you believe it or not."

"Is it?" I asked, looking over my shoulder. "So you're telling me that if I were to run after those Guardsmen and report you, you would do nothing to stop me?"

"Correct." He turned and kept walking. Apparently, my threat had done nothing to deter him. "Of course, they would want to question you. To learn why you were in the company of a wanted Valdfae. And the moment they realized who and what you are, they would lock you in their dungeon. Marqueyssal's lord has no idea how valuable you are, Leta, or trust me, he would be sending every man he has to comb the streets for you instead of the likes of me."

I laughed. "Valuable?" I spoke breathlessly, trying and failing to keep up with him, "I'm afraid you don't know me very well."

"Then tell me—why did Prince Corym hold you close for so long? Why did he want so badly to marry you? A prince, who could have anyone in the realms—even the most Gifted of mortals. Why would he want *you*?"

My cheeks heated, though I wasn't certain if I was offended by the question, or merely shocked that he knew so much about me. "How do you know about that?"

"Come now—all of Kalemnar knew Corym was planning a lavish royal wedding to Leta Martel."

I scowled at the thought that the news had gone public even before Corym and I had set an official date. "He only wanted me because he lost his chance with my sister at the Blood Trials. I was the consolation prize."

"That's *not* why he wanted you, or why he wants you still,"

Thalanir replied coldly. He took hold of my shoulder, and for a moment, I thought perhaps he was hoping to reassure me, to comfort me. But instead, he steered me around the corner and down the street to our right.

"Fine. Then why?"

He stopped again and turned my way, staring into my eyes, assessing. "Have you already forgotten what happened at the pub? The fire raging inside you? Are you still going to tell me there's nothing special about you?"

My eyes stung with tears at the memory. "Special. Yes, I suppose that's one word for it." I wiped my eyes quickly. "I thought I was going to die back there. It was like...like something had taken me over and turned me into a monster. And before you ask—Corym didn't know my body could light itself like a torch, because I didn't know, either."

"You really don't know what you are." Thalanir inhaled the air and looked into the distance. "No. I suppose you don't. The truth has been hidden from you this whole time by that bastard Corym and everyone else, all in the name of protecting you. You haven't yet seen what your sister has become."

"Wait!" I shot, taking hold of his arm. "My sister? What do you know of Lyrinn?"

"More than you imagine," he replied, looking down at my hand.

I pulled it away, taking his expression as one of irritation, and, clenching my hand into a fist, tucked it away at my side.

Instead of explaining further, Thalanir began to walk again. "The inn is up ahead," he said, drawing his hood up around his face to ensure his ears were hidden from view. "For the purposes of concealment, you are my wife. We have been married a year. We've come from Belleau, traveling south to see your ailing father. Do you understand?"

The bastard was speaking to me like I was a child. A fool.

I wanted to tell him off. Of course I bloody understood.

But instead of unleashing the chain of expletives lingering on the tip of my tongue, I simply nodded.

We entered the inn—a place that smelled enticingly of smoke and lamp oil—and found the innkeeper. A jolly, short man with a long gray beard, a red face, and a bald head to match.

"Lookin' for a room, are ya?" he asked with a grin.

"Yes, for my wife and myself," Thalanir said, and I snickered at the absurdity of the statement before reminding myself what was at stake if I gave the game away.

"We've been married a year," I said with a shy smile, taking the Fae's arm and letting out a disingenuous giggle before adding, "He and I are *madly* in love."

"I'll bet you are, handsome couple like you," the innkeeper said, eyeing each of us in turn. "Well, that'll be five silvers for the night. Room's up on the second level, third door on your right."

Thalanir opened a small sack and extracted several coins, handing them to the man. I counted ten silvers.

Either his math was terrible, or he hoped to buy the innkeeper's loyalty.

"There's a fine pub down the way," the red-faced man said, his eyes lighting up when he saw the coins. "If you're in need of that sort of thing."

"Thanks so much," I replied, and as Thalanir began to lead me toward the staircase, I called out over my shoulder, "But I suspect we'll be spending all our time in our room, if you know what I mean."

Thalanir's grip on my arm tightened with warning as we began the climb up a set of creaky wooden stairs to the second floor. "That'll do with the horny wife act for now," he hissed through gritted teeth.

"Aw, come on," I chirped. "I'm just getting started."

We found our assigned room unlocked, and a large iron key awaiting us on the night stand.

The bed was narrow—barely big enough for two adults. I supposed Thalanir would sleep on the floor, or not at all. A so-called Valdfae didn't exactly seem like the type who slumbered for eight hours each night—though I didn't much feel like asking.

As I stepped over to the bed, stretching my arms over my head, a sudden, wretched realization hit me.

"My rucksack," I moaned, grabbing at my shoulder. "I must have left it behind in the pub in Duggat. Damn it. I have no clean clothing—or dirty clothing, for that matter."

"Some of the shops are still open," Thalanir said, turning back toward the door. "I'll find you what you need. Stay here."

"Wait!" I called out before he had a chance to go. "You're just leaving me here?"

I should have been pleased. With him gone, I could simply take off for the woods again and head north. I'd already survived for weeks in the wilderness, after all. Surely a few *more* weeks wouldn't kill me—and I would be free of his watchful, judgmental eye.

But for some inexplicable reason, I couldn't fathom being separated from him. I ached at the very thought of it—of being torn away from him, even for an hour.

I ground my jaw, chastising myself once again.

My desire for him isn't real. It's not even mine. It's...hers.

Whoever she is.

Besides, the Thalanir I had seen in my mind's eye didn't seem anything like the one standing a few feet from me. *Vision-Thalanir* was gentle and good-natured. There was a softness to him, a sweetness—whereas this Thalanir was hard as stone, and ice cold.

But when he left and closed the door behind him, I knew in my heart there was nothing in the world that could persuade me to leave this room before he returned to me.

CHAPTER EIGHT

After locking the door behind the Fae, I set the iron key back on the night stand and stepped over to the window. I simply wanted to take a look at the city view, I told myself. It had nothing to do with a desire to watch *him*.

But my eyes betrayed me when they turned to the cobbled street below rather than the buildings across the way. I waited with bated breath then watched as Thalanir slipped out of the inn and began striding up the road.

He seemed to know exactly where he was going, like a cat out on a prowl of his territory. I couldn't help wondering how he was so well acquainted with the city. Was he in league with Lord Dubois after all? Had he brought me to the inn to imprison me until someone came to take me away?

As I watched him move up the street with that strange, smooth stride of his, those powerful legs and the cloak that concealed his face and ears—I knew I was only being cynical. If he wished to hand me over, he would have brought me directly to the palace.

With a sigh, I turned away from the window. I hadn't slept

properly in days and finally had a bed at my disposal—and a locked door. For the first time since I'd left Domignon, I felt safe.

I lay down on the bed and closed my eyes, silently questioning my sanity for remaining in this room instead of fleeing. But when a flash of light blinded me and I found myself once again witnessing a moment swiped from someone else's life, I succumbed quickly to the desire to stay in the comfortable quarters.

The memory had me standing under an evening sky, staring into Thalanir's eyes. He cupped my cheek with his hand, his lips parted.

"Please," he said. "Don't do it. For your sake and mine."

"You don't understand," the feminine voice replied through lips that once again felt as if they were my own. "I have no choice."

He pulled back, torment in his eyes. "You always have a choice," he said. "You just need to choose right over wrong."

And then he was gone, the brief memory with him.

I struggled to piece it together—to try and remember what they were talking about. What was she about to do that was so terrible? What had happened to make him wary of her?

But no answer came to me. Instead, sleep overtook me as if the flitting moment had been too much for my tired mind and body.

Sometime later, I awoke abruptly, sensing that I wasn't alone. The room was filled with shadow, the moon shining high over the city's rooftops. A silhouetted figure stood a few feet from the foot of the bed, and in the dim light, I could just make out a pair of glinting eyes.

"Is that...you?" I asked, not daring to say his name.

When he stepped forward to reveal his face, I breathed a sigh of relief.

"I brought you a few things," he said softly, as if afraid he would be heard from the outside. With a flick of his hand, a lantern that sat on the night stand flared to life. The room was instantly engulfed in warm light.

Thalanir gestured to a small table where a pile of garments were tidily laid out, as well as a large leather pack. "There should be something to suit your every need."

I slipped out of bed and over to the clothing, picking up one piece, then the next, and examining each of them. He had brought me silk, linen, leather. Dresses, trousers, boots, even, which he had set on the floor.

"How did you pay for all of this? I mean, I will be sure to pay you back, once I—"

I couldn't finish the thought. The truth was, I had no money. And even if I found my way home to Dúnbar, I would still be poor. The only time in my life I'd ever felt close to wealthy was at the palace in Domignon—but that wealth had never been my own.

He held up a hand. "No need," he said. "It's all looked after."

I put down the blouse I was holding and stared at him. "Someone *did* hire you, then. Who was it?"

He ignored the question and averted his eyes, looking toward the window. "There are signs of the Cloaks in town," he said. "We must be wary."

"Cloaks?"

"The Crimson Cloaks, a so-called 'Brotherhood' that's simply a militia made up of Fae conspiring with mortal rebels. They've banded together in pockets throughout the realms, all in hopes of taking on the forces of Tíria when the war moves northward. Small packs of them are moving through Kalemnar, seeking out allies as well as any threats to their cause. Rumor has it the mortal lords support them—they see them as an army more mighty than any mere human one, capable of taking on Tírians with their gifted magic users. If the Brotherhood were to find us, it would likely not end well."

"If they found *you*, you mean," I said with a nervous laugh. "I told you, I'm no threat to anyone."

His head twisted around, his eyes flaring as they bore into mine. "There was a time not too long ago when your sister would have said the same of herself," he said sharply. "You need to understand the threat you pose to the Crimson Cloaks and everyone else, Leta."

"How could I possibly be a threat?" I asked sharply. "What is it you're not telling me?"

He ground his jaw for a moment, then shook his head as if dislodging a thought. "It is not for me to tell," he said. "I had hoped—"

A quiet fury began to build inside me.

"It *is* for you to tell, actually," I retorted, interrupting his thought. "Because if you don't, I will leave—and this time I promise you, I will make sure you don't find me. Who paid for these clothes?" I asked, lifting the blouse and shoving it in his face. "How do you know my sister? What *is* all of this?"

"Do you really want to know?" he replied, grabbing me by the wrist. I could feel the extent of his strength as he did so, absolute and terrifying. He could have broken me like a fragile porcelain vase, shattered me into a hundred pieces if he so desired.

Still, I managed to lift my chin in defiance. "*I want to know.*"

He let go of me and turned away. "It was Mithraan, High Lord of Fairholme. He...wanted me to find you."

"Mithraan?" I shot. "You mean Lyrinn's..." I tried to absorb the words, to grasp what they could possibly mean. "Why would he...?"

Thalanir growled over his shoulder. "You know the answer perfectly well. He hired me because he loves your sister—and she loves you. They heard you'd left Domignon, and knew you would be in grave danger out in the wild."

"From Corym, you mean."

Thalanir shook his head, turning back to face me. "Corym is little threat, not to you. Not anymore. Look—there are things you don't yet know about yourself."

"I think I know myself pretty well, actually." My tone was haughty, arrogant. "I don't need some winged sell-blade to swoop in and explain my own nature to me."

Thalanir's lip curled into a crooked grin. "That's where you're wrong. You need to learn what you are before you can begin to understand what the future holds for you, for your sister—for all of us."

"What's that supposed to mean?"

"It's complicated, Leta," he said. "More than you can begin to imagine. Come—sit on the bed. Please."

I did as he said, my heart pounding in my chest, fear shuddering its way through me. I wanted to prove him wrong—to insist that there was no deep, hidden secret inside me. But if the last few weeks had proven anything, it was that my mind and body teemed with secrets that no one—including me—understood.

"The Blood Trials," Thalanir said. "That was the last time you saw Lyrinn, correct?"

"At the Trials' beginning, yes," I replied. "The palace wouldn't let me watch any more than that. The king said it would be too painful for me."

"*Too painful*," Thalanir scoffed. "As if King Caedmon is so benevolent as that. No—he wanted to keep the truth from you about what your sister really is. Because he didn't want you to know what *you* are—not yet. Easier to keep you in check if you think you're weak. Besides which, admitting the truth would have meant admitting his son was about to break a mortal law."

He was rambling like a madman, and his words made no sense, which did little to quell my fear.

"I...don't understand..."

Thalanir raked a hand through his hair and, breathing hard, said, "You didn't see the last event at the Trials."

I stared at him, irritated that he wasn't getting to the point. "No, I didn't. You mean when Mithraan stole Lyrinn? When he took her away from me, from Kalemnar?"

Thalanir looked away, wincing, his eyes fixed on some distant place. He still seemed pained when he said, "You're right to think it was a powerful Fae who took her, and that your sister would never have left you of her own will. But the Fae who abducted her wasn't Mithraan."

"So who was it?" I asked, pulling myself to my feet and reaching for him. "Tell me, please!" I pressed my palm to his chest, a shock running along my flesh. A flash, lightning-like, that moved over my skin like flame.

"The answer lies within your own mind, Lahnan," he replied softly. "Close your eyes, and you will see."

"What? How?" I snapped, my voice strained. "How can I possibly..."

He placed a hand over my own, which was still pressed to his chest. "Breathe," he said. "And trust me—but more importantly, trust yourself."

Terrified but desperate for the truth, I obeyed.

I found myself instantly reeling, falling through space. Rapid-fire visions came to me like a massive flock of flying birds

—brief flashes of events that had occurred since Lyrinn and I had last been together.

Through a wall of swirling mist, I saw my sister on a ship that sailed over the choppy waters of the Elden Sea. She was arguing with someone. *Shouting* at him.

It took me a moment to realize that Kazimir, the High King of Aetherion, stood a few feet from her, a smile of pure arrogance on his lips.

*Kazimir...**he** was the one who took her from the Trials?*

But why would he do such a thing?

I fell once again, barreling through time and space, then stopping abruptly. Only Thalanir's hand over mine kept me tethered to the present, to reality. Only he managed to prevent me from crashing to the floor as my mind barreled downward.

From a distance, I now saw Lyrinn in a palace, surrounded by wondrous beauty...yet sadder than she'd ever been. She breathed my name, told me she missed me—that she would find her way back to me, back to Mithraan.

She was torn away from him...just as she was torn from me and from this land.

I saw a red-haired woman—no—a Fae—who looked so much like me that I had to remind myself I wasn't looking into a mirror.

Our mother.

Morsel after morsel came to me, feeding my famished mind, explaining to me in a million ways what Lyrinn had endured.

What she was.

What *I* must surely be.

Finally, I saw Lyrinn, despairing, surrounded by darkness. Flames and light crashing in the sky high above her. I could hear Mithraan crying her name, desperate to keep her safe from a threat greater than either of them. Greater than any I could imagine.

But what the threat was, I could not see.

The visions ceased, and my eyes opened.

A sob rose in my chest, and I grabbed at my head with both hands, trying to force the demons away from my mind.

"Where is Lyrinn?" I cried. "Is she alive?"

"Ask yourself the question," Thalanir breathed. "The answer lies in your bond with your sister."

I closed my eyes again, and then an image came that answered a hundred questions at once, but raised a million more.

It was Lyrinn, a set of beautiful, glowing wings springing from her shoulders. Wings like the ones I'd seen spread from Thalanir's back, except that Lyrinn's glowed white with black veins that swirled like silken thread through gossamer.

She looked exquisite, strong...and utterly reborn.

And at last, I knew what Corym and his parents had hidden from me all those weeks in the palace and why. I understood why I was a threat—why it wasn't just the prince who might hunt me.

"Lyrinn and I..." I whispered, the memories dissipating like smoke. "We're..."

Thalanir nodded gravely. "Lyrinn has found her wings. It is only a matter of time before you find yours."

When I stared at him with disbelief, he said, "You're a High Fae, Leta, just as Lyrinn is. The burns that afflicted you so long ago, concealing your ears—they were a deliberate act, meant to hide the truth—even from you. A protective measure, because if anyone knew two Fae born of Lightblood and Tírian parents were living in a mortal town, you would have been in grave danger, to say the least."

The logical thing would have been to ask how this had happened. How on earth I had spent my entire life ignorant of my origins, of the terrible power simmering inside me.

But I understood that, too. In that brief, shocking moment, I had seen my sister's mind, and I knew all of it. Why our adoptive father had lied to us all our lives. What had happened to our mother after we were born—and *where* I was born.

Domignon.

I should have screamed with fear and shock at the revelation—but as the massive wall of knowledge slammed into my consciousness, it all made a strange, terrifying sort of sense.

So *much* of my life in Dúnbar, my nature, my scars—finally made sense.

Kazimir...he is our father by blood. And our mother was...

"Our mother was the daughter of the High King of Tíria," I said, my voice breaking, my heart overwhelmed with emotion. Tears streamed down my cheeks when I added, "And she's dead."

Fear gripped me then. I was terrified of what was happening to me, of the power trying to take hold. Terrified of my own nature and of what was yet to come.

"Are you all right?" Thalanir asked.

"What's going to happen to me?" I asked weakly, my fingers touching my ear. "When will I become...like Lyrinn?"

"I don't know. You aren't...quite like other Fae I've known. Which means you're not quite like your sister, either. There is a force in you that binds you to someone else, Leta—one that transcends time itself."

Narrowing my eyes accusingly, I asked another question— the one that had plagued my mind since the night I had fled Domignon.

"Who is she? The woman from my visions? Is she a Fae, too?"

Thalanir's face went white and cold, his irises flaring. But he didn't utter a word in response.

"I've just had my world turned upside down," I growled,

straining against the desire to scream. "My head is pounding from the surplus of information that just bombarded it. And you won't answer a couple of simple questions?"

"What you're asking of me," he said. "It's..."

"What I'm asking of you is to help me. I'm asking you to explain to me why this is happening. Why I feel like I'm losing a little more of my mind with each day that passes. I'm asking you to help me to preserve the last of my sanity, Thalanir."

"She was a Fae," he snapped with finality.

But I defied him.

"Why is she inside my head?" I pressed. "What are you not telling me?"

His eyes burned with blue flame when he warned, "Do not ask me any more about the matter. I cannot—*will* not—speak of her."

Irritation gnawed at me, and all of a sudden I wanted anything but to be trapped in this room with someone who refused to provide me with the answers I so desperately needed.

"If you won't talk," I said, "then I'm going to get a drink. After everything that just exploded in my mind, I'm sure you'll understand."

I headed for the door, embarrassed that I'd allowed him to witness so much fear and torment in my eyes. I hated being vulnerable around him—I hated that he knew my weakness.

"I'm going to the pub," I said over my shoulder. "Come with me or don't, I don't care. I'm powerful, right? I mean, my veins glow like lava, and apparently I make grown mortals crap their pants with fear. You've seen it yourself—I'm a force to be reckoned with."

"You may be powerful," he said, stepping forward to block my path to the door, "but you still have no money to pay for drinks—and you do not know the spells required to pull coin out of thin air."

"Money?" I scoffed. "My *body* is my currency. Or haven't you figured that out yet? Every foolish man who has ever wanted something from me has started by staring me up and down like I'm a slab of meat. It's how we women get by in this vile world of ours. Now if you'll excuse me, I'll be on my way."

CHAPTER NINE

Thalanir had never looked at me as if I were something to consume.

He often eyed me with distant curiosity that bordered on familiarity, but never with the kind of grotesque hunger so many men exhibited when ogling me or other young women.

Right now, he looked like he wanted to slap some sense into me. But I knew in my heart that he would never lift a hand to me for anything.

"Don't be a fool," he growled. "Now is not the time to do something impulsive."

"Me? Do something impulsive?" I asked innocently as I reached around him and tried to pull the door open.

Damn it, it was still locked.

I glanced over to see that the iron key hadn't moved from its original position on the night stand.

"You didn't use a key to get into the room earlier. And I didn't let you in," I said. "How did you..."

His face darkened. "I have lived a long time, Lahnan. If I couldn't make my way through mortal-locked doors, I would probably have died hundreds of years ago."

"Hundreds?" I tried and failed to grasp the magnitude of such a lifetime, my rage dissipating. "Really?"

"Yes."

I had never thought about Thalanir's age, though perhaps I should have. In my visions, he looked the same as he did now—twenty, at the most. And though I knew Fae could live long lives, he had never *felt* ancient to me...whatever an ancient soul is supposed to feel like.

There was something about Thalanir that felt young and wise at once, as if he had experienced a hundred consecutive lives and amassed knowledge from each.

Still, I had always imagined that an Immortal his age would feel like an ancient tree caving under weighted limbs, and not vivacious and powerful as he was.

"Look—I'll go with you to the damned pub," he said with a sigh of surrender. "It's not safe for you out there, and especially not tonight, of all nights. A heavy truth has just fallen on your shoulders, and it would not do for you to be alone."

With a twitch of his fingers, he cast a spell to unlock the door, which flew open. He stepped through, and I followed.

We walked along the street outside in silence, grim-faced and dour.

In my earlier days—the days before the Blood Trials and before Prince Corym—I would probably have found all of this amusing, even exciting. The truth about Lyrinn and me. The anticipation of powers I couldn't fathom, of learning what it felt like to have Immortal blood flowing through my veins.

But now, it felt like my world had been upended. As if everything I had ever known—everything I had ever loved—had been a lie set in place to deceive me. I was the very thing the people I'd known in Dúnbar had despised and feared. I was the enemy, and so was Lyrinn.

My sister had endured the Change without me. The last

time I saw her, had she known what she was? Had she known about our true father—that he was mere feet from her at the Trials?

Something told me the answer had to be no. She couldn't have kept such a secret from me, even if she'd wanted to.

Could she?

In the pub, Thalanir and I found ourselves sitting in a shadowy corner with two pints of ale. He kept his hood up and his head down as mortal men and women paraded around the place, flirting, belching, laughing, and arguing loudly.

As I stared out at the crowd, I spoke softly. "What's happening in my mind—the visions...they're not part of a simple Coming of Age, are they?"

"No," my companion said. I turned his way. Only his lips and nose were visible, but it was enough to reveal his stern expression. He was bracing himself for another outburst from me, no doubt.

I couldn't exactly blame him.

"You, Leta," he said, turning to look at me, "will not come of age as some do. But it's not because you're a Fae. It's because you came of age long ago."

"That makes no sense. It's not possible. I'm only eighteen—"

"That's not what I'm saying. Look—have you ever heard someone call another person an 'old soul?'"

I nodded. "My father used to say that about me—though I always thought Lyrinn was more deserving. She was more mature than I was. More serious."

"Ah. But that's not what an old soul is—not exactly. You, Leta, are what is called a *Násuire*. It's a word in the old tongue that refers to one whose soul—what we Fae call an *Essence*— has passed through multiple lifetimes. The memories that torment you now may not be yours—but they *are* connected to your body and mind, whether you like it or not. They belonged to the last Fae who held the Essence inside her that has now invaded you. In passing the memories to you, she is offering you information—a warning of sorts, I suppose. It's how the Násuire learn, how they grow. There is an old story that tells that one day, a Násuire will rise, flying on wings like those of no other Fae. That she will save all her kind and the entire world."

I stared at him, searching for another answer, yet frightened of what it could be.

"I have no wings," I said. "So obviously I'm not her."

"I suppose not," Thalanir agreed.

"Is Lyrinn a...a Násuire? Like me?"

"No. Lyrinn is a High Fae, and has had her own battles to fight— her own demons. Your fate, I'm afraid, is quite different from hers."

I took a sip of ale, then set my cup down.

"Whose memories have I been seeing?" I asked in a near-whisper. "How is it that you're part of them?"

Thalanir let out a breath. "She was...someone who died long ago, Lahnan. You know why you see me in her memories."

No. That wasn't good enough. "She was your lover," I said. "She was something more to you than just some Fae you knew."

Her memories were part of me now. *He* was part of me— and clearly, there was a reason I felt so close to him.

She had felt it too. She had loved him—that much was clear.

"I was her lover, yes," he finally confessed. "But you know that already. Every answer you seek is in those memories. You just have to know how to make your way toward the truth."

"Or I could just ask you," I sneered.

"You could. But there are some truths I will not divulge."

"Why not? You and she seemed pretty damned happy together. Why wouldn't you want to talk about her?"

His hand rolled into a fist and he brought it down hard on the table, causing the cups to jostle violently.

"Because, Leta, they were not all happy memories," he said. "Now please—stop."

"You were there," I hissed, leaning in close. "You're hiding something from me. You know what will happen to me, don't you?"

"If I am hiding anything from you, it's for your own protection, Leta Martel," he said, then took a massive swig from his cup.

We sat in stony silence for a time before I finally spoke again. There was no point in asking anything more about the visions. It was clear that Thalanir was not willing to open that particular vault.

So instead, I took another angle.

"Tell me something. Were you trapped in Tíria for the last thousand years? With the mist and the Grimpers?"

He didn't move his eyes to mine when he said, "No. In fact, I spent a good deal of those years *away* from that land. I was one of the few Fae who managed to come and go in spite of the obstacles keeping me from that land."

"How?"

At that, he glanced sideways at me, looking *almost* playful. "Wouldn't you like to know?"

"How?" I repeated irritably. I wasn't sure if it was the ale or some other compulsion, but I found myself moving closer to him, staring straight into those wild blue eyes.

"I have certain Gifts," he replied. "Talents that allow me to move freely—and that help me evade those who wish to capture me."

"Tell me about them."

"It's easier if I show you. And if my suspicions are right, I'll have a chance to do so in a few seconds." At that, Thalanir's eyes shot toward the door.

He reached out and grabbed my wrist just as a series of figures in red cloaks marched into the pub.

"Say nothing," he whispered, leaning in close. "Nothing at all, unless they ask you questions. Let me do the talking."

I was too busy leering at the strange procession to notice that his voice had changed to something a little higher—thinner. It wasn't until I looked back at him that I realized his face—his perfect, handsome face—had morphed into that of someone else—someone mortal and at least forty years old, from the looks of it. Thalanir had shifted into a pallid, weak-chinned man, his eyes droopy, his hair thinning and blond.

He pushed his hood down and hunched over pitifully, rocking a little in his chair like he'd suddenly grown intoxicated.

"You're a shape-shifter?" I hissed under my breath as the party made their way toward us.

Thalanir snarled, "I told you to say nothing," before glancing up at the Crimson Cloaks.

"Gentlemen," he said with a wide gesture of his arms, his speech slurring. "What can I do for you?'

"We've had reports of a High Fae traveling with a young woman who looks like her," the group's leader said with a nod toward me. His eyes were bright caramel-colored, his cheekbones sharp enough to cut glass. He was a Fae, which was enough to entice me to slouch down in my seat for fear he would see what I really was. "I don't suppose you know anything about it?"

Thalanir's fake lips broke into a grin, then he started laughing. It was maniacal, the cackle of someone unhinged, or at least highly inebriated. "Do you know how many plain-looking redheaded women there are in this city alone?" he asked through gasping laughs. "Come, now. There are any number of them, and *this* one is my daughter, fellows. Besides, as you can see, I'm no High Fae. You're barkin' up the wrong tree, you are."

Plain-looking? I thought, shooting him an angry look.

"Is that true, Miss?" the leader asked me. "This drunken fool is your father?"

"Unfortunately, he is," I replied. "I'm just seeing to it that the arse gets his daily medicinal pints before I drag him home."

The leader eyed me suspiciously, but after a moment, he nodded to the others, pivoted on his heel, and they turned to leave the pub.

"Plain-looking?" I hissed under my breath when they'd gone.

Thalanir glanced at me sideways through the stranger's eyes, sunken as they were into dull, grayish skin—and said, "Does that really bother you?"

He drew his hood up again, shifting into his original face.

"No. Of course not."

I refused to look at him, telling myself I shouldn't care what he thought. He wasn't my friend, after all. He was the temporary hire of my sister's lover—a Fae I didn't trust as far as I could throw him. He was nothing to me.

I scolded myself silently for giving a crap what he thought about my looks. My vanity was a curse inflicted on me by years of unwanted attention from men and boys. I had come to take for granted that others would find me pretty, or at least pleasing to the eye. It was the one power I had always held over most men—*and* many women.

Yet Thalanir had, from the start, seemed utterly uninterested in my looks. Only in those distant memories that haunted my mind had I ever seen him look at me with desire—and then, it wasn't *me* he was looking at.

Why should it matter to me if some Fae thinks I'm hideous? It's not as if I find him...

Attractive.

What a lie *that* was.

Since the first moment I'd seen him in that clearing, I had wanted to touch him, to press my face to his chest and feel his arms wrap themselves around me. I had wanted desperately to taste his skin, his tongue. To take possession of him, body and mind.

But I told myself it was folly brought on by the coming Change. Nothing more.

As I drank in silence, I noticed him eyeing me sideways once or twice, but I refused to look at him—speak to him.

"It pains you to think I may not be attracted to you," he said after a time, the amused, crooked grin on his lips once again. "After everything that has happened—everything you've learned about yourself today...*that* is the thing that irks you?"

My brows met. "I couldn't care less what you think of me. I'm just tired. That's all."

He sat back and let out a low chuckle. "I don't think that's true at all. You want the entire world to find you as beautiful as the boys back in Dúnbar did."

"Wrong."

"Mmm-hmm," he said, taking a swig of ale, then slamming his cup down. "Come, let's get back to the inn before the Brotherhood returns. I wouldn't want to have to tell them again that I find you homely. It might send you into a fit of rage that would blow the roof off of this place."

"Piss off."

Sullenly, I rose to my feet and accompanied him out of the pub and back to the inn.

When we were in our room, I readied myself for bed, going through the clothing Thalanir had bought in search of night-clothes.

"There's nothing for me to sleep in," I said, my voice clipped like that of a spoiled child, and I hated myself for it.

"What do you normally wear to bed?"

"A nightgown," I said. "Or at least a long shirt."

"A long shirt it is."

He proceeded to peel off the white shirt he was wearing, which looked remarkably clean, all things considered.

I told myself to look away as my eyes met a sculpted torso and arms that looked like they could lift a house. An abdomen that appeared to have been carved of the finest marble by a craftsman in love with his subject.

At averting my eyes, I failed utterly. Instead, I stared—no, gawked—at him, my cheeks burning, desire assaulting me again in spite of myself.

Damn you for looking like that, Fae.

Along his flesh here and there were scars I hadn't seen in the memories—marks of a past fraught with conflict. A map of all the battles he'd ever fought, displayed in graphic detail.

Some feral part of me wanted to move toward him, to trace my fingers along the scars, along every line of him. Because despite my protests to the contrary—I wanted him now, more than ever.

He was wrong about one thing, though.

I didn't care what the young men back in Dúnbar thought of me. I never had.

But for some insane reason, I cared what *he* thought of me.

Far too much.

Pathetic, I told myself, realizing for the first time ever how much I envied Lyrinn. My sister had never placed any stock in her looks, never worried about whether or not any man desired her. That was part of her allure—part of what made her so independent, so strong.

Why had I always valued myself on so superficial a level?

What did it matter if this Fae thought me beautiful? I had far more to offer the world than pretty eyes and a mane of red hair. Didn't I?

But as I stared at the lines of his body and inhaled his scent, I *knew* why I cared. As much as I wanted to deny it, there was something between us far deeper than a surface attraction—something I didn't yet understand. I had been drawn to him since before I'd ever met him. I had felt love for him before we'd ever exchanged a single word.

So yes. It hurt that he didn't want me—that he saw me as nothing more than a commodity to be traded for coin. I was a job, a task.

A pain in his admittedly exquisite ass.

"Turn around," I commanded when he'd handed me the shirt, and he did so, revealing an equally remarkable back.

Tearing my eyes away, I pulled the sweat-stained clothing from my body and slipped the garment on.

"All right. I'm done," I said.

When he turned back around and his eyes landed on me, moving down to my legs then back to my face, his expression softened, his face altering. His features hadn't exactly changed, but I felt suddenly as if I were looking at the version of him from my visions—the one whose eyes seemed perpetually filled with longing and affection, and not the cold-hearted Fae who kept me relentlessly at arm's length.

He had once been a creature of pure desire, of warmth and love.

What had happened in his life to turn him to ice?

"What is it?" I asked, struggling to keep my voice in check. "Why are you looking at me like that?"

"Because," he replied, "You—"

Before he could finish the thought, the room began to spin... and then everything turned to blackness.

CHAPTER TEN

"WHAT HAPPENED?" I asked when I found myself lying in bed, the sheets covering me, with Thalanir seated on a chair next to me.

"You fainted," he replied softly, pulling closer to examine my eyes. "How are you feeling now?"

The second I turned to look his way, the room began to twist and spin, forcing me to slam my eyes shut. "Drunk," I moaned. "That ale is strong."

"It's not the ale. This is something else entirely. You are..."

He stopped speaking, reaching a hand out and pushing my hair back off my sweat-soaked face. I reveled in his touch, savoring it for an instant before reminding myself yet again that he was *her* lover.

Not mine.

I had only witnessed moments of intimacy through her eyes. I had invaded his privacy, fallen for a dream.

I opened my eyes again and looked away. "I'm what?"

"Changing," he said. "Your true nature is beginning to force its way out. Slowly, but it's happening. It all began with the memories you've seen. And as the days pass and the memories unfold, your strength will increase. You will find your senses heightened. Your powers will show themselves."

My head twisted around and I glared at him. "How can you possibly know that?" I asked. "For all we know, the memories are just..."

"What?" His voice was soft, gentle. "Fantasies crafted by your mind?"

"I didn't say that."

Thalanir's lip twitched, threatening a smile, but he pulled back, pain sweeping across his features. "I've watched it happen before. That's how I know."

"With her," I replied. "You saw what happened to her when she came into her powers. You're telling me she had visions, too?"

"She did, yes." He let out a sorrowful breath. "I watched her grow and alter. I watched as she trained her body and mind, as she became one of the most powerful Fae I've met in all my years. She had been graced with many Gifts—but cursed with them, too. Her power proved her downfall, as happens far too often in this world of ours."

I pushed myself up, pressing my back to the headboard. My breathing had steadied, my heart slowing, and I summoned the courage to ask the question that had been plaguing me for far too long.

"The woman—or Fae, or whatever she was—I see in the visions...what was her name?"

"Leta," he said, a gentle warning in the two syllables.

"I need to know. Please."

He looked away then, as if staring into my eyes would be a betrayal. "Gallia. It was Gallia."

"Gallia," I repeated. "You loved her. Didn't you?"

He winced his eyes closed, shaking his head once. "She was my lover," he said.

It wasn't exactly an answer to my question.

"Were you true mates? Was that it? Destined to be together?"

He didn't reply.

"Why in all the hells is she showing me memories of you?" I pressed. "Of your time together? Why is she..."

Torturing me.

Why would she think I'd want to feel the touch of his lips, of his hands on my skin, his tongue...

"I told you that you will not come of age," Thalanir said. "Gallia has been dead for many years, Lahnan. The memories are not under her control, not really. Her Essence—her soul—is passing to you, as it was always meant to do. The memories are nothing more than a consequence of that."

I rolled onto my side away from him, my jaw clenched tight. The more answers I sought, the less I understood what was happening.

Thalanir climbed into the bed, his heat engulfing me as it had in the memories when I had felt safe, desired, comforted.

I wanted to tell him to go away, to leave me be. I wasn't Gallia. I wasn't his lover. I was his *job*. And I was a victim of a fate that was creeping closer daily, one that I didn't begin to comprehend.

I wondered with a shudder if he was enjoying this—if it gave him pleasure to watch me suffer.

He slipped a hand onto my waist, pulling himself closer, and said, "Your sorrow is mine, Lahnan. I feel it because you do. I will not let you suffer alone."

I rolled onto my back, turning my head to look at him. "Why?" I asked in a whisper, a tear running down my temple. "Why would you say that? I see how you look at me...like I'm nothing but a thorn in your side."

One side of his mouth twitched, a smile threatening to reveal itself again. "You really think that's how I look at you?"

I nodded.

The smile bloomed on his lips, his eyes brightening, but after a moment it was gone.

"Well, then," he said, rolling onto his back. "I suppose we should both be grateful. It's for the best, after all."

"Right. Fine," I said, turning my back toward him. "Good night."

Irritation simmered inside me. Or perhaps it was embarrassment.

His silent rejection was almost worse than a spoken one.

But he was probably right.

It *was* for the best.

By the time morning came, I felt as if I hadn't slept for a second.

But I must have, because Thalanir had already risen, dressed, and left the inn long enough to acquire some fresh bread and water for us both.

As I rubbed the sleep from my eyes, he seated himself at the foot of the bed and handed me a torn-off piece of crusty, steaming bread.

"Thank you," I muttered, taking a bite then resisting the desire to moan with pleasure. It was, without question, the best bread I had ever tasted.

"Today, we head north," he said, pulling himself back to his feet. "Best to get away from this place before we spot more Crimson Cloaks."

I nodded, and when I'd popped the last of the bread into my

mouth, I climbed out of bed and slipped over to the pile of new clothing.

I chose a pair of gray trousers and a white blouse, as well as a jacket and a pair of supple leather boots.

"Would you give me a minute?" I asked the Valdfae, who was glancing out the window, watching the passersby below.

"A minute?" he replied, turning to face me. When he realized I wished to dress, he nodded. "I'll be in the corridor."

I threw the clothing on quickly and, just as I was about to call him back in, another violent flash of memory took hold of my mind. I reached out for the bed, but too late. I went tumbling to the floor, crashing to my knees and crying out in pain.

Thalanir burst into the room, his hands instantly on me, lifting me easily onto the bed. He sat me down then crouched before me, cupping my cheeks in his hands.

"Are you all right?" he asked, searching my face for an answer.

"Fine," I nodded. "It's nothing. I just..." But there was no point in lying. The truth was, the spells were getting more and more violent, more unpredictable.

The memory that had just flashed through my mind had come at me like a ball of vicious flame.

In it, I had felt the blow of a sharp weapon to my chest.

And then my legs had given out beneath me.

That was all I knew—but it was enough to terrify me.

"What is it?" Thalanir asked. "What did you see?"

I stared at him, assessing his eyes. He looked concerned—frightened, even.

My eyes veered down to my chest.

There was no sign of a wound there. No mark from any weapon.

It was my imagination, I thought. *Nothing more.*

And then, I felt something—some powerful new force— clawing at my mind, trying to infiltrate it. Narrowing my eyes and crying out in anger, I pushed it away, refusing to let any more destructive thoughts inside my head.

"No!" I cried. "Stop!"

Thalanir went flying backwards and slammed against the room's far wall with a ferocity that shook the bed.

"Gods!" I cried, leaping to my feet. "What was that?"

He was on the floor, knees tucked up, a strange laugh rising up in his chest. He raised an eyebrow. "You have the capacity to become an impenetrable fortress, Leta Martel," he said, wiping his eye with the heel of his hand. "You should be pleased with yourself. Not many people—or Fae—can keep me from their thoughts."

But I wasn't nearly so amused as he was. How had I done that? How—how had I flung a Fae as powerful as Thalanir across the room with nothing but my thoughts? "That was you?" I stammered. "You were trying to see inside my mind?"

He nodded. "If you must know, I wanted to make sure you were all right. I have to say, I've never been rebuffed quite so effectively."

I crossed my arms over my chest, glaring down at him. "You shouldn't delve into people's minds. It's...intrusive."

He pushed himself to his feet, lowering his chin and fixing me with those penetrating eyes. "I apologize for the invasion. But be aware that you will encounter others who will try and get into your mind, and you must not let them. Some aren't so friendly as I am."

"Friendly," I scoffed. "Yes, you're just as warm and cuddly as a puppy, aren't you?"

"Some puppies take a little while to open up."

"You're trying to tell me there are introverted puppies in this world? Really?"

"Absolutely I am."

At that, I couldn't help but laugh, despite the fact that part of me still wanted to slap him. "Anyhow, I don't intend to let anyone into my brain. I can't imagine who would want access, anyhow. It's a horror in there these days."

He smiled a little. "Part of me would love to know what goes on in there. But another part is convinced that learning your thoughts would devastate me beyond words."

I wanted to believe him—to think he *wasn't* teasing me. I wanted to believe I could hold such power over his emotions.

But I reminded myself once again that I was nothing to him but a mission. A young woman in his charge. He'd made as much clear last night, after all.

"We should leave," I said curtly.

CHAPTER ELEVEN

Coldness ate at my mind as we strode through Marqueyssal's sun-dappled streets, twisting and shoving our way between slow-moving pedestrians heading out to the city's morning markets.

Occasionally, Thalanir reached back to take me by the hand and pull me along. For the most part, though, I was his shadow, following as quickly and closely as my legs would carry me.

Once or twice, I had to stop to press a hand to a signpost or wall as I fought off another spell. The visions were growing more frequent, coming at me like bolts from a powerful crossbow.

They were also growing more frightening. Gone was the idyllic nature of the first memories—Thalanir's smiling face, sunny fields of wildflowers, the bliss of his touch, his lips.

Now, all I saw was a flash of a blurred face here, a bleeding wound there—but never any clarity. Shots of pain assaulted my chest, and I gasped for breath, my body convulsing with agony before I could catch my breath and move on.

Was I seeing a war that had taken place long ago, or a battle to come?

"We must keep moving," Thalanir urged. "I'm sorry, Lahnan." His hood was pulled so far over his face that all I could see were his lips and stubbled chin. I glanced up to realize a small group of Guardsmen were patrolling not twenty feet from where we stood, and fear seized at my chest.

Thalanir wrapped a supportive arm around me, guiding me in the opposite direction.

"Why don't you shape-shift?" I asked weakly. "Or use glamor? If they see you're a Fae—"

"Those both require energy—which I need to preserve, in case we find ourselves caught up in a bloody fight in the near future."

Eventually, we came to a large town square crawling with locals. We began to cut across it, heading straight for a narrow street on the other side. But when we had almost reached our destination, the sound of hard-soled footsteps met my ears, and before we could react, a series of armored men emerged from the shadowy street to form a line before us.

Thalanir's hands were on me then, pulling me behind him as I gawked at the men dressed in tunics decorated with a dove —the sigil of the lord of Marqueyssal.

It will be all right. He'll talk his way out of this...

The men parted to allow another figure through—one taller than the rest, his skin dark, eyes blue-green, hair silver-white. He wore a cloak of deep blood-red and a malicious grin.

Like the Crimson leader we'd met last night, he was a Fae.

But he was far more daunting than his predecessor.

"A Lightblood in Kalemnar," Thalanir said. "Allied with mortals."

"A Tírian Valdfae," the other Fae replied with a disturbing grin. "Here in the South. Interesting. A pretty sum must have brought you so far from home." With that, he peeked around Thalanir to meet my eyes and added, "Or perhaps a pretty face."

"I am escorting this young lady home," Thalanir replied, and the quiet hostility in his tone raised the hairs on the back of my neck. In the air around us, power crackled, and I could see the mortal militia members shuffle uncomfortably on their feet as they, too, felt it.

Whether it was coming from Thalanir or the Lightblood Fae, I couldn't say.

"I see," the Crimson Cloak replied. "And where, exactly, is home?"

I pulled myself up to stand next to Thalanir and summoned the courage to look him in the eye. "Belleau, Sir," I replied with an accent not entirely my own. As I spoke, I strained against his attempt to delve into my mind, to learn my true identity.

"Belleau," he parroted, grinning. "I see. Well, then, I'm sure you won't mind taking a slight detour and accompanying us to Lord Dubois' palace for a tour."

"And why would we do that?" Thalanir snapped. I could feel the searing heat coming from him, anger rising inside him as his body readied itself for a fight.

"You'll do it because you don't want this lovely young woman's blood spread over the cobblestones," the other Fae replied before nodding toward the guards. "Seize them both," he commanded.

An obedient guard lunged for me, and instinctively, I leapt backwards, pulling away from his grasp with a speed greater than I had thought myself capable.

I turned to Thalanir, my eyes wide, horror throbbing in my chest.

What was that?

The guard's brow furrowed and he looked puzzled.

"A Gifted," the Lightblood said, chuckling. "Well, I shouldn't be surprised. Why would a Valdfae bother to accompany any lesser mortal such a long distance? Unless, of course, he had other motivations..."

He didn't complete the thought, but it didn't take a genius to deduce that he was insinuating Thalanir and I were together in more ways than a Valdfae and his bounty should be.

"Did you know," he said, taking a step toward me, "that bonding between mortal and Fae is strictly forbidden? The penalty is death."

"That's of no consequence to us," Thalanir growled, thrusting himself between us. "We are not bonded."

"And I am not a—" I said, but Thalanir reached for my arm, squeezing hard enough to make me wince.

Do not tell him you're a Fae.

His voice was clear in my head, though I told myself I'd imagined it.

The Lightblood stepped toward him and sniffed him as if he was a piece of cheese that might have gone bad. "No," he said. "Indeed, it seems you are not."

He moved toward me and sniffed my neck. It took everything in me not to recoil in disgust. "You may not have bonded," the Fae said with a knowing smirk, "but there is desire between you."

"There is not!" I protested far too quickly, my voice too shrill.

Laughing, the Fae grabbed me, taking my upper arm in hand. I tried to pull away again, but he anticipated my resistance and his fingers locked on me brutally, pain shooting up to my shoulder as I bit my cheek to suppress a yelp.

"I beg to differ," he said, and then under his breath, added, "mortal whore."

With a roar, Thalanir leapt forward and grabbed him by the neck, pressing him back against the stone wall and lifting him at least a foot off the ground. The mortal Guardsmen reached for their blades, but their Fae leader simply let out a choked laugh as he hung suspended from Thalanir's powerful hand.

"Just as I thought," he chuckled, his voice a rasp.

Thalanir dropped him and he landed gently as a feather on the ground, a hand rubbing his throat for a moment before he asked, "Now, Valdfae—are you going to come quietly, or will we need to battle it out?"

"We will not be going with you, no," Thalanir spat. "I have a responsibility to the young lady, and I intend to fulfill my promise."

"Very well, then," the Crimson Cloak said, stepping back. He lifted a hand into the air and shot a shard of ice at Thalanir, which missed hitting him square in the chest only because he managed to react with lightning speed.

Thalanir countered with an attack of his own—a barrage of what looked like a series of wooden spikes hurtling through the air. Some of them hit a few of the mortal guards in the chest or abdomen, and the men went crashing to the ground.

The Fae, however, managed to evade the projectiles. He raised his hands in the air, this time turning toward me.

"Whoever you are," he said, "Whatever your importance to him—I cannot let you live."

Thalanir reacted by shooting a hand out, summoning a wall of blue flame between us and the Guardsmen which instantly spread twenty or more feet into the air.

"Run!" he shouted, and I tore after him back across the town square and down a laneway that zigged and zagged through the city.

We sprinted at full speed for what felt like several minutes before Thalanir finally pushed open a rickety-looking wooden door embedded in a stone façade and pulled me inside, a finger pressed to his lips.

The space around us was cold and damp, its earthen floor

covered in straw. We had found our way into a stable—and from the looks of it, it hadn't been used in some time.

Pulling me toward the shadows of the far wall, Thalanir gestured vaguely with his fingers. The air hummed quietly and rhythmically with a strange, pulsing force before silence once again met my ears.

He signaled me to stay quiet.

Seconds later, the sound of barreling footsteps echoed through the gaps between the wooden slats of a sealed-up window. I could just make out the shadows of what remained of the small party tearing down the street. Their red-cloaked leader strode after them, apparently too dignified to run.

When they had passed, Thalanir whispered, "I've warded this place. We're safe here for now—but we need to stay put for a little."

"Isn't it strange?" I asked "A Lightblood, all this way from Aetherion?"

"He's a Braïthe—a traitor Fae, come to win the favor of mortal lords by doing their dirty work for them. I'm afraid there are many more of his kind out there—Tírian and Lightblood alike. Power-hungry, the lot of them."

Breathing heavily, I pressed my back to the wall, only now realizing how hard my heart was beating. I set my bag down and dropped to the floor, pulling my knees up and wrapping my arms around them.

"Was he serious?" I asked. "About bonding being punishable by death?"

Thalanir sneered. "I've heard it's the king's decree, though it's based on ancient law. Caedmon doesn't want mortals bonding with Fae, because their children might be stronger than that simpering prince he calls a son. A little hypocritical, given that he wanted Corym to wed you."

I winced at the mention of the prince. "Do you think he would actually kill people for taking Fae lovers?"

With a shake of his head, Thalanir said, "Fae would never tolerate such rules. If the king were to try and harm one of our kind or someone we love...suffice it to say King Caedmon would quickly meet his end."

His irises flared with anger as he spoke the words.

"But you don't need to worry about such threats," he added. "Never. You are of royal blood. You will wed someone powerful, a High Fae worthy of you. Your future will be filled with wonder —and I intend to make sure that future begins as soon as possible. I will help you to find your way to the life you deserve, Leta. I promise you that."

The words were kind. Generous, even.

But still, they hurt.

They were further confirmation of the rejection he'd issued last night—evidence that he didn't want me as I wanted him.

Still, when he seated himself next to me so close that our shoulders touched, I sank into the sensation, reveling in it for as long as I could.

I turned to face him, studying his profile. His perfect, angular nose. His full lips. His chin...that jaw...

"What if I don't wish to wed someone like that?" I asked. "What if I don't want a prince or a High Lord?"

When he turned to me, our faces were so close that I could feel his breath caress my lips. He smiled, but it quickly faded, and he pulled his eyes away again. "You're a princess," he said. "You could have any Fae you desire."

Desire.

The Lightblood in the red cloak had spoken of it.

Even he knows how much I want you.

"What if the Fae I desire chooses to forego his title of High Lord?" I asked quietly. "What if he's someone I've seen in my mind a thousand times? Someone I can taste, just by thinking of him?"

He stood up, shaking his head as he took a step away from me.

"Don't," he murmured, rounding on me.

I pushed myself to my feet, stepping toward him, and it took all the strength I had just to meet his eyes. "If you don't feel the same desire, then just tell me," I breathed. "Tell me now, so I can push these thoughts away once and for all. Because I see you in my waking dreams, Thalanir. Day and night, I see your face, hear your voice. I've felt your lips on mine so many times. I've asked myself a hundred times what it would be like to be with you. It's a torment—torture for my body and soul. But I feel like—like there must be a reason I've been gifted *these* memories in particular. A reason I...I want you so badly that it hurts."

I sucked in my lower lip, my cheeks flaming.

I had laid it out for him. I had rendered myself vulnerable to the point where he could easily tear me down.

Now, it was his turn to speak.

"If you think I do not desire you," he said, his eyes roaming down my body as he eased closer. "If you think I wouldn't give everything and anything to claim you as my own, right here and now, Leta of the hundred lives...then I'm afraid you are very, very wrong. Your body and mind have called to me for longer than you know. And as much as I try to resist, I want nothing more than to give in to the craving that's built hour by hour inside me, to the point where I fear it might destroy me."

His mouth was an inch from mine now—so close that I could taste him on the air.

"Tell me," I said softly. "Tell me what would happen if you surrendered to that craving."

He reached out, taking a twisting wave of red hair in his

fingers. "When I look at you, I feel a part of me that died long ago come back to life—a part that I thought would never live again."

He stroked the backs of his fingers down my cheek, his eyes shifting to my lips, my neck, my breasts, then back again.

"I didn't know I was still capable of desire," he whispered. "Of wanting—*needing* to protect someone with my life. I didn't know I could want anything quite so badly as I want you. You are exquisite, and it is torture to wonder constantly what you taste like. It's torture to be so close to you."

"And you said I was plain," I replied. But this time, I smiled.

He shook his head, his expression earnest. "I might as easily say I find the mountains, rivers, and valleys of the world dull. You are the most beautiful creature I have ever set eyes on."

My lips parted slightly in anticipation of the kiss I was sure to come. The kiss I had been craving so desperately for so, so long.

"If you surrendered to your craving," I breathed, "then what would you do?"

"I would consume you," he whispered back, his lips stroking my cheek now. "I would claim you. I would pledge my soul to you, because once I had you, I would never have the strength to leave. I would be yours forever—yours to bend as you wished. Yours to command, Lahnan."

I closed my eyes, my body tightening as Thalanir's hand slipped down my stomach, then pushed down, and then down some more into my trousers, until I found myself squirming with the pleasure of it.

His fingers found the place between my legs, slipping over my slick sex, and he let out a sigh that shattered me. He pulled his hand free and stroked his tongue over his fingertips, his eyes narrowing as they locked on my own.

Flame swirled in his irises as he pushed me back against the wall, and for a moment, I was back in the place of memories—standing in that open field, no obstacles between us. Nothing keeping us apart—nothing and no one forcing us to resist our attraction.

And then his mouth was on mine, his arms trapping me on either side, his tongue stroking my own. I tasted him back, reveling in the unquenchable need between us, the feeling of falling—yet feeling entirely safe, locked between his powerful arms.

I opened my mouth to his, inviting him deeper. He obliged with a stroke of his tongue, and I moaned with the taste of him —of my sex on his lips. I raked my fingers into his thick hair, forcing myself onto my toes.

He lifted my chin and kissed my neck, and for a moment, nothing in the world mattered.

His hands moved to my hips, then my waist, and then, as one hand slipped over my breast, the pad of his thumb flicking over the rigid peak, he moaned with pleasure. Any lingering doubt that he desired me as much as I desired him was gone. I could feel him harden against me—feel the desperate need like a raging fire between us.

I needed him to claim me, to take every inch of me so that I was destroyed...yet whole, for the first time in my life.

"Gods help me, I want you," I breathed against his mouth.

Those, it seemed, were the wrong words.

He leapt backwards, a look of horror flashing over his features.

"I'm sorry," he growled, twisting away to hide his face from me. "I'm sorry. I shouldn't have done that."

I reached for his shoulder, expecting him to recoil, but he remained for a moment, frozen under my touch.

"Why not?" I asked, stepping closer. "Why can't we be together?"

"Because you would grow to despise me," he snarled. "For what I am. For what I've done."

"No," I protested. "I could never—"

He spun around to face me then, a look of something close to fury in his eyes. "You have no idea what I am, Leta. Don't speak of things you don't understand." He let out a deep breath. "But you will know it all soon enough, I fear."

"No thanks to you," I scolded, pulling back, hurt creasing its way across my features. "You won't tell me anything about yourself. About who she was—why I have these...these memories of you. They're no gift, Thalanir. They're cruel and teasing —and they've made me want something I can never have. Which is...insane. Because I feel like those were *my* memories. *My* life. I feel like—like I know what it is to be in love with you."

"Then know this—loving me would be your downfall, Lahnan."

Pain shot through my chest, but I swallowed it down and forced out the words, my voice fracturing. "What happened between you and her? Why do you fear love so much?"

At that, his blue eyes flared again, this time with some hidden emotion.

"You will see the truth," he said. "And when you do, you will abhor me for it. You may think you know what it is to love me— but there is no doubt in my mind you will soon hate me."

I shook my head. "No," I said. "I *want* to hate you, Thalanir. I do. I want to force myself so far from you, to tell myself I never wish to see you again. But it would be a lie."

Tears stung my eyes.

Pain colored his features as his hands took hold of my face. "Do *not* allow yourself to care for me," he said under his breath. "I am empty. Hollow. Devoid of a soul. There is nothing in me to love, despite what you may tell yourself. I am hatred, rage, and darkness, Leta. Learn that now, and move on. Live your life. You deserve so much better than me."

To that, I had nothing to say.

His words broke something inside me, and the pain that coursed through my body was so great that when he released me, I fell against the wall, my hands clenched protectively against my chest.

Turning away, Thalanir spoke icily. "You'll find what you seek in the North. I am not what you should ever want. Remember that, if you forget all else. I'm a fool. It was a mistake to kiss you."

"A mistake," I repeated with a bitter laugh. "That's what I am to you."

"No." He couldn't bring himself to look at me when he said, "What you are to me is a curse."

CHAPTER TWELVE

By the time the sun had set, Thalanir and I had paced, sat, and slumbered through hours on end of hostile silence, locked away in that abandoned stable.

Each time I considered speaking, I warned myself against it.

He's nothing but a paid escort—A Valdfae who hopes I will end up bound to someone else.

He does not care for me. He never will.

I told myself that besides, I was foolish to feel so hurt by a man—a *Fae*—I had only just met. One who, for all intents and purposes, could well be my enemy. For all I knew, he'd lied to me about Mithraan hiring him. Maybe that High Lord bastard just wanted me kept away from my sister. Perhaps he saw me as a threat.

Hell, for that matter, Thalanir and his friend might have been hoping to collect and split a ransom from Corym and the king for my return.

Bitterness grew inside me as the hours wore on, every imagined scenario painting Thalanir to seem worse than the last.

By the time he finally spoke, I was close to convincing myself I despised him.

Darkness had just begun to creep into the stable when he said, "We need to leave."

Without another word, he opened the stable door, and in an instant, I felt the oppressive spell that had protected us all day fade away. We were now without a shield, vulnerable to the outside world.

I stepped out into the narrow street. Not a soul was in sight —which frightened me more than it should have.

"How far to the outskirts?" I asked, my tone sullen.

"It will take us twenty minutes to reach the edge of the city, if all goes well," Thalanir replied, turning right and beginning the march. "If I fly us out, we'll be seen. So that's not an option."

With my pack over my shoulder, I followed in silence, trying not to feel like a pony trotting behind an elegant stallion as I once again struggled to keep up with his quick, long strides.

I drew my hood over my head, my eyes warily darting this way and that, my heart leaping each time I saw a shadow move.

To my utter surprise, we made it to the edge of town without incident, altering course only when we'd reached a narrow lane flanked by tall, well-groomed shrubberies.

I expected to continue hiking all night, but instead, Thalanir led me another mile or so until we reached a house next to what looked like a smithy, its glassless windows glowing with welcoming red-orange light. The place reminded me of our father, Martel, who had died so recently. The wound of his passing was still deep and painful.

Thalanir knocked on the smithy's door, and when a gruff-looking man of fifty or so opened it, the Valdfae said, "We need a horse. A large one, if you can spare it."

"I only have two, and I need one of them," the man grunted, eyeing Thalanir and me warily. "I suppose I can spare Surly, my gelding. He's the bigger of them—practically a draft horse. What are you willing to give me for him?"

He eyed me up and down as if to imply that I was the price he charged for a steed.

Disgusted, I found myself easing closer to Thalanir in spite of my resolution to treat him with cold hostility for the rest of my days.

With a look of warning, the Valdfae pulled out his seemingly bottomless sack of coins and handed a few to the man. These ones were shining and gold—incredibly valuable pieces the likes of which I had never seen in person—not even in Domignon's palace.

"That'll do nicely," the gray-haired man said, immediately losing interest in me. "Come around the back, then."

Thalanir and I headed around the smithy only to spot a small stable with four stalls. A black horse with an exquisite mane seemed to be awaiting our arrival, his head jutting out of his stall's half-door as we approached.

"Surly here's a good lad," the smith said. "Reliable. Steady. He won't throw you for anything, and he can easily carry the both of you."

"Thank you," Thalanir said, opening the stall door to let the horse step out. "I'm sure he'll do nicely."

"What about tack?" I asked. "Bridle, saddle?"

Thalanir shot me a look that betrayed amusement. "There's no need to shackle our friend here."

"He's been trained with a bit," the smith said. "You won't get far without it."

"I'll retrain him, then," Thalanir snapped. "I don't believe in cramming steel into a horse's mouth. They find it unpleasant."

The smith watched as Thalanir lifted me easily up onto the horse's back, slinging my pack over his own shoulder before leaping up behind me.

The Fae leaned forward, his chest pressing against my back,

and whispered something to the horse in a language I was certain I had never heard...yet I understood it perfectly.

Make haste, my friend. Go north, and when we arrive at our destination, you will be rewarded handsomely with fields of lush grass.

The smith looked stunned as he stepped back and the gelding took off at a fast trot, heading for the road that led north out of the city.

"What language was that?" I asked when we were out of earshot.

"It's òran," Thalanir said. "A dialect used by the Valdfae."

"I see. The language of sell-blades and bounty hunters."

He tightened behind me. "Among other things, yes."

"Though it's weird to call you a sell-blade. I haven't seen a dagger or sword on you in the time I've known you. I suppose a more appropriate title for you would be 'Cold-hearted killer.'"

He fell silent for a moment before replying, "If that's what you think of me, then so be it. I wouldn't want you to have too high an opinion of the likes of me."

"I've struggled to form *any* opinion of you, actually," I replied. "Given how you run hot and cold. One minute, you're risking your life to protect mine and the next, you're insulting me in one way or another. It's hardly fair."

I could feel the slow throb of his heart against my back. "Nothing in this world is fair, Leta Martel. The sooner you learn that, the better."

I went silent again, my hips moving in conjunction with the gelding's gait, which slowed to a walk as we entered a narrow path leading into a dark wood.

"How does he know where to go?" I asked, curiosity superseding my urge to give Thalanir the silent treatment. "With no reins, I mean. You're not even pressing your hands to his neck. How do you steer him?"

It was true—Thalanir's hands were resting in fists pressed to his thighs, clearly avoiding any risk of contact with my body. I could still feel him too acutely behind me, though. The rhythm of his pelvis as he moved with me; his chest against my back; his breath penetrating my cloak. It was impossible to relax. Indeed, it was impossible not to be swept up in desire for him, and I despised myself for it.

"I have a way of linking my mind with animals' minds," he said. "Valdfae are often intimately connected to nature—it's why we're natural wanderers."

"I see. And just how long have you wandered and charmed horses?"

"Again with the questions," he said, but I detected a hint of amusement in his tone. "For many years, I have walked the trails and woods of Kalemnar and Aetherion."

"Alone?"

"Yes."

"And you intend to be alone forever."

He hesitated, then said, "Perhaps."

"Then I'm sorry for you. That's a sad way to live."

"Maybe it is, but it's the only way I have known, for hundreds of years."

After the brief exchange, we rode in cold silence for an hour, maybe more.

Memories began to shoot through my mind again—briefer flashes than ever now, and they made little sense. The second I tried to focus on any one of them, it disappeared into the ether, pointless and forgotten. I dismissed the visions, telling myself they were little more than quick blinks of my mind's eye.

I was grateful, at least, not to be teased with lengthy, graphic scenes of intimacy with the Fae riding behind me. Perhaps it helped that I told myself he was now off limits for eternity—that I needed to free myself of him, body and mind.

The sooner we arrived at whatever destination we were headed for, the better.

When the glowing windows of a series of welcoming houses came into view in the distance, Thalanir said, "We're heading to the village of Lapis. They're friendly enough, and I know the innkeeper. We'll stop there to water the horse and get a bite—and perhaps some drink. You must be hungry by now."

I hadn't wanted to say anything, but he was right. We hadn't eaten since the bread that morning, and I was famished.

Thalanir—or the horse—or both—guided us into the town until we came to a stone inn, where the gelding turned to slip down a narrow laneway until we stopped at a small paddock. Thalanir dismounted before helping me down, and we released the horse into the enclosure, where he had access to a trough of clean water and a fresh bale of hay.

We strode back to inn's entrance, and Thalanir pushed the door open.

Inside, we were greeted by a tall man with a grim face who took a long step toward us, a short sword at his waist. His hair was brown and scraggly, his face coated in spiky graying stubble.

Nothing about him looked even remotely welcoming.

He ignored me while assessing Thalanir, like one male lion eyeing another to decide whether or not he was a threat to the pride.

"Where's Lachain?" Thalanir asked, apparently caught off-guard. "The innkeeper?"

"He sold the place and moved to Belleau months ago," the man grunted. "*I'm* the new owner."

"I see."

"You're a Valdfae, aren't ya?" the man asked, a hand resting on the hilt of his sword as his eyes veered to me. "And who's this lovely creature?"

Thalanir's body went rigid at the words. Instinctively, he stepped forward to place himself between the man and me.

"Who wants to know?" he asked.

The innkeeper let out an amused snort. "Don't worry—I couldn't care less about either of you. But there's a lady Fae in the back who's been waiting for you for hours. She must've known you were headed this way."

"Lady Fae?" I asked.

Thalanir sniffed at the air, his expression grim. When he caught the Fae's scent, he reached for me, taking my hand in his. "Leta," he whispered, "we need to leave this place."

"Perhaps," a feminine voice said from somewhere behind the innkeeper, "you should let the young lady decide."

I moved around Thalanir to see a woman stepping out from a dark doorway at the back of the room. She was dressed in a long silver cloak, a veil covering her face. As she eased toward me, she lifted it to reveal exquisitely beautiful features and a set of pointed ears.

Something about her felt vaguely familiar, though I knew I had never laid eyes on her in my life. For a moment, I wondered if I'd seen her in one of my flashes of memory.

I stared into her eyes and she looked into mine, a warm smile slipping over her lips that made its way enticingly to every feature.

"You've come at last," she said softly. "It's so nice to see you."

"Who...*are* you?" I asked, dazed by her beauty, her voice. I felt intoxicated, as if someone had poured a flagon of wine down my throat, and my head was trying to wrap itself around the ensuing dizziness.

Thalanir's hand pressed itself to my shoulder, and he said again, "We have to go. Now."

Taking my arm, he tried to pull me toward the door, but my

feet were planted—no—*welded* to the stone tile beneath me. I could not move—nor did I want to.

Nothing could have compelled me to abandon the feeling that had settled inside me—this sensation of perfect bliss and comfort.

"She isn't going anywhere, Valdfae," the female Fae said, extending an inviting hand. "She belongs with me. Don't you...Leta?"

CHAPTER THIRTEEN

THALANIR DROPPED my arm and leapt in front of me toward the female Fae, shielding me with his body.

But it did little to subdue her allure.

"If you want to take her," he snarled. "You'll have to go through me, Priestess."

Priestess?

I didn't even know there was such a thing as a Fae Priestess...

Or did I?

Did it even matter? *Did anything matter?*

I chuckled as I contemplated the questions. No—nothing mattered right now. Nothing except the knowledge that somehow, this Priestess, whoever she was, was the answer to all my woes.

"Leta," her velvety voice purred again. "Are you really going to let this murderer control you—or would you prefer to make up your own mind and choose your own destiny?"

Yes, a voice inside me whispered—and it took me a moment to realize it was my own. *She's right. He is a murderer. A cold-blooded killer. One who teased you, took you captive, and held you in*

that dank stable for hours on end. One who put your life at risk more
than once. He is dangerous, and **she** *is safe.*

"Don't listen to her, Leta," Thalanir snapped, turning to me.
"She is a Goldtongue. She's trying to lure you by playing on
your weaknesses. You don't know what her kind is capable of—
but I do."

"Capable?" she laughed. "You, Valdfae, should know better
than anyone that I am weakened in recent days, as are all of my
Sisters. It was your friends who stole our power...or have you
already forgotten?"

I stepped out from behind Thalanir, rendering myself fully
vulnerable to her.

"She won't hurt me," I said, my voice a strange monotone.
"She's not here to do me harm."

"She is one of the Sisterhood of the Fallen," Thalanir
snarled. "Formerly known as the Order. They are fanatics who
lost their wings when..."

The female Fae cocked her head to the side, smirking as if
waiting for him to complete the thought. "Well?" she asked.
"Aren't you going to tell her who took our wings from us? Or is
that one of the many secrets you refuse to share with your
captive here?"

"Your wings rightly vanished when the Elar died," he
snarled, his voice low, feral, threatening. "No one *took* them
from you. Your kind should never have had them in the first
place. They were stolen from the High Fae by that wretched
entity—they were never rightly yours."

"Wrong." Her voice was ice. "The Elar granted us the Gift of
flight in return for our devotion. And though she is gone, we
remain devoted to her cause." She glanced at me and, in a tone
fit for a five-year-old child, said, "Leta—I am Dauphine, and I
have been looking for you. You're safe now. That is all that
matters."

I took a step toward her, some invisible force drawing me closer. But after a moment I stopped, a small, nagging voice in my mind compelling me to ask, "How do you know who I am?"

"Because you're special, my dear. We all know who you are, just as Thalanir here knew."

"She'll use you," Thalanir warned. "She will destroy you, Leta."

Dauphine laughed, her eyes flaring with silver flame as she shot him a glare. "You tracked her for money—hunted her—and you dare warn her of danger, Valdfae? Tell her what else you've done to your fellow Fae, why don't you?" She gestured to me, the motion of her hand elegant, beautiful even. "Tell her how you've killed without remorse too many times to count."

"She knows I have killed," he said, his voice so tightly coiled that it sounded as though it might snap like a too-thin steel thread at any moment. "And I will happily kill you where you stand if you try to harm her."

"Yes," Dauphine replied, still smiling, apparently unperturbed by his warning. "You would, wouldn't you?" Turning back to me, she added, "Your friend here thinks I mean to harm you. He doubts my motives. But what could be more benevolent than wishing to reunite two beloved sisters after a long separation?"

"*Sisters?*" I echoed, pushing away thoughts of what had just transpired between the two Fae. My mind swam with pleasure. Talk of killing and threats were of no concern to me. "Are you telling me you can bring me to Lyrinn?"

Thalanir shook his head. "She is a liar," he said, his voice strained with fury. "Whatever she is making you feel right now, it's only an illusion. She's twisting you to her will. Do you hear me?"

I turned to him and looked up into his eyes. He was so beautiful, so devastatingly attractive, and in my bliss, I wanted so badly to kiss him one last time. But even as the thought coursed through me, it vanished...and all I could think of was the promise of seeing my sister again.

"Where is she?" I asked, turning back to Dauphine. "Where is Lyrinn?"

"Not far from here," she promised. "But I should tell you, if you come with me, you must leave the Valdfae behind—which I don't suppose will be difficult, given what he has done to you." She offered up a sympathetic smile, her head tilting when she added, "He has made you desire him, has he not? Forced you to long for his touch?"

"I..." I turned back to Thalanir, eyeing his clenched jaw, the fire in his eyes. "He has, yes. I have desired him so much that... that it hurt."

Dauphine clicked her tongue, chastising. "It's a common tactic of their kind. They like to lure their prey before reeling them in. But it's easy enough to sever the connection. Come with me, and I promise—you will be free of him. Free of the hold he has on you."

Some far-off voice told me I didn't wish to be free of him— that I wanted the connection to deepen between us. But it was impossible to feel anything in that moment other than a sense of joy at the prospect of seeing Lyrinn.

You don't need him, a soothing, ethereal voice whispered to my mind.

Gallia's voice—or was it mine once again?

You don't want him. It's all a game he's been playing with you— a series of twisted lies.

He is a monster.

"Don't go," Thalanir cautioned. "Please, Leta—it will not end well for you."

"Would you like me to tell her what will happen if she chooses to stay with you, Valdfae?" Dauphine asked, her voice turning acidic. "Or would you rather walk away now and leave it to her imagination?"

The words had a dagger-like effect on Thalanir, who stepped back, pain scrawled across his face and body.

"I would not hurt her for the world," he whispered.

"Oh, but I think you would," Dauphine purred, stepping toward him and laying a silken hand on his stubbled cheek. "I think you would revel in it."

"Leta," he said softly, drawing back from the Priestess. "I will not force you to stay with me. Not if you wish to leave. But you must say the words. Tell me what you want. Ask me to let you go, or I will have no choice but to stay by your side."

Backing away, Dauphine held her hand out to me. "What do you owe him? He pushed you away. He toyed with you—teased you. Your desire for him has eaten away at you, and he's watched all this time with cold amusement."

"Do *you* know where Lyrinn is?" I asked Thalanir, my tone chilly as the darkest winter night. "If you do, then tell me right now."

"Leta," he breathed.

"Do. You. Know?"

"No," he confessed, his chest heaving. "But I would guess that neither does this witch."

"Witch?" Dauphine tutted. "Come, now. We prefer harpy or shrew, if you insist on insults. Witches are *soo* last millennium." She slipped a hand under my chin, pulling my eyes to her own. "Tell me, Leta, do you wish to see your sister?"

"Of course I do," I said, looking her in the eye. The comfort of her face was drawing me in relentlessly, despite a quiet desire that had taken root again, warning me to stay with Thalanir. But I forced that desire away, telling myself he was poison. "More than anything."

She nodded. "Good. Come with me, and before you know it, you will have your arms around Lyrinn."

"Leta," Thalanir warned, his voice quietly intense. "Ask me to let you go, and I will. But if you do not ask, I will do whatever it takes to keep you from her. I have no choice in the matter."

I pivoted to face him again, my face contorted with sudden anger. "You told me that I'm a curse—you've made it clear over and over again that I'm nothing more to you than a task, a job —a sack of coin. I have no desire to trudge along after you for hundreds of miles while you break my soul slowly, *Valdfae*. So let me go. Please." With the final word, a stab of pain shot its way through my chest that was almost unbearable. My voice was thin and strained when I said, "I wish to see my sister. And I never wish to see you again."

"Then come with me, dearest," Dauphine said, turning to walk out the door at the back of the room.

"Lahnan..." I heard behind me as I started to follow, and I stopped and turned my head slightly.

"What?"

He was silent for a moment before he murmured, "You're nothing but a fool if you go with that manipulator. Corym twisted your mind—and now you're letting it happen all over again. Don't do this. Don't let her control you."

So, that was all he had to offer. No plea for me to stay. No kindness. No affection. Nothing but judgment and coldness.

"I suppose I'm a fool, then," I replied, raising my chin as tears fell down my cheeks. "Because if there's the slightest chance that I might see Lyrinn by accompanying the manipulator, I'll take it. I'd sooner be a hopeful fool than one who desires a Fae she can never have."

Without another word, I headed out the door.

CHAPTER FOURTEEN

I DIDN'T EXACTLY WANT to walk away from Thalanir.

I only *told* myself I wanted to. I told myself that if I could just step away from him—from his scent, his eyes, his touch—everything that had consumed me for far too long would fade, and I would begin to mend.

I would forget he ever existed.

The Priestess had offered me something he had not—something more than vague hints and mysterious connections.

She had offered me my sister.

And for that, I was willing to snap the thread binding my heart to the Valdfae.

When Dauphine and I were outside, she guided me to a small paddock where two saddled horses awaited us.

I stopped in my tracks, a jolt of fear freezing me in place. For a moment, it was like my mind cleared, and I could see the folly of what I was about to do.

"You knew I would come here. How?"

Dauphine smiled at me, and instantly, I lost myself again, her eyes rendering me drunk with a sensation more pleasant than almost any I'd ever known.

"I heard some time ago that you had fled Domignon," she explained. "I tracked you, just as the Valdfae did. It took me some time to find the trail, but when I discovered you were with that cruel bastard, I made haste." She looked over her shoulder, but there was no sign of Thalanir. It seemed he'd already surrendered to the notion that he wouldn't be earning his bounty, after all.

Dauphine leaned in close to me and said, "Don't let yourself regret your choice. He is a thing of beauty, I'll admit—and I know it's difficult to leave him behind. But that breed of Fae... they're devious creatures, out only for themselves. Thalanir is one of the worst of them, capable of entering the minds of those he wishes to manipulate and forcing them to yearn for him. But make no mistake—he is a monster. Had you stayed with him a moment longer, I fear that you would have seen it for yourself."

I heard the words, absorbed them, nodded.

But still, I turned to see if he was standing in the doorway. To see if there was any chance he was sorry to watch me go.

"Leta," the Priestess said when she saw me glancing back at the inn. "You are facing a momentous battle in the days ahead, and you will need powerful allies. I intend to help you."

My eyes shot back to hers. Suddenly, I was desperate to leave this place. To get as far from Thalanir as I could, as fast as I could. "Then help me. Where is she? Where is Lyrinn?"

The smallest, mildest flicker crossed Dauphine's features— a look of quiet triumph—then it was gone.

"At a convent set deep in the woods, some distance north of here. The convent used to belong to a sect of mortal Priestesses, but it was abandoned years ago and was recently claimed by my Sisters and myself. Come. Let's go see your dear sister."

With that, she handed me one of the horses' reins. I nodded one last time, issuing a final look toward the door.

My stomach rolled over on itself as my eyes met the empty doorway.

I don't feel right. This...this feels...

"Leta," Dauphine said, cutting through my mind. Her voice was cold, commanding. "Make haste."

I obeyed, my body tight. With each passing second, an uneasiness was spreading through my mind, twisting like ivy through my thoughts.

What was I doing, going with this Priestess? I knew nothing about her other than that she claimed to know something of Lyrinn. But she had offered no evidence of it. It wasn't as though she'd given me any reason to trust her other than a smooth voice and a pretty face.

"It's all right," she said, seeing the look in my eyes. "You have nothing to fear."

With that, she urged her horse to break into a trot down a narrow path leading out of the paddock, and I followed in sullen silence.

When we reached the outskirts of the small town, we began our long trek along a broad dirt road, and Dauphine urged me to ride beside her, eyeing me sideways as my mount caught hers up.

"So," she said, "you know."

"Know what?" I replied.

She laughed softly. "About your sister—about yourself." She looked into my eyes, and her own swirled with color as she studied me, the horse now moving at a steady pace beneath her. "You know you're a Fae. But you don't yet know why those like the Valdfae and I have been searching for you—or the *true* reason Prince Corym wants you for his wife."

"Prince Corym," I repeated, horrified to hear his name on her lips, "doesn't want me for his wife—not anymore. Maybe he did once, but it was only because he wished to steal my Gifts."

"Ah. The Gifts that haven't yet shown themselves. Your Change hasn't fully taken hold, has it?"

I didn't need to reply. She pulled her eyes back to the road and said, "Your ears are still rounded. Your scars still show. But soon enough, you will alter and find your strength."

"How do you know any of this?" I asked her. "About Corym —about Lyrinn? About...me?"

"I knew your mother," she said simply, and a flash of memory came to me—an image of my mother as Lyrinn had known her, of her beautiful but frightening face. Her flaming red hair.

"You're wondering what she was like," Dauphine said.

"I'm curious, yes," I told her, shifting uneasily in the saddle. "But I suppose Lyrinn will fill me in when I see her."

"Yes, of course she will. I can tell you in the meantime that your mother was the most powerful Fae I ever met. She was a wonder, and her loss was a tragedy for all our kind."

I wanted to ask how she had died, but something kept me from it—some tacit warning deep in my soul.

The Priestess kept her eyes locked straight ahead when she said, "Your mother once counted herself among our ranks. A High Priestess, like me. Ah, but she was powerful. Her father is powerful still. No doubt he will be pleased to learn you're alive and well."

"Rynfael? Have you met the High King of Tíria?"

Dauphine gave her mount a gentle squeeze of her legs and he sped up, as did mine. We were suddenly moving like the wind, though the horses didn't seem to be over-exerting themselves. This was some spell, some magic silently cast by the Priestess, and I was beginning to understand how much stronger she was than she had initially appeared.

"I have encountered King Rynfael, yes," Dauphine replied. "Long ago now. Some call him a High Lord, but you're right to refer to him as High King. It's my hope that you'll meet him one day very soon. But come—we must hurry if we're to reach our destination by dusk. We will stay there tonight. You will eat and drink, and you can have a proper rest. You look as though you could use it, after the ordeal the Valdfae put you through."

"I *am* tired," I confessed, looking back over my shoulder. A sudden pang of remorse collided with a place deep inside me, truth fighting with lies.

What, exactly, had the Valdfae put me through?

I had told myself he'd been cruel. That he had imprisoned me.

But...had he?

He had kissed me, stroked my neck. He had rendered me weak with desire and pushed me away when I asked him for more than he was willing to give.

But now that there was some distance between us and my head had cleared a little, I could be honest with myself. He had *never* been cruel. Aside from a little teasing, which I deserved for my vanity, he had been nothing but respectful and protective.

And in return, I had told him I never wished to see him again.

Dauphine had not said a cruel word to me, either. Her voice was still velvet-smooth, her demeanor perfectly pleasant.

But with each moment we spent together, my dread grew. Her pleasant words were beginning to feel like a mask covering something dark and foreboding. Poison seeped through them, infiltrating the air itself.

For a brief moment, I considered turning my mount around —I even yanked on the reins once to see if he would obey. But he surged forward as though a tug of the bit had no effect on him whatsoever. He was under Dauphine's control now—and I was trapped.

"Don't think about leaving me," she warned. "You don't want to fall back under his spell, do you?"

"No," I replied, my mind soothed once again by her voice. "I don't."

We rode in silence for what felt like hours more before Dauphine finally steered the horses off the road onto a wooded path. They walked at a quick pace along the trail, as if our mounts knew they were headed home.

"The convent is just up ahead," Dauphine assured me. "I'll show you to your quarters when we arrive."

"Thank you...but," I replied, agitation churning inside me. "I don't care about quarters. I want to see Lyrinn. You told me she was—"

"All in good time," she said, flicking her fingers toward me, and with a jolt, my mind calmed, and any worry that had begun to eat away at me disintegrated into a sense of peace.

"Yes," I repeated, a smile curling on my lips. "All in good time."

The sun was falling below the horizon by the time we entered the convent grounds, which comprised a series of unadorned gray stone buildings that bore more than a passing resemblance to a prison compound like one I had seen during my time in Domignon.

I told myself it made sense that the place wouldn't be hospitable or beautiful. Convents weren't exactly meant to be palaces, after all. Those who worshiped the gods were supposed to be devoted—contemplative and lacking in superficiality or care for material things.

As we approached the large stable tucked away behind what seemed to be the main building, a feeling of panic set my heart racing, replacing the calm that Dauphine had just renewed in me.

A quiet voice whispered to me, warning me to swing my horse around and flee this desolate place before it was too late.

No. If Lyrinn is here, I scolded myself, *how could I even think of leaving?*

Just as I was looking up at the windows, seeking out any sign of life, something flew by my head—a large insect such as a wasp, or a bee, the flitting of its wings clearly audible.

But as I glanced around, I saw nothing.

Dauphine whistled, and a stable hand stepped out from the shadows. Dressed in gray linen, she was small, her face coated in a layer of dust. Without saying a word, she took hold of the horses' reins, and the Priestess and I each dismounted then began the walk to the convent's back entrance.

I followed Dauphine inside to a plain white foyer where a few veiled figures milled about slowly. Disinterested, they pulled their gazes toward me for only a moment before looking away again. Some of them were Fae—their pointed ears were visible in spite of the veils. But others—those who kept their heads down in apparent submission—looked like mortals.

"I thought you said the mortals had left this place," I said to Dauphine, but at first she ignored me, heading for a stone staircase at the far end of the broad, open space. When we'd climbed halfway up, she finally replied, "I said the convent was now the property of the Fae," but that was all the explanation I was to receive.

She guided me to a room on the second level—one with a thick wooden door on iron hinges, which she pushed open.

"Your quarters," she said. "I hope they're satisfactory."

When I had stepped inside, I turned to her and said, "Which room is Lyrinn in?"

But instead of replying, Dauphine smiled and took a long step back into the hallway. With a simple gesture of her fingers, she sealed the door shut, and I heard the grind of a turning lock.

I leapt forward and reached for the doorknob, which wouldn't budge. I knocked, then pounded on the door, calling out to her to set me free.

But to no avail.

Panicked, I turned to assess the room that was now my prison cell. It was small and dingy, its walls made of cracked plaster, its layers of paint long since peeled most of the way off. One smallish window was wide open to the outdoors, and I stepped over to see if there was a way I could climb down the side of the building. But it was a sheer drop, and a perilously long way to the stone-hard ground below.

I really was trapped.

Worse, I had proven myself the very fool that Thalanir had warned me about.

Your pride made you push him aside, and you listened to her soothing voice instead of common sense. He warned you, and you ignored him because you didn't want to subject yourself to aching for him for a single second longer.

Stupid, stupid, stupid.

There was no bath in the room—only a ewer on the nearby dresser, and I splashed some water on my face before throwing myself onto the bed, my eyes stinging with tears.

Too much had happened since I'd left Domignon. Too many words and thoughts now swirled through my head. Too much madness. I had lost my ability to trust anyone, including myself. I was nothing more now than a naive girl in a world of cunning deceivers.

Back in Dúnbar before the Blood Trials, life had been so calm, so peaceful. I'd always lamented how dull it was, how predictable.

Now, I would have given anything to have it back.

"Who *are* these Priestesses?" I asked in a half-whisper, my eyes locked on the ceiling. "And what do they want with me?"

"I can answer the first question," a strange, low voice said. "But I'm afraid I don't yet know the answer to the second one."

CHAPTER FIFTEEN

"Who said that?" I asked, shooting upwards, my palms flat on the bed. "Show yourself, or I'll..."

I'll what?

Threaten to burn him alive, like I did to the men in the pub a few nights ago?

The rapid flutter of a small creature's wings met my ears once again, just as it had done outside.

Only this time when I turned to look, I could see where it had come from.

A tiny person—no, not a person, but some sort of faerie, his minuscule wings fluttering wildly behind him—was hovering in the air a few feet away. He wore a small suit of mail and leather, a sword sheathed at his waist.

"You are Leta Martel," he said, his expression stern.

"I am," I replied. "And I suppose I shouldn't be surprised by anything in the world right now. But..."

"You find *me* surprising."

"You're very...small."

A look of annoyance contorted his face slightly. "You're very tall, and yet you don't see *my* eyes going wide with wonder."

"True."

"I'm a sprite," he added with a roll of his eyes, as if he'd had to explain this same thing far too many times. "From Aetherion. There are many of us in that realm."

"A sprite," I repeated. I had heard of their kind in my younger years, in stories told by old men and women—folk tales. The small magic-users were said to be cunning, devious, mischievous.

But I had always thought they were nothing more than a fiction.

"My name is Lark," he added. "I know your sister Lyrinn quite well from our time together on the other side of the sea."

At that, my heart performed a dangerous flip in my chest.

"Where is she?" I asked, my voice coiling tightly in my throat. "Is she all right?"

"She's in transit, as far as I know," he said. "Traveling to Tíria by ship."

"She's not here in the convent?"

He looked stunned. "Of course not," he snapped. "She's hundreds of miles away."

I had to fight off the tears that were threatening to form in my eyes at the revelation.

This was proof that Thalanir had been right all along. I was a fool. The Priestess had lied to me, and I, charmed by whatever spell she had cast over my all too eager mind, had fallen for it, just as I'd fallen for Corym's tricks.

"When was the last time you saw her?" I asked, trying to conceal the tremor in my voice.

"A week or so ago."

"Is she all right? Is she..."

I couldn't finish the question. Is she still with Mithraan? Has she forgotten me? Is she entirely changed?

"She was fine, the last time I saw her. Though..."

He stopped there, lowering his chin and averting his eyes for the first time.

"Though what?"

"I am sorry to say this to you, but your sister has been through some difficult times."

Recollections of my visions flashed through my mind then, all at once. I remembered with vivid clarity the painful image of Lyrinn crying out, tormented by some unseen enemy. Mithraan's voice as he called to her. Fire in a dark sky...

"I've seen something of her pain," I said, "but no explanation for it. Please, tell me what you mean. I need to know what's happened to her."

Lark shook his head apologetically. "Let her tell you herself. She needs you, Leta, which is why I came to find you—though I must confess that she did not send me. I came on my own as a service to her. To tell you the truth, I'm surprised to find you in the company of the Sisterhood—or should I say *captivity*? I heard the Valdfae had gone looking for you. I was hoping he would remain by your side until you were safely in Tíria."

The Valdfae. "You...You know Thalanir?"

Lark stiffened in mid-air. "I know *of* him," he said. "But we aren't well-acquainted. He's a friend of Mithraan's, and as far as I know, he's loyal to the High Lord—which means he's loyal to your sister."

All right—so, that much was true, at least.

"That's right," I said, but shame overtook me when I added, "I...doubted him. I think it was the Priestess who did it to me— she made me feel like he was my enemy. I don't entirely know how to explain it...but when Dauphine—the Priestess—told me Lyrinn was here, I *chose* to accompany her. I told Thalanir I didn't wish to see him again."

The truth, of course, was far more complicated. Some part of me had desperately wanted to distance myself from Thalanir.

He'd hurt my pride. My feelings. My *everything*. I was all too easy a target for anyone who could have wished to turn me away from him.

"The Priestess is a Goldtongue," Lark said.

"Yes," I replied. "Thalanir tried to warn me."

Lark nodded, his stern expression unwavering. "They're smooth talkers in more ways than one. It's almost impossible to resist their persuasive methods—but given who Thalanir is, it probably wasn't terribly difficult to convince you he was an enemy."

"Who Thalanir is? What does that mean?"

"Cold and hard to read," Lark said with a quiet chuckle. "Am I wrong?"

"No—but why would you say that? You said you don't know him well."

"He's quite well known among my folk. Let's just say that he...has a reputation. I've heard speak of him many times over the years. They say he's a Fae of few words, a mystery—but by all accounts, a very worthy tracker. They call him the Wandering Ghost, because he makes his way through the lands like someone whose soul was long ago stolen from him."

Wandering Ghost.

The nickname saddened me. Perhaps it was the accuracy of the moniker—the notion that he was so alone in the world. After all, it was true; he did seem soulless at times. Or maybe it was just that he kept such a thick, impenetrable shield around his mind that it was impossible for even the most empathetic person to delve inside his thoughts or emotions.

I had tried so often to read him, to understand him. To prove to myself that he was capable of more than mere coldness. But with every effort I had made to get close to him, he had managed to thicken the wall between us. And in the end, it was the reason I'd left him behind—though it pained me deeply now to think I might never see him again.

"Do you know what happened to make him this way?" I asked quietly.

"No. But if I were to guess, I would say it was heartbreak."

"Yes, I suppose that makes sense," I replied, a pang of sorrow needling at my chest. "Someone he loved long ago died. Perhaps it was her loss that did it."

Lark sighed before adding, "Where is he now?"

I bowed my head, not wanting the sprite to see my pain. "I left him in Lapis. I assume he's long gone by now, looking for his next opportunity to earn a few gold coins."

"I wouldn't be so sure," Lark replied. "It seems he vowed to Mithraan that he would find you and bring you to Lyrinn. A Valdfae's word is good. It takes a great deal for them to back down once they have made a promise."

"Except that he did find me—more than once," I protested. "He offered to bring me north. I told you—I chose to leave."

"Did you *ask* him to let you go?"

I narrowed my eyes. "What if I did?"

"An honorable Valdfae will not hold a lady against her will —not if he respects her. Even if it means losing out on hundreds of gold coins."

"But how honorable was it to release me into the hands of the Sisterhood?" I asked. "Surely he knew what he was doing. He had a choice."

"Not if you asked him to release you, he didn't. Valdfae have a code of conduct, you see. And you were not Thalanir's prisoner. He was your protector—and you asked him to break the silent contract between the two of you. As for why he released you to the Priestess, I suppose he knew she was unlikely to hurt you anytime soon. It seems you're valuable to the Sisterhood, just as your sister was—though why, I can't say. Lyrinn no longer has any purpose to serve for their kind."

"Wait—what do you mean?" I stammered. "What did Lyrinn have to do with the Sisterhood?"

Lark stared at me, and a flicker of realization seemed to spark in his eyes. With a flutter of his diaphanous wings, he set himself down on the night stand, crossing his arms and leaning against an iron lantern.

"The Sisterhood—called the Order, before it fell apart in recent weeks—tried to use Lyrinn to gain a great deal of power. They failed, Leta. But I suspect the Priestesses mean to use you to regain something of what they lost. In all likelihood, they plan to hold you here until you Change. They want you at your full strength. To what end, I can't begin to guess. Revenge, perhaps."

"How do they know I'll even have powers? How does anyone? I could be an utter weakling, for all anyone can predict."

"The daughter of a High King could never be weak." He glanced at me as if trying to assess whether or not I was aware of my lineage. When he saw that I was unsurprised, he continued. "You, like your sister, will very probably prove incredibly strong. Which means we need to free you of this place before the Sisters get what they want."

I leapt to my feet. "Fine," I said. "Then let's go. Let's leave this place. Can you bring me to her—to Lyrinn? I don't care if she's hundreds of miles away. I'll gladly make the journey. Just get me out of this oppressive place."

In truth, as much as I wanted to see Lyrinn, it was Thalanir I most wished to find. To apologize, to make amends for what I had said when I was under Dauphine's spell.

I couldn't bear the thought that he was roaming the wilderness thinking I despised him.

Lark glanced toward the locked door. "I came in through the window—but *you* can't fly, and it's a long drop, in case you hadn't noticed. I can pick a lock under normal circumstances, but the Priestesses have cast a spell on that one. They don't want to lose you, now that they have you."

"I don't care what they want!" I snapped, my voice nearing a shout. I winced at the volume, realizing if one of the Priestesses was in the corridor, she would surely hear me ranting—apparently to myself. "I need to leave. I can't stay here. I can't..." My heart sank before a burst of excitement exploded in my chest. "Maybe *you* could find Thalanir. He can help us. He's incredible. He..."

I stopped myself singing his praises any further. I didn't know Lark well enough to pour my heart out to him quite yet.

The sprite frowned. "A Valdfae who does not wish to be found won't be found."

"But you said you suspect he'll stay close. You said—"

Lark's lips formed a tight line, and he took off into the air, his wings flitting so fast that all I saw was a frenzied blur. "You told him you wished to leave. It's possible he took you at your word. Still, I can hunt for him if you like. But the fact is, you're stuck here for the time being. Perhaps you would do well to learn what the Sisterhood means to do with you."

"I'm not sure I really want to know," I replied with a frown.

"Well," Lark said, eyeing the window, a hand on his sword, "Whatever it is, they will not hurt you until you've shown your strength—so I advise you to be careful on that front. You have my word that I will spend the rest of my life serving you and your sister, if that's what it takes to bring you back together. Just stay alive long enough for me to orchestrate a reunion, please."

With that, he pivoted and fluttered toward the window.

"Wait," I said, halting him in mid-air before he could leave.

"Why would you make such a vow to Lyrinn or me? What's in this for you?"

Lark looked taken aback by the question, so I took in a breath and tried again. "I only mean that most people aren't so benevolent. Yet here you are, far from your home, helping someone you've never met in your life. Why?"

"Because I need to make amends, both to you and Lyrinn, for something I did to you both."

"Amends?" My brow crinkled with confusion. "What exactly did you do to us?"

"Something that cannot be undone," he said, his voice a grim monotone. "I had no choice—that much I'll concede—yet it still pains me deeply. So, I offer my sword to you, Leta Martel. I will not rest until you are reunited with your sister. She is eager to see you, to put it mildly. She missed you terribly when she was in..."

"In our father's captivity," I said, nodding. "It's okay. I know about Kazimir's cruelty. I know a good deal. But not everything, clearly. Help me get out of here and find Lyrinn and the answers I seek, and I promise, we'll call it even."

Lark bit his lip, then turned back to the window. "I'll be back soon," he said. "If all goes well, I'll soon have news for you of our friend's whereabouts."

CHAPTER SIXTEEN

WHEN LARK HAD LEFT, I walked over to the window and peered out to see that the trees surrounding the convent grounds had taken on the air of an ominous army of sentinels, silhouetted as they were against a violet evening sky.

In the modest gardens below—a series of gravel pathways leading between neatly trimmed hedges—shadowy women in long robes wandered in silence, their faces veiled, heads bowed. From my vantage point, I couldn't tell which were mortal and which were Fae, though here and there, I was sure I spotted a set of bright eyes shining through a veil.

None of them seemed aware of my presence, or in fact interested in much at all, and I was beginning to wonder if I'd simply been left in this room to rot.

"Is that your revenge?" I muttered. "You aim to starve me to death?"

As if in response, a hard knock sounded at the door.

I spun around, my fists clenching as I searched the room for something I could use as a weapon. But unless I figured out how to subdue my visitor with a pillow to the face, I seemed to be out of luck.

Before I could call out, the door creaked open, and a female Fae walked in—one dressed similarly to Dauphine, in a long, flowing white cloak and a matching dress underneath. Her veil had been pulled back so I could see that she had jet-black hair and green eyes. She was a combination of beautiful—her features teeming with knowledge and wisdom—and youthful-looking.

In that regard, at least, she reminded me painfully of Thalanir.

When she moved toward me, I found myself recoiling in apprehension as if a powerful weapon were making its way over to where I stood, its threat growing with every step.

"My name is Elodea," she said, halting when she seemed to sense my fear. "And I am here to assess you, Leta."

"Assess?" I asked, my voice a mere squeak, and I cleared my throat to try again. "Why would you do that? Dauphine said my sister—"

"Come, now." She raised a hand to silence me. "If Dauphine had told you why you were really being brought to the convent, you wouldn't have agreed to accompany her. She didn't wish to harm you or the Valdfae, so she did what she needed to in order to persuade you to walk away from him."

She spoke as if Dauphine were some kind-hearted soul who had done me a favor by charming me into leaving Thalanir behind—when the truth was, she had taken me from the only person in the world whose sole interest lay in protecting me.

"She *lied*," I snarled between gritted teeth.

Elodea shrugged. "She told you what you wished to hear, and now, you are free of the Valdfae. For that, you should be grateful."

I wanted to tell her I wasn't—that every fiber of my being wished right now that I had remained with Thalanir. He was complicated and confusing as all the hells combined. He had withheld information from me plenty of times, and yes, he had driven me to distraction with his impossible-to-read moods.

But as far as I knew, he had never outright lied to me.

He had cared for me when I was disoriented. Carried me to safety when I was threatened. And I had abandoned him— accused him of abusing me, when it wasn't true. That had been my pride talking and nothing more.

Perhaps one day I would even learn to feel grateful that he had kept me from falling too much in love with him.

Quiet torment wove its way through my bloodstream as I strained not to scream.

"What, exactly, are you assessing me for?" I asked.

Elodea eyed me up and down. "I need to see how far along you are." She walked around me, examining me like I was a marble statue in a gallery. "Tell me, have you cast any spells yet?"

I was about to say no, but then recalled what had happened in Daggut, when I had shot my hands toward the asshole called Teryns in a fit of rage. The pub had filled with blinding light, everyone vanishing except for one lone figure. I could still vividly recall Thalanir's face as he stepped toward me through that sea of white light, a calming beacon in a storm of confusion.

But maybe I was wrong. Maybe it was the Valdfae who had cast the spell. For all I knew, my flick of the hands had done nothing at all.

"I'm not sure if I've cast," I replied. "I...can't say for certain."

"I see." Elodea sounded irritated, impatient. "Yet I was told you were beginning to show signs of your Coming of Age."

She reached out and pushed my red hair behind my ear, examining my scars. "You have not spoken to your sister Lyrinn since the Blood Trials."

It wasn't a question.

"How does everyone know so damned much about me?" I spat, suddenly too irritated to be intimidated.

"Because you have the potential to be an important weapon in the war that is now raging in the realms," she said as if it was the simplest thing in the world. "I'm sure by now you've seen the patrols of Crimson Cloaks, yes? Fae and mortals doing battle in the streets of Kalemnar's towns and cities. King Caedmon is amassing a vast army of mortals, and things are only going to get worse. The Sisterhood's hope is to prevent the war from escalating. To end it quickly, with the pure-blooded Fae as the rightful victors. And for that, we need you, Leta."

I narrowed my eyes, skeptical. "I see—and how do you hope to do such a thing? How could I possibly be a weapon? I told you already—I'm not even sure I've cast a single spell."

"You do know what you are, no?"

The way she phrased the question confused me. "I know I'm a Fae," I retorted. "I know who my father is—or *was*. I know about my grandfather."

"That's not what I mean." Elodea backed away, her eyes flicking to my hands, then back to my face. "I'm talking about the memories. About what you've seen on your left ring finger."

My jaw dropped open in spite of myself. I wanted to deny that I'd seen memories, the glowing image of a dragon on my flesh. But clearly, there was no point. Elodea knew the truth of it already.

"Tell me what it feels like," she said. "When it happens."

"My left hand?" I said, holding it up, and she nodded with an off-putting eagerness. "It's...like it's been licked by flames. It burns and trembles, and then the sensation passes."

"Ah," she replied, a slight smile curving her lips up at the corners. She stepped closer, her eyes flaring briefly when she said, "You've seen *her* in those memories, haven't you?"

"Seen who?" I shot back, wilting a little under her stare.

"The one he loved," she said, her voice like silk. "The one who died. The one with a similar mark."

My heart pounded in my chest to hear her say it—to hear someone else acknowledge that the visions came from some-place real—some*one* real.

"I haven't seen her, not exactly," I replied. "I've...*been* her. I don't know if that makes sense, and honestly, I don't care. I have felt her memories, seen through her eyes."

"The memories will keep coming, if all goes according to plan," Elodea said. "And in the end, you will receive whatever Gifts—whatever powers—she wishes to grant you. When it is yours, you'll begin to understand who and what you are, Leta Martel—and that you are unlike any other living Fae, including your dear sister."

My brows met. I was just about sick of cryptic clues. The Priestesses were more vague than Thalanir, even, at handing over information—and I wouldn't have imagined that was even possible. "What do you mean, she wishes to grant me a Gift? Gallia is long dead, is she not?"

"She is dead, yes. But her Essence lives on—and is almost entirely passed to you now. It's only a matter of time before the transition is complete and you become whole."

When I looked taken aback, she said, "You know what I'm talking about. I'm sure the Valdfae told you what a Násuire is. You know that Gallia is part of you, just as you're part of her. It has always been so, from the beginning of time. Now, we have only to wait a little longer."

She stepped toward the door, but before she reached it, she turned to face me.

"Are you going to tell me what I'm doing here," I snarled, "or—"

The Priestess held up a hand, gesturing elegantly with her fingers, and a charge of white, crackling light erupted from her fingertips. It bore an eerie resemblance to lightning, and fear filled me at the thought of it coming anywhere near me.

"Do you think you could defend yourself if I attacked you right now?" she asked.

"No," I said. "I don't think so."

It was an honest answer, at least.

Elodea thrust her hand toward me, a searing bolt of lightning crashing through the space between us. With a speed I had only exhibited once before, I shoved my hands up, palms out, shielding my torso.

The lightning slammed into my palms, wrapping around my hands like coiling twine. It tightened around my flesh, digging in until I bled.

I cried out in pain, fighting the urge to fall to my knees. Rage overtook me then—rage at Elodea for doing this to me. At Dauphine for bringing me here. But most of all, rage at myself for ever doubting Thalanir's word.

"Fight back!" Elodea cried out, her eyes as cold as ice now. "Or do you intend to let me burn you until your hands are useless?"

Determination combatted the anger inside me. I took a step toward the Priestess, my wounded, bloody hands pulsing orange-red, my veins swimming with flame.

"Do not push me, Priestess," I snarled in the voice that belonged to *her*. "Or I will have your head."

My eyes widened when my fingers splayed open, forcing the lightning away, and a ball of fire shot toward Elodea.

The Priestess stepped out of the way and let it slam into the stone wall behind her, leaving behind a broad circle of jet-black.

The fire under my skin calmed, my chest heaving with the power that had just surged up within me.

"It's a start," she said, unimpressed as she reached for the door knob. "Still, you're not there yet. You will need a good deal of training before you can take full control of what lies inside you. I'll come for you in the morning, and we will work together to hone your skills. You need to become a fighter, Leta."

"I have no wish to fight," I moaned, collapsing back onto the bed, my energy sapped. "I just want to go home."

"Haven't you figured it out yet?" Elodea replied, and in a tone that chilled me to the bone, added, "You *have* no home."

CHAPTER SEVENTEEN

AN HOUR OR SO LATER, when I had stewed, raged, and cursed under my breath what felt like a thousand times, a veiled woman—this one a mortal—brought me a tray with some fruit, bread, cheese, and water, as well as a carafe of red wine. She laid the tray on a small table set against the bedroom's far wall.

I watched her, wondering silently if I could kill her and escape. Wondering if my rage would be enough to turn me into a murderer.

Apparently, the answer was no, because in the end, I simply watched her go.

Over time, I grew restless, bored, eager to see Lark again and to learn if there was news of Thalanir. But the sprite had not returned—and I found myself worried that I may have sent him to his death.

I wasn't sure what the Priestesses might do to him if they learned of his presence...but I couldn't imagine it would be anything good.

Absentmindedly, I took a piece of bread and some cheese from the tray the mortal had brought, and took a bite. It was surprisingly delicious. The cheese was sharp, the bread fresh, and for that, at least, I was grateful.

I moved toward the window, leaning against the stone sill to look out toward the dense, now dark woods beyond the convent. A flicker of light caught my eye at the forest's edge, and I stared down, narrowing my eyes until I made out two glowing dots aimed in my direction.

I told myself they were the eyes of some wild animal—though some deep part of me hoped, as I watched the two bright spots in the darkness, that it was something else entirely.

No. It can't be. He didn't follow me here; he's long gone.

I'm alone and hopeless.

When the eyes disappeared, I told myself that maybe Lark was right. Thalanir didn't want to be found. I could hardly blame him if he never wished to see me again.

I laid down on the bed and closed my eyes, an arm draped over my forehead. My journey from Domignon had been rife with problems and obstacles. But this—being trapped like a bird in a cage—was easily the worst of it.

Each day I spent here was a day I wouldn't see Lyrinn.

A day I wouldn't see *him*.

"If you can hear me, Thalanir," I said under my breath, "know that if I had to do it over again, I would try my best to fight Dauphine off. I wouldn't leave you. You were right. I was a fool to walk away."

It felt like many hours had passed since I'd last suffered through one of the visions that had plagued me so violently for weeks. But now, as if inspired by thoughts of the Valdfae, I was swept up in a flash of blinding light.

This time, Thalanir and Gallia were indoors, for once—in a large chamber inside what looked like an elegant palace. Ornate carvings and murals decorated three of the walls, and a large, arched window took up most of another.

The two lovers were arguing, and my emotions surged in waves as I slipped inside Gallia's mind and body.

"You cannot do it!" Thalanir shouted. "You don't understand the consequences, Gallia, if you go through with this!"

She reached for him, and I watched as she grabbed at his powerful arm, nails digging into his flesh. The winged marking on her ring finger was glowing orange-red and fiery, flaring with heat just as mine did.

I watched the moment unfold, my own hand seared with a now-familiar pain, and I winced, trying to force it away and focus on the vision.

"It's too late, Thalanir," Gallia said. But this time, instead of sounding playful and loving, there was a hard edge to her voice —something frightening and angry. "It's a part of me now. You know I have no choice."

"There is *always* a choice," Thalanir replied, his voice choked. "Please—Don't do it. They'll kill you. They'll—"

The vision ended with a jolt, and I sat bolt upright, breathing hard. I was back in the convent now, the cool evening air wafting in from outside.

Some revelation was inside me—crawling under my skin, creeping insidiously toward my mind like a parasite intent on taking me over.

Who? Who was going to kill her? And why?

"Is that what happened to you, Gallia?" I asked in a whisper. "Did someone murder you because you grew too strong?"

"Highness?"

It was Lark's voice. I turned my head to see him hovering by the window, a look of concern in his eyes. "Are you...all right?" he asked.

What could I possibly tell him? *No, I'm absolutely not. Sometimes I hallucinate, and it feels like my mind is melting.*

"I'm fine." I lied. "I was just thinking about something, that's all."

"I'm glad to hear it," he replied, perching on the window ledge. "For a moment, you looked like you'd left this world entirely."

I took in a deep breath, then asked, "Any sign of him?"

The sprite shook his head dolefully. "Nothing. Then again, he's a shape-shifter, from what I understand, and a skilled one. It's entirely possible that he's standing outside right now, disguised as a shrub."

I couldn't help it. I laughed. Yes—it was entirely possible, I supposed.

I recalled the set of bright eyes I'd seen staring up at me earlier, and for a moment, I wondered...

No.

If Thalanir were that close, surely he would have broken into the convent by now.

"Any word on what the Priestesses expect of you?" Lark asked.

"All I know is they want to train me," I said with a frown. "Apparently, they want to see what I'm made of."

Lark nodded as if this news was unsurprising. "Don't let them use you, whatever may come."

I nodded, choosing my words carefully before I asked, "What exactly did they do to Lyrinn?"

Lark tightened, and I pushed myself off the bed and stepped toward him. "Look," I said under my breath, "I understand your reticence. You think this is between her and me—and truly, I appreciate the respect you're showing us both. But I'm locked inside this place like it's my prison for life, and I need to know what I'm up against. So please—tell me what the Sisterhood did to her."

Lark raised his chin and met my eyes when he said, "They made her promises, then tried to kill her. They intended to sacrifice her as a means to give power to a living goddess—a creature so malicious that it might well have destroyed our world. I know that sounds mad, but it's the absolute truth." He slammed his mouth shut, and I knew I couldn't hope for much more by way of explanation.

It was enough.

My visions of my sister were beginning to make sense. Lyrinn's pain—her torment. Mithraan's desperate cries.

But in the end, they had faced the Sisterhood and survived.

So would I.

"What should I do, Lark?" I asked softly, lowering my chin. "How do I fight them?"

"You can't fight them and win—not by any traditional means. But perhaps you can learn something about their motivations," he replied with a gentleness matching my own. "Whatever happens, do not let them break you, Leta. We will get you away from here and reunite you with Lyrinn, I promise you that. I will keep searching for your Valdfae—he seems like our best hope. I'll begin the hunt again in the morning. For tonight, though, I intend to camp outside in a tree. I'll keep watch from that vantage point, and if anything should happen, you'll be the first—and only one—to know."

I nodded. I wanted to thank him. Hell, I wanted to *hug* him, though he was so small that I feared I would break him if I did.

If he managed to bring me Thalanir, I would forgive the sprite even the most egregious sin. Whatever he had done to Lyrinn and me—whatever wrong he had committed—would be rendered insignificant in comparison.

I only hoped I could someday forgive myself for sending Thalanir away in the first place.

CHAPTER EIGHTEEN

WHEN MORNING CAME and I'd taken a few bites of a breakfast tray left by one of the Priestesses, Elodea shoved my door open and stepped inside my room.

"Follow me," she commanded coldly. "We have work to do, you and I."

Dressed in my leather trousers and a gray linen shirt, I slipped out of the chamber after her. I reminded myself as I strode along the corridor of what Lark had said the previous night. *Don't give her anything of yourself. Don't let her see what you're capable of.*

We were headed to the first level, and when we moved through the convent's foyer, it was all I could do to hold myself back from trying to rush through it.

I could make a run for it—get out of this place and leave it behind forever. Maybe if I—

"Stop," Elodea said, halting and forcing me to do the same. "There will be no pondering escape."

My eyes widened. "But I wasn't..."

She glared at me, fire in her eyes. "Do you take me for a

fool?" she asked, her voice hard-edged and hostile. "Do you think I can't see your mind?"

Something came to me then—the moment when Thalanir had tried to delve into my thoughts, and I had pushed back so hard that he went flying across the room.

No, I thought. I will not let you inside. Neither you, Elodea, nor any of your terrible Sisters.

More gently this time, I locked my mind down just as I'd done to Thalanir. I watched as the Priestess's eyes went wide with the jolt of pain my quiet rejection inflicted on her. She seemed almost pleased to realize I was capable of such quiet violence.

"Stay out of my mind," I whispered sharply. "My thoughts are no business of yours. Besides, I was brought to the convent under false pretenses. Dauphine lied to me outright. Why would you be even remotely surprised to discover that I want to leave?"

At that, Elodea's expression softened a little, the licking flames leaving her irises. "Perhaps if I told you exactly why you're here, you would feel a little more cooperative."

"Fine." I crossed my arms over my chest. "Tell me, then."

"We want—need—your help, just as Prince Corym did. The mortal realm sought your allegiance, Leta, because of what you are. And I am—*we* are—asking you to help the Fae. It's us against mortals, Leta, and they have an advantage at the moment. There are more of them, and they are amassing a small force of Fae traitors to increase their numbers. You and your sister are the only two in all the realms who share Light-blood and Tírian bloodlines. Which means you have the potential to be two of the most powerful Fae in existence. If you should choose to side with the humans, we know our cause would be lost."

"We won't," I told her, almost amused by the notion. As if I would ever side with Corym or his duplicitous father. "But I've said it before—I'm not a warrior. I don't wish to do battle. Lyrinn is more of a fighter than I ever was or will ever be. All I want is to find her. If you let me go, I will persuade her to do battle against Corym's army. I know she'll agree to it—"

Elodea shook her head. "Your fate is not that of someone who sits on her hands while the world erupts in war around her. You were built for something far more important, Násuire."

"So let me find Lyrinn. Why can't I train with her instead of here? Why keep me locked in a small room, away from everyone I care about?"

Which admittedly means very few people.

Lyrinn.

Thalanir.

That's all.

Elodea looked frustrated when she said, "Understand, Leta, that you don't yet know your strength. You haven't yet gotten your wings, and wouldn't you prefer to fly over battles than trudge through the mud alongside sword wielders? We're here to help you. Don't you see?"

Fly.

The thought rendered me breathless.

I'd seen Lyrinn with beautiful wings of light, veined like stained glass, much like Thalanir's. But that was only in my waking dreams. It hadn't sunk in yet that she really *was* a High Fae now—a fully developed, powerful being with a High Lord for a mate.

My sister was a full-fledged Fae princess. And one day, she would be a queen. Those extraordinary wings were a part of her, just as a set might one day become a part of me.

"If we sent you out into the wilderness now," Elodea added, "and if the Change came over you when you were vulnerable, you could die. We want to help you through the coming days in a controlled environment. It may seem harsh, but trust me when I tell you it's for your own good."

Defeated, I exhaled.

I didn't trust her as far as I could throw her. But she was right about one thing, at least: the idea of being out there, alone somewhere in the wild while my already addled mind ravaged me from the inside, and my body flared with agony—it wasn't a pleasant thought.

With my mind still concealed behind the blockade I'd erected between Elodea and myself, I finally replied, "Fine. Let's train. But I warn you—you'll probably be disappointed."

"We'll see."

I followed as she began to walk again, commanding myself to pretend I didn't despise this place. She needed to think I was here willingly, happily. That I truly wished to help her cause.

I had always been good at lying, at charming people. At deceit.

Ironically enough, I might have made a good Valdfae.

I reminded myself that the Sisterhood had done nothing so very terrible to me, other than lying and locking me up. They fed me well, they gave me a pleasant, albeit small, damp room to stay in, where at least I felt safe—which was more than I could say about most places I'd found myself over the last few weeks.

Things could be worse, I suppose.

Then again, I felt safe when I was with Thalanir. Safe, and...

No. No thinking about him. Focus, you idiot.

Elodea led me outside to a cloistered courtyard—one with only a single door leading in and out. There was no chance of escape, not unless I spontaneously sprouted the wings everyone seemed to think I would one day acquire.

A series of human-shaped targets was set up at the courtyard's far end, awaiting some kind of assault.

Elodea seated herself on a stone bench, looked me up and down, then said, "Go ahead. Destroy them."

I let out a laugh, thinking she was joking. But her stern expression never faltered.

"What exactly do you think I'm going to do?" I asked, staring at the wooden targets. "Choke the life out of them?"

"You shot a fireball at me yesterday," she reminded me. "Surely you can do the same now."

"You hurled *lightning* at me. I was just defending myself."

"So pretend those targets are as threatening as I am."

Oh? Pretend they're cold bitches?

"Fine."

I hadn't forgotten what Lark had said about making sure I didn't show the full extent of my powers.

But what he and the Priestesses failed to understand was that I had little to no control over what meager power I possessed. Every spell that I had conjured until now had occurred in an act of desperation or fear. Inanimate objects did nothing to inspire me, and I couldn't imagine the targets lined up like shrubberies would do anything to turn me into a wrathful fire-demon.

Still, I needed to at least *pretend* I was trying.

I lifted both arms, fingers pointed toward the targets, and closed my eyes, commanding myself to focus. *Do something. Anything. Give her just enough to satisfy her.*

I shot my hands forward, fingers splayed, envisioning a ball of flame hurtling through space.

To my utter shock, when I opened my eyes, I saw that my attempt had succeeded.

Sort of.

The fireball was more like a marble...and by the time it had sputtered halfway to the first target, it fizzled into ash and cascaded down to earth in very small, very non-threatening embers.

"Damn it," I muttered under my breath.

"Try again," Elodea said.

"But I..."

A hard edge rose in her voice. "Try. Again."

I did. And again. And again. And then, ten more times, each with the same result. When she asked me to try other spells—light, or ice, or shards of glass—I failed just as badly or worse.

When she handed me a small dagger, I considered stabbing her with it, but quickly realized such an act of violence disgusted me—besides which, I probably had fifty other Priestesses standing between me and the convent's nearest exit.

I flung the dagger at one of the targets and it went flying off to the right, only to land with a clatter on the cobblestone pathway surrounding the courtyard.

Lyrinn used to tease me at how terrible I was with projectiles, how uncoordinated. My only skill in the world lay in charm and flirtation—and against an army of foes, it would hardly do.

I had discovered in recent weeks how weak I really was when confronted by a group of angry men.

I asked myself quietly why I was so unable to cast a proper spell, and the answer came to me in Gallia's voice.

~*You're not angry enough, Leta.*

I am angry, though, I protested silently. *I'm angry that I'm here. Angry that they lied to me. Angry that I left...*

~*It's not enough. You haven't yet learned to use your rage to your advantage. You let it weigh you down, when it should elevate you to greater heights.*

So what do I do?

~*Think of him,* she said. *Think of what the Priestesses have done, taking us away from him. They have robbed us of our lover.*

He's your *lover. Not mine. He was never mine, and never will be.*

At that, Gallia laughed, and the sound echoed around my mind like a torment.

~You want him, she said. *I've felt it in you. You ran from him because you wanted him so badly that it was killing you. You ran because you were afraid.*

Stop it.

~I'll stop when you stop lying to yourself. Admit that he drives you to distraction. Admit that you would give anything to wrap your legs around his waist, and...

Shut. Up. You're dead. You're not really talking to me.

~My body died long ago, but my Essence is part of you now. We are one, you and I.

With a violent snarl, I forced her away, stared at the targets, and repeated to myself, *He's not my lover. He never was.*

Another laugh rose up somewhere deep inside my mind. *Her* laugh.

Gods, she hadn't left.

~I know him. I know his eyes, his lips. The way the muscle in his jaw twitches when he wants something. He wants you, Leta. Desperately. He's lying to himself out of the same fear you feel.

I glanced down at my left hand, which was burning with raging heat. My ring finger twitched, trembling slowly at first, then wildly, and I grabbed it with my right hand to steady it.

~Find your rage, Gallia said. *Kill the Priestess. Kill them all, and free yourself of this horrid place. Find him...and one day, perhaps you'll find happiness.*

I swung around to face Elodea, staring her in the eye. On her face was a look of terror, and I realized after a moment that I had raised my hands to her, my fingertips glowing with licking blue flame.

~You can do it, Gallia urged. *You are stronger than she is, and soon, you will possess might greater than any army of men.*

"NO!" I shouted.

I lowered my hands to my sides, rolling my fingers into fists.

"I'm...sorry, Elodea," I stammered. "I don't think I have it in me right now to do as you ask. Maybe we should try again tomorrow."

The Priestess nodded, relief shading her features. "Yes," she said. "We can try tomorrow. Go back to your quarters. I'll see to it that your lunch comes soon."

I headed through the door and strode down the hall to the staircase, realizing just how close I'd come to succumbing to Gallia's temptation.

I was beginning to see something of her true nature. Beyond the joy and laughter, the absolute love she had felt for Thalanir, there was something dark, almost cruel. All the affection in the world—all that he had given her—it wasn't enough to keep her demons at bay.

And that knowledge terrified me.

Each morning at the same time, Lark flew off in search of Thalanir, and Elodea would come fetch me for a lesson that turned out to be not so much a training session as a Priestess-repeatedly-watching-me-fail session.

Elodea never grew impatient with me or criticized. If anything, she was remarkable in her stoicism as my spells sputtered and died. I could almost feel her relief when she would call an end to each session.

I managed not to have another angry outburst or threaten her again. In moments when I felt my rage growing, I pushed the emotion down and away. Instead, I filled my mind with thoughts of Thalanir. Of his face, his smile, the kindness I had seen in his eyes in our best moments together.

I thought of the pain I had seen in him, of what I would give to be able to take it away and replace it with joy.

I reveled in my failure each day, and each time I returned to my room, I lay down on my bed, as relieved as Elodea felt. I had come far too close to killing her on that first day—too close to unleashing a monster that lay dormant somewhere inside me.

Each evening when Lark returned to me, we spoke of his own lack of progress in finding Thalanir.

On the seventh day after my arrival at the convent, just as I was finishing dinner, my door opened and Dauphine walked in, her eyes locked on my own.

"Elodea has filled me in on your failures," she scolded, disappointment dripping from the words. "It seems you are resisting your Change, Leta."

"I..." I rose to my feet from the bed, my chin low in mock-defeat. The truth was, her acknowledgment of my shortcomings felt like a triumph. "I'm sorry. I know you must..."

Dauphine held up a hand. "I don't care about contrition. Tell me—how have you been feeling? Any dizzy spells? Visions? Have any new memories revealed themselves to you?"

I pondered the questions for a few seconds, then shook my head.

The truth was, ever since Gallia had spoken to me that day in the courtyard and I had pushed her back, the visions had ceased—as had the dizziness. I almost felt like my old, mortal self, in fact.

I missed Thalanir's face. I missed seeing him in my mind's eye.

But I definitely did not miss the feeling of torment that often accompanied those moments.

"I thought as much," Dauphine said. "So, I've found a way to move things along. It's time we got you back on track, Leta."

She stepped to the door and opened it, leaning out to speak to someone in the hallway.

"Bring him in."

Him?

Who's him?

My heart pounded, my breath tightening.

Had they found Thalanir and dragged him to the convent in hopes that seeing him would stimulate my mind or drive me to some kind of passionate, fiery outburst? Were they going to force me to fight in order to keep him alive?

For that privilege, I **would** *fight. I would kill.*

I would do anything.

But first, I would embrace him. Kiss him. Apologize a hundred times for how cruelly I pushed him away. I'd make up for all of it.

Brushing my hair away from my face and patting down the wrinkles in my shirt, I steeled myself for the encounter.

But when Elodea appeared in my doorway pulling a thin, braided rope, I could see that it wasn't Thalanir she was leading behind her like a dog.

It was someone else entirely.

The last person on earth I wanted to see.

CHAPTER NINETEEN

A FAMILIAR FIGURE stepped through the doorway after Elodea, his chin down, a set of defeated eyes aimed squarely at the stone floor.

When he drew his gaze up to meet mine, the deep red grooves carved into his cheeks flared with some indecipherable emotion.

"Corym," I murmured, my jaw dropping open. "How...?"

The Sisterhood had managed to capture the Prince of Kalemnar.

Not only that, but they'd somehow dragged him across hundreds of miles of rough landscape to the convent where we now stood.

"Why would you do this?" I cried, my eyes burning into Dauphine's. "If war weren't already brewing between Fae and mortals, this alone would instigate it!"

"Ah, but war *is* raging already," Dauphine said. "And the prince is here to help us develop our most potent weapon. Aren't you, Corym?"

"Surprise," the prince muttered, a pathetic smile on his lips.

Some distant instinct told me to hug him, to ask if he was

all right. But I quickly reminded myself that he was not my friend. He never had been.

He was a lying bastard who had twisted my mind into desiring him—one who had cruelly played with my emotions for his own gain.

He was, at the very best, a handsome stranger to me now.

At worst, he was my enemy for life.

"You two have a bond—or so the prince seems to think," Dauphine said with a smile. "He believes you are meant for one another—that you're true mates. He has informed us that you, Leta, began having visions on your last night in Domignon—and dizzy spells. That alone is reason enough to bring him to your side."

"The visions mean nothing," I replied, nausea swelling inside me. "Surely it doesn't prove he and I are really—"

Gods. If they were confident enough to kidnap him, they must have had little doubt that he and I really were fated for one another.

The thought that they could be right...it was unbearable. I didn't love him; I never had.

My feelings for Corym, even at their most intense, have only ever been a mere fraction of what I feel for Thalanir.

And they were based on a vicious lie.

The realization made me want to weep.

I had spent several moons with Corym, wandering the castle grounds, feasting in the palace's endless beautiful chambers, meeting important aristocrats. I had lived a dream life with him for that stretch of time. But my attachment to the Valdfae I'd only known a few days was so much deeper, so much more...real.

"The visions aren't absolute proof, no," Dauphine said. "But if the prince is right, then his presence here *will* precipitate your

Change. We have no time to waste, Leta. Corym is here to force your evolution."

"*Force*?" I breathed, my chest tight.

The word was a horror. It could mean only one thing, and I would sooner die than let it happen.

Elodea yanked Corym into the room, and the rope around his neck disappeared.

"Enjoy yourselves," Dauphine said before turning to leave, with Elodea behind her. The door closed, and I could hear the lock grinding, a torment to my ears.

"You're happy to see me, clearly," Corym said weakly, his hand moving to his throat as if to wring the raspiness from it.

I stepped over to the night stand and poured him a cup of water, handing it to him. "Of course I'm not," I said. "Not after what you pulled for all those weeks, *mind-bender*."

Sipping the water, he glared at me.

Inside, I was all conflict. Apprehension mixed with reluctant relief at seeing a familiar face.

But I reminded myself again that he was my enemy. I had half-starved, suffered assaults, and nearly died, all while trying to escape his clutches. Yet locking him into this room with me was more awful than anything I could imagine.

Still, I had a thousand questions raging through my mind.

"How..." I asked as he drank greedily. "How did you even come to be here?"

"I was looking for you, of course," he said, wiping at his mouth with the back of his hand. "I had traveled with a host of men to Marqueyssal. It seems the Sisterhood had heard I'd left Domignon. They found me. Told me they would bring me to you."

"And you're telling me you simply came with them?" I stammered. "You just left your men behind?"

"Of course not!" he half-yelled, glaring at the door. "Do you think I would ever have come here alone if I'd had a choice? Given the opportunity, I would have brought an army, had my men storm this place and take you captive to drag you back to Domignon behind my horse."

I almost laughed at the irony.

And here you are, dragged to this place behind a Priestess's horse, no doubt.

It was almost poetic.

He slammed the cup back down on a small table by the door, meeting my eyes, his anger focused now.

"You left me!" he cried. "You fled the palace and made me look like a fool! We were to be married, you and I—and like an absolute madwoman, you decided I wasn't good enough for you."

I glowered at him, keeping my distance and suddenly wishing I could summon Lark to my side.

I could use his blade about now, if only to get the bastard to stay back.

"You were using me," I said coldly—evenly. "Just as you tried to use my sister. You thought I couldn't see what you really were—that I would remain oblivious to your tricks. And you almost succeeded. I did want you for a time, Corym. I wanted you to be the prince I'd always hoped you were—and yes, I wanted to marry you." I felt my blood chill when I added, "But that night, when you told me about the wedding, I saw you clearly for the first time. I am not your plaything, Highness. I do not belong to you. I never have."

"Yes, you do, by rights!" he snarled, taking a step closer, but when I recoiled, he stopped, tightening as if some quiet force had frozen him in place. He struggled to calm his voice. "You *are* mine. You were to marry me. We are—we're true *mates*. Whether you like it or not, it's a fact."

I shook my head. If there was one thing in the world of

which I was certain—one thing I knew above all else—it was that he was *not* my true mate.

I did not love him.

I hated him.

"Even the Sisterhood knows it!" he exclaimed, his voice shrill as he gestured toward the locked door. "They know we are meant to be together, you and I." He shifted his weight, trying to calm himself. "Look—you're hesitant. It's understandable—your fear is perfectly natural. But surely you see it. You must know we're meant to be, Leta."

I shouldn't have laughed. I should have taken him seriously and feigned respect, if only out of a sense of self-preservation.

But I couldn't help myself.

I snorted.

"I was *never* meant to be with you," I said with amused tears in my eyes, watching as his cheeks reddened around the angry scars Mithraan had torn into his flesh. "Neither was Lyrinn. If anything, you are meant to die alone in your damned fortress of a castle. I wouldn't wish you on my worst enemy."

The disrespect was enough to send him over the edge. Corym leapt at me, a growl rising in his throat, and raised a hand to strike me.

When he swung his arm, a deep instinct took hold of my mind and body, and without thinking, I shoved my hands out, palms forward.

He flew backwards, slamming against the far wall and sending a painting of a deer in the woods crashing to the ground.

With the wind knocked out of him, he slid down to land hard on the floor next to the now-broken frame.

"Bitch," he scowled when he had recovered his breath enough to speak. "You need to be taught a lesson."

This time, he tried to assault my mind rather than my body.

Rising to his feet, he narrowed his eyes viciously. I could feel his substantial strength as he strained to bend me to his will, to force me to desire him once again. It was a violation, an intrusion into the deepest reaches of my thoughts and emotions, and I pushed back still harder this time, driving him from me with all the rage I could muster.

He crashed back against the wall again, his head cracking horribly into plaster.

"You can't control me anymore," I snarled as he moaned in pain. "Never again will you lie to me with impunity. I am not your puppet, Corym—and you are not entitled to any part of me, body or mind. Try to infiltrate either again, and I promise you—I *will* kill you."

I hadn't found my strength in the courtyard with Elodea. My rage had never been sufficient to wish her, or even Dauphine, dead.

But Corym was another story entirely.

I did *not* belong to him. If I belonged to anyone, it was the Valdfae I had abandoned so coldly.

But even Thalanir had no claim of ownership over me. I was not the property of anyone in the world—nor did I ever wish to be.

Corym fell to his knees, his breathing strained, just as the door flew open and Dauphine stormed in.

"What in the hells is going on here?" she asked when she saw me standing against the far wall and Corym, winded, writhing on the floor.

She turned to me, a look of surprise on her face. I didn't have to be a mind-reader to guess that she was pleased.

To her, my attack was proof that I was growing stronger, and that Corym was the cause of this sudden burst of power. Proof that he had already accelerated my progress to the point where I was now throwing full-grown men against walls with nothing but my mind.

Little did she know I had done the same to Thalanir when he, too, had tried to delve into my thoughts. Little did she know Corym was nothing to me, other than an irritating gnat.

"If you want one of us to die, Dauphine," I told her, my chest heaving, "by all means, lock us in here together. But I would strongly suggest that you take him away, because I will *end* him if he tries anything more. He and I are no more destined for one another than a lion and a gazelle. He is not my damned mate."

The Priestess eyed Corym warily, then me, then she relented and threw a hand toward him. A long chain of silver tangled itself around his neck and she grabbed hold of it.

"Come along, then," she said, yanking on the end of the chain.

His attempts to resist proved futile in the face of her spell. He looked suddenly like a rag doll being dragged by a giant.

With the door sealed behind them, I sat down on the bed, relieved beyond words to be rid of the bastard.

Noises came at me through the wall—the sound of doors opening and closing, of nearby voices. A few minutes later, the door opened again. Dauphine stepped inside and said, "He is in the room next to yours, locked inside. As close as he can be without physically inhabiting the same space as you. But if we see no progress from you in the coming days, then I will personally escort him into this room each night until you two consummate your bond. We will see you come to power, even if it makes you miserable beyond comprehension."

"You can't!" I shouted. "You can't force me—"

But I shut my mouth. Because the truth was, she could force me to do whatever she wanted. I wasn't anywhere near strong enough to fight the likes of her—even if I *was* capable of slamming princes into walls.

"I hate him," I finally said with a sneer. "You don't know how much.'

"Insist that you hate him all you like," Dauphine laughed, "but I can feel a power rising in you already. I can feel the Change coming stronger now that the prince is here. Bonding isn't so unpleasant as you think, Leta. I suspect you would grow to enjoy it very quickly. If you two decide you can get along, then this will be much easier for you."

I shuddered. "I will *never* wish to bond with him."

There's only one person in the world—a certain Valdfae—with whom I would ever want to bond.

But that will never happen. If ever there was a chance, it's gone now.

"Your wishes are insignificant to me," Dauphine said with a scornful laugh.

"You realize you're accelerating the war by imprisoning him, don't you? This will end in many deaths."

"The war is already in full swing in parts of Kalemnar," she said, padding over to the window and glancing out. "And Corym is a valuable asset. A bargaining chip. His father will doubtless do anything to get him back—and we intend to take the mortal king up on whatever offer he presents us. As far as I'm concerned, this situation is a win-win for the Sisterhood."

As she turned to leave, I could hear Corym in the next room, his breath coming in hard gasps as if the chain around his neck had half-killed him. Had he been anyone else, I might have knocked on the wall and asked if he was all right.

But I couldn't bring myself to care.

I *wanted* him to suffer.

"My father will come for me!" he howled as Dauphine sealed my door. "He will descend on this place with armies of men, beasts, and the Fae who have pledged allegiance to the

Crown. The Sisterhood will fall, and I will see to it that your vile heads are displayed at Domignon's gates!"

"Yes, yes," Dauphine's voice said as her footsteps echoed in the hallway, fading into the distance. "Of course you will."

For the next hour or so, Corym and I did not speak. I paced my room, grateful that daylight still flowed in through the window. Occasionally, my eyes veered to the woods beyond the convent grounds in search of the gleaming eyes I'd seen once...but there was no sign of them.

"This is barbaric!" Corym finally shouted. "I can't stay in this hell-hole!"

When I glared over at the wall separating our rooms, I spotted something I hadn't noticed before—a small wooden hatch built into the wall, painted the same color as the plaster. I stepped over and opened it, peeking in to see the prince, red-faced, pacing frantically.

"This convent is more luxurious than the house where I grew up," I said. "More luxurious than the houses of most of your subjects, your *Royal Highness*. Then again, I don't suppose you've ever taken the time to speak to any of them about their living conditions, have you?"

Corym snarled, then, spinning around to face me, said, "You know, don't you?"

"Know what?"

He leapt toward the hatch. "You bloody know what you are. That you're like *them*," he said haughtily, jutting his chin toward the door to his room.

"I'm not like them in the least," I grunted.

"No. *You're* High Fae, and they're...they're nothing but

Fallen Immortals. Not that you have your ears or wings yet. I suppose that's why I'm here. Those will come after we..."

He stopped talking when I shot him a look of warning.

"We will not be doing *anything*," I hissed. "When I was with you in Domignon, I let you shove that vile tongue of yours into my mouth far too many times to count. But if you ever try it again, you'll find yourself mumbling incoherently for the rest of your pathetic life."

All of a sudden, Corym's eyes were wide. His body was tense, sweat beading on his brow.

"What the hell is wrong with you?" he asked, backing away as if he'd just spotted a monstrous predator. "Why do you...look like that?"

I lifted a hand to touch my neck, only to find searing heat once again radiating from my skin, my scars pulsing with fire. I knew without looking at my reflection that my skin was glowing bright again, throbbing with flame.

I was no Fae, not yet. But there was no denying the power surging through me as I glared at Corym, wishing him a thousand miles away.

I slammed the hatch shut and pressed my back to the wall, breathing hard.

Over the next days, I would probably have no choice but to listen to him whine and moan about his lot in life.

But for a few hours at least, I wouldn't have to look at his lying face.

CHAPTER TWENTY

LARK RETURNED in the early evening, a look of quiet concern adorning his fine features as he flitted over to the night stand.

"You've heard about our new neighbor, I assume," I said in a whisper.

"I have," he replied softly. "I heard the Sisters talking about him outside. I'm sorry I wasn't here to defend you against him —though it sounds like you did all right on your own."

"It seems my hatred for him fuels my powers."

Lark let out a quiet laugh then and seated himself.

"Do you suppose he knows everything about who I am?" I asked. "About my father, my mother?"

Lark's concern morphed into anger, and he nodded. "The prince has known from the first," he said. "He knew about Lyrinn—it's why he and his dastardly father were so insistent that she compete in the Blood Trials. No doubt he intended to keep you in the dark until you were wed—until it was too late for you to realize he'd duped a Fae princess into binding herself to him. But I assure you, Highness—if he tries anything with you, I will kill him. He may be Prince of Kalemnar, but I am a sprite of Aetherion who doesn't care much for mortal titles."

At that, I couldn't help but smile.

The sprite was small but fierce. And there was something so earnest about him that I found it impossible to doubt his word for a second.

He was the opposite of what I might have expected of his kind. I'd always heard sprites were tricksters, mischievous and cunning. Yet Lark was anything but. He was all seriousness and vows of loyalty. He was, in fact, the most noble creature I'd ever encountered.

"I appreciate that," I told him. "But I wouldn't want you to deny me the pleasure of killing Corym myself."

When the dark of night fell and a knock sounded at the door, I half expected it to fly open and for some Priestess or other to throw Corym back into the room with me.

"Come in," I said, hesitantly rising to my feet and throwing a look of warning toward Lark, who disappeared.

The Sisters usually didn't wait for my approval before barging in. But whoever this visitor was had the decency to wait a moment before pushing the door open.

As it turned out, it wasn't Corym or a Priestess who walked in, but a male Fae...or so he appeared.

He was dressed in a long black cloak, his ears pointed, his hair blond. He had a wise, interesting face with light, aqua-colored eyes, and he was beautiful just as all Immortals were... but something about him sent a quiet warning shooting through my bloodstream.

"Who are you?" I asked, taking a step back. There were so few places to stand in the small room that I had little choice but to press myself to the wall.

"My name is Erildir," he said. "I know your sister Lyrinn from her time in Aetherion."

My legs felt like they might give out under me, and I wondered if Lark had heard him.

"You do?" I asked, my voice trembling.

"Yes. Quite well, in fact."

"Why are you here?" I reminded myself that if the Sisters had allowed him in, he was probably no friend of mine. "Have you come to make me false promises? To tell me you'll bring me to see her?"

He shook his head, his expression solemn. "Such an honor would be more than I deserve," he said. He turned hesitant, as if he were trying to work out how much he could tell me before invoking my wrath.

But finally, when he realized I was awaiting further explanation, he said, "Your sister and I were actually friends for a time. I trained her in spell-crafting. Your sprite friend can attest to that." With that, he gestured toward the window.

"Sprite friend?" I asked with false naiveté. "I don't know what you're—"

"Lark," Erildir said, "you can show yourself now. It's not as if I'm not aware of your presence."

At that, Lark appeared in front of the window, flapping over to hover protectively above my left shoulder.

"Erildir," he muttered. "How unpleasant it is to see you."

Our guest's lips turned up slightly. "It's been a while, hasn't it?"

"Not nearly long enough."

"Lark?" I said, crossing my arms. "Can you confirm that this...*man*...and Lyrinn were friends?"

"In a manner of speaking, they were, yes. But only for a short time," the sprite replied. Quiet rage underscored the words. "He betrayed your sister. And he betrayed your father the High King, as well, when he—"

"You may be interested to learn that Kazimir lives," Erildir interrupted, and I felt Lark jerk to attention next to me.

"Where is the High King now?" I asked coldly. "Where is my...father?"

It was so strange to use that word for Kazimir. All my life, I had had only one father—the mortal named Martel. He was the only man who deserved the title. The only man who had raised me, clothed and fed me. Nurtured and taught me.

Kazimir, on the other hand, was a stranger—and by all accounts, a cruel one.

"In Aetherion, I assume," Erildir said, "presiding over his realm. A healer in Nordvahl helped him through his...*illness*. After that, he returned home—as far as I've been told."

"Illness," Lark scoffed. "A pretty word for what you did to him. Why don't you tell Leta about it?"

My eyes shot daggers at Erildir, and I only wished they could do so literally.

He bowed his head when he said, "I don't deny it. I did try to kill him, but the High King is powerful and not so easily ended. I'm sorry for the part I have played in all of this. Truly. But I want you to know I have come to make amends."

When I turned to Lark to study his expression, I saw nothing but skepticism in his eyes.

"My friend here seems to doubt your word," I told Erildir. "Tell me—why would the Sisters let someone into this convent who claims to be my ally? You do realize they're holding me against my will, don't you? Dauphine and the others must think you're on their side. Which means you probably are."

"Normally, I would agree," Erildir said. "But you see, the Sisters trust me because I was a close confidant of your mother's. I don't suppose you know she was once a High Priestess of the Order, do you?"

"My mother," I said, recoiling. I didn't yet know the whole story behind what had happened to her—what had transpired between her and Lyrinn. I only knew my mother was dead—and that when I thought of her, a shadow passed over my mind. "I don't know anything about her. But I get the feeling she was not all sweetness and light, so forgive me if I have difficulty bringing myself to trust you, Erildir."

He raised his hands, gesturing as if to say, "I mean you no harm."

"If I wanted to hurt you, Leta," he said, his eyes narrowing, "I could kill you with one stroke of my fingers on the air. Lark can attest to that."

"If you so much as think about it," Lark snarled, "I will slit your throat before you can blink."

Erildir shot him a knowing glare and said, "I am perfectly aware of your skills with a blade, sprite. I only wonder if our friend here knows exactly what you're capable of."

Lark bowed his head, his face reddening, and fell silent.

Turning back to me, Erildir added, "Please. Sit. I don't have much time before the Sisters grow suspicious, and I have something in my possession I'd like to show you. A gift."

"I think I'll stand, thank you."

"Fine."

When Erildir reached under his cloak, Lark fluttered to position himself between him and me, his blade drawn in his small hand.

A moment later, Erildir extracted something from a sheath at his waist. At first, I thought he was holding a dagger, but when he held it out to show me, I realized it was merely an ornate hilt of silver and gold. Adorning its grip was a small, delicate set of feathery wings that seemed to glow in the room's pale evening light.

Erildir offered it to me, his arm outstretched.

"I don't understand," I said. "What is this?"

"It was in your mother's possession for many years," he told me. "It's the hilt of the Blade of Dracrigh, crafted by your grandfather Rynfael of the Dragon Court. I'm sure you know he is the High King of Tíria."

"Yes. I know." I took it from him and examined it, marveling at the craftsmanship.

"The blade has yet to be forged," Erildir explained. "That is by design. Your mother took the hilt from the king before she left Tíria, knowing its potential if ever it was completed—the power it might one day hold for its wielder. For a long time, she intended to destroy it, and for many years, I assumed she had. I only discovered after her death that she still had it in her possession."

Turning it over in my hands, I asked, "Why would she destroy something her father made? Why not keep it and wield it herself?"

Erildir smirked then, and when I pulled my gaze to him, I thought I detected a hint of bitterness in his cold eyes. "Your mother was complicated, as was her relationship with her father. The blade, too, is a complex matter. It would take two High Fae to forge it—and those two Fae must possess the bloodlines of a Tírian and a Lightblood."

I jerked my head up, my eyes moving from the hilt to Erildir's eyes. "Lyrinn and me," I said breathlessly. "But—when our grandfather forged the hilt, we hadn't yet been born, surely."

"No. You weren't. But there are some in this world— powerful Fae—who can see the future as clearly as some of us see the past. Your grandfather is one of them."

I wasn't sure if I detected a hint of sympathy in his voice then, as if he knew about my visions—the memories Gallia's Essence had thrust into my mind.

"And yes. You and your sister are vital to the forging of the blade." He glanced at Lark before finishing. "It's part of the reason you're a valuable asset to the Sisterhood, Leta."

I tightened. "Is that why you've come? You want me to help craft this weapon for you to—what? Kill someone with it?"

"Not at all. I brought the hilt to you in hopes of beginning to mend open wounds. So that one day, when you and your sister are reunited, you might use its strength to save the realms from disaster."

My shoulders relaxed slightly, though what he was saying made little sense. How could a blade solve all the world's ills?

"Why should Leta care about this hilt?" Lark asked. "What's in it for her?"

"The hilt is laced with High Magic," Erildir explained. "It is much more than a mere weapon. When the blade is forged and wielded by its proper bearer, they say it will be instrumental in ending the War of the Five Realms." He took a step toward me. "Leta, tell me. Are you in possession of a pendant? One that has perhaps faded over time—silver, with a small design on its surface?"

I stared at him in shock. I had been wearing the pendant for ages now—so long, in fact, that I'd almost forgotten about it. It was one of a pair, identical in every respect. I had given the other one to Lyrinn just before the Blood Trials.

Our father had told me they had once belonged to our mother, and I wore mine for purely sentimental reasons. I had always thought it rather ugly and dull...but it was one of the few reminders I had of my father.

I extracted it from under my tunic and held it up. Erildir stepped closer and took it in his fingers, murmuring a few words in an ancient tongue as he stroked his thumb over its surface.

When he pulled away, I took the pendant in hand and looked at it. It gleamed silver now, and for the first time, I could clearly see the image of a dragon engraved in its surface—much like the one that had appeared on my left hand in recent days.

"Your sister has the same one, yes?" Erildir asked.

I nodded.

"Good. Keep yours close—and safe."

"Why?"

Glancing at Lark for a moment then back at me, Erildir smiled. "Your sister is strong now—stronger, even, than your mother once was. But the two of you together may prove unstoppable. The Sisters want to pull you to their side—to siphon your power—before you and Lyrinn can reunite. They don't want you anywhere near your sister—because the moment you forge the Blade of Dracrigh, you will have the potential to take control over the realms—which means the Sisterhood would never reclaim its former glory."

Lark thrust himself forward then, still defiant. "What's in all of this for you, Sidhfae?" he snarled. "The great Erildir does not offer gifts without an ulterior motive."

"No indeed," Erildir replied with a chuckle. "The answer lies in your question, sprite." Meeting my eyes again, he said, "I am a Sidhfae, as our friend just pointed out. Half Elf, Half Fae. I was taken from my home, the realm of Naviss, many years ago, and because my land is sealed off from this one, I am unable to return. They say that when the Blade of Dracrigh is forged at last, it will be sharp enough to slice through stone and even through the air itself, from one realm to the next. I cannot return home, as my realm was long since sealed off from Kalemnar. I ask only that when the blade is forged and the war won, you let me return to my place of birth to be with my kind."

"And if we lose the war?"

"Then I will have lost, too," he said. "And I will cease to be —because my time in these realms is coming to an end, one way or the other." He held a hand out. "The hilt, please."

My grip tightened around it. "You said it was a gift."

"Indeed. But if the Priestesses find it in your possession, they will take it from you—and they could well destroy it. Don't worry—I will see to it that you get it back before your time in the convent ends. I promise you that."

With a sigh, I handed it over. It wasn't as if I had a choice, after all.

"Leta," Lark's low voice warned. "Are you really going to trust this vile—"

"It's all right," I said under my breath. "He's not wrong—the Sisters would find it and steal it. It's safer in his hands."

"Keep an eye out for me," Erildir said. "You'll be seeing me again soon enough."

When he turned and opened the door to leave, I told him to stop.

"What do they really want from me?" I asked, shifting my eyes toward the hallway to ensure no one was listening in. "If my captivity isn't about the blade, then what can I possibly do for them?"

"They want what they feel they are owed," he replied with a tight-lipped smile. "They believe your sister stole their power from them—and I can't deny that's exactly what she did...with a little help from our friend here." He narrowed his eyes at Lark, who growled.

"Well, I won't help them," I declared. "Not for anything. I'd sooner die."

Erildir chuckled. "You and your sister are not so different, you know. I'm not sure I've ever met two Fae quite so brave—or so stubborn."

With that, he headed out the door, which locked behind him.

CHAPTER TWENTY-ONE

AFTER CORYM'S ARRIVAL, Elodea stopped showing up to escort me to my training sessions.

It seemed I was now officially a prisoner in my chamber, destined to remain as close as the Sisters could keep me to Corym without risking putting us in the same room.

The prince and I bickered through the wall occasionally, but most of his activity seemed to consist of yelling threats at absent Fae or hurling random objects at various walls. Once or twice a day while he twisted himself into a fit of rage, the loud crash of a chair thrown against the door would meet my ears, followed by a string of expletives.

But nothing he did was enough to break out, and nothing he said to the Priestesses was persuasive enough to convince them to set him free.

It was beginning to look like my best hope for escape was his repeated promise that King Caedmon's men would show up and liberate us. At this point, I would almost have preferred to be locked away between Domignon's walls than in the convent —though the thought of being bound to Corym through marriage was still repulsive beyond any words I could muster.

To say I missed Thalanir would have been like saying one misses a vital organ when it's been removed. Each day that passed meant one more day when his face lost a little of its focus in my memory. One more day when his scent faded, his touch, his smile.

The visions had disappeared again, and Gallia's voice, at least for the time being, was gone, too. I didn't even have my frazzled moments of disorientation—moments when I had so vividly recalled Thalanir's touch—to console me.

And, though I would never have admitted it to anyone in the world, part of me feared he would quickly forget about me.

One morning, while Lark was out on his daily hunt, hopelessness settled over my mind to the point where I was desperate enough to initiate a conversation with Corym.

I opened the hatch between our quarters and, when I saw that he was awake and dressed, I asked, "Why has your father not sent his army to find you? He is the most powerful mortal in Kalemnar, after all."

I had no doubt the words would anger the prince, but I was at my wits' end. Erildir had not returned, nor had he tried to help me find my way out of this horrible place, and Lark had had no luck in finding Thalanir.

I couldn't begin to imagine what the Sisters would do to me if I failed for too much longer to show any signs of the pending Change.

"I have no doubt my father has sent out legions," Corym snarled, his face visible through the opening in the wall, his brows knotted together in irritation. "The only reason his men haven't found me is that the damned Priestesses have warded or veiled this convent, hiding it from view. All my father's men couldn't find it even if they walked right past it. Not without the help of a Valdfae."

My heart leapt at the sound of the word.

"Valdfae?" I asked, struggling to keep my voice in check. "Why would they want one of their kind?"

Corym snickered. "You know what they are?"

I hesitated. "I...heard about them when I was younger. They're hunters of sorts, right?"

Corym began to pace, chewing on the skin around one of his fingernails. "Yes, they're hunters, and much more. The Valdfae roam the wild, seeking out Fae and mortals alike—anyone they're hired to locate. Their skills at tracking are unmatched. If they wish to find someone, no amount of magic can keep them away for long—not even a powerful warding or veiling spell. They're killers, too. Some say a Valdfae could infiltrate a palace and take down a king if they so desired—but fortunately, regicide goes against their limited moral code."

I didn't care about Corym's assessment of anyone else's morals. I just wanted to know what the chances were of getting out of this oppressive place. "Do you actually think your father might hire one of these Valdfae to find us—I mean you?"

"Of course. My father needs me. I'm the leader of his damned armies. He can't fight the war without me."

"No," I said, jittery with something close to glee at the thought that a certain Fae sell-blade might soon show up to the convent. "I'm sure you're right about that."

For once, I was grateful for Corym's presence. A rush of joy had filled me at the thought that maybe—just maybe—the king's men would track down Thalanir, and he would find his way back to me. Maybe he would be the one who...

But just as quickly as the joy came, it left me.

Thalanir would never accept such a task. Why should he? I

had been horrible to him. I'd abandoned him, after he'd risked his life more than once to keep me from harm. He had pledged himself to me—promised to reunite me with Lyrinn—and I had ditched him for a complete stranger, even after he'd warned me about her.

I didn't deserve his help, let alone his affection.

I shut the hatch and turned around only to see that Lark had just returned from his flight and was perched on the window ledge.

He looked frustrated when he said, "Still no sign of your Valdfae. But I came upon a few small militias, roaming the trails through the wood. They were dressed in red—a strange mix of Fae and mortal alike."

"Crimson Cloaks." I swallowed. "We can only hope—"

The sound of a creaking hinge silenced me. Lark vanished, and I spun around toward the door to see Dauphine bringing in a plate of delicious-looking pastries. She laid it down on the small table next to the window and turned to face me.

"Anything?" she asked.

She had posed this same question every day since Corym's arrival, and I knew exactly what it meant. *Had I become the powerful being she hoped would magically appear before her one day?*

"Nothing," I told her, revealing my still-rounded ears to her. "Perhaps I'm not what you think I am, after all. Maybe you should let me go, Sister. I'm no weapon of war. That should be obvious by now."

She took a step toward me, her eyes flaring bright, and growled, "I told you, if you and your *mate* cannot find a way, I will lock you together in this room. I will tell him to have his way with you, to claim you as many times as he likes until you show your true colors. Do you understand me?"

Her voice was tinged with a flicker of fury that threatened to explode into an all-out conflagration.

I backed off, nodding submissively. But the truth was, I wanted to say, *I will fight like a wild animal if you should lock him in here with me.*

She stepped away and opened the door. "Keep searching your mind. Find your power, or Prince Corym will find it for you. And trust me, it won't be so pleasant for you as it is for him."

When she'd left again, Lark reappeared, rage painted across his delicate features.

"If Thalanir really is gone, you need to ask around until you learn Lyrinn's whereabouts," I whispered. "Send word to her of where I am—and that Corym is here, too. She'll know what that means—she'll understand better than anyone the danger I'm in."

"I *cannot* leave you here," he hissed. "If they put Corym in this room with you, it will not end well."

"For *him*."

"For you, Leta. He is stronger than we may know, and *your* full strength has not yet come to you. The risk would be too great if you two were locked together."

"Then do as I ask. Find my sister. I've seen her wings. Perhaps she can get here quickly."

When the sprite seemed skeptical, I said, "Please, Lark, I'm begging you."

He looked like he wanted to protest again, but the sound of Corym speaking to someone next door quieted him. No doubt Dauphine was issuing him the same threat—or promise—that she'd thrown my way.

Lark whispered, "I'll do what I can to get you out as soon as possible. Just—stay here."

"Where, exactly, do you think I would go?" I asked, managing a half-smile.

"Fair enough. But don't do anything rash. All right?"

I nodded, and he disappeared out the window.

I seated myself on my bed, hopeful for the first time in days that I might soon find my way free of this prison.

For two days after that, I didn't hear a word from Lark. Each morning and afternoon I paced my room, waiting for something to happen—for the king's men or someone else to arrive —but the most interesting events of each day consisted of Dauphine's brief visits to bring meager helpings of food and ask if anything had changed yet.

Each time she asked the question, I showed her my ears, my neck, knowing the rage that would reveal itself in her eyes upon realizing I was the same useless young woman she'd seen the previous day.

"You have four more days," she told me one afternoon, "and then I will have no choice but to bring the prince back in here— even if it means tying you to the bed to keep you from murdering him."

My hopelessness deepened with that horrid thought.

It was the following day that a vision came to me for the first time since Corym's arrival. I was pacing the room quietly, my mind racing, when the room began to spin uncontrollably.

I threw myself onto the bed, holding my head in my hands, my eyes sealed shut in an attempt to access the vision with any clarity.

And then it came, along with a blinding flash of white light.

I saw myself standing outdoors, the wind whipping at my hair, sun beating down on my skin.

Thalanir stood some distance away, his eyes bright, intense. Dressed all in white, he moved toward me, his arms outstretched, and I took off at a sprint, racing toward him.

But when I was a few feet away, something grabbed at my feet, my ankles, wrapping itself around my legs.

I looked down to see that vines had sprung from the ground and coiled themselves around me, stopping me in my tracks.

Thalanir took a step toward me, halted, stared me up and down, and said, "You have chosen wrong. That is why we can't be together. If you doubt me, look to the power. Ask yourself if you can control it—then ask yourself if you even want to."

With those cryptic words, he turned and walked away.

"No!" I tried to call out, but my voice faltered, coming out as a mere whisper on the air. "No—please. I don't understand. What do you mean? What power..."

The next thing I knew, I was lying on a soft bed, with a small window open to my right.

The sun was beaming in, a cool breeze stroking my skin. And for the first time in days, I inhaled a deep breath, allowing my lungs to take in the air, to embrace it as if for the very first time.

I was still in the convent—back in my room. And for once, it was a relief.

I sat up, my left hand pulsing with heat. When I looked down at my fingers, the dragon seared into my skin glowed orange-red, throbbing with the hard pulse of my heartbeat.

"That was quite a dream," a masculine voice said from the direction of the door.

I looked up to see Erildir leaning against the door frame, dressed in black trousers, leather boots, and a white tunic.

"I...yes. It was," I replied, not wishing to tell him anything about my visions. I glanced down at my hand to see that the dragon was gone, my skin returned to its former state.

"The memories are melding with your dreams," he said, stepping into the room. "You are beginning to learn what really happened back then—which means it's almost time. The Change is upon you, Leta."

He closed the door behind him and moved toward the bed, and I found myself scrambling to sit up straight, brushing my hair out of my face.

His tone was making me nervous, and the way he was looking at me—it was too intense. Too familiar.

You shouldn't look at me that way.

Where was Lark when I needed him?

"Where's Dauphine?" I asked, more out of fear than curiosity. Something about Erildir felt...*different,* as if his intentions since our first meeting had changed. He was staring at me with an expression of need—almost of desire—as if he wanted something from me that I wasn't prepared to give.

"Dauphine is indisposed," the Sidhfae said. "For the time being, at least."

"I see," I said. "And Corym? Do you know if—"

"He's still next door. I believe he's asleep." Erildir cocked his head and added, "Are you concerned about his well-being? After all, he is your true mate, is he not?"

"Of course not!" I snapped. "I dislike him intensely."

"Then how do you explain this?" Erildir reached for my left hand, stroking his thumb over my ring finger to reveal the faint outline of the dragon. "If your true mate isn't near, then why is the dragon revealing itself? Why have your visions returned?"

"I don't know what that mark means," I replied, my voice trembling. "Why it's even there. But it can't mean Corym is my true mate—it can't. I don't..."

"You don't what?" he asked, slipping closer still.

He was staring at me with such intensity that I couldn't bring myself to meet his eyes. I glanced down at my hand, at the dragon, cursing it, wishing it away.

"I don't love him," I said miserably. "I don't want him."

"I see. Tell me, then—is there someone else you desire? Perhaps your true mate *is* nearby...but you haven't yet figured out who he is."

His voice had changed now, growing deeper, warmer. There was something so familiar in it...

Finding my strength, I met his eyes again.

"Yes," I said. "There is someone. But he's far from here, and I'm afraid I destroyed any small chance I had of being with him. I pushed him away—I was cold and awful to him—and he didn't deserve it."

"Perhaps he did. Perhaps he was cold to you, when he should have told you how much you mean to him. How much he aches for you." Erildir slipped a hand onto my cheek, pushing a lock of red hair behind my ear. "What would you say to him if he was here with you?"

My brow wrinkled. I should have snarled at him to go away and leave me alone—this was no business of his. But instead, I replied, "I would tell him I'm sorry. That I want him—that I never stopped wanting him. That I have missed his face, his voice. I've missed *him*."

"He's missed you too, you know," he replied, then, pressing a kiss to my forehead, added, "*Lahnan*."

CHAPTER TWENTY-TWO

"What did you just call me?" I asked, yanking myself backwards.

Erildir's eyes were still fixed on mine—but as I stared into their depths they altered, his irises ebbing and flowing like ocean waves until they settled into a blue the color of the clearest sky on the brightest day.

His other features followed, changing slowly so that, for a moment, I thought I was having another spell, someone else's memories stealing away my sanity.

But even as he morphed and altered, hope began to seep through my insides then broke through in a torrent. A raging flood of joy overtook me, and it was all I could do to keep from crying out.

Those eyes. Those lips.

I didn't dare speak his name. Didn't dare tell myself he was real—that this was anything but one of my vivid waking dreams.

Slowly, so slowly, I reached a hand out, pressing it to his chest. When I felt the strong beat of his heart under my palm, tears came to my eyes.

"It's really you," I murmured. "You came."

He nodded, his expression somewhere between a smile and a frown, as if he was trying to assess whether I was truly pleased to see him.

In response, I took hold of his tunic and pulled him to me, kissing him with all the need, all the want, all the desperation that had built up inside me over the days since we'd parted.

I didn't care anymore if he rejected me. I didn't care about my own fear.

I needed him to know my heart, if only this once.

He kissed me back, his tongue stroking mine, his hands on my neck, holding me so gently yet so possessively that I gladly drowned in the sensation of his grasp.

For all the depth and passion I had felt in the visions—all the painful need, the quiet desperation...

This kiss was more. It was everything.

It was pure honesty. Vulnerability.

It was a baring of souls.

When I'd pulled away, but not so far that I couldn't kiss him again, I said, "I'm so sorry, Thalanir. Forgive me for what I said to you."

"Forgive you?" he asked with a chuckle that was so unlike him, so amused and easy-going, that I almost wondered if I'd just kissed the wrong Fae. "I should be the one asking for forgiveness."

"I told you to let me go. I was horrid to you. I pushed you away, all because..."

"Because she was telling you lies—lies that only took hold because I had pushed *you* away," he replied. His eyes moved toward the window. "I was never very far from you—though it took me some time to find my way into this place. The Sisterhood's warding powers are strong, and the spell they used seemed specifically aimed at other Fae. I couldn't use the usual means to get into the grounds. It wasn't until Erildir came to me in the woods a few days ago that I discovered a way in."

"Wait—he came to you?"

I had assumed Thalanir had watched Erildir leave and taken on his identity as a means of entry. Certainly not that the Sidhfae had sought him out.

Thalanir nodded. "He gave me this," he said, reaching into a small sack at his side and extracting the hilt Erildir had shown me. "He said you'll know what to do with it when the time comes."

As I took it from him, he reached out and gently pulled the chain from my neck, examining the pendant I was wearing.

After a moment, he let it go and pressed his forehead to mine. "I will get you to your sister," he said. "Whatever the cost to me or anyone else. I will not let you go again—do you hear me? You can beg, insult me, scream at me, and I will not set you free. You are my prisoner now, and I intend to hold onto you like grim death—or beautiful life."

I nodded, a sob rising up in my chest at his vow.

I didn't know how long my willing imprisonment would last. All that mattered was that he would stay near me until I saw my sister again.

"When I left with Dauphine," I said, "When I was so awful to you—did you..."

"Did I understand why?" He looked at me, stroking a hand through my hair. "I've told you before, Lahnan—I feel your pain. I feel your joy. I felt your anger, your hurt, in that moment. Of course I understood."

"How?" I swallowed a sob. "How do you understand me so acutely? How do you know?"

He smirked. "When you've lived as long as I have, you learn to read bodies. Movement. You read faces, most specifically eyes. But you don't need to live centuries to understand others' emotions, Leta Martel. All you need is to open your mind to an empathy most people lock away. It's understandable—it's nothing more than self-preservation. It's hard knowing how much pain is in the world. It can break a person down. But *you...*"

He kissed my cheekbone, his lips lingering there for a moment.

"You are even capable of caring about the prince being held captive next door, despite all he did to you."

"Corym," I breathed. "Did you know he was here all this time?"

"I did. I kept an eye and ear out. And when we are safely away, I'll send word to King Caedmon of how to find him—with the help of one of my kind. The Sisterhood will no doubt negotiate some sort of trade—they won't want to let the prince go without a price."

"I don't *really* care about him, you know," I said. "I don't like him in the least."

Thalanir smirked. "Liking and caring are two very different things. You don't want him to suffer, and that is noble of you. But no—you don't like him, which is understandable. He's a morally deficient goblin of a man, after all, and if I had a little more time, I would burn his door down and tenderize his insides with my fists."

I laughed. "Does it make me a bad person to admit I'd like to see that?"

"Not at all."

I fell silent for a moment, chewing on my lower lip, before meeting Thalanir's eyes again. "Do you know what I'm feeling right now?"

His jaw tensed, the muscle twitching, and he nodded. "I do. And we will speak more of it later. Leta...there are things you don't yet know about me. Things that may affect how you feel."

His fingers moved to my left hand and he lifted it, examining the faint, light outline of the dragon ring that now seemed
a permanent fixture on my flesh. "But you will know everything
soon. The time is coming when the truth will be revealed—by
your mind or someone else's."

"Nothing that I learn could affect how I feel about you," I
said, reaching for his face, his stubble deliciously rough under
my palms. "I'm tired of pretending not to feel, Thalanir. The
Sisters—they threatened me with Corym. Told me they would
force us together. The thought was like a blade in my heart—to
think it might mean I could never be with you."

"I want you, Lahnan," he replied, the words barely whispered. "I have wanted you from the first. But that doesn't mean
I can have you. It doesn't mean I deserve you."

The sound of someone clearing their throat met our ears.

Thalanir and I both swung our heads toward the window,
startled. Lark was hovering there, his arms crossed, an expression of deep irritation set in his features.

"I have been searching for you for days on end, Valdfae," he
said. "Why the hell didn't you show yourself to me?"

"Because," Thalanir said, standing and raising himself to his
full height, "you would have told Leta I was out there staring up
at her window each night."

Lark asked the question I was thinking. "And what would
have been so terrible about that?"

"Had the Sisterhood suspected Corym wasn't her true mate,
then it would have gone badly for her."

My chest tightened at those words.

If he was so certain Corym wasn't my true mate, did that
mean...

"They may lack the wings that used to adorn their backs,"
Thalanir continued, "but the Priestesses are powerful still. I
needed them to feel safe here—isolated. I didn't want them to

panic and take Leta elsewhere in an attempt to force the Change." He turned toward me with a warmth in his eyes that set me quietly aflame. "Let's just say I couldn't bear the thought of losing her again."

"Fine," Lark retorted coldly. "So, what's your plan? Or do you even have one?"

"Lark!" I snapped. "He's here, isn't he? He came for us. We should be grateful, not resentful."

"You trust him?" the sprite asked. "In spite of everything? I've told you—these Valdfae can be shifty characters." But his tone had softened, and I could tell his concern lay only in ensuring I felt safe.

"You know I do," I said, rising to my feet to stand next to Thalanir. "I trust him with my life."

Lark bowed his head in submission, and when he raised it again, he said, "Let's get out of this wretched place, then."

"Wait—have you learned anything about Lyrinn's whereabouts?" I asked Lark, remembering what he was up to the last time we'd seen one another.

"Word has it she's searching for you—moving south from Belleau with a party of Fae. If we head north, there's a chance that we may meet her halfway."

I turned back to Thalanir.

"Are we trapped here?" I asked. "The Priestesses..."

"The Priestesses," he said, his lips twitching into a grin, "are currently no threat to us."

CHAPTER TWENTY-THREE

With a flick of Thalanir's fingers, the door flew open. He stepped over and glanced into the corridor to ensure we were safely alone.

"Come," he said, disguising himself once again as Erildir—which almost made my heart break. Everything about him changed—not only his face and body, but his scent, too. He embodied every element of the Sidhfae, down to his cryptic expression and cold eyes, and I found myself instantly craving the absent Valdfae.

"I'm still here, Lahnan," he whispered over his shoulder.

Along with Lark, I followed him out into the corridor, only to spot two Priestesses standing at the far end in their veils and robes. I gasped, thinking they were headed in our direction. Their bodies appeared to be in motion. Each had one foot lifted, the other firmly planted on the floor.

But neither so much as moved an inch, even when we began to move toward them.

"Don't worry," Thalanir whispered as he strode down the corridor. "I cast a paralytic spell—which means their world has slowed to a crawl, and their senses are dulled to almost nothing. To them, we're little more than quickly-moving dust motes."

"Will they be all right?" I asked as we walked by the two Sisters.

"Do you want them to be?"

"If you're asking if I want them dead, the answer is no. They aren't my favorite beings in the world, but they haven't hurt me, exactly."

"I vote yes to hurting *them*, if I get a vote," Lark said almost under his breath. I turned to him, shocked, and he shrugged. "The Order has never been kind to my people," he said. "I have no love for their ilk."

"They're losing their hold on our world as each day passes," Thalanir assured him. "One day soon, if all goes well, sprites will hold far more power than the Order ever did."

We walked in silence down the stairs and along another long corridor and kept moving until we were clear of the convent. On our way out of the grounds, we passed Elodea and Dauphine, who were frozen in mid-conversation. Here and there, other Priestesses sat around on benches or tended to the gardens.

They looked peaceful. Gentle. Not at all like the Fae who had forced me into a locked room against my will and threatened to allow a prince to violate me repeatedly.

I scowled at them as I walked by, considering for a moment whether I was really benevolent enough to resist punching each of them in the face.

None of us said a word until we had advanced a few hundred feet into the woods. When I turned around to look back, I could see no sign of any trail we might have left behind.

"Impressive," Lark admitted as he, too, assessed our seemingly easy escape.

"I've covered our tracks," Thalanir explained, altering once again into his proper appearance. "So that no one follows."

"Corym is still back there," I pointed out, and I wasn't sure whether I felt relief or guilt at having left him behind. "You're certain he'll be all right?"

His eyes flaring, Thalanir glared back at the convent. "He'll be fine," he said. "Which is bad news for the realms. When I walked by his room earlier—before I applied the paralyzing spell—I felt his thoughts, Lahnan. He has no good intentions for our lands or our people."

"Why then didn't you slay him?" Lark asked, his voice cold. "You could have saved lives, Valdfae. You could have—"

Thalanir interrupted him. "It is not his destiny to die, not yet. And it is not for me to decide the fate of a prince, besides. I kill when necessary—not when the mood strikes me. An impulsive Valdfae is a danger to everyone." With those words, he cast me a long look filled with meaning that I wasn't able to discern.

As we began what would doubtless be a long hike, I reached into my waistband for the hilt Thalanir had given me—the one my grandfather the High King had forged. Pulling it free, I asked him, "Do you know anything about this?"

"I know it's powerful," Thalanir said. "I can feel its magic on the air even now. I have some idea of its purpose—Erildir told me a little when he gave it to me for safe-keeping."

"It's meant to have a blade," I said. "But I still don't understand why it's in *my* possession. Lyrinn knows how to use weapons, but I don't. I've always been terrible with them."

"The Blade of Dracrigh is more than a mere weapon," Thalanir replied. "I'm sure Erildir told you that much."

"He did—but he didn't really explain what I'm supposed to do with it when the time comes, other than to help him get home."

"There are many powerful objects in this world imbued

with ancient magic. And when the time comes to use them, they have a tendency to reveal their purpose—which often proves extremely dangerous. Until we understand the hilt, Lahnan, you should keep it hidden. Don't show it to anyone— not even other Valdfae. Understood?"

I nodded, shoving it into my waistband once again and covering it with my shirt.

"I have no intention of letting anyone in on any secret, ever again," I assured him.

Other than you.

It seemed like hours before we finally came to a dirt road and hours more before we spotted what looked like a town in the distance, its walls crafted of thick stone. Squat watch-towers rose up every fifty feet or so along the fortified barrier, and in each tower stood a sentinel.

I stopped in my tracks, suddenly fearful.

"This looks almost like a fortress," I said under my breath.

"It's all right," Thalanir replied. "It used to be. But it's now a town known as Tarroc."

"Tarroc?" Lark asked. "That sounds like a Fae word."

"It is. It means 'comfort.' The fortified town fell and was abandoned by mortals long ago, and in recent weeks, Fae have taken control and renamed it. They use it as a gathering place, a location where our kind can rest when we're weary from our travels. There are similar outposts set up throughout Kalemnar, now that Tírians are able to roam freely."

"Will we find members of the Sisterhood between its walls?"

"No. Those who were once part of the Order are not

welcome here, nor do they even know about it. It is shielded from their eyes. We three can see it easily enough, but to our enemies, the land before us appears to be nothing but dense wood."

"And mortals?" I asked. "Corym's men?"

"Even less welcome than the Sisterhood—though they can enter if invited."

As we approached, Thalanir hastened his stride. He was several feet ahead of Lark and me when his glowing wings sprang from his back, spreading behind him like magnificent sails.

I stopped in my tracks, catching my breath in wonder as I beheld him.

As if in response to his signal, the town's thick wooden doors creaked open, and Thalanir gestured to us to enter alongside him.

"Come," Lark said softly. "It looks like we're safe for the time being."

With his wings still spread, Thalanir led us into the town and down the broad Main Street until we stopped at what looked like a welcoming inn. But before we could pull its front door open, a tall, dark-haired Fae stepped out, looking Thalanir up and down. In one hand, he held a long pipe. At his waist was a gleaming silver sword. His build was powerful, his neck as thick as his jawline.

I froze, more terrified than I cared to admit, as I watched him and Thalanir size one another up.

"A High-blooded Valdfae, waltzing into Tarroc like he owns the place," the other Fae said. "This town is going straight into the bowels of the lowest hell."

"I would have thought it was already there, given that your stench is permeating every corner," Thalanir retorted.

The large Fae stepped toward him, his free hand reaching

for the hilt of his sword. Thalanir held his ground, standing firmly between us and the behemoth until their chests nearly touched.

They looked like two rams preparing to do battle, bracing themselves for impact.

"I have a bad feeling about this," Lark whispered. I looked over to realize he'd turned invisible, and I couldn't blame him for it. I only wished I could do the same.

But when I glanced back toward the inn, Thalanir and the other Fae were hugging each other tightly and laughing.

The sight, I had to admit, was beautiful.

"This is Rieth," Thalanir said, turning to me and slapping the larger Fae on the shoulder. "A very old friend of mine."

I managed a weak smile and nodded my head. "I'm...Leonora," I said, wincing at the too often used alias.

"Leonora," Rieth said with a wink, as if he knew full well who I was. "You are most welcome here for as long as you need to stay. We will guard you from any pursuers and delight in tearing them to shreds, should they try to penetrate our walls."

"I...thank you?" I was horrified, yet secretly delighted by the promise.

"We need a room for the night," Thalanir said. "Possibly longer."

"I can give you one room with two beds," Rieth replied jovially, throwing Thalanir a conspiratorial look. "That's the best I can offer."

My cheeks heated. I had no idea where I would sleep tonight—whether in Thalanir's arms or not. But I told myself all that mattered was that we would be together. Safe.

Far from Corym and those wretched Priestesses.

Thalanir followed me into the inn, then Rieth led us up the stairs to our room. Somewhere behind me, I heard the flutter of Lark's invisible wings.

The room was surprisingly large, with a view overlooking a small town square. As promised, there were two beds, though one was significantly larger than the other, with soft-looking white bedding.

I threw myself down, claiming the larger one immediately, and Rieth laughed.

"Women," he chuckled, and Thalanir said nothing in reply but went and set his small bag down on the next bed over.

"I'll be back to check on you three later," Rieth said, heading for the door.

"Three?" I asked.

"If your sprite friend thinks I can't feel his presence in my own inn, he's not as clever as he thinks."

Lark reappeared the second the door had closed behind the innkeeper, flapping over to perch on the windowsill and scan the town square, one hand on his sword.

"Are you sure these Fae of yours are to be trusted?" he asked, and Thalanir stepped toward him, glancing outside.

I climbed off the bed and looked, too, only to see a couple of Fae—one female, one male—looking briefly up toward our window then continuing along their way.

"*No one* is to be trusted entirely—none except those of us in this room," Thalanir whispered. "Understood? This town is a safe haven, but it's crawling with Valdfae, some of whom are easily corruptible for the right price. If they were to learn Leta's value—or what she has in her possession—let's just say some of them would happily kill you and me without thinking twice, sprite."

"Yet you brought us here," Lark snapped. "Why?"

"I…" Thalanir said, casting a sideways glance at me. "I have my reasons."

"You still trust him?" Lark asked me.

I nodded. "I do. Besides, I feel safer here than I have in any mortal town since I left Domignon. This place—I don't know. It feels...comforting."

"Fine. I'm going to scope out the town. I'll be back in a few hours—but don't expect me to sleep in this room with you. I'll stay outdoors, where it's safe."

I smiled at the idea that he felt more secure out in the elements than inside a warm, cozy room.

To each his own.

CHAPTER TWENTY-FOUR

WHEN LARK HAD FLOWN OFF, Thalanir closed the windows.

"Is there anything you need?" he asked, turning my way. He was all business again—the Valdfae hired to look after me, rather than the one I'd kissed passionately not so long ago. But something in him was changed. The coldness he had so often exhibited toward me was gone, replaced by a sort of tentative warmth.

I stretched my arms over my head. "A bath," I said, my eyes taking in a large copper tub sitting at the room's far end. I stepped over and sighed, seeing that it was empty. When Thalanir sensed my disappointment, he moved close and gestured lightly with his hand, his eyes landing on mine.

The tub instantly filled with a bath of hot, soapy water, and my heart surged with wonder and awe—and affection.

"I'll take my leave for a little," he told me, his voice gentle. "So you can have some privacy."

I nodded, disappointed but understanding. Things were still confusing between us—and unsettled. I couldn't very well just strip naked and climb into the bath in front of him, could I?

Much as I wanted to...

A minute later, Thalanir had left, and I settled into the copper tub, soaking away every anxiety, every fear, every stress that had eaten away at me over the last several days. I pressed my head back and closed my eyes, allowing my mind to wander to another vivid waking dream.

Gallia had returned, as if it was Thalanir who had summoned her.

I became her once again, and once again I was standing in a familiar, vast field. Long, blowing grass and wildflowers surrounded me. I lay back, the sun stroking my skin, and then he was over me, kissing me. I could smell him, taste him, all over again.

A smile slipped over my lips.

"I want you," he said, and I beamed up at him as he pulled back, silhouetted, his face in shadow.

"And I want you," I echoed, pulling him closer. "Too much for my own good."

"Yes," he replied, his eyes turning cold. "Too much."

"What is it? What's wrong?"

He turned away, shaking his head. "Why have you done this? Why have you forced this upon us all?"

Forced what? I wanted to ask, but Gallia was in control of this memory, imposing it upon me. I had no say in what words were spoken; I was merely an observer.

"It's my fate," she said through my lips. "And my choice."

"It will be your end." His voice had turned to ice.

"No. It is only my beginning."

Agony assaulted me, a spasm of searing pain in my gut.

I let out a cry as my eyes opened.

I was still in the tub, now surrounded by darkness as if I had drifted off hours ago…though as usual, the memory had only seemed to last a few seconds.

"Lahnan," a voice said from behind me.

The water was cold by now, the bubbles gone, and I crossed my arms over my bare chest, turning to see him standing close by.

Thalanir was looking down at me, his eyes like two lights shining in the room's shadows. As my eyes adjusted to the dark, I began to make out his face. A look of affection, of kindness, of concern. An expression so familiar, one that I felt like I'd seen a million times.

But never outside of the memories.

"It's all right," he said. "You're safe."

He held up a large white towel, and, without thinking what I was doing, I rose to my feet and allowed him to wrap it around my naked body.

"Were you gone long?" I asked, shivering. He pulled me close, sensing the cold that had assaulted me.

"A few hours. I thought you could use some time to relax."

I nodded. His muscular arms were still wrapped around me, and I didn't want to move despite the fact that I was still cold, my legs surrounded by the chilly water. I didn't want him to let me go.

"What happened to her all those years ago?" I whispered, and I felt Thalanir breathe on my neck as he exhaled sharply, then release his hold on me, backing away.

"What did you see just now?"

I twisted around, the water ebbing gently at my thighs.

"Another vision," I said, looking down at my hand. The dragon ring was faint on my skin, though I thought I detected a subtle glow of orange, pulsing under my flesh.

"What did you see?" he repeated.

"I saw you—speaking to her. I felt pain. Excruciating..."

"It's trying to force its way on you," he replied. "The Change." He stepped forward and offered me his hand. I took it and stepped over the tub's edge, and he led me to the bed. "But something is holding it back. Fear, perhaps—of what will come."

"What *will* come?" I replied, shivering again. "What is going to happen if...if I change?"

"The truth will come out. You'll gain the appearance of a Fae. Your senses will be heightened, your ears pointed. But eventually..."

"Eventually?"

"I've told you already. You will despise me."

I shook my head, seating myself on the bed and looking up at him. "I could never despise you," I told him. "I'm not capable of it. Not even close." In spite of my unease, I chuckled. "Every time I've tried to tell myself I hate you, I've failed. It's only made me want you more. Whatever my connection to Gallia—the Essence that binds us—I seem to have inherited her affection for you."

He looked so sad then, so pained, and I wished I could read him as he read me—I wished I could see inside his mind.

"That's only because you see me as a protector," he protested. "You see me as someone benevolent. You don't know the truth about me. About her..."

"I know enough," I replied. "I know your heart, even if you think I don't."

He lowered his chin, shaking his head. But he said nothing.

"You know it's true—don't you? The Change is coming because of who you are to me, isn't it?" My voice was trembling. "It was never Corym, and you've known it all along. You're my true mate. It was *always* you...wasn't it? You're my destiny."

Thalanir sank to his knees before me, and I took his face in my hands, leaning down to kiss him—but he pulled back.

"Destiny," he repeated. "Yes, it has guided me to you after so many centuries. It has brought us together, Lahnan. But I'm not yet convinced it wasn't a cruelty cast upon us by some god or other. Destiny has caused us both more pain than anyone should endure in a lifetime."

"What do you mean, a cruelty? How can it be cruel for two people to find their way to one another?"

"There is nothing cruel in how I feel about you," he whispered, stroking my cheek with his thumb, moving closer to me. "But it is cruel of fate to tease us with a taste of one another, unless fate then allows us to remain in this world together."

"Why wouldn't it?"

The second I asked the question, I regretted it.

Gallia.

He had loved her and lost her. And it tortured him to this day.

I should have felt jealous, perhaps, that he still seemed to harbor deep feelings for her. But I didn't. I simply wanted to understand.

"She loved you," I said. "I've...felt her. I've felt her heart while she looked into your eyes. Felt her desire, her need..."

"Yes." He nodded, turning away. "She loved me, and for a time, she trusted me above everyone. But she shouldn't have, and neither should you." He stood and stepped away, turning toward the door. "I...I desire you. You know I do. But I can't do this. It wouldn't be right. It would be dishonest, Leta, to pretend I am anything other than a broken man."

He had just reached the door, his hand on the knob, when I spoke again.

"Don't," I pleaded. "I won't let you leave me. Love her if you must—love her more than you love me. But don't leave me. Please."

"Love her more?" he asked, twisting around, his eyes burning into mine. "Is *that* what you think?"

"I've...I've seen how you looked at her, Thalanir. I know you cared deeply for her. I've reveled in it—wished you could feel that way about me. But I know it's too much to hope for."

"Oh," he replied, laughing bitterly. "I loved her once, in my youthful folly. But the visions you've seen—they're carefully selected. They're what her Essence—all that remains of her—has wanted you to see. A moment of bliss. But in the end, there was so much pain—and only now are you starting to feel the sting of it. Leta—my fear is not that I can't love you enough. It's that I will love you so much that it will break us both when the time comes. I fear that you will be my end, or I will be yours. I could not bear that fate for either of us."

I rose to my feet and stepped closer to him, pressing a hand to his chest to feel his heart once again, to seek courage from it.

"You're not my end," I assured him, his pulse beating beneath my palm. "You're my beginning."

He bowed his head, his eyes shifting away, reluctant to meet my own. "I don't deserve your love. I *want* it—I would be a fool not to. But I don't deserve it."

"Perhaps no one really deserves love," I told him. "We're all broken in our own way. But our future doesn't need to be an unhappy one, Thalanir. It can be beautiful, and filled with light and joy."

He shook his head. "There can be no light. Not when you cast a shadow as long as mine."

He looked as if he held in his mind a secret that would break us both.

"I am not goodness personified," he said. "I'm a killer, Leta. For hundreds of years, killing has been my life, and my heart has been frozen, devoid of feeling."

"I don't care what you did in the past." I stroked his cheek, drawing his eyes to mine. "If you can forgive yourself, then so can I—easily. What I want above all else is you. Don't you see?"

"If I give myself to you," he replied, taking my hands in his and kissing one then the other. "If I claim you as my own—then you will change irrevocably. You will see what you have never seen before. Feel as you've never felt. You will never again be the same Leta you've been all your life. Is that really what you want?"

My gaze slipped over his features, and I took him in, memorizing every line, every contour. If I changed, would he seem different, too? Would my feelings for him alter?

"I know my heart," I said. "But I can't promise that I know what will become of me when I change. I can only promise I will never stop desiring you."

"That's not a promise you should make lightly, Lahnan. You don't know what you're saying."

"Thalanir—I may change. But you won't. Which means my desire for you will never diminish."

"I will fight for you and defend you until the end, even if you should become a Queen of Nightmares. My desire for you...it's a force that I fight every minute of every day. Tell me what you want. If it's all of me, then that's what you will have."

"My decision is made," I said. "It was made for me before I ever saw you in that clearing. Even in my mind's eye, I knew what you were to me—though I'll admit I feared you. I feared this feeling, this desire. I had always controlled men easily, and never wished to let myself be controlled by one. I had never surrendered my heart to any man. But *you* are no mere man—you're so much more."

"You have my heart, Lahnan. For you, I will do whatever it takes to make your world beautiful."

I felt as though we'd just exchanged the most solemn of vows. A promise to love one another, whatever may come to pass.

"All it takes to make my world beautiful is for you to be a part of it," I whispered.

He leaned over me. "I believe you. I believe you," he said as he kissed my lips, my neck. "I believe you, Lahnan. And when war comes for us...then at least we will have shared a few perfect moments of bliss."

CHAPTER TWENTY-FIVE

I STOOD and let the towel drop to the floor. He backed away, taking me in, his blue eyes gleaming bright.

Kneeling before me, Thalanir cupped my breast, taking my nipple gently between his teeth, flicking its tip with his tongue.

I moaned with the pleasure of it. The painful tightening at my core, the agonizing desire for him, burned into me like a brand in my flesh.

Something inside me ignited under his touch, and I no longer cared if we were in danger. I no longer cared about anything but claiming him as my own.

Falling back onto the bed, I pulled my legs apart, my eyes locked on his.

"Protect me," I breathed. "From the feeling that has been tearing me apart since we met. Save me from my own desire—because more than anything in this world, I want you, and I will be in agony until I have you."

He was over me in an instant, pushing my red hair back behind my ear, my neck, his teeth raking my flesh. And then he was just where he had been so often been in those lost memories, his face so close to mine, his breath warm and sweet against my lips.

Only this time, he really was mine.

"If I do as you and I both desire," he said, leaning down, his lips stroking my chin and neck as he spoke, "then I will be setting in motion events that will change not only you and me, but the lives of many others, as well. I'm asking you one last time—is that what you want?"

"Yes."

His lips were on my breast again, his mind reading my pleasure, and I writhed, my hips bucking under him, my legs parting further, demanding his length between them. But he moved slowly, slipping down my body, his mouth on every inch of me, his tongue tasting my flesh.

When he arrived at the V of hair between my legs, he paused, then crashed to his knees again. He inhaled deep before stroking his tongue over me once, twice, slowly, exploring and torturing me at once.

I moaned with a pleasure unlike any I had ever known.

Just as I wanted to beg for more, he pulled away to stare up at me with the eyes I had only ever seen in dreams. But his fingers followed where his tongue had been, gliding over my slickness, making me writhe as he pushed them deep inside me.

"You're so wet, Lahnan," he said. "So ready for me."

"Yet you insist on taunting me," I purred. "You know what I want most, but you seem intent on keeping it from me."

"Let me savor you just a little longer," he said with another lap of his tongue against the bundle of nerves between my legs. And then another, and another, his tongue flicking in small, careful circles. I could feel his smile when I moaned—when he felt the depth of my pleasure, the ache of need that he was satisfying so expertly.

Just as I thought I would explode from the delectation of it, he stood, pulling off his shirt, then letting his trousers drop to the floor, unleashing his substantial length. I took in a breath, trapping it inside my chest as he climbed over me, his lips and tongue tasting of my sex, of my craving for him.

His tongue stroked mine as he teased me again, the broad, swollen head of his steel-hard cock pressing into my slickness, promising at last to grant me what I had craved for so long.

I took his face in my hands and kissed him, raising my hips, willing him deep inside me. He obliged with a hard thrust of his hips, sheathing himself and splitting me apart as I let out a howl of the purest pleasure mixed with the sweetest pain.

My body burned with the bliss of it—the feeling that he had broken me in two, yet I was more whole, more empowered than I'd ever been in my entire life.

The world spun again as it had so many times in recent memory, but this time when it steadied, my eyes focused as they never had before. I saw his face more clearly than I ever had, and he appeared more beautiful than I had ever known. In his eyes there were a million colors; in his lips I tasted a million scents and flavors. Everything he had experienced over the course of his long life—all that was a part of him—became a part of me.

His fingers traced my breast, his thumb stroking over its peak as he moved against me—his face caressed my neck, the tip of his tongue slipping along my skin as I pulled my chin up to ask for more. Each time he buried himself inside me, I met his thrusts and my hips rose to take him in me, deeper, deeper, until my head swam with the bond tethering us inexorably to one another's souls.

This—*this*—was what they spoke of when they talked of bonding, of two souls intermingling and two bodies becoming one. It was the sweetest, deepest pain imaginable. I reached around, grabbing at Thalanir's muscular ass, drawing him deeper, deeper inside me before letting him break free once again.

He pulled out entirely, smiling down at me, then rammed himself deep again. He was reveling in my pain, knowing the pleasure in it...because it was his own. Everything I felt—the ache between my legs, the thickness of him—he could feel too.

And I *felt* his pleasure. The throb of his swollen length as he held back, struggling to keep himself from exploding inside me. The scent on his lips, his tongue. The sensation of my body claiming his greedily, taking him into my tight, swollen slickness.

I stared up at his beautiful face, knowing he could feel the love I felt for him—that he knew its purity, its unmarred perfection. He knew, in that moment, that my desire for him was real and true—and that it was everything in the world.

"I will not let you down," I promised him, sensing fear in his eyes. "You don't need to be afraid of this—of me."

"I'm not, Lahnan."

He slipped a hand down between us, his finger stroking me as he drove himself harder into me, faster, as he felt me moving closer to the edge. I could feel how close he was, too—how deep the throb, the ache in him—

And then—

We cried out together, my arms around him as he unleashed inside me and my body convulsed with a shattering pleasure. My teeth chattered, my extremities numbed, as if every nerve ending had focused momentarily on the place where our bodies met.

I held him for a long time as our chests heaved, our breath moving in and out of us as one. I pressed my face into his shoulder, tears streaming now, another moan escaping my lips as pain set into my neck, my ears, my back.

"Gods help me," Thalanir said. "But I love you, Leta."

He pulled away and I rolled onto my front, my arms under my face, which I turned to him as I smiled.

"I love you," I told him. "I always have—though I may not have understood it."

He stroked a finger over one shoulder blade, then the other, and I watched his face as he did so.

"Are you frightened?" he breathed.

"You know how I feel. You don't need to ask."

He smiled. "You're apprehensive."

This time, it wasn't a question.

"Yes," I confessed. "But not for the reasons you think. I'm not frightened of what might happen to my body. My sister went through it, and it seems she came out stronger for it. My only fear in the world right now is losing you, Valdfae."

He slid his fingers over my skin, which flamed in the wake of his touch. "I will not leave you unless you ask it of me. I will never betray you. I will stay with you through your pain, and I will do what I can to alleviate it."

"I know," I said, mumbling into my arm as a shot of pain assaulted my chest. "You know what might help?"

He leaned down and kissed my back, slipping a hand down between my legs, which moved apart instinctively. "Yes," he said, his fingers pinching me gently, teasing. I squirmed then, the pain disappearing as he stroked his fingertip over me. "What say we try to precipitate the Change again?"

"I say that's a very good idea," I laughed.

He slid down to the end of the bed with me still on my stomach, and shoved my legs apart. His mouth was between them again, and every shot of pain that assaulted my body was met by a lick, a suck, a stroke to counter it. He took his time, turning my agony into ecstatic shudders.

Thalanir kept at it for the entire night. When his mouth wasn't between my legs, he was taking me hard again, or slowly, carefully, his eyes locked on mine. Sometimes, my mouth was on him, taking him in, stroking, sucking, licking. Try as I might, I couldn't satisfy my hunger. But the pleasure of my effort was greater than any bliss I'd ever known.

We didn't sleep until dawn, when we collapsed, exhausted, a tangle of limbs.

He was still holding me when I awoke to the sensation that something in my body had altered inexorably.

The air smelled different. More vivid—filled with aromas I had never know. I could smell distant wildflowers. Trees, grass, even the scent of sweat wafting up from someone on the street below.

In the ceiling beams, I could see each faint line of wood grain, however narrow. Every pore in the rough surface, every minuscule mark where a chisel had carved slightly too deep.

I could hear Thalanir's heart beating in his chest. The sound was music, a beautiful, sweet, pulsing rhythm telling me he was alive—that I had stirred something inside him, and he inside me.

Gently pulling his arm away from my body, I slipped out of bed and stepped over to the mirror above the dresser, hesitant to see myself. And for the first time, I knew what Lyrinn must have felt when she awoke as a Fae—the first time she truly felt who and what she was.

My eyes, which had always been large and blue, now gleamed like sapphires, flickering with quiet embers threatening to ignite into flame.

I reached cautiously for my waves of hair, taking it in hand and pulling it back to reveal the ears whose scars I had worn with a quiet pride, the neck lined with markings that I had accepted as a part of me long ago.

My ears were tipped and pointed like Thalanir's, their scars no longer red, but narrow, twisting lines of cobalt blue so beautiful that I ached to see them. The scars on my neck, too, now looked like curling designs painted on my skin by some extraordinary artisan.

Naked as I was, I turned my back to the mirror, glancing over my shoulder to see that the lines continued down the center of my shoulder blades.

Did I have wings? If so, where were they? How did I summon them?

I forced out a sigh, letting my hair drop.

It was Thalanir who had granted me this gift—however frightening it was. I now had a new identity. A new life. One that I did not fully understand yet but for which I was eternally grateful.

"You're beautiful."

His voice wafted through the air, caressing every part of me. I turned to see him pushing himself up onto his elbow, eyeing me up and down.

"But then," he added, "you always were."

I slipped over to him and sat on the edge of the bed, my left hand touching his face as if I were trying to assure myself he was real.

Around my finger, what had once been the faint trace of a dragon ring was now inky deep and dark, an unmistakable mark in my flesh. It wasn't the same design as Gallia had had on her own skin, but similar.

"You made me this way," I replied, staring at my hand.

He shook his head. "You would have ended up here eventually," he said. "I simply helped the process along."

He took my hand in his, kissing it.

"How do you feel?" he asked.

"Surprisingly fine," I told him. "I thought it would hurt more—or at least mess with my mind more. But I feel...*good*."

Smiling, he nodded. "Like I told you, you endured the true

Coming of Age many, many years ago, Lahnan. Your Essence is as old as time—it was only your body that needed to shift and alter. I'm glad you were spared some pain."

"I'm grateful to you for saving me from it." Returning his smile, I climbed on top of him, straddling his hips, a groan escaping his throat as I ground gently into him, feeling his length harden under me.

"I still envy her, you know," I said quietly. "I think I've envied her from the first. Knowing she had you then—in the days when you were happy."

Thalanir shook his head. "I wasn't happy with her. Not like you think. But let's not speak of her, okay?"

He was right. It wouldn't do to talk about the ghost that seemed to haunt us both. Not now—not after the perfection we had just shared.

"Besides, I'm happy now," he said, wincing with pleasure as I lifted myself gently, grasping his shaft in my hand and lowering myself again onto him. As I took him in, inch by inch, he murmured, "*So* happy."

"You're *horny*," I told him with a laugh, leaning down to kiss him. "That's hardly the same thing. I want you properly happy."

In one quick motion, he pulled my body to his, rolling me onto my back. Sheathing himself inside me with a hard thrust of his hips, he said, "Lahnan—if anyone can make me happy... it's you."

CHAPTER TWENTY-SIX

WHEN WE HAD MADE love twice more and then bathed together, I slipped into a white dress and a thick brown leather belt selected from the clothing Thalanir had amassed for me in Marqueyssal.

"While we're here in Tarroc," Thalanir said, "I want to seek out a couple of my friends. Perhaps they will be kind enough to offer you some training before we head north."

My throat tightened at the word. "Training?"

I had no desire to train—not after my awful sessions with Elodea, where I'd discovered how frightened I was of my own rage. I could only imagine what would happen if I learned to harness my fury properly—and I had no desire to find out.

Before I could protest too much, Thalanir replied, "You woke up this morning much more powerful than you were last night. You need to learn how to focus that power—or you could prove a danger to yourself and others."

"So, why don't *you* train me? I'm sure you're very capable. And I'd rather..."

I'd rather spend time with you than anyone else.

He smirked as he pulled on a pair of trousers and buttoned

them. "I'm capable of a good deal. But there are other Fae who are far better teachers. Trust me on that."

"Fine," I sighed. "As long as you promise not to leave me alone with any of them for too long."

His head jerked my way. He strode over and, taking my chin in his hand, kissed me hard, his tongue finding my own. "I will never leave you," he said when he'd demonstrated his devotion to something approaching a mutual satisfaction. "I will never betray you or forsake you, Lahnan. Understand?"

I nodded, overcome with a fierce desire to get him back into bed.

He grinned. "Not just now," he said, reading my mind a little too easily—or perhaps he was only smelling my desire. "Come—let's find some food and a few Fae."

When I'd slipped the Blade of Dracrigh into my bag, we left the room and headed downstairs and out to the street. There, Thalanir steered us toward a small tavern called the Crescent Moon. The sun was high in the sky already, but the air had grown chilly, and a few flakes of snow tumbled lazily toward the ground, melting as they collided with the earth.

"Snow!" I exclaimed, stopping outside the tavern. "I didn't expect it so far south."

"War tends to bring winter," Thalanir said bitterly. "It always has, since I can remember."

"Have you been through many wars?"

"More than I'd like to say," he replied. "The world changes when they assault our lands, as if the trees themselves feel the fear that trembles inside people's bones. The sky loses its beauty—the water runs with blood. Nothing good ever comes of war, and I fear the coming conflict will be no exception—unless we can conclude it quickly."

I took Thalanir's hand. "Erildir told me something," I said. "About the Blade of Dracrigh. He said it might help our side to win—to avoid all the carnage of so many wars that have come before this one. I think he believes Lyrinn and I might be the keys to ending the conflict before too many lives are lost."

"Let's hope he's right," Thalanir replied, kissing my hand before pulling the door open.

Inside, he scanned the place until he spotted a lone female Fae seated at a table at the tavern's far end. She was dressed in black leather from head to toe, which, from a distance at least, gave her the appearance of someone both intimidating and stealthy.

"Ah," he said. "Janyn is here."

"Who's Janyn?" A quick flash of possessiveness flared in my chest before I pushed it away.

"She's another Valdfae—a highly skilled one. We've known each other for many years. Come, I'll introduce you."

As we approached, the Fae rose to her feet. She was small— a half a foot shorter than me at least—with neatly-trimmed, short hair that framed her face so that she reminded me of a sprite.

Unsurprisingly, she was beautiful, with a delicacy that reminded me of fine porcelain.

She looked at me, then at Thalanir, a cautious twinkle in her eye. "Thal," she said. "You're the last Fae I expected to see this side of the sea."

"Janyn," he replied with a bow of his head. "I had business here."

"*Business,* is it?" she replied with another glance my way, her tone filled with the quiet insinuation that I was far more to him than a mere job. She sniffed at the air, then smiled. "Ah —*that* sort of business."

My cheeks heated. I had expected the bath would wash off the scent of our love-making. But clearly, I was wrong.

"She is freshly Changed," Janyn said. "Huh. This will be interesting."

"I was hoping someone could give her a few pointers," Thalanir said. "I don't suppose you'd be willing."

"Of course I would," she laughed. "I do love a challenge."

She looked me up and down, her eyes stopping when they landed on my left hand.

Her expression altered instantly from one of mischievous amusement to horror.

She reached for my hand and pulled it up, examining the dragon ring that had engraved itself into my skin. When I yanked my arm away, her look of horror faded, but only slightly.

"You're a Násuire," she said softly, moving closer to me and staring up into my eyes. "You have the Essence."

I nodded, glancing sideways at Thalanir, whose expression had turned stony. "That's...what I've been told," I said.

Janyn's eyes shot to Thalanir's. "Do you have any idea how dangerous it was to bring her here? What the hell were you thinking? Why would you do this, after..."

She stopped speaking, her voice seemingly trapped in her throat.

I watched the silent interplay that followed, then, growing weary of guessing, asked, "What happened, exactly?"

"He hasn't told you?" Janyn said under her breath, seating herself with a thud in her chair. "He brought you here—he bonded with you—and he hasn't *told* you?"

I pulled up a seat next to her, and Thalanir joined us at the table. "I know there was a time," I said under my breath, "long ago, when he was with someone like me. I know she died...if that's what you mean. Thalanir has not lied to me."

Janyn glared at me scornfully and said, "She didn't just die.

She *had* to die. She gave the world no choice but to rid itself of her. She was a goddamned nightmare."

"Jan—" Thalanir said, a note of quiet rage in his voice. "Enough." He took my hand in his under the table and said, "Leta is not Gallia, and she never will be. The mark on her finger should tell you as much. It's entirely different."

"It's a damned dragon," Janyn retorted. "You somehow think that means she's not dangerous?"

Thalanir sat back, exhaling sharply. "She is the granddaughter of Rynfael, and the daughter of Kazimir. And she has a sister who has already found her wings—you know who Lyrinn is already."

At that, Janyn looked winded, as if a large stone had collided with her chest. She eyed me again, sucking in her cheeks, trying to find a reason—any reason—to think I was to be trusted.

"Yes," she said. "I know of Lyrinn's exploits. I know she endangered us all when she did battle against Mithraan in the Blood Trials."

"She loves Mithraan, and he loves her," Thalanir countered. "Either of them would have died before harming the other."

"And you two?" Janyn asked, looking from one of us to the next and back again. "Will you die before harming each other?"

"Leta knows I will never hurt her," Thalanir said coldly.

"And I would never hurt him, of course," I added. "Why would I?"

Somehow, the reassurance only seemed to make the Fae angrier. "It is a dangerous thing," she said, "to be bonded to a weapon. To love an asp. It makes us all vulnerable."

I glanced over at Thalanir, who said nothing at first.

"I trust him," I said. "He has never lied to me—never steered me wrong."

"He has kept truths from you," Janyn retorted sharply.

"Everyone in the world has kept truths from me," I snapped.

"All my life. But I don't believe for a second Thalanir would have...*been* with me...if he thought it would endanger me."

Janyn snickered. "It isn't you I'm worried about, Násuire," she said. "It's the rest of us."

I wanted to ask what the hell she was talking about—what had happened to make me seem terrifying to anyone. So, I had a dragon etched on my skin. My grandfather was a High King who dwelt in the Dragon Court. It was in my blood, after all.

"She's our best hope, Jan," Thalanir hissed.

"If *she* represents hope, I may as well hang myself from the rafters."

"Could someone tell me what's got you two so riled up?" I croaked. "I thought I was here for a bite to eat—or to train—or something. What's all this hopeless talk? Aren't we all on the right side of the war?"

"The right side?" Janyn scoffed, pushing her chair back from the table. "Thanks, but I won't be training you. I have no intention of helping you to destroy what's left of our folk after so many of us were stripped of our souls and turned into Grimpers a thousand years ago. I tried to help a Násuire once before—and I have no interest in subjecting myself to any of this madness a second time." Her eyes locked on Thalanir. "It seems you've forgotten the pain you endured so long ago," she said. "But I haven't. I will not watch you self-destruct a second time."

With that, she rose to her feet and stormed out of the tavern.

As I watched her go, a flash of bright light exploded somewhere inside me, and a vision crashed through my mind's eye. It was more vivid, if that was even possible, than those I'd had before the Change.

This time, though, I wasn't watching from inside Gallia's body. Instead, I found myself looking at her from behind as she stood in a beautifully decorated room of carved stone, with intricate tapestries lining the walls. A row of tall windows on one side led out to a view of rolling green hills and pure, blue sky.

"Are you ready?" a female voice asked, and I spun around to see Janyn stepping lightly toward Gallia, dressed in brown hunting leathers.

Neither of them saw me; I was nothing but a shadow, a creature who had not yet come into existence.

Gallia turned, smiling, and for the first time, I saw her clearly.

She was lovely, her hair dark brown, her eyes green as emeralds. Her cheekbones were high, her lips full and pink. As I stared at her, I understood why Thalanir loved her. She was alluring, with kind but mischievous features that drew me in and made me want to step closer to her, to examine every inch of her.

When Gallia looked puzzled, Janyn laughed and said, "Are you forgetting we have a training session, my Lady? The first of many I have planned for you."

"I—" Gallia replied, but she stopped there, like she was momentarily confused. "Right—of course. I suppose I *had* forgotten."

Something felt off.

I glanced down at her left hand, only to see that the swirling image of a ring wasn't yet there. Which meant that whatever event had brought about its existence hadn't yet happened. This memory—it was from the more distant past, before Gallia had fully come into her powers.

Clearly, Janyn had trained her. She had helped her along the way, aided her in unleashing the powerful Fae inside her.

But if that was the case, then why was she now refusing to help me so many years later?

With a flash of white light, the vision came to an abrupt

end, and I glanced down at my hand again, seeing the dragon still starkly outlined there.

How did such a harmless mark make me a threat to any Fae? What had happened to inspire so much fear and anger in Janyn?

"Tell me, are you hungry?" Thalanir asked, laying a hand on my own, and I sensed that he was trying to take my mind off the nagging questions.

I nodded, though the truth was, I had no appetite. I felt like I could have gone for days with no food, no drink. I was deflated, like a sail with no wind, left to waft uselessly in the breeze.

I pulled my eyes to his. "Am I a threat to you? Is—is that why you didn't want to get close to me before?"

He stroked his finger over the dragon image that was now a permanent part of me. "Never," he replied, pulling my hand to his lips. "Never. You are too good, too kind, to be a threat to me or anyone. Do you hear me?"

I nodded again, though I wasn't sure I believed it. I reached for his mind, not trying to read his thoughts, but his emotions. I could feel truth in the words, but a quiet reserve, as well—as if he wasn't entirely confident I wouldn't explode at any moment.

"I'll ask the chef to send some food to us at the inn," he said. "Come—you didn't sleep much last night, and neither did I. Let's get some rest, then we can assess our next move. If I need to train you myself, I will. It was foolish of me to bring you here. I was hoping..."

My voice was weak when I repeated the word. "Hoping?"

Rising to his feet, Thalanir said, "Hoping my fellow Valdfae had forgotten the past. But it seems we are all doomed to live with the memories of those days until our last breath leaves our bodies."

CHAPTER TWENTY-SEVEN

My sleep was fitful at best.

The midday sun outside was too bright, and my mind was too worked up for rest to be a possibility. The few times when I did manage to drift off, I awoke every couple of minutes to see Thalanir seated by the window, his eyes fixed on the town below.

"You're not going to rest?" I asked, saddened that he was so close to me yet felt so far away.

"Eventually," he replied.

I could feel that he was a million miles away, his mind straying to thoughts well beyond the town's walls.

"Why do you look as if you're on high alert? Aren't we safe here, around your kind?"

"I trust most Fae, yes," he replied, keeping his eyes locked on the view of the street. "But I've begun to feel something awry in this town—a corrupting force on the air. I feel it with each breath—yet I have to confess that I can't pinpoint exactly where it's coming from." At that, he turned my way. "It's possible I made a mistake, bringing you here. Perhaps we should find Lark and leave town sooner, rather than later.

After Janyn's reaction, I'm not entirely sure we're welcome here."

His words saddened me. As frustrated as I was, as confused by my new place in the world and as eager as I was to find Lyrinn, I felt genuinely safe in Tarroc—for the first time in a long time. The distance we had put between ourselves and Corym was a relief, as was knowing we were far from the Sisterhood. With each mile that separated us from them, I felt more secure, more free.

And yes—I wanted to leave soon, to head north toward Lyrinn. More than almost anything, I wanted to reunite with my sister at long last.

But a quiet, selfish part of me wished to remain here in this place where Thalanir and I had first bonded.

I wanted to enjoy a little freedom and contentment—to take pleasure in my time with him. If only for a little while.

I didn't care about training. I didn't care if other Fae wanted nothing to do with us. He was mine, and I was his. That was all that mattered.

"Couldn't we stay?" I asked meekly. "Perhaps just a few days?"

Thalanir's eyes glowed bright in response, and I thought I detected the merest hint of a smile in them.

"You'd really like to, wouldn't you?" he asked, rising to his feet and stepping over to the bed. "Are you quite certain?"

I pulled the covers aside, encouraging him to climb in beside me. He slipped off his boots and did so, and when he lay down, I rested my head on his chest and reveled in the sensation of his fingers gently combing their way through my hair.

"I need to feel secure for a little," I said, "but to tell you the truth, there's something more, as well. I...feel like I've always belonged in a place like this." I let out a laugh. "I suppose it makes sense." My fingers slipped over my ear, confirming that I hadn't dreamed the moment when the Fae concealed inside me had revealed herself at last.

"You belong with your family," Thalanir said. "With Lyrinn and your grandfather Rynfael. And I will die if that's what it takes to ensure you are reunited with them. I will even find a way to get you to your father Kazimir, should it come down to it —and if it's what you wish for."

"I have no desire ever to lay eyes on that bastard again," I replied bitterly, pulling my head up to look into Thalanir's eyes. "Not after what he did to Lyrinn, torturing her for weeks on end. Not after the hell he put her through. High King Kazimir can burn, for all I care."

Thalanir stroked his thumb over my cheek. "Don't judge him too harshly. High Fae are complicated creatures, and High Kings even more so. Kazimir is reputed to be cruel but fair—and rumor has it that he's coldest to those closest to him. Some say it's because he wishes to protect them, even if it means earning their ire. Others claim it's because his wife—your mother— drove him to madness. Only Lyrinn can confirm or deny this, I suppose."

"Do *you* believe it?" I asked, scoffing at the notion. "Can anyone really blame that asshole's awful behavior on a woman?"

Thalanir let out a laugh, then he pondered the questions for a moment. "No. His behavior—his coldness—they're in his own hands, under his control and no one else's. But to be fair, Lahnan, there have been plenty of times when you've thought me cruel. Cold. Heartless. Even though every action I have taken since the moment we met has been with the intention of protecting you. Even the act of letting you go when you asked me to...*my Lady*."

The way he uttered the last two words felt like possession, like want. *Need.*

And I reveled in it. Never had I wanted a man to take ownership of me. But Thalanir wasn't trying to rule me or force me into submission.

He only wanted me to be safe and happy.

"Well, then," I said, easing my body over his then yanking off the long blouse I'd thrown on before climbing into bed. "Perhaps you should remind me now just how protective you can be."

"What did you have in mind?"

I pushed my hands up under his shirt, marveling for the hundredth time at the muscles that met my fingers, my palms. I gasped as he exhaled, and the gap at his waistband expanded so that I could slip my hand inside his trousers.

The sigh that slipped past my lips when I grasped his length was one of pure joy—and the languid growl that escaped his throat was one of pure desire.

When I began to undo his trousers, he shook his head. "Not fair," he said.

"I thought you wanted to look after me," I pouted.

"I want nothing more, as a matter of fact."

"Then let me satisfy my craving. If you don't, I fear that I will perish, and you'll have no one to blame but yourself, Valdfae."

"No one ever died because they were denied the opportunity to take a Valdfae's cock in their mouth."

"You don't know that. The dead can't speak for themselves. For all we know, there have been thousands of corpses of unsatisfied women left in the wake of every Valdfae in history."

With a laugh, he surrendered, lifting his hips and allowing me to yank his trousers down at last.

I slipped my tongue along his shaft, the substantial thickness, throbbing head grasped in my palm and squeezing just enough to elicit a whimper of delight. I wrapped my lips around him, my tongue lapping at the drop of liquid that had gathered at the tip and drawing a full-on groan from him.

When I took him into my mouth, I felt him again—his pleasure, every nerve in his body tingling in anticipation. The sensation of pure arousal that had overtaken him, making his head spin.

But there was something else, too.

A deep, cruel feeling of inadequacy. A sensation that he didn't deserve this. Didn't deserve *me*.

You're wrong, I thought, my hand stroking him, my mind linked to his own, my body pulsing with the same pleasure he felt as I tightened my grip, my fingers barely able to meet around his substantial thickness.

He raked his fingers into my hair, holding my head as I pleasured him, his hips driving him slowly, deeply, until I felt the rushing wave of his release like a violent earthquake.

I drank him down, reveling in the taste of him, the power I held over him right now, and he over me. And when we had finished, I slid my tongue over him, showing him just how much he deserved my affection, my attention. My love.

And then, pushing him back onto the bed and climbing on top of him, I showed him all over again.

CHAPTER TWENTY-EIGHT

WHEN NIGHT FELL OVER TARROC, Thalanir was asleep in our bed—a rare and beautiful sight—and I found myself still wide awake.

I rose to my feet and stood before the mirror once again, a hand reaching for my shoulder blade, wondering about the wings that hadn't yet shown themselves. I glanced down at the outline of a dragon on my hand—the strange marking whose meaning I didn't entirely understand. Would those be the only wings I ever had? Was my body teasing me with the promise of something that would never come?

They didn't resemble Thalanir's beautiful, glowing wings, elegant and translucent as they were. They were webbed, aggressive, dark, and grim. Still, there was a beauty to them—something wild and forbidding.

As quietly as I could, I dressed in what had become my favorite pair of trousers and a blue linen shirt. With a sigh, I glanced over at Thalanir. He looked so peaceful that I didn't wish to disturb him...but I was undeniably hungry.

I told myself it wouldn't be the worst thing if I slipped out to the tavern to get a bite to eat. He was a Valdfae, after all—he would quickly figure out where I'd gone, and follow me if he so desired.

With a quiet *Thank you for this,* I took a couple of silver coins from his small bag and headed downstairs, confidently striding out of the inn, my head held high as the realization hit me that for the first time since leaving Domignon, I felt no need to wear a cloak, to hide my face. This was a town run by Fae—run by my kind.

What a strange thought that was.

I inhaled deeply as I stepped out onto the street, and the scent of spices, bread, pastries and roasting meat met my nose in a barrage of delights. As I began the walk to the tavern, the sound of lilting music lured me to my destination.

I could hear the lyrics clearly, though I was still some distance away—something that would never have been a reality a few days ago. It was a song about a maiden with silver hair—a Lightblood, perhaps—who had died. Her body was left on a giant leaf to float down the river, and her lover wept as he watched her go.

As I stepped inside the tavern, the minstrel, a male Fae with a lute in hand, sang.

Fate called on her to die...
So that another might live.
She was the most noble of maids,
And he the most grateful of men.

Something in those words sent my heart reeling, sadness ravaging my insides...though I had no idea if the lyrics were pure fiction or not.

"It's quite sad, isn't it?"

The deep voice came from my right, and I glanced over to see a tall, black-haired Fae leaning against a carved wooden pillar, a cup of ale in hand.

"A story too often repeated in the lore of our kind, I fear," he added.

His eyes were fixed on mine, and something in his look was impish—but appealing. He felt like an old friend, despite the fact that we'd never spoken a word to one another.

"You're the Násuire," he said, taking a step toward me. "You have her Essence about you. *She who lives again.* It really is remarkable..."

I thought I caught him glancing down at my left hand, but he quickly shifted his gaze back to my face, as if realizing it was inappropriate to stare.

"What's remarkable?" I asked, feeling suddenly self-conscious.

"The resemblance," he said. "Not so much in physical attributes, but in presence. She had the same...energy."

I didn't need to ask what he meant. He was referring to Gallia—which meant he had known her all those years ago.

"And you are?" I asked, pushing the thought from my mind.

"Rowland," he replied with a bow of his head. "You can call me Row. Has that scoundrel Thal not mentioned me?" With a laugh, he responded to his own question. "No. I don't suppose he has."

Thal.

So strange to hear his name shortened. But nice, in a way, to meet someone who appeared to be his friend.

Then again, Janyn had appeared to be a friend, too, and that hadn't exactly gone as either of us had hoped.

"I'm Leta," I replied with a smile. "And no, *Thal* hasn't said a word about you, I'm afraid."

"Ah. Well, he was probably worried that if he described me in graphic detail, you would immediately leave him for me."

I crossed my arms and stared him down. "A little arrogant, aren't you?"

"Always have been." With a gesture of his hand, he summoned a small table with two chairs that pulled themselves out as if in invitation. "Come. Sit."

I took a seat opposite him, wary of his so-called charm. In my experience overly confident males weren't a breed to meddle with too closely—though admittedly, there was something enjoyable about him.

"So, you're the secret Thalanir has been keeping," he said, flicking a finger toward the table and conjuring a pint of ale, which appeared in front of me. "I'd been wondering why I haven't seen him in some time. Normally, we run into one another on the road with some frequency."

I took a skeptical sip and had to confess to myself that the ale was delicious. A moment later, a plate of roast chicken, potatoes, and green beans appeared before me, complete with silverware.

"I don't know what you mean," I said, grabbing a fork and stabbing a potato. "It seems I'm hardly a secret. Everyone I've encountered seems to know everything about me. I'm beginning to take it as a threat."

Rowland leaned in closer and whispered, "Don't worry; I'm not a threat. Only curious about you—I've heard rumors on the wind, you see. They say you and your sister are quite special."

"Are you from Tíria?" I asked, ignoring him.

He half-nodded, then seemed to think better of it. "Yes and no. I'm a Valdfae, like our friend Thal—of Tírian blood. But technically, I was born on a sailing vessel. I've made myself scarce on the seas since before Tíria was laid to siege, hiding out on this ship or that when the need arose, roaming Aetherion and the isles to its west, and seeking my fortune."

I smirked. "I see. And have you found it?"

"My fortune?" Row let out a laugh. "Hardly. I'm no Thal.

That one knows what side his bread's buttered on. He understands where the money is, and he always seems to find it."

I tried not to sound overly defensive when I asked, "What do you mean by that, exactly?"

Row glanced around to ensure no one was sitting too close to us and said, "Just that your...*friend*...has always had a knack for finding the best of all the bounties. Don't get me wrong— he's talented as all the hells. Best tracker around. But he's also blessed with an endless spate of good luck." He sat back, linked his hands behind his head, and added, "What do you reckon he's getting paid for tracking *you* down and dragging you back to that sister of yours?"

The question bit into my mind and heart, and I dropped my fork onto my plate, glaring at Row. "He didn't come seeking me for money."

"No? Are you sure about that?"

His eyes flared bright briefly, and for the first time I noticed their color—a sort of mix of hazel and violet, veering from one to the other depending on the shadows.

"He had other reasons to seek me out," I replied, my tone clipped.

Row reached out and pushed my hair behind my ear, smiling. I yanked myself backwards, glaring at him.

"Yes," he said. "I see that he did. You're newly bonded, aren't you?"

"Thank you for the food," I said, threatening to rise to my feet, but he held his hands up and chuckled.

"I meant no offense. I apologize profusely. Please—keep eating and drinking. I was only toying with you because you feel...familiar. Like we know one another from another life. I suppose I got carried away. Truly, I'm sorry."

Another life.

This time, I was the one who leaned forward when I whispered, "Did you know Gallia?"

"Ah. Yes. I knew her intimately." With a wink, he added, "What would you like to know about—"

"If you don't want me to conjure a thorn-covered gag and wrap it around your entire head and neck, you'll shut your mouth, Row."

The deep voice came from behind me.

With my heart hammering in my chest, I turned and looked up to see Thalanir standing immediately behind me.

I couldn't tell from his expression if he was genuinely angry or if his words were in jest, but when I felt his warm hand on my shoulder, I ceased to care. A hard breath escaped my lips at his touch, the moment of pure tactile pleasure overwhelming me.

"Thal!" Rowland said, shooting to his feet. "Speak of all the devils in all the hells. There you are. Such a pleasure to see you."

"I wish I could say the same," Thalanir said, pulling up a chair between us and crossing his arms over his broad chest. He looked my way when he said, "Row here has a habit of divulging far too much information to far too many people. It's one reason he's a rubbish Valdfae. He could no more be stealthy than go a month without trying to charm some poor young lady's pants off her."

Row ignored the barb and turned his attention back to me. I tightened, the tension in the air growing exponentially. It seemed a silent competition had just begun to unfold between the two Valdfae.

"Leta," he said, "I sense that you're itching to learn about your new and changing body."

"Watch yourself, Row," Thalanir warned. "Leta doesn't need to hear from you on that front."

Rowland raised a hand and said, "Don't worry. I simply

wondered if Leta might like a little training in the ways of Valdfae."

"I can teach her anything she should wish to know," Thalanir said possessively.

"Ah, yes. You could teach her to pick a lock, charm an albatross, or grow some weeds quickly. But you're no blade-master —nor are you an archer. I can teach her to use weaponry of all sorts—it will help her to get by until her spell-casting has developed." He glanced at the dragon on my left hand again, and said, "I'm beginning to suspect she's a flame-wielder. I can help her there, too."

My breath caught in my chest.

A flame-wielder.

I had summoned flame with my fingertips. I had threatened to burn Elodea alive with the blue fire that had erupted from my body.

But the truth was, it frightened me half to death.

"No doubt you can help," Thalanir said. "But I'm not entirely sure spending time with a beast like you is in Leta's best interests. I'm trying to keep her bloodlust at bay—not increase it."

The two stared at each other for a long moment, then slowly, laughter rose up in both their chests.

"Fine. Leta," Rowland said, reaching for my hand and pressing a kiss to its back, "Meet me fist thing in the morning in the courtyard behind this awful place. I'll show you what a *real* Valdfae can do."

With that, he rose to his feet, bowed his head slightly, then left.

Thalanir reached a hand out and stroked my cheek gently, and I leaned into his touch, quietly euphoric at the semi-public display.

"Are you all right, Lahnan?" he asked.

"Why wouldn't I be?"

"The Change can hit hard," he replied. "It can be unpredictable. I want you to know that you can ask me for anything you need."

I nodded, grateful, and smiled at him. "I do have one question," I confessed.

"Tell me."

"He said he knew Gallia...intimately. Did they...?"

At that, Thalanir stiffened and pulled back. For a moment, I thought he was going to ask my meaning, but we both knew perfectly well that he was well aware of what I was saying.

"They were...close friends." His jaw tightened in the way it so often did when he didn't want to divulge anything more. "Row has a habit of bringing out the worst in people—and he had a hand in her downfall. That's all you need to know."

The pain in his voice was palpable, and I sat back, taking a sip of ale.

"If you don't want me to train with him," I said, "it's fine. I don't need to."

Thalanir shook his head. "I said he had a hand in Gallia's downfall," he replied. "Not that it was entirely his fault. Just promise me one thing."

"Anything."

"Don't let him convince you that violence is the only solution to the world's problems. The truth is, violence is usually the beginning of the end—something I know better than anyone."

CHAPTER TWENTY-NINE

WHEN WE'D RETURNED to our room at the inn, we made love again—this time quietly, needfully, as if it would perhaps be the last time—and I lay with my head on Thalanir's chest, his arm locked around me.

"She was a talented Valdfae," he said quietly after a time.

Without asking, I knew who he was speaking of. I raised my head and looked into his eyes. He looked pained, and I knew how hard it was for him to release the words, to speak of her at all.

Still, I wanted—needed—to know more.

He reached for my left hand and caressed the mark of the dragon with his thumb. "This is a harradh. A mark only Násuire have."

"What does it mean?" I asked. "I saw hers in my visions—a set of wings, but not a full dragon."

"Each one is different. I've heard that long ago there was a Násuire whose harradh was an image of a horse. Another had flames raging around her finger. Gallia's...it was something else entirely. She struggled to understand it, and there was a time when she believed her wings would sprout, that she would be able to fly longer and faster than any other Fae. But in the end, they never came."

I pressed my head back down, listening to his heart. I wanted to ask what happened to her—to ask how she died, why it tormented him so much to speak of her. But instead, I simply listened.

"She was complicated," he said. "She was in demand as a Valdfae, for her skill—her strength. She was like your friend Lark, in that she could vanish at will. She had a reputation for her ability to infiltrate any building, any fortress or castle. She thrived on it, reveled in it. She grew wealthy, and her reputation was extraordinary. In those days, she was the most feared of all the Fae."

"Why?" I asked. "Why fear her?"

"Because she was a killer, like all Valdfae. Her weapon of choice was a blade—at least, for a time. When her full powers came to her, she grew far more dangerous."

"What do you mean by 'full powers?' What changed?"

I felt him tense beneath me, his breath growing more shallow.

"Nothing that you need to concern yourself about," he said. "Let's just say she...gave in to temptation. When you're powerful—and when others want to buy that power from you —it's easy to succumb to corruption. It's happened to many of my kind over the generations. Gallia was no different. And though she was strong, when an offer came that was too great, she couldn't help but accept it."

He stroked my hair, falling silent for a minute.

"My mother was corrupted, I think," I told him. "At least, from the little I've seen in my visions."

"Yes," he replied. "She was. There was an ambition in her that ate away at her soul, I think. She was..."

"Destructive," I replied with a nod. "I don't know exactly

what happened between her and Lyrinn, but I've felt it. My mother's wrath, her hatred. There was something festering inside her."

Thalanir's jaw tensed, and he let out a breath. "As your powers grow—as you train—you will be faced with choices, just as Lyrinn was, and as Gallia was. Cruelty will be a temptation, as it is for all those who hold power."

When I pulled my head up and began to protest, he shook his head. "I love you," he said. "I do. I see all the good in you, Leta—even good that you yourself aren't aware of. But do not think yourself above the capacity for evil. We are *all* capable of it. I have perpetrated more than a few dark deeds in my time, and perhaps, if you hadn't come along, I would have been guilty of far more. The shadows have come close to consuming me over the years."

"But they didn't. You fought them back, and you won."

He smiled slightly, stroking his fingers down my neck. "It was only my own visions that kept me going—visions of a future with you in it. Hope kept me going. It kept me alive. I only hope our future is as sweet as I have imagined it to be."

The last words should have been light and optimistic.

Yet he spoke them with all the weight of a thousand years of pain.

"Why are you so afraid of what may come?" I asked, taking his hand, bringing it to my lips. "I can't imagine anything but brightness—I see a home the likes of which I never thought I'd have. And I'm not talking about a great house, or a castle, or anything like that. I just mean...I never thought I would feel myself become a part of another person. I never expected *you*."

Thalanir managed another faint smile, leaned over and kissed me gently, then pressed his forehead to mine. "If you knew the hope that still tries so hard to flourish in my heart," he said softly. "If you knew how much I wish I could believe our future would be idyllic..."

"It will," I assured him. "We've found each other. We've broken down the barriers that were keeping us apart. Why shouldn't we be happy? Why should we give in to despair?" I pushed myself up to a sitting position and smiled. "We will go north. We'll find Lyrinn and Mithraan—and we will help our side to win the war before it escalates. That was the promise of the hilt Erildir gave me. We'll forge the blade, Lyrinn and I. And everything will be perfect."

Thalanir moved to sit next to me, laughing. "Your optimism is boundless, Lahnan," he said. "It's almost infectious."

"Good. I want to infect you. I want you to understand I will not let anything come between us." I slipped over him, my hands draped around his neck, my legs around his waist, forcing him closer to me and drawing a moan from his lips. "I fought my feelings for you. I told myself you were an enemy—something sent to add to my misery. But I know now that you're my joy."

He had begun tracing a hand down my chest, but he froze at those words, turning his face away.

"You may discover soon enough that I'm the opposite of joy," he said.

"Don't say that. It's not true. It can't be."

He shook his head. "It is. You will be tested in the coming days. The power will try to overwhelm you. The truth will come out—and when it does, then I fear it will break us both."

"Then be my strength when I need it," I said, taking his face in my hands and pulling his eyes to my own. "Help me through it."

As I looked at him, a flash of white blinded me.

No.

No, no, no...

I was in Gallia's body again. She, too, was staring at Thalanir, speaking quietly, and as she spoke, she said, "Be my strength. Help me through it."

"I cannot," he said. "I'm not strong enough to do what you ask of me."

The flash of light came again, and then I was in the present day, back in my own body.

My breath was tight, my eyes wet with tears.

Thalanir, too, looked brought down by sadness, and I knew without asking that he was recalling that very same moment.

"I'm sorry," I whispered, climbing off him and lying on my back, my hand pressed to my forehead. "I...didn't mean to burden you."

He inhaled, his chest expanding, and trapped the breath there before releasing it. "She hoped for happiness," he said. "As did I. But I wasn't enough. We can't always force our wishes to come true."

"I'll never wish for chaos," I replied. "I will never wish for anything but happiness—and you."

"That may change. And sooner than you think."

CHAPTER THIRTY

IN THE MORNING, before Thalanir headed out to roam the town, he assured me again that he supported my desire to go to my training session with Rowland.

"You're not worried?" I asked him. "Last night—"

"Last night was not this morning. I have faith in you—as should you. Row is a dick, but there's no reason you can't handle him."

"True. I've been handling dicks all my life."

When Thalanir raised an eyebrow, I added, "Okay, that came out a little wrong."

With a kiss, we went our separate ways, and I strode up the street toward the tavern where Rowland and I were to meet.

Lark's voice startled me just as the sprite appeared, fluttering in the air before me. "Aren't you forgetting something, my Lady?"

"Forgetting?" I asked, stopping in my tracks.

"Me," he replied. "I'm here to watch over you when Thalanir is not. You shouldn't be roaming this town on your own. There's danger about."

I glanced around, then breathed, "What have you seen?"

With a hand on the hilt of his sword, Lark said, "Rumor has it there are traitors among the Fae here. I overheard a few discussing it last night in an alleyway toward the outskirts of town."

"Overheard?" I repeated. "Or eavesdropped while invisible?"

"Both."

I snickered, crossing my arms. "Okay, then. Who are these so-called traitors?"

"They didn't divulge names. Only said there were a few in town who are in league with the enemy. It's not entirely surprising—sell-blades sell their blades, after all. Still, let me accompany you to the tavern, Leta."

With a nod, I began walking again. "Of course," I said. "I appreciate your protectiveness. But I'm fine, I assure you. I'm just going to meet with one of Thalanir's old friends."

Lark grunted slightly but said nothing as I stepped up to the tavern door. "I'll be fine," I said, turning his way. "Just...go listen in on some more private conversations. And watch your very tiny back."

With a roll of his eyes, Lark vanished, and I stepped into the tavern.

Inside, I found Row seated with two male Fae, who rose to their feet as I approached, bowed their heads slightly, then turned and left without a word.

"Friendly, aren't they?" I asked, trying to sound less nervous than I actually was, now that I was in the presence of the Valdfae who was supposed to teach me how to harness my dubious powers.

"Don't mind them," he said with a wave of his hand. "They're cold bastards, here in town on a job. They were just asking me a few questions."

"About?"

"A Fae who was through here a few weeks back—one who's long gone. I sent them on their way." He rose to his feet, clapped his hands together, and said, "Let's get to it. I'm sure Thal will want you back as soon as possible, and the last thing I want is to inspire his wrath."

We headed out to a small, mud-filled courtyard behind the tavern. At one end were three large, round targets that looked like prettily-designed moons covered in various scorch marks, and next to them against a stone wall below a sagging thatched roof were three dummies made of straw and burlap. Each was wounded in its own way, either with slashes from a blade, scorch marks, or other horrible injuries.

"You've probably guessed we use this place for target practice pretty frequently," Row said with a grin, his breath coming out in a puff of white vapor.

I nodded, my jaw set. The place reminded me a little too much of the target practice Elodea had subjected me to in the convent, and all of a sudden I felt like a prisoner again.

"It's all right," Row said. "I'm not going to keep you here against your will. I'm only here to help."

"Fine," I said, laying down my leather bag on the ground, stretching my arms over my head, then locking eyes on him.

"What's in the bag?" he asked.

I hesitated, asking myself why I'd ever brought it. All it contained was a clean shirt and the hilt of the Blade of Dracrigh —which I had scarcely let out of my sight since Thalanir had handed it to me. I had left most of my clothing behind in our room at the inn.

"Not much," I told Row. "Nothing important."

He smiled, then leaned down and picked the bag up, opening the buckle that held it closed. "May I?"

I was about to tell him I'd rather he didn't when he reached in and pulled out the hilt.

A surge of rage worked its way through me, my skin burning with a brutal desire to snatch it away from him.

"Give it back," I snarled.

But Row wasn't listening. Instead, his eyes were locked on the gleaming object, his eyes filled with something that too closely resembled lust.

"Do you have any idea what this means?" he said, his gaze a thousand miles away. "Do you..."

"No," I replied, taking it from him and shoving it back into the bag. "And I'd appreciate it if you didn't go rifling through my things again."

Rowland stepped back, his eyes refocusing on me, and he nodded. "Yes," he said. "Of course. I apologize."

But instead of beginning our training session, he said, "Do you know how Gallia died, Leta? Do you know who killed her? Or has she kept that one memory from you?"

My rage, which had abated slightly, renewed itself. "How do you know I've seen her memories?" I spat.

I felt suddenly naked, as if he had peeled back several protective layers and revealed my insides to the world. Was I that transparent to all Fae? Did I have no capacity to keep my secrets to myself?

"Because I knew her when..." he said. "When she suffered through the same torments that you have endured. When the Násuire who came before her—who possessed the Essence before Gallia, before you—showed Gallia *her* memories. And so it goes with each Násuire."

My heart was in my throat when I asked, "Do you know anything about what she saw?"

Row shook his head. "Not much. She told me of an ancient power that had manifested in her mind. The memories terrified her—then invigorated her. In the end, they nearly killed her."

"Nearly," I repeated. "You asked if I knew how she died. You said *someone* killed her."

He nodded. "It's true," he said. "You know, I loved Gallia."

My eyes widened, my brows arching in surprise. "I didn't know that," I told him. I hadn't seen him in the memories or felt his presence. "I..."

I didn't know how to ask if it was unrequited or something more. I wasn't sure I wanted to know.

"Near the end of her life," he said, sighing. "Not that we knew it was the end. By then, Thalanir had distanced himself from her. He didn't like the way she was changing—the way her personality had altered. But I thrived on her. I was infatuated." He leaned in conspiratorially when he added, "Don't tell Thal I told you. He might not like it."

My stomach churned. Gallia had altered and Thalanir had moved away—away from the woman he had seemed to love so much.

Would the same happen to us? He had promised he would never leave—but still...

"Why would he care?" I asked, forcing control into my voice.

"No man likes being reminded that his lover cheated on him," Row said with a smile that was part arrogance, part indifference.

"Cheated? You were with her when they were still together?"

"Officially, yes," he said with a shrug. "Though I can't say Thal cared much that she and I were together. Like I said, he'd moved away emotionally. Though there was a moment when I thought he might murder me..." He laughed. "Still, I'm here now, so I guess we patched things up sufficiently, didn't we?"

I wasn't interested in hearing about Row's exploits, and he was starting to irritate me again. "Who killed her?" I asked, straight and to the point.

Row stared into my eyes, then shook his head. "Out of respect for her, I will let her memories speak for themselves. If her Essence hasn't shown you the truth yet, then it is not for me to reveal it to you. When the time is right, you'll learn it, one way or another."

"I see," I replied coldly, my irritation growing. "And the hilt? What is so special about it?"

Rowland inhaled, then looked away, pursing his lips. "It's a powerful object, crafted by a High King and imbued with High Magic. It's not the first such object I've seen. Every Násuire in existence has possessed one at some point, but never the same one twice." He met my eyes again. "Do you know what Násuire means, Leta?"

Sucking in my cheeks, I replied, "I assumed Nás had something to do with rebirth."

Rowland shook his head, his chin low. "No," he said. "It means 'Death.'"

My eyes widened, nausea roiling inside me. It was Thalanir who had first called me Násuire—who had first told me what I was. But he hadn't explained the full depth of its meaning

Was this his way of protecting me yet again—by withholding an ugly truth?

"I don't..." I stammered.

"You are dangerous, Leta," Row said. "I'm not going to lie to you about it. Gallia, too, was dangerous—it's why Thal and she fought bitterly in the end—and every Násuire who came before her was a threat, too. That's why you need to learn to control the flame inside you."

"I'm not dangerous," I insisted. "I'm as harmless as anyone's ever been. I've never hurt anyone. I..."

But the truth was, I had come close. I'd summoned flame and, in my anger, had come close to killing Elodea. I had thrown Thalanir—and Corym—against stone walls. They had only survived the impact because each of them was impossibly strong.

I had the potential to be a monster.

I just hadn't wanted to admit it to myself.

CHAPTER THIRTY-ONE

"Leta."

Rowland's hands were on my shoulders, his eyes locked on mine. But my mind was far away, searching for the answers I hadn't yet uncovered.

Jerking myself out of my thoughts, I pulled my attention to him at last.

"You'll be fine," he said with a warm smile. "I'm sorry I frightened you. It was just—the hilt threw me."

I nodded, though I was far from convinced.

"Look," he added, "This is all the more reason you need to train. Some Fae are arrogant and assume they already know everything. Don't make that mistake, and you'll be fine."

"I'm not so sure about that," I shot back. "I'm not just some Fae. I'm someone who, until not long ago, thought she was mortal."

Rowland laughed outright at that. "Being raised as a mortal, believe it or not, may prove your saving grace. Those who are raised Fae tend to have inflated notions of who and what they are—we all think we're so mighty and powerful and forget there are others out there who are far stronger than most of us.

Just stay humble and remember that you're learning. It will serve you well in the end."

With a sigh, I said, "Fine. Teach me, then. I may as well start somewhere."

"Let's begin simply," Row said, glancing toward the far end of the courtyard. "See the target over there? The round one on the right?"

I nodded again.

"See if you can hit its center."

"With what?"

"Whatever you like. A fire bolt. Ice. Whatever your mind calls up."

"How can I know if I haven't trained?" I asked, frustrated. "I'm not some Champion who's done this her whole life. The few spells I've cast have been random or uncontrolled."

Row turned my way, his handsome face betraying his amusement. "Leta—have patience. No Fae is born knowing what their skills might become. It's a little trial, a lot of error. You must try, and you will naturally fail more than once. That's not a shortcoming—it's part of the process."

I was about to protest again but realized I was being too much like Lyrinn, who had doubted herself since our youth to the point where I sometimes wanted to scream at her to grow a backbone and recognize her talent.

When had I ever doubted myself back in Dúnbar? When had I ever questioned my ability to get a task done? I was Leta Martel, damn it. I was as confident as they came.

As I inhaled, I felt a pressure on my lower back then and realized it was Row's hand, gentle and supportive. I should have welcomed the sensation, but instead, I winced and pulled away from him.

Don't you dare touch me, I thought. *You have no right.*

On instinct, I thrust my hands in front of me, quiet ire

simmering inside my mind as I shot a bolt of the purest white at the target, flying like a blade of blinding light through the air.

The target sliced clean in half, falling to the ground in two pieces of solid wood with a horrible clatter.

"Oh...gods," I said, cupping a hand over my mouth. "Sorry, I didn't mean..."

Row let out a laugh. "Well, well. Never has my touch rendered a woman quite so enraged," he said. "Impressive. I suppose it should come as no surprise that you can summon light-blades, given that you're Kazimir's daughter."

"No, indeed," a voice agreed from behind me.

I didn't need to turn around to know that Thalanir had found us. My heart began hammering in my chest with the knowledge that he was near—that he had witnessed what I had just done.

I raised my hands again, and this time, I tried to focus on the dummy to the left of the round targets.

With another narrow blade of white light, I severed its stuffed head, which hit the ground with a thud and rolled several feet.

Row laughed again, and this time I turned around, smiling, to face Thalanir—who was unamused.

If anything, he looked almost angry.

"Your powers are growing," he said, and there was a lament in his voice, a sadness, as if my show of strength had hurt him.

"They are, aren't they?" I asked, then laughed. "Soon I'll be able to take on the world."

"Yes," Thalanir replied. "I'm afraid you will."

"Come on, old man," Row said, clapping Thalanir on the shoulder. "You should be pleased. You've uncovered a secret weapon."

"Not secret anymore," Thalanir retorted, his eyes narrowing at his old friend. "Is she?"

"I don't know what you mean by that," Row replied, but Thalanir grabbed him by the front of his shirt and yanked him close.

I, too, was confused. Why was Thalanir so enraged? He knew I was intending to train, after all.

"You've seen it," he growled at Row. "Haven't you?"

Rowland looked like he was going to deny knowing anything, but finally, he nodded. "Thal—it's nothing to worry about."

"You *know* that's not true." Thalanir's grip tightened and he dragged Row closer. "You know how important it is."

"What the hell are you two going on about?" I asked, trying in vain to thrust myself between them.

"Go on," Thalanir said, pulling back and shoving Row away. "Tell her what's on your mind."

"Come on, Thal," Rowland said with a laugh that sounded more frightened than amused.

"*Say. It.*"

"You're frightening me," I said, grabbing his arm. "Come, let's just go back to the inn. We've done enough for one day, anyhow."

"I want Rowland to tell you why he was so intent on 'training' you. Why he wanted to get you alone. I didn't see it at first —I was fool enough to think he was being friendly. I'd almost forgotten what he did last time."

"I only wanted to help," Row said. "Really, I..."

"You're meddling in things that don't concern you," Thalanir replied. "Just as you meddled back then." He pivoted and stepped away, a hand raking through his hair, clearly agitated. "You wanted to control Gallia, but you couldn't—and you hated that. I will not let you sink your claws into Leta. Do you hear me?"

"What?" I snapped. "He hasn't done anything—"

"Hasn't he?" Thalanir charged at Rowland, and this time he reached around him and extracted something from his waistband.

The hilt of the Blade of Dracrigh.

"He...stole it from my bag?" My voice was trembling, as was the rest of me. "Why...why would you take that, Rowland? What good could it possibly do you?"

"I..." Row said. "I'm sorry. I was only trying to protect you, Leta. It's a dangerous weapon. In the wrong hands, it could cause chaos."

"Bullshit!" Thalanir shouted, lifting a hand as if intending to cast a devastating spell. "You were trying to protect *yourself*, Valdfae. Your interests. Tell me—who hired you this time?"

"What?"

"Who hired you to follow Leta and me to this town?"

I stared at Thalanir, confused.

"I spoke to Rieth," he said. "I know you stepped into town an hour after we did. You were tracking us, weren't you?"

"Thal, come on. We've been friends for centuries. You know I'd never do anything to hurt you."

"Oh, do I?" Thalanir snarled. "Have you forgotten what you did all those centuries ago?"

"That wasn't my fault, and you know it."

"No. I suppose it was mine." Grabbing my hand, Thalanir said, "We're leaving, Lahnan—and we will not be returning."

CHAPTER THIRTY-TWO

THALANIR HELD onto my hand as we surged through the tavern and out onto the street beyond. I could feel his rage in his touch, but there was something else, too.

Fear.

"What were you two even arguing about?" I asked under my breath as we made our way up the street toward the inn. "Are you upset because Rowland saw the hilt?"

"I'm upset because I was an idiot," Thalanir retorted. "He is power-hungry; he always has been. And he knows about the weapon now—he knows you intend to forge its blade. He took the hilt, intending to destroy it or present it to some master or other. He is aware that you're a danger, Leta, even if we don't yet know what *manner* of danger. Like the Sisterhood, he and others wish to wield you like their own personal weapon."

"Well, for the gods' sake, they can have the hilt!" I cried. "I never wanted it. I've said it again and again—I don't know how to wield a blade. I'm no warrior, and I never will be. I just want to live in peace."

Thalanir seemed to calm as the words met his mind. He stopped, turned toward me, and took my face in his hands.

"Understand that the Blade of Dracrigh is no mere weapon. Not in the way you imagine. Its purpose is far more significant than that of most blades—only, we don't know what it is, not yet. No one knows its full potential. Your grandfather alone will be able to tell us what it's for—which means we have to get to the High King. We have to leave Tarroc."

He proceeded toward the inn, and I went with him, breathless in my confusion and fear. When we got to our room, Thalanir pushed the door open. I stepped inside, tears welling in my eyes.

"I feel like a fool," I confessed, "bringing the hilt so close to him. It's my fault this is happening."

"It's not," he replied. "Row is a traitor—a Fae whose very soul is for sale. I should have seen this coming. It wouldn't be the first time he'd..."

He stepped closer, pulled me to him, and kissed me deeply.

I wondered if he'd stopped himself from revealing what I already knew—that Rowland and Gallia had been lovers.

"I don't want to lose you, either," I said. "But I'm frightened. I feel something terrible is going to happen."

Thalanir drew me to him and held me, and I felt the full power of him around me like a wall of steel, protective and warm, his heart raging in his chest. "I have seen two futures," he told me again. "And either is possible. You will thrive, Leta— if we can get you home. You *need* to find your way to the Dragon Court—your grandfather's home. You need Lyrinn. I will not make the mistake of introducing you to any more Valdfae. No one is to be trusted. Forgive me for my error in judgment."

"There's nothing to forgive," I said. "You were trying to help me through the Change—to help me understand my powers."

He took my hand and kissed it. "I only *ever* want to help you," he said, his voice smooth and sensual. "I want to grant you every pleasure imaginable."

"Every pleasure?" I asked, raising an eyebrow, and Thalanir chuckled, moving closer and pushing my hair away from my neck. He kissed me there, sending me into a quiet fit of delight, my pulse accelerating as I inhaled his scent. All of a sudden, I forgot my worries about Rowland, the hilt, or Janyn.

Nothing mattered but Thalanir's eyes on my own.

"Every pleasure," he repeated, slipping a hand down the front of my trousers, his fingers dipping between my legs.

But with a sudden, swift movement, he pulled away, leaping toward the window and looking down at the street.

"Grab your things," he whispered, gesturing to me. "We need to leave."

I strode over to where he was standing. "Why? What's happened?"

It was then that I saw a sea of red below us—a small army of Crimson Cloaks. One set of eyes was turned to look up at us, and I recognized the same Fae Thalanir had fought in Marqueyssal.

"They've found us," I said softly.

"Found, or were led to us?" he replied, his tone bitter.

"You think Rowland called them here?"

"Most likely. I think he was waiting to confirm you were a Násuire. It's why the bastard wanted to assess your skills. He wanted to be certain you were who he suspected—and when he saw your dragon mark and the hilt, there was little doubt left in his mind."

"Lark," I shot out, spinning around, a sudden realization gripping me. "Lark, are you here?"

There was no reply.

"We can't wait for him to return," Thalanir said. "He'll have to find us, and something tells me he won't have any trouble doing so."

I nodded and grabbed hold of my bag to fill it with my clothing. "I'm ready," I breathed when I'd finished.

Thalanir pulled the door open and glanced out into the corridor, wary and alert. When he nodded silently, we raced down the stairs to the inn's back door and out to the stable.

But we were already too late. Outside, two red-cloaked guards, one a male mortal and one a female Fae, stood waiting for us.

I saw them before Thalanir did...

But I was too slow to react.

Without a word, the Fae raised a hand and shot a fire arrow that hit Thalanir square in the chest.

I let out a cry, then without a second's hesitation, retaliated, shooting a light-blade that pierced clean through her chest before I twisted toward her companion and shot another, slicing his neck open.

Both fell lifeless to the ground, their eyes staring up at the sky.

I didn't have time to register the horror of what I'd just done. I grabbed Thalanir, who was still on his feet but pale and weak, his chest bleeding and grim.

The scent of burning flesh met my nose, enraging me.

"Can you ride?" I asked him.

He nodded. "Grab a horse," he said, his voice strained. "Quickly."

I did as he commanded, opening a stall door and taking hold of the only horse that was wearing both a saddle and bridle. Unlike Thalanir, I didn't have the skill to charm an animal into submission, so I was grateful for that small blessing.

When I'd steered the horse out of the stall, I climbed into the saddle, then Thalanir, mustering all his strength, leapt on behind me.

"Which way?" I asked over my shoulder.

"Go north," he replied, his voice heavy. "North..."

The second *North* was a mere whisper.

I will not let you die, I thought. *I will not lose you.*

"Lean on me," I told him. "I'll get us to safety."

I urged the horse forward, and we made our way down a narrow back laneway leading toward the edge of town and away from the rest of the Crimson Cloaks.

When I heard a commotion behind us, I glanced over my left shoulder to see the small army in pursuit, pushing its way down the lane.

"They'll catch us," I said, squeezing my heels into the horse's sides. "The horse can't gallop—not until we're out in the open."

Thalanir raised a hand weakly into the air, and behind us, a massive wall of twisting, thorn-covered ivy sprang from the ground, blocking our enemies' route. It grew as we moved, thickening and braiding itself together into an impenetrable barrier.

I felt Thalanir collapse against me, and I leaned forward, whispering to our mount.

"Please," I said. "Get us to safety. I'll give you anything if you just help me keep him alive."

CHAPTER THIRTY-THREE

I HAD no idea how many minutes or hours had passed before we finally came to a stream, and I felt confident enough to stop and dismount.

I leapt off, leading the gelding to the water so he could drink. All the while, my eyes were locked on Thalanir, on his shaking, weakening form.

He was pale, his face beaded with sweat, his tunic soaked with blood and the sort of blackness that only flames could inflict. I helped him climb down, guiding him over to a nearby tree so he could seat himself on the ground, his back seeking support against the trunk.

Hesitantly, I pulled at his cloak, then gently lifted his tunic. He tried to bat my hand away, but I shook my head.

"I need to see the wound," I said. "I'm sorry—but you know it's true."

At that he surrendered, his head bobbing slightly.

I pulled the garment up to see a vicious wound in his chest, worse even than I'd feared. Red at its center, black as soot around its edges, it looked excruciating. Surrounding its perimeter, inky veins were beginning to form as if the burn had shot some dark poison into his blood.

"We need a healer," I said woefully. "I've tended wounds before, but this one is polluted by some foul spell."

"Leave me here," he rasped. "Go north. Find Lyrinn. If you seek a healer, it will only slow you down."

"No," I said. "I'm not leaving you for anything."

"Leta..." He grabbed my wrist and pulled me close. "I will die before any healer gets to us."

The laugh that escaped my throat shocked me. But I couldn't help it. It was funny to me, to think he would ever imagine I would leave him to die.

"I'm not going anywhere," I told him again. "So don't even think about insisting."

"You *must* go."

"You're not my lord," I told him sharply. "Nor are you my keeper. I will do as I please—and I want to stay with you."

He leaned back, his eyes closing, a moan escaping his lips.

"I don't deserve your care," he whispered. "I don't deserve your affection. I never did. It was a dream, that was all. One that we both knew would be short-lived. All these years, I dreamed of you, and all these years, I knew I couldn't ever hope for the happiness I saw in my mind's eye..."

He was delirious; I was sure of it. Of *course* he deserved me —he had saved me more than once from hideous fates. He had watched over me from the first, keeping me safe. Caring for me —even when I'd been cruel to him.

He deserved my love more than anyone.

Tears rolled down my cheeks, and I took his hand, bringing it to my lips. "Stay with me," I said. "Don't you dare go. You promised you wouldn't leave me, remember?"

His eyes rolled open, and he offered up a faint smile on his pale features. "Actually, I promised I wouldn't let *you* leave."

"Don't you dare argue with me," I murmured through a sob.

"I won't go," he said. "Just for you, I'll stay right here. I won't leave until you tell me to, Lahnan."

"Lahnan," I repeated in a whisper. "You've called me that since the beginning—since we first met. Tell me what it means."

"Ah," he replied. "I knew you'd ask again one day." He gestured for me to come closer, and when I did, he looked into my eyes and said, "It means 'my love.' That is what you've always been to me, Leta Martel."

I choked back a sob, my hands on his cheeks, my forehead pressed to his. I could feel the life leaving his body—the weakness overtaking him.

"It seems, Lahnan," he breathed, "that the future I envisioned for us is not meant to be."

"Don't say that," I wept. "Don't. Please. You have to hold on. You have to stay with me. Our future will be wonderful, Thalanir—I promise you that. Just stay with me."

Desperate, I raised my face to the sky, silently pleading with some unseen entity for guidance. What do I do? How can I help him?

"My Lady!"

The low voice came from somewhere behind me, along with the flutter of wings. I spun around to see Lark approaching rapidly.

"Help me," I said. "His injury...it's..."

Lark shook his head, glancing down at Thalanir. "I am no healer. But your sister—she once used her powers to heal Mithraan, or so she told me."

"Do you know how she did it?"

Shaking his head, he replied, "Only that she said she was terrified of losing him—that she called on her own strength, and it came to her. Perhaps you share the Gift."

Not wishing to waste a second, I knelt down before Thalanir, closed my eyes, and pulled my face to the light of the sky, pressing my hands toward his chest, careful not to actually touch him.

"With everything in me," I said, "I wish—I *need*—to mend him. I need him. I want him. I cannot let him go—we have so much more life to live, he and I. Please, bring him back to me."

His chest heaved, his breaths coming hard and swift. His face was soaked with sweat, and when I glanced down, I could see that the wound on his chest appeared worse than ever.

"Please..." I repeated, closing my eyes again, my voice shattering. "If there is any strength granted me by my forebears, let me show it now."

I felt it then—a surge of warmth in my hands that quickly turned hot. Only this wasn't violent and raging as it had been in the past—it felt like comfort, like joy. I opened my eyes to see a sphere of white light rotating slowly between my palms and his chest.

"Is it working?" I asked.

"I don't know," Lark replied. "I..."

Thalanir's hands shot up and grabbed my wrists, and for a moment, I recoiled in fear, thinking I must be hurting him.

But he held my hands there, his eyes clear and bright, the color returning to his cheeks as the sphere continued to twist and turn.

He stared into my eyes as the light moved between us, his gaze imprisoning mine until the ball of light disappeared, and there was nothing between us but cool air.

He took my face in his hands and pressed his forehead to mine once again. I looked down to see his chest mended, with little other than the faintest scar where the ghastly wound had been a moment earlier.

"Leta," he whispered. "Thank you...for giving me my life."

I pressed my lips to his, tears in my eyes. It was a soft, careful kiss—one of pure affection and gratitude for his survival, for this one more moment I had been gifted to spend at his side.

Whatever might confront us in the coming days couldn't possibly be harder than what we'd just endured.

I was certain of it.

He smiled at me, all the warmth in the world contained in those extraordinary blue eyes, those sometimes-playful lips.

Behind me somewhere, Lark cleared his throat.

"I hate to interrupt," he said, "but I hear hoofbeats in the distance. I'm afraid we need to leave."

CHAPTER THIRTY-FOUR

WHEN THALANIR HAD CHANGED into a clean shirt and disposed of his tunic, we mounted the horse once again and headed along the stream, meandering away from the road. In the distance, I could hear the hoofbeats Lark had mentioned, but Thalanir, newly strengthened, was decisive when he whispered that we had nothing to fear.

"They're nothing but mortal travelers," he said. "Probably headed south toward Marqueyssal."

I nodded, reassured but still wary. After what had occurred with Rowland, I was convinced that no one outside our small party was to be trusted anymore.

When we'd ridden for a time, my head began to spin more violently than it ever had before. I found myself closing my eyes against the sensation in hopes of making it disappear.

But instead, it made things worse. I was dizzy to the point of nausea. Images spun through my mind, a twisting tale of a time long past.

Through Gallia's eyes, I saw Thalanir dressed in white and silver, looking like an ancient Noble as he moved toward me, an expression of mischievous desire in his eyes. He took me by the waist and spun me around, laughing.

He kissed me.

I was laughing, too, with the purest joy—but I pulled back, looked into his eyes, and asked, "You would never betray me—would you?"

His brows met and he let out a chuckle of his own. "You know the answer to that question already."

Something surged through me then—something greater and more powerful than any happiness imaginable—and I kissed him again.

But in an instant, the vision ended, and then I was surrounded by darkness, shadows lurking and menacing, all around me.

I squinted into the velvety blackness, trying to make out the shadowy shapes until finally, my eyes settled and I realized I was inside Gallia's body and mind once again. But gone were the comforting field of flowers and the sun beating down on my flesh.

This time, I was standing in a dense wood, a foreboding night sky cloud-covered overhead.

A male Fae stood before me, a hood drawn over his eyes. "You will do as I command, will you not?" he asked, and I told him that yes, I would obey.

"Just as I always have," I told him, Gallia's voice like silk on my tongue. "I won't let you down...*Lahnan*."

Lahnan?

The Fae she'd spoken to wasn't Thalanir—that much I knew. And from his voice, he didn't sound like Rowland, either. Who was he? And why was she referring to him with such affection?

What did you agree to, Gallia? I asked urgently, silently. *What*

happened back then? Did you fall in love with someone else?
Someone who came into your life after Thalanir, after Rowland?

I must have been mumbling, because Thalanir told the gelding to stop and laid a comforting hand on my shoulder. Light blinded me, and then I was back in the present with him.

"Leta," he said, trying and failing to draw me out of my trance. "Lahnan—can you hear me?"

I could—and yet, he sounded a thousand miles away. I wanted to touch him, to speak to him, to have him tell me everything was all right.

Why could I not speak—why couldn't I see the world around me?

"What's wrong with her?" I heard Lark say.

"She's still enduring the effects of the Change," Thalanir replied. "And it's taking a toll. I fear it's my doing."

He sounded pained, and I knew without being able to ask that there was more to this than a simple worry that I felt unwell.

Something was coming.

Something that would hurt us both.

"What do you mean, Valdfae?" Lark growled, his anger raging through the air. "What have you done to her?"

"I asked too much of her. Perhaps I pushed her too soon toward her power. We must get her somewhere safe, and soon. The next hours will be difficult for her."

There was silence for a moment. I tried again to speak, to interject, to explain—but no words came. My head rocked back and forth on my neck, and I felt myself fading once again, even as Lark said, "Fine. I'll fly ahead and see what I can find."

"Leta," Thalanir said when the sprite had left. "We're going to follow him. We'll find shelter for the night. You will be all right—do you hear me? I'll help you through this, whatever occurs."

I stiffened slightly, stealing a little strength from his words. "What happened to us?"

Thalanir wrapped his arms around me, pulling me close. "Nothing," he whispered. "Nothing at all. You're having visions —it's the Change, that's all."

"No—I...I don't mean *us*—I mean you and Gallia. You need to tell me what happened. What did she..."

"Please," he pleaded. "I'm sorry, Lahnan—but don't ask me to recount the events of that night."

He spurred on the gelding, and the horse began to move swiftly through the woods. A few minutes later, Lark found us once again and said, "There's a stone house not far from here— abandoned. We can spend the night there. Come."

"Lahnan," Thalanir whispered as we moved. "Nothing from the past matters in this moment. Don't let ghosts haunt your mind. Whatever happened back in those days—it isn't important just now."

"I died," I said, my head reeling with confusion. "I died back then. I want to know why."

"You didn't die...*Gallia* did, as all living things die."

"But..."

"You must rest," he said gently. "Tonight, you'll get your answers. I promise you that."

The spell had passed somewhat by the time we reached the cabin in the woods. But in place of dizziness, there was now a churning, biting pain deep inside me—like a knife twisting slowly, deliberately, inflicting pain on every organ.

Instead of letting me lose consciousness, the memories were now forcing me awake—forcing me into reluctant alertness.

I winced, nearly doubling over with the pain of it, when Thalanir lifted me down from the gelding and helped me inside.

The house was sparsely furnished, with a small bed and a

couch in one tiny room, a little kitchen with a wood stove in the other.

"I'll keep watch outside," Lark said, his voice strained with concern. "But let me know if she needs me."

"I will," Thalanir promised.

He helped me to the bed, laying a wool blanket down before I seated myself, then fell back, too dizzy to sit upright.

The sky was darkening, and I found myself craving light, so I flicked a hand toward a candle crookedly positioned in a sconce on the wall. Moving my eyes to the window, I felt myself luring the meager daylight to myself, drawing its strength to ignite the candle's wick.

My breath caught in my chest when I realized what I'd just done.

"How..." I stammered. "Where did that spell come from? What did I just do?"

"You pulled the light from the outside world," Thalanir replied grimly. "It was a...a Gift of Gallia's. She could move light from one place to another—and likewise for shadows and darkness. Now, I suppose, it's *your* Gift."

I shuddered. When I had flicked my hand—when I had cast the spell, a horrible feeling had passed through me—something malevolent and ugly. A flicker of another memory—one filled with misery and fear.

"Thalanir," I said, pulling my face weakly toward his, "why is this happening to me?"

It was light that had healed him. Light, which I had summoned with my mind. Why now did I feel as though I were filling with darkness?

He ground his jaw, then said, "There are two forces at play inside you, Lahnan. Two paths, diverging. It...it happens to all Násuire at some point in their lives. It's in that moment when they must choose their fates."

"Gallia made such a choice," I replied, the revelation unfolding in my mind. "Didn't she? Is that why she died? Did she...choose wrong?"

Thalanir looked me in the eye then. "You know the truth. It's inside you, Leta. It's locked away in those memories, so close to coming to you."

"I've wanted it," I breathed. "So badly. To understand who she was—why she died. But now, I *fear* it. The closer I get, the more frightened I become." I pushed myself up to a sitting position, leaning back against the headboard, my breath coming easier now. "What happened to her?"

Thalanir stepped away, watching me from the doorway, as if readying himself for a quick escape.

"Ask her for the truth," he said. "It's time you learned it."

CHAPTER THIRTY-FIVE

I CLOSED my eyes and called to Gallia, to the Essence that bound us together.

"Show me," I whispered, my lip quivering with apprehension.

There had to be a reason Thalanir kept the truth from me. A reason he couldn't bring himself to speak it.

I had thought for so long that it was because he loved her—because it pained him to speak of losing her.

But as the memory unfurled in my mind—the final memory from her too-short life—something told me I had been wrong all this time.

When the vision came, I found myself standing *outside* Gallia's body for the second time. A mere shadow, concealed in darkness. In the dead of night, I watched her cloaked form move smoothly and quickly through an elegant palace garden, lit only by the moon and stars high above.

The palace reminded me of Domignon's grounds, but it was more grand, more...ethereal. The castle was elegant and ornate, its features carved of beautiful black stone.

As Gallia advanced, a figure stepped out from behind a tall shrubbery, as if he'd been lying in wait for her.

"You startled me," Gallia said with a breathless laugh. "I forget sometimes how quietly and swiftly you can move."

"I forget the same about you," he replied, stepping closer. He, too, was dressed in a long cloak, and when he was near enough, Gallia yanked his hood down to reveal a head of thick, dark hair.

"Thal," she said coyly, lowering her chin and smiling up at him. "You look upset." She took hold of his cloak and pulled him close. "Did you come to chastise me?"

I recalled what Rowland had said—that Thalanir had grown distant from her in their final days together. That she and Row had become lovers.

Was that what this was about? Was he being cold to her because of her betrayal?

"Did he send you?" she asked, smiling up at him and laying a hand on his cheek. "Was he hoping you and I would patch things up—or did he want you to change my mind?"

"No one sent me," Thalanir replied gently, and I thought I detected a note of sadness in his voice. "I came of my own volition."

"Well, good. I'm glad to hear you've come to your senses."

She kissed him then, a deep, passionate kiss that filled me with an envy I had never felt when I'd been inside her body—when I had been the one tasting him, reveling in his touch on what had felt so much like my skin, my tongue, my lips.

But there was something else eating away at me, too—a warning deep in my mind that all was not as it seemed.

Too late, I became aware of a stiffness in his form, the pain in his features as he reached under his cloak.

And then, even as I watched it unfold, I *felt* it. The brutal pain that had assaulted my chest so many times over the weeks —a twisting, agonizing sensation searing through every nerve.

The shocking jolt she had felt in the moments before she died.

It was her pain, not mine—yet she had passed it to me like a cry for help.

I leapt forward, crying out—but no sound managed to escape my throat. I was shadow and wind, and nothing more. A specter invading the past.

Gallia fell to her knees before Thalanir, and he stepped back, a sob rising in his chest.

When she drooped to the ground, a pool of dark liquid forming around her, I knew she was gone.

My eyes searched for Thalanir once again, but already, he'd turned and fled, leaving her body in his wake.

Alone and forsaken.

CHAPTER THIRTY-SIX

A FLASH of white light collided with my mind, and I returned to the present.

I couldn't breathe.

Thalanir was still standing at the other end of the room, his back to me as if looking me in the eye, knowing what I now knew, would be too painful.

"You killed her," I choked out.

"I did," he replied. "There is no denying it."

"Yet you kept it from me, all this time. You let me think you loved her...and in the end..."

He turned to face me, tears in his eyes. Were the tears for her? For me?

For the realization that I would never look at him the same way again?

I couldn't say—because in that moment, I told myself I didn't even know who he was.

He was a liar. A manipulator. Just like Corym. Just like all the rest of them.

"I told you," he said softly. "I did love her for a time—at

least, I thought I did. I was young, Leta. I was a fool. I did not see her for what she really was. And when she—"

I rose to my feet and took a long step toward him, rage filling me. "I don't care what excuse you throw at me!" I snarled. "I don't care that she was unfaithful to you. I saw her mind and felt her heart. She *loved* you, Thalanir, and she thought you loved her. It doesn't matter why you did it. Nothing can redeem you. Not after that." I swallowed a sob, then said, "If you could do that to her, you can do it to me. That much is clear."

Pain marred his features, setting in so deep that I may as well have thrust a knife into his chest and dragged it slowly downward.

"Your *Highness*," he replied sharply with a clenching of his jaw. "I did not expect you to understand what could have driven me to such an act. How could you? You weren't there." He took in a deep breath. "You know the truth of her death now, and clearly, you do not intend to forgive me for it."

I went to speak, but he raised a hand, telling me to wait a moment.

"I promised you I would never let you leave," he said, "even if you begged me to. But if it's what you want, I will break that promise. I do not wish to cause you pain for anything in the world. I never have, and I never will."

My hands were fisted so tight that my nails dug into my palms. I could feel my blood burning through my veins, heating my skin as rage and hurt filling me. But even now, I couldn't bring myself to tell him I hated him. I loved him, and it was *because* I loved him that I hurt so deeply.

It was love that now felt like a jagged weapon tearing at my heart.

"Then I'm asking you to break your promise," I said. "I

trusted you. I gave myself to you, body and soul. All this time, you could have told me the truth, and like a coward, you kept it from me." At that, I laughed bitterly. "How ironic that everyone insists on telling me how dangerous I am—how dangerous *she* was. No one—not even your dear old friends—had the decency to warn me that *you* were the dangerous one all along. Not even Rowland. I suppose there's some quiet rule among you Valdfae, isn't there? You protect one another. Except you didn't protect *her*."

"No. I did not." He raised his chin and said, "I have always said you would learn to despise me, Lahnan."

"What a fool I was, telling myself you were simply selling yourself short—pretending inadequacy. If you *really* believed it, you should have saved me the trouble of loving you." Another sob was perilously close to exploding from my chest.

With a lowering of his chin, he said, "I am sorry that I have wasted my time and yours. I thank you for healing me—for saving my life. For your part, I hope..." He fixed me in his stare, his irises searing with tortured emotion. "I hope you live a long and prosperous life, with many joys."

With that, he bowed quickly and moved aside.

I grabbed hold of my pack, stormed past him and out the door into the woods, where the gelding awaited me.

I took hold of his reins and mounted, steering him immediately north. I did not look back at the cabin to see if Thalanir was watching me.

For the second time, I was leaving him—and I told myself I didn't care.

He had broken my heart, and my mind reeled with the pain of it.

I rode for several minutes, maybe more, before a voice met my ears.

"My Lady?"

Wiping my eyes, I turned to see Lark flying toward me, his sword drawn, eyes darting this way and that.

"What's happened?" he asked. "Where is the Valdfae?"

"I left him behind," I said, pulling my eyes to the distance. "You and I are going north without him."

"Leta—What is it? What's happened?"

I was shaking then, my body convulsing with sobs. I pulled the gelding up and Lark sheathed his sword and flitted over, landing on the saddle's pommel. Softly, he repeated, "My Lady."

"He...killed her," I managed between uncontrolled breaths. "He killed her—Gallia—the one whose Essence I share. I saw it. I've tried to sort out why—what could possibly have driven him to do it. And all I can think is that it was jealousy. She had taken a lover, and Thalanir couldn't bear it."

"Did he tell you that?"

"No. But what else could it possibly have been?"

"Leta," Lark replied, rebuke in his tone. "Thalanir would never—"

"Yet he did!" I cried. "He did. I saw it. I felt it. I saw the pain in his eyes. If not a crime of passion, then explain it to me, Lark. How could he do such a thing? Even if he no longer loved her. How..."

He shook his head. "I can't possibly answer that. But you and I both know Thalanir would never willingly kill one he loved—not unless he saw no other way. What happened, I can't begin to guess. But he is not so callous, nor so cruel as that. Even I know that much."

I stifled a sob, narrowing my eyes at him. "I *saw* it!" I repeated.

"You saw him kill her? Or you saw him explain why?"

"What's the difference?"

"There is a world of difference, my Lady."

I stared down at Lark, confused. Why would he take Thalanir's side—as if it was the Valdfae who deserved sympathy in this scenario?

"I don't understand why you're defending him," I snapped, urging the horse forward as Lark took off to fly along next to me. "Gallia may not have been perfect, but that is no reason to kill someone. Surely she wasn't so terrible that she deserved a blade in her chest."

"You don't know that."

"I've been inside her mind, Lark. I've felt her love for him. I've..."

"Tell me, then. Have you seen every thought she had in those last days? Do you really know what led up to the moment of her death?"

"Well, no—but..."

"Leta." Lark's voice was calm and quiet—but there was a tension in it that reminded me of my father's tone when he used to prepare himself to lecture me. "Thalanir is not the only one in this world who has ever killed someone he admires. Sometimes it's a necessary evil—for the greater good."

Tears streamed down my cheeks.

"What greater good?" I asked. "That's ridiculous. How could he—" But I stopped speaking. I tried to focus on Lark's face, to read his expression as he turned to me, but it proved impossible. "You're speaking from personal experience," I murmured. "You killed someone close to you...didn't you?"

For the first time, I could feel Lark's pain. A sorrow he had been hiding from me since we'd met. His façade of quiet strength, of stoicism—they were just that. A façade. A mask.

I could see his face now, contorted with sorrow, and feel his heart. He had suffered a wound so great that it had nearly toppled the small but mighty warrior—and all this time, I had been oblivious to it.

"Someone I admired for many years," he said with a grim nod. "I wasn't in love with her—but I did feel affection for her, and sympathy for what I perceived to be a painful lot in life. I admired her and thought her brave. But when the time came to make my choice, it was not as difficult as you might think. And, as much as it hurt me to do it, I would do it again in a heartbeat—because it saved the life of someone who was important to me. And to *you*."

For the first time, I was beginning to understand what Lark had meant when he'd told me long ago that he had to make amends to Lyrinn and me. *For something I did to you both.*

My mind reached for the answer, but I couldn't quite bring myself to say it.

"I had a choice," he said. "I could let her kill Lyrinn, or hope Lyrinn killed her. But there was a third option, too. One that would save Lyrinn from suffering the worst pain imaginable. I couldn't bear to see her fall into an abyss of her own making. I knew my pain would be great—but not such a torment that I would never be able to look myself in the eye again."

"You..." I said again, but once again, I failed to complete the thought.

"Yes." Lark nodded. "I killed your mother, Leta. Because I can only imagine the burden your sister would have carried for the rest of her days had she done it herself." His face tightened then, his lips a thin line. "I wanted to tell you from the first. I wanted to be honest with you. But how does one..." His voice cracked, and he inhaled, trying to regain control. "How does one tell someone he's just met—someone strong, beautiful, noble like yourself—that he is the reason she will never know her own mother? How could you ever look at me as anything other than a villain, if you knew?"

I pulled the gelding up, my breath coming in short bursts. Not only in reaction to his revelation, but because I was beginning to feel something else—something that made me want to cry out in pain.

Thalanir had killed Gallia—that much I knew. And I had seen it as a black-and-white scenario. I had told myself he was a murderer, plain and simple.

But it wasn't so simple as that. It couldn't be.

She had concealed something from me, too. I had felt it deep in my gut, though I couldn't grasp why she would do it. She had hidden away some aspect of herself—her nature. Her memories had only revealed to me how much she loved him—how much she had wanted him during their early days together. I had witnessed happy times spent frolicking in fields. I had seen a few brief moments of conflict but nothing else.

She had never revealed her moments with Rowland or the ones she had spent talking to whoever it was who issued her orders. The Fae she had called Lahnan.

I had never seen anything that seemed to warrant her death. But I didn't really know her, either.

Something—some massive evolution—had occurred to bring her relationship with Thalanir to such a violent tipping point. Something I hadn't witnessed. And I hadn't given Thalanir a chance to explain—because I had stubbornly insisted there was no excuse for killing someone you love.

I had meant the words when I'd said them. But Lark was right.

Thalanir would never kill anyone he cared about—*not unless he had no other choice.*

I swung the horse around and urged him back toward the

cabin. He galloped through the woods, deftly avoiding branches, leaping over fallen trees.

When we arrived after a few minutes, I leapt off his back and charged into the small house.

"Thalanir!" I cried, "Are you here?"

When I saw no trace of him, I ran to the cabin's front door and looked out...but there was no sign of his whereabouts, no trail leading away into the woods, other than the one we had forged.

Thalanir had become the Wandering Ghost once more, and it was my fault.

"He thinks I despise him," I told Lark, who was hovering by the door. "He saw this coming the whole time—it's why he always claimed he didn't deserve me. But you're right. There has to be more to it. Thalanir would never kill her out of spite. He had an opportunity to kill Corym, after all—and he simply walked away. Gods, I'm a fool." I sobbed when I added, "When he did it—when he stabbed her—I saw the pain in his eyes, and I mistook it for wrath. But it wasn't envy or rage. It was pure agony. Heartbreak."

"I suspect that he despises himself," Lark said. "I fear he has hated himself for centuries, my Lady, because of the burden he has carried. I'll admit I've been hard on him—untrusting and hostile. But I have always known he is not evil, and he never has been. Many Valdfae do good in the world, ridding it of cruelty through acts the rest of us are too cowardly to perform. Chances are, he doesn't deserve your hatred—unless I do, as well."

I swallowed, the truth of Lark's words colliding with my heart.

"My Lady," the sprite said, flying over to land briefly on my shoulder. It was a reassuring gesture, one that felt almost like a comforting hand.

"Hmm?" was all I could muster.

"Let's find Lyrinn. It's time."

"I can't," I told him with a shake of my red hair. "Not without Thalanir. I need to talk to him. I need to tell him—"

"You will. I promise, you two will find one another again. But for now, we must find your sister. Trust me when I tell you the Wandering Ghost is gone and will not be easily found. We must leave him be for now."

CHAPTER THIRTY-SEVEN

MY SPIRIT SAPPED, I rode north all night with Lark occasionally perching on the pommel, sometimes flying ahead to look for threats.

Gallia's memories had ceased to torment me.

I wondered with an odd sensation of emptiness if I had seen the last of her.

Part of me hoped so—hoped I would never have my mind overtaken again. But another part wanted her to return. I needed to understand Thalanir, or I feared I would go mad. I needed to see his mind, his reasons for what he did. Because Lark was right. The Fae I knew was not cold-blooded. The Fae I'd seen in the visions had been kind and loving.

Perhaps it was ironic, given that he was a sell-blade...but even the fiercest killer can be loyal, after all.

As our journey progressed, I began to comprehend what Lyrinn must have felt when she and Mithraan had been separated. I understood how she must have felt tethered to him after they'd bonded, linked to his heart, his mind, his soul—and how she must have ached with a fierce pain when Kazimir had stolen her away from him.

With each mile we rode away from Thalanir, I felt myself growing weaker and stronger at once. Weaker for his absence, for the pain of knowing I may not see him again.

But stronger in the knowledge that I had loved. I had allowed myself that vulnerability, that potential for pain and sorrow. I had freed my heart.

And though I was suffering for it, I was grateful for what he had given me of himself—and what he had taken in return.

How twisted am I, I thought as Lark and I trekked northward, *to love someone who killed his lover?*

Yet I knew it was no simple matter. What Thalanir had done had broken him, nearly shattered his soul. And now, after witnessing his crime, I had issued the final blow. He had carried a wretched weight on his shoulders for so long that he didn't know how to exist without it. He had not allowed himself happiness for centuries—and when he had finally tasted a little of it, I had snatched it away in a moment of anger, of fevered impulsiveness.

As we trudged along in silence, Lark's bright eyes on the lookout for any possible threat, I could feel a new sensation of power flowing through my veins. I was suddenly light, like I was floating on air rather than a gelding's back. Never tiring, never fading. I never grew thirsty or hungry. I never felt a need to rest.

It seemed that with Gallia's last memory, the final surge had come. A final transition from my mortal life to an Immortal one.

So, this is what it feels like to be a Fae.

Except that I still have no wings.

Thanks to Lark's ability to fly up to nearby treetops and scan the area, we managed to find a series of long trails leading directly north toward the realm of Belleau. It would take us a few days to get there, no doubt—but so long as I managed to rest our horse now and again, something told me we would be fine.

"Do you suppose," I asked Lark after a time, "I'll ever get my wings?"

"Your sister did," he replied. "And like her, you're High Fae. So I assume it will happen soon."

"When did she acquire them?"

"After..." he said, but the one word seemed to die in his mouth. "After your mother's death—and that of the entity known as the Elar when the spell she had cast long ago died with her. The wings she had stolen from all High Fae returned in that moment."

"Ah," I sighed. "So, I just need to wait for some momentous occasion, and mine will magically appear. Or...perhaps they'll never appear, because I don't deserve them."

"Only time will tell, my Lady."

"That's the wrong answer, sprite. You're supposed to tell me I do deserve them, and that they'll come to me any day now."

"Apologies. You deserve wings, and I'm sure they'll be delivered anytime now, probably by a roving wing salesman. I hear the woods are crawling with them."

"You know, for someone so small, you're an enormous smart-ass sometimes."

"Thank you."

We continued along the path for some time. While Lark watched for threats, I kept my eyes peeled for any sign that Thalanir had come this way. I was doing my best to put on a brave face and not reveal how deeply I ached at the thought that he might be gone forever.

But Lark saw through me.

"We *will* find him, my Lady," he assured me.

I swallowed, holding my chin high as I trudged onward. "What if he never wants to be found? What if those few days spent together are all I'm ever to have of him? Perhaps this is our fate."

Lark swooped down to fly in front of me, flittering backwards as I rode. On his small face was a dubious expression, almost one of amusement.

"You can't be serious," he said.

"Why not?"

"Because I've seen how he looks at you. How you look at each other. That Valdfae is in love with you—and I would bet good money he never loved anyone else as much, whatever you may tell yourself. He will find his way back to your side once he's confident that you won't..."

"Kill him?" I asked, my tone slightly cheeky.

"I wasn't going to say that, exactly. You can be a little...intimidating."

"Intimidating? Me?" I snorted.

"You're not exactly an open book, Leta." Lark spun in mid-air and began to fly forward again. "You may think you are, but you are more impenetrable than most of us. Thalanir has some difficulty knowing your heart just as the rest of us do."

I was about to argue with him, but I silently conceded that he was right. Most of the time, even I didn't know my own feelings. I had denied my attraction to Thalanir, though it had been there from the start; I had pushed him away and fled from him with the Sisterhood. And now, like a coward, I had left him behind again.

What a fool I was.

CHAPTER THIRTY-EIGHT

OUR SECOND NIGHT in the wilderness had begun to fall when Lark held up a hand, signaling me to pull the gelding to a halt.

My shoulders slumped with relief. It was time for a rest, anyhow. The horse had trekked heroically along miles of trail, resting only briefly every few hours, drinking at any creek we happened across, and scarfing down whatever grass we could find. But he needed sleep, as did Lark and I.

When a harrowing sound met my ears, though, I knew sleep was not going to come anytime soon.

A faint rustling came at us from several directions at once, as if something or someone were making their way through the undergrowth toward us.

I froze in the saddle, shooting a glance at Lark, whose small sword was drawn.

"It's a party of six or more," he whispered. "Moving on foot. By their light tread, I'd guess they're Fae."

The words should have been reassuring—after all, the idea of Fae was more appealing than mortals at this point. But for all I knew, they were Rowland's ilk, those allied to the Crimson Cloaks. Traitors to Fae-kind.

I dismounted, guiding the horse behind a thicket and crouching down in hopes of seeing the intruders before they spotted us.

The rustling drew closer, and finally, I could see branches being pushed aside, silhouettes of cloaked figures shoving their way through while whispering to one another.

"This way," a soft voice said. "I'm certain it came from here."

Someone stepped out from behind a tree, a set of bright violet eyes shooting left and right. It was a male Fae with lightish hair, his chin held high as he sniffed at the air.

After a moment, he twisted to face me, his eyes landing on my own.

"Over here!" he called over his shoulder.

I leapt to my feet, but Lark was faster. In a flash, he had landed on the Fae's shoulder, his small blade at the intruder's throat.

"Tell them not to hurt her, or I'll kill you on the spot," he hissed.

"Whoa, there, little fellow," the Fae said. "Easy."

"He doesn't enjoy being called *little*," a female voice called out from behind them. "Do you, Lark?"

I *knew* that voice...

Without thinking, I surged forward, scrambling through branches and brambles until I was at the edge of a tiny clearing where the small party of Fae had gathered. At their center stood a female, with glowing white wings laced with black veins.

When she turned my way and our eyes met, she smiled, her teeth gleaming in the moonlight.

"Well, what do you suppose the chances were of us finding each other in the wild like this?" she asked, stepping toward me. Around her neck, gleaming in the bright moonlight, was a pendant like mine—silver, with a dragon engraved on its surface.

"I...can't..." I stammered.

Her wings faded from sight, and she leapt forward, throwing her arms around me. Never had I been squeezed so tightly, and never had I wanted quite so badly for a hug to last forever.

"I can't believe it's really you," I said, tears in my eyes.

"Believe it," she replied. "Oh—Leta. You've come of age. How is it possible?" She pulled back, her hands on my shoulders, and looked me up and down. "But something else has happened, too." She glanced at Lark, who had re-sheathed his sword and joined us, hovering in the air next to my sister.

Lyrinn's ears were pointed, her scars turned to beautiful swirls of black along her skin. Her eyes were bright, and she was more beautiful than ever, her hair a twisting masterpiece of dark and silver combined.

"A lot has happened," I confessed, struggling to keep my voice in check.

"Thalanir," she said. "He was sent to look for you. Did he..."

My cheeks heated, and I bowed my chin. "He found me some time ago. Did you know...Did he—"

"Leta? What is it?"

But I was too close to tears now, so I simply shook my head and swallowed down a surge of emotion. "I'll tell you everything. Just—let me catch my breath first."

"Of course." Lyrinn signaled to one of her Fae to grab hold of the gelding and lead him over to the other side of the clearing.

"You're not on horseback," I observed.

"No. We flew here."

I looked over at the party, noting that Mithraan wasn't among them. "All of you?"

"All, yes," she laughed. "It's faster to fly with a party of High

Fae than move on foot. We've been looking for you for days. Mithraan flew out a few hours ago on a scouting mission. He should be back soon. Come, sit by the fire."

She led me to a fallen log, and when we took a seat, I glanced over at the gelding whose saddle and bridle were off now. He dipped his head down to graze, content to be free at last of his tack.

"He won't go far," Lyrinn assured me. "And if he does, we'll just summon him back."

I let out a chuckle. "You're awfully comfortable in your new skin. My sister, the confident High Fae."

"When you've been through all that I have, everything afterwards seems almost easy," she said with a wincing smile, glancing over her shoulder. "Wouldn't you agree, Lark?"

The sprite nodded solemnly.

Lyrinn leaned toward him and spoke a few quiet words. He flew off, and she turned her attention back to me.

"What did you say to him?" I asked.

"I told him he doesn't need my forgiveness or yours," she said. "I know what he did and why. And so do you."

"I do. Though I'll admit, I wish I'd had a chance to meet her." I hesitated briefly before asking, "What was our mother like?"

"Complicated," Lyrinn replied. "And devious." I thought I saw a twitch of her lips when she added, "She broke my heart, Leta. In so many ways. Be glad you never got to know her—and be glad you're not like her."

Not like her.

The words sent a chill through me. Perhaps I was more like her than I cared to admit. Volatile, impulsive.

Stubborn.

"What was wrong with her? I mean—how did she fall so far?"

"Power surged through her blood—more power than she could control," Lyrinn said. "She thirsted for more. She wanted the world to burn in her name, at any cost. She would have destroyed me, you, anything that got in her way. I wanted to believe in her—to think she was simply ill, and that she could be helped. But there was no helping someone like her—not after she got a taste of her own ambition. Power is the most corrupting force I've ever encountered, and it's frightening how quickly it can turn someone kind and rational into a monster."

I let out a sigh. "I'll never know what you went through—you, Lark...Mithraan. But I do know you spared our world the fate of a cruel queen. I may not have known her—at least, not well enough to love her. But she..." I took her hand in mine. "She let *you* love her—and I can feel your pain even now. For that, I will never forgive her, as long as I live."

I hugged Lyrinn to me. As much as I might try, I would never be able to fully imagine the pain she'd endured in the Broken Lands.

"What Lark did for me—it was the greatest act of mercy," she said, her voice heavy. "He saved me a lifetime of insufferable pain, and I will always be grateful to him for that. I just hope he knows it."

I pulled away and nodded, my eyes fixed on the dancing flames before us. "I'm beginning to understand what that lifetime of pain must feel like. I've been witness to its consequences—and it is cruel."

Lyrinn took my hand, and, surrendering to my sadness, I allowed myself to lean my shoulder against hers.

"Tell me about him," she said, wiping a tear away.

"Who?"

The question seemed innocent enough, or so I hoped.

She glanced sideways at me and let out a chuckle. "If you think for a second that you can keep anything from me, Leta, I should tell you right now that you're very wrong. So, tell me about Thalanir. I've met him, you know."

"Yes—he told me." I was almost scared to ask what she thought of him. But in the end, she saved me the trouble.

"He was quiet. Hard to read. But there was something in the way he looked at me—like he was searching my face for a secret. It wasn't until Mithraan explained his ancient connection to you that I understood. He was already searching for you by then, and I was glad to know you were in good hands."

"Wait." I tightened. "Mithraan knows about Thalanir's past? About Gallia?"

"He and Thalanir are good friends. He knows a great deal about the Wandering Ghost, like what makes him such a determined tracker—and what sorrows torment him. Though I must say, he didn't tell me any details until I forced them out of him a few days ago. About how, when we were in Aetherion, he had asked Mithraan if he could be the one to search for you—"

"Wait!" My heart flipped in my chest. "*He* asked Mithraan? It wasn't the other way around? I always thought—"

Lyrinn laughed. "You thought Mithraan had paid him to locate you for my sake. Yes, I'm sure that's what he wanted you to think. From what I understand, it's just like Thalanir to hide his true intentions and feelings."

"Well, yeah," I said. "I always thought someone had handed him a sack of coin. He spent so much money on me—on clothing, horses, food, you name it."

Lyrinn shook her head. "Mithraan never gave him a single copper piece and has no intention of doing so."

In that moment, my heart filled—and for the first time since leaving Thalanir, the slightest spark of hope flared inside me.

It had never been about money. Never about fulfilling a duty to someone else. He had sought me because it was his fate and mine to meet in that clearing, all those days ago.

"How did I ever doubt him?" I whispered.

"Fae are complicated creatures," Lyrinn replied. "Infuriating at times, with their secrecy and noble acts that feel more like subterfuge half the time." She laughed again. "In our early days together, Mithraan sent my mind reeling so many times that I thought I would go mad. But enough about him. Tell me— where is Thalanir now?"

"I don't know," I lamented. "I...found something out about his past, and I panicked. I left him behind, and when I went back to find him, he was gone. He's out there somewhere—and he thinks I despise him."

"Ah. But you don't, of course."

I turned and looked my sister in the eye, the licking flames reflected in her irises. "I could never despise him. I love him. Whatever he did all those years ago—he must have had his reasons. I only wish I could ask him what they were."

A shrill cry rang out in the sky above us, and Lyrinn said, "I happen to know someone you could ask about Thal's past," before rising to her feet and drawing her eyes skyward. "I suspect he will have all the answers you could want."

CHAPTER THIRTY-NINE

A MASSIVE SILVER eagle came in for a landing on the other side of the campfire, shifting instantly into the High Fae I knew as Mithraan.

He strode toward us, taking Lyrinn by the waist and kissing her before turning to me.

"Leta," he said with a smile. "I can't tell you how happy I am to see you."

"I'm pleased to see you too, my...Lord," I replied, leaping awkwardly to my feet.

"Call me Mithraan. Please." He looked around, then back at me. "Thalanir?" he asked. "Where is he?"

Lyrinn pulled away from him and said, "I think I'll leave you two to talk. I'm going to check on Lark."

Mithraan nodded and gestured to me to sit once again.

I set myself down on the log by the fire, inhaling a deep breath in preparation for what was to come.

"How much do you know?" I asked. "About why Thalanir wanted to find me, I mean."

Mithraan eyed me intently, then said, "I know about Gallia. I know she was a Násuire and that Thalanir was convinced her

Essence had passed to you. He had seen you in visions—dreams of a future he confided to me one night, after several pints too many." He snickered. "He was convinced that fate was leading him to you. To tell you the truth, had you not escaped Corym on your own, I suspect Thalanir would have come and broken you out of Domignon's palace himself."

I tightened, unable to derive any amusement from his words. "Do you know how Gallia died?"

"Yes," he said with a nod. "I do."

I watched the flames for a time, working up the courage to ask another question.

"Why did he kill her?" I asked at last. "How could he do such a thing? For two days, I've been riding through the wilderness, trying to understand—to tell myself there had to be a reason for it. But I've struggled, Mithraan."

"You know that your sister came close to killing your mother—and if Lark hadn't done it, Lyrinn would have had no choice. She would have done it to save the realms. To save *me*."

I nodded. "I know. Lark told me about that. To tell you the truth, I'm still wrapping my head around it."

"My point is," Mithraan said, "I happen to know a little of why Thalanir did what he did—and the fact that he didn't tell you only reminds me how noble a Fae he is. Even now, after all that happened back then, he is still protecting Gallia."

"Protecting?" My heart was racing now, and I breathed deep, trying to calm it. "Please—I want to understand. I need to, if he and I are ever to...well, if we ever see each other again."

Mithraan looked into the distance, his amber eyes bright as he summoned a memory of his own. "Once, a few years ago when he was with me near Fairholme, Thalanir revealed the truth to me. He told me it had been gnawing at his insides for so many years that he could no longer bear it—and so, he conveyed his memories to me, releasing them and freeing

himself of a little of the pain. He told me that he had killed her
—and why."

"Tell me," I whispered.

"Gallia had grown strong, as all Násuire do. A High Fae—
one who loved her—had hired her for a killing—and in
exchange, he had promised her a gift unlike any other. It was a
powerful object, a charmed flute. The instrument's purpose
was to summon dragons to its player's side so that they could
control the beasts."

"Dragons?" I repeated, my eyes wide. "Are you serious?"

Mithraan nodded. "There were many dragons in the North
in those days," he said. "They say the beasts were beautiful and
majestic—and dangerous as raging storms on an open sea.
Many Fae had already tried and failed to tame them. But
according to legend, the charmed flute—Fathuír was its name
—was powerful enough to grant its wielder dominion over the
creatures. The High Fae had told Gallia that once she had
fulfilled her duty, he would unearth the instrument from its
hiding place."

My hands knotted together in my lap. "What duty? Who
was she supposed to kill?"

Mithraan rubbed his fingers along the stubble on his jaw,
agitated, then met my eyes. "She was to murder the High King
and High Queen of Tíria—the Fae who ruled over the Dragon
Court in those days." He stopped there, moving his eyes up to
the sky for a moment. "For a little while, Tíria's future was in
grave danger. Gallia was a skilled assassin. The best there was.
If anyone could get to the king and queen in secret and slay
them in their beds, it was her."

I was almost afraid to utter the words when I asked, "What
happened?"

"Gallia had been handed the potential to upend the realm
—and she took full advantage of it. She murdered her

employer the High Fae—the one who adored her, and who thought, apparently, that she adored him. But she only did it after forcing him to reveal the flute's location. Her plan, it seemed, was to assume control over the dragons—and then to kill the king and queen and take the throne for herself. That much power in any Fae's hands would have been unthinkable."

Emotion twisted and churned inside me, shock and anger braiding into strands of nausea that swam along my insides. The Essence I had inherited from Gallia, which had revealed so much and infected me so profoundly, still held so many secrets.

Gallia had started out as an innocent Fae in love with Thalanir—and somewhere along the line, she had turned into something unrecognizable. And I had never seen so much as a hint of it.

Or had I?

"So, Thalanir stopped her," I breathed. "He killed her to save the king and queen and keep them on the throne."

Mithraan frowned. "I'm afraid you're getting ahead of yourself." He turned to face me, his expression sorrowful. I had never seen such vulnerability in his features, and it disconcerted me more than a little.

"Why do I get the feeling this tale gets worse?" I asked, my voice trembling.

"Because it does," Mithraan confessed with a solemn shake of his head. "To obtain the flute, Gallia had to infiltrate a village in Tíria's north. Her employer had revealed its hiding place, hoping she would spare his life in return. But when she killed him and went in search of Fathuír, she discovered the Fae had lied to her about its specific location. Yet she could still feel its power on the air and knew it was close. It was indeed concealed somewhere in that small village."

Tears came to my eyes. Without Mithraan saying another

word, I could *feel* his thoughts and emotions. The sense of loss permeating his flesh—his bones.

"Instead of taking the time to hunt for the flute," he said, "one evening, she moved like a shadow into the village and cast a sleeping spell over its residents. Gallia burned the village in the night, knowing the flute, spell-protected as it was, would survive the flames. She killed every Fae—male, female, children —in their sleep, and retrieved the instrument. And when Thalanir learned what she had done, he discovered there was not a shred of regret in her—not a single sign of a conscience."

"Gods," I breathed.

I had suspected Gallia had hidden some terrible moment from me, but never in my darkest imagination could I have envisioned such blatant cruelty—and such callous disregard for life.

"Did Thalanir ever tell you that he sometimes has visions of the future? Waking dreams of what may come to pass?" Mithraan asked.

I nodded. "He did, but not what he saw—not exactly."

"He told me once that when Gallia began to change, he began to see not only one future, but two possible ones, branching off left and right, like paths in the woods. One path guided him toward a world of war, pain, and death. The other guided him to this world—the one we see before us now. A world filled with promise and beauty."

"But there's death and pain in this world," I protested. "The war is raging, from what I hear."

"The war has not yet fully begun," Mithraan said with another shake of his head, "and if we are fortunate, it never will. You see, this world contains two powerful elements the other did not—two things that could bring peace to the realms."

"What?"

"You...and your sister."

I cocked my head, my brow furrowing. "I don't understand."

"The thing is," he said, "Thalanir had seen that the High King and Queen that Gallia was to murder would eventually have a son—a prince. They would name him Rynfael, and he was the very Fae who would become your grandfather. Thalanir had seen him in his mind's eye. He knew the importance of the future High King—he knew that without Rynfael, there would never be a Lyrinn. Or, more importantly for him, a Leta."

My breath was trapped deep inside me. It was all so mad— so twisted.

"Thalanir killed her to save Lyrinn and me," I rasped. "He did it to steer the world in our direction."

Mithraan nodded. "He had a choice: Let the world fall into chaos or try to salvage it. With the second option came a world in which you exist—and that, I believe, is what drove him to take her life. When Thalanir had his visions of the future back then..." He paused, staring up at the twinkling stars above us and inhaling deep. "In them, he felt an emotion so profound—"

I bit my lip, summoning a shot of courage. "So profound that what?"

"It seems he fell in love with you hundreds of years ago, Leta. He knew you in his visions—the version of you I see before me now—come of age and filled with endless questions and wisdom, all at once. He told me he used to have conversations with you—he saw the potential for a future filled with light and joy—one in which Tíria flourished and beauty reigned. So, he was confronted with a choice: Let Gallia murder the prince and watch the world to fall, knowing you and he would never be born—or protect the prince, protect the realms, and know that one day, your paths would cross."

"But, couldn't he have reasoned with Gallia? Convinced her not to—"

Mithraan shook his head. "She was too far gone," he said.

"I'm afraid I must warn you, Leta—a Násuire has a burden of their own to carry. A great power will soon be handed to you, too, Leta. Though in what form, I can't say. Perhaps Thalanir has already seen that future for you. Maybe he already knows what will befall you, and he wanted to see you fulfill that destiny. Whatever his reasons, I can tell you that he has carried the consequences of what he did to Gallia with him every day of his life since that night so long before you or I were born."

Mithraan closed his eyes, seeming to feel Thalanir's pain, to take it on for a moment, then release it into the wind.

"He has paid for his actions a million times over," he said. "Every time he takes a breath, he remembers what he did. And it doesn't matter who tells him he did the right thing, or why. He has never forgiven himself for it, not to this day." Raking a hand through his hair, he sighed. "Understand, Leta, that he was the only Fae who could get close enough to her—the only one she truly trusted, though she had broken *his* trust countless times. He had to be the one to kill her; it was his fate. I only hope you can find a way to forgive him—to understand why he felt such a relentless need to stop her."

"Of course I forgive him." Tears streamed down my cheeks now, a torrent I couldn't hope to hold back. "I need to find him," I murmured. "I can't let him go another day, hating himself as he does. I have to let him know..."

"I'll go on the hunt tonight. Hopefully, I'll learn something of his whereabouts by morning. In the meantime, you should get some rest. I'll send your sister to watch over you while you sleep."

All I could muster was, "Thank you."

When he'd left, I closed my eyes and called out for a presence I hadn't felt since the moment I left Thalanir behind. A presence I had hoped never to encounter again.

Are you there, Gallia?

A few seconds passed before her voice came to me. A voice that had always been silken and smooth, sweet beyond compare, now sounded icy and hostile, sharp as a blade.

~*You've heard the truth now. What more do you want from me?*

I want you to show me what really happened on the night he killed you. I want the truth.

~*You already know what happened.*

Not all of it. I want to feel your mind—your emotions. I want to feel what it was like to be you in the moment when you died. Please, Gallia—do this one thing for me. Then, I promise you—I will let you rest.

A moment passed, and I thought she'd abandoned me, never to show herself again.

But then, a flash of light exploded in my mind's eye, and one last time, I found myself inside her body and mind.

I was standing outside the palace of black stone, darkness engulfing me. I had already pulled Thalanir's hood away—already revealed his face. He stood before me, his face stricken, his cheeks pale.

"Did he send you?" I asked, smiling up at him and laying a hand on his cheek. "Was he hoping you and I would patch things up?"

"No," Thalanir replied. "I came of my own volition."

I let out a laugh. "Well, good. I'm glad to hear you've come to your senses," I said, a hand reaching under my cloak.

It was then that I felt it—the cold hilt of a dagger, tucked away at my side. The weapon was intended to slit the king's and queen's throats that very night.

But first, it would take another life—one that Gallia had once valued above all others.

No! I cried silently, struggling to turn the vision—to alter the unalterable past. *Please...*

But there was no stopping it. I may as well have tried to rewrite history on the minds of all those who had lived it.

I kissed him—knowing full well that it would be the last time our lips met before I plunged the weapon into his heart.

Only it wasn't me, of course. It was *her*—and everything inside me shook and cried out in silent warning...

Yet I could do nothing.

I could feel the malice inside Gallia's heart, the sickness that had eaten away at her for too long now, stealing from her all the sweetness, light and joy she had felt in those early days with Thalanir. There was no bliss now—no love. Only a cold bitterness.

My hand—no—*her* hand—grasped the dagger tightly, slipping it out of its sheath.

It was in that moment that I felt it once again. A jolt of pain so fierce that my mind reeled with it.

And then, in an instant, the entire world disappeared.

My mind flashed with an explosion of white light, and then she was gone, and I was once again in the small clearing, a fire dying a slow death before me.

She was going to kill him, I thought.

I wonder if Thalanir knew.

CHAPTER FORTY

DARKNESS STILL SURROUNDED the clearing when I awoke to the sound of voices.

I sat up to see that Lyrinn was on her feet and moving toward a tall, broad-shouldered Fae. In the faint light, I could just make her out as she threw her arms around him.

It seemed Mithraan had already returned from his latest scouting mission.

I pushed myself to my feet, smoothing out my hair a little, and stepped forward.

"Were you successful?" I asked breathlessly. "Did you find him?"

He nodded, his eyes dark and serious. "Yes and no. As I flew north, I spotted two mortal guards patrolling the roads. I swooped down to listen, as I could hear them speaking of a prisoner taken to Castelle's Lord and Lady yesterday morning. I couldn't imagine who would be so valuable that they would drag him so great a distance, so I landed. And..." He looked at Lyrinn when he concluded, "Well, let's just say I interrogated them."

"Oh dear," Lyrinn said with a wince. "Poor humans."

"They're none the worse for wear," Mithraan half-shrugged, "though I told them I'd be back for both of them if the bastards breathed a word of my little visit to anyone."

"What did they tell you?" I asked, my heart feeling like it had frozen solid in apprehension.

"They said he's a Valdfae. Another guard had found him wandering the woods after he'd flown some distance north. According to one guard, the Fae looked weak, broken, and he didn't put up a fight. He said the Fae...looked like a mere shadow of a living thing."

A cry cut through the air, and it took me far too long to realize it had come from me.

Lyrinn laid a hand on my back.

"Is it him?" she asked. "Can we know for sure?"

Mithraan nodded. "From the description, he did sound like Thalanir. He must have flown quite far north if he made it to Castelle. The guards said he's in the palace's cells already—the lord and lady's men are trying to extract information from him about Fae movements in the mortal realms. Though they're fools if they think he'll ever talk."

"What will they do to him?" I choked out.

"Nothing—at least, not if we get to him soon. Leta—don't despair. We will free him, even if we have to kill every member of Castelle's Guard. You have my word on it."

"I need to see him," I lamented, pulling my eyes to the sky, which was already beginning to lighten. "I need to tell him I know the truth. How long will it take us to get there?"

"If we fly?" Lyrinn asked. "Two hours, maybe."

Tears rimmed my eyes when I said, "You're forgetting that I don't have wings—and I can't ask the gelding to gallop such a distance."

Lyrinn managed a smile. "My dear sister, you're forgetting that Mithraan can turn into a massive eagle with giant talons—but he also has the wings of a High Fae and extremely strong arms. Take your pick."

I barely pondered the question when I wiped my eyes and said, "Eagle it is."

CHAPTER FORTY-ONE

AFTER I HAD THANKED the gelding for carrying me so far and freed him into the wild, Mithraan shifted once again into an enormous silver eagle. He was beautiful, his eyes intelligent and dangerous, his beak curved and blade-sharp.

As I looked at him, I wondered at my choice to ride such a creature.

"It's all right," Lyrinn laughed when she saw me hesitate slightly. "You can climb onto his back. He won't bite."

In response, Mithraan let out a shrill cry. I glanced one more time at my sister, who nodded her approval, then leapt onto the eagle's back, perching at the base of his neck, my legs hooked just ahead of his wings.

"Two hours," Lyrinn said before the exquisite white wings sprang up behind her, and she took off into the sky. Mithraan followed, and I leaned into his neck, letting out a faint cry of fear as I felt him surge upward.

My heart soared as we flew over woods, rivers, valleys, and the mountains rising to our east. Towns and villages unfolded below us and occasionally, I spotted smoke and flame ascending from this or that mortal stronghold. The war really was raging, disorganized and jumbled though it was.

But when we flew over a broad road, my heart sank when I spotted a massive army of men, marching in perfect, ordered synchronicity. Even from a great distance, I could see their swords, pikes, spears, and daggers gleaming in the sunlight.

Lyrinn banked and flew over.

"You see them too," I shouted.

"They're hard to miss. Those are Corym's men—and Caedmon's. And I guarantee they're not setting out to attack Castelle's lord."

"You think they're headed to the Onyx Rise?" I asked. "Toward Tíria?"

"Yes. Which means they'll want to climb the Onyx Stair."

"Which means..." I said, my heart aching. "They'll pass through Dúnbar—and kill anyone who gets in their way."

"Not a lot of our old mortal friends would dare try and stop them," Lyrinn assured me. "So at least there's that. I'm more frightened of what they might do when they reach the Rise's peak. Fairholme is not far from the Stair—it's the first Fae stronghold they'll come upon. It's been rebuilt since the Mist ceased and the Grimpers fell—but if we're not there to stop the assault, I fear what might happen. Mithraan's friends Khiral and Alaric are protecting it, but we must warn them."

"How long will it take the mortal army to get to Dúnbar?" I asked.

"Three days, perhaps four. Mortals need rest—and food. We have a little time—but our best chance is to speak to our grandfather and gather some of his forces to stop the onslaught in its tracks."

"I don't see how Corym thinks he can take on Tíria," I said, but even as I spoke the words, I realized just how large the army below us was, stretching for what seemed like miles.

"There are Fae among their numbers," Lyrinn told me, glancing downward, and I realized her senses were more honed than mine. "Traitors to our kind...including Valdfae."

"You can see all of that from up here?"

"And more. For instance, I noticed Corym and King Caedmon are not among their numbers."

"Where do you suppose they are?" I called out, my voice fighting the wind. Could Corym still be with the Sisterhood? It had only been a few days since I'd last seen him, after all.

"A scout I spoke to two days ago said the prince had been spotted with his father heading west toward Domignon. Perhaps they're mustering more troops."

"Perhaps," I agreed, though a nagging feeling had begun to eat away at me.

"I'm going to fly up ahead and tell a couple of our friends to head straight to Fairholme," Lyrinn called out, soaring off to speak to the two Fae at the front of our flying party. Instantly, they banked and headed north-west, toward Dúnbar and the Rise.

When we finally touched down in Castelle's main city square, a group of gathered townspeople regarded our small party with horror and interest combined, whispering to one another or fleeing, depending on just how terrified they were. Mithraan shifted into his Fae form, and we moved quickly toward the palace gates, only a few hundred feet from where we'd landed.

As we drew near the palace, I felt a familiar stirring—an energy emanating from the palace grounds, drawing me toward them. My heart hammered in my chest, my feet wanting to break into a sprint.

"He's there," I said under my breath as Lyrinn moved next to me. She reached for my arm, squeezing it gently.

"You're certain?" she asked, and I nodded.

"Absolutely sure of it."

"Let's pick up our pace, then."

When we arrived at the palace gate, four guards had already been sent out to greet us, swords in hand. One of the men—a guard of thirty or so, tall with thick stubble—stepped forward, his chin raised.

"What's a party of Fae doing in Castelle?" he asked with a clear dose of disdain. "Do you not realize there is a war lapping at our borders? We are not friends, and the High Lord and Lady are not fond of intrusion."

"Then you might wish to ask them why they have taken one of our friends captive," Mithraan said, stepping toward the man, who immediately recoiled. Mithraan's amber wings spread out behind him, and I knew without looking that his eyes were flaring bright with the dancing, threatening fire of a powerful Fae.

"The Valdfae came of his own free will," the guard insisted.

"Did he?" Mithraan asked. "Perhaps you'd be so kind as to allow us to ask him ourselves."

My heart danced in my chest at the prospect, which seemed too good to be true. Thalanir was so close I could almost taste him—yet I would need the lord's blessing before I could make my way to him without risking a miniature war of our own.

"Take us to the lord and lady," I commanded, striding toward the guard, who eyed me suspiciously.

"Where are your wings?" he asked.

My cheeks heated with shame when I said, "I have no wings."

"Then you're not a High Fae," he scoffed. "The High Lord will not accept an audience with the likes of you."

"No?" I asked, flicking my hand toward him.

He fell to his knees, hands at his throat. No noise came from him, but he looked panicked—terrified.

"Your windpipe has sealed itself," I told him as the other guards took a step toward me. "You will not breathe again until I allow it. But I suppose if I'm not a proper High Fae, you can fight off my spell...can't you?"

The guard waved his hand at me, begging silently for release, and with another flick of my fingers, I set him free.

I had never used that spell before, never even known I could.

But I'd seen Thalanir cast it the first time we'd met. And now, reaching into my memories, I understood what had compelled him to action.

He had reached inside his mind and done it to protect me.

And now, I had cast the same spell to protect *him*.

The guard, still unable to speak, gestured to the others to open the gates. They obeyed, staring at us with furrowed brows and wide eyes as we stepped through into the palace grounds.

We moved as one through the palace's corridors, our senses telling us just where to go to find the lord and lady.

We discovered them in a dining chamber, where they were feasting on an enormous breakfast, complete with several bottles of red Castelle wine.

Two guards tried to keep us from entering the room, but with a swipe of Lyrinn's hand they fell to the ground, writhing in pain.

"Lord Dewlyn, Lady Dewlyn. We wish to speak to you both," she said, her chin raised as she beheld the lord and lady.

"What's this about?" the lord shouted, leaping to his feet. "How dare you infiltrate the palace?"

But after a moment, his eyes narrowed. He stepped toward Lyrinn and Mithraan both, and said, "I recognize you two." He stared at Mithraan when he said, "You're the Tírian. The High Lord. And you—" he added, looking at Lyrinn. "How is this possible? You're a mortal, from Dúnbar!"

"I'm not," she replied. "I lived in that town, but I was never mortal. Now, we believe you're holding our friend prisoner. A Valdfae."

The lord laughed, spinning around to face his wife, who was also guffawing. "Your presence alone is proof of the Valdfae's value," he said, turning back to us. "I will not turn up my nose at a potential bargaining chip to negotiate with Tíria's High King—or with King Caedmon in Domignon."

Lyrinn was about to speak again when I reached out for her arm. She turned to me, and I shook my head.

"Let me," I said quietly.

My sister gawked at me, baffled, but when Mithraan said, "Listen to Leta," she backed away with a half-bow.

"Be my guest."

CHAPTER FORTY-TWO

"Lord Dewlyn," I said, and he looked down at me, his chin held up in the manner of someone who had convinced himself that this was how a man of his status behaved. "My Lady," I added, nodding to his wife. "You two must love one another very much, yes?"

Lady Dewlyn rose to her feet and glared at me then, a flash of rage in her eyes. What sort of audacious, disrespectful fool asked such a question? Who did I think I was?

But when she saw the sincerity in my eyes, her face softened.

"Of course we do," she said, stepping toward me. "We have been married for thirty years. We have six children together."

I smiled. "Do you—my Lady—remember how you felt in the early days, when you first met the High Lord? How you could do little but think of him, how he consumed your every thought?"

I flicked my fingers slightly by my side, sending a jolt of energy to her mind, seeking out a memory I knew was in there somewhere. I could *feel* it inside her—feel her lust for him, long dormant but still alive, waiting to find its way out again.

Confusion shifted and ebbed on her face—then, all of a sudden, she looked enraptured.

"I do," she said. "I remember all of it." She turned to her husband and smiled, reaching out for his hand. "Do you, darling?"

Between them, almost so faint as to be invisible, tendrils of light flickered and flamed, drawing them closer together.

"Of course I do," he replied, pulling her to him and kissing her gently. "I think of it daily."

"What," I said, "would you two have done in those days, if someone had stolen the one you love and imprisoned them, keeping them away from you?"

"I would have died to get her back," the High Lord said. "I still would. I would burn cities, move mountains, empty oceans to find her again, if ever someone tried to take her from me."

"Then you understand what I will do if you do not release Thalanir to me," I said, flames burning in my irises. "I will have no choice, I'm afraid."

"You...love the Valdfae?" Lady Dewlyn said, her eyes flickering back to mine.

In spite of the clear threat I had just issued, she had reacted with sympathy and sorrow. Her heart had filled with benevolence, all hostility vanished.

I had her fully in my clutches...and I had turned her into an ally.

I nodded. "Very much. But I lost him, you see—because he thought I had given up on him. He didn't know how deeply I love him...and I suppose I didn't, either."

"That's why..." the High Lord said, his eyes filled with empathy. "The poor fellow looked so downtrodden—I didn't understand how anyone so powerful could look so weak."

"He is heartsick, clearly," his wife said, squeezing his hand tighter. "The poor thing. My darling, we must reunite these two immediately."

Somewhere behind me, Mithraan let out a little snort of amusement, and I heard Lyrinn shush him.

"May I...may I see him?" I asked.

"Of course!" Lady Dewlyn said, swinging a hand wildly in the air. "Guards! Bring this lovely young lady to the dungeons at once. Give her everything she needs."

"And the prisoner?" one of the guards asked.

Lady Dewlyn looked to her husband, who nodded once. "Release him," she commanded. "A Valdfae isn't so valuable as all that, is he? After all, we have no need of his services here—and it's not like he's going to tell us anything of importance. They have a code of honor, those ones."

Suppressing a cry of triumph, I thanked them both and turned to accompany the guards down to the dungeons. Lyrinn and Mithraan followed, and I smiled to hear the whispered words between them.

"It seems her true power is persuasion," Mithraan breathed with a low chuckle.

"It always has been," said Lyrinn. "Ever since she convinced our adoptive father that he was firmly wrapped around each of her fingers, she's proven countless times that she can convince most people to do pretty well anything she wants."

"Almost," I replied. "But I've discovered lately that I'm not always successful."

"Something tells me that's about to change," Lyrinn snickered.

But I wasn't concerned about my growing powers just now. All I wanted was to get to Thalanir—to tell him what I had learned. To pour out my emotions and express all that I still felt for him—and to promise him nothing would ever tear us apart again.

There would be no more fear of rejection. No more hiding from the past.

Only truth, and trust.

He will know I love him...even if those are the last words he ever hears from me. Even if he tells me to leave.

I'll make sure he understands that no one in this world deserves love more than he does.

My heart thundered when my foot collided with the stone floor at the bottom of the staircase. The air was cold and damp, the corridor dark.

I could feel him around me, his scent entangled with the dungeon's dampness.

I pushed ahead of the guards until I stood outside a cell whose door was nothing but a set of worn iron bars. A door Thalanir could easily have opened at any moment since he'd been locked up, yet he'd chosen to stay in this awful, dingy place.

He'd chosen this fate as punishment for his sin so long ago.

I grabbed the bars, my knuckles white with tension, and stared into the shadows of the cell. I could see him there, seated on the floor, his knees bent up, his head down. His hair hung in thick strands around his face.

He looked like a broken man.

"Thalanir," I said softly, feeling the iron bars melt away beneath my touch as my need for him grew.

The guards stepped closer, their eyes bulging in wonder. One of them let out a gasp, turning away to run back up the corridor, but Mithraan stopped him with a hand to his chest and a shake of his head.

Slowly, Thalanir raised his face a little. His eyes glowed slightly as I walked toward him, but still, he didn't meet my gaze.

"I know," I said softly, slipping over to stand before him.

His gaze moved up to meet mine, but he remained silent.

"I know why you did it," I said. "And I am so sorry that I allowed myself to doubt you."

His lip twitched slightly. Whether into a potential frown or smile, I couldn't say.

"It doesn't matter," he finally rasped, his throat so dry that it sounded as if he'd been swallowing sand. "She was flawed in so many ways, but it was not for me to be her jury and executioner. I went against my code of honor. I chose to kill her of my own volition, despite her faith in me—she still trusted me in spite of the chasm that had grown between us. That I would take advantage of her trust makes *me* untrustworthy and unworthy of your love."

"No," I said, crouching before him, my hands slipping onto his knees. "It makes you worthy. It was noble, what you did. You could have taken the easy way out—you could have let her live and thrive, and your conscience could have remained clear of one sin while the world fell into ruin. I *know* you loved her. I know how it crushed you." I blew out a breath, fixing him in my gaze and seeking strength. "In the end, I felt her cruelty. After we parted, you and I, I saw what she had become. Her heart had turned to ice, and she was incapable of love, or even of true hatred. She was driven by a force too powerful for her to resist. But none of that matters. All that should ever have mattered was my faith in your goodness, and I allowed that faith to fracture. Please forgive me."

At that, a spark ignited behind his eyes, but he remained silent.

"I won't leave here without you," I told him. "Because I love you. I will not let you rot in a cage, unless I get to rot alongside you."

He shook his head. "No. I won't allow that."

"You don't get to choose my fate. I do. And I choose to be

with you. From this day—if you'll have me—you and I will live the life you saw in your visions of the future. We'll find the happiness you hoped for. I promise you, I will never betray you as she did. I will not let any power, no matter how great, take hold of my heart."

At that, a spark erupted in his irises, and I could feel a warmth flowing through his mind the likes of which he had not allowed himself in many years. A quiet conflagration, building up over centuries to ignite now in a flame, lighting him from within.

The betrayal had never been his...but hers. She had sold her soul and left him no choice but to stop her. His foresight, a curse that haunted him all his life, had shown him the future she would force upon the world.

"Besides," I added with a smile. "I owe you. You saved my life back then, long before I was ever born. You saved Lyrinn's life—and our grandfather's before us."

"Then it was worth every moment of torment," he replied, letting out a long breath that seemed to have been trapped forever in his chest. "I suppose I can begin the process of forgiving myself at long last." He slipped a hand onto my cheek, tentative and affectionate. "I've spent so many years despising some part of myself, numbing my heart against emotion, that I had forgotten what it was to feel until I saw you in that clearing —until I dared hope our future might come to pass."

"And now?"

He smiled. "I am nothing right now *except* for intense emotion—but still afraid of what it all means. Afraid that this is nothing but another dream crafted by my cruel mind."

"Then come with me," I said, rising to my feet and stepping backward. "The lord and lady have agreed to release you. We'll head north. We have a great deal to do, and Caedmon's army's are on the move. We need you, Thalanir. *I* need you for the next task. I need your strength—because something is awaiting me in the North, and I don't know what it is."

He stood and moved toward me, and when he was close, I pushed his hair away from his face and smiled up at him.

"All this time," I said, "I was afraid of what would happen if you and I were allowed to be happy. I kept finding reasons to push you away, to tell myself you didn't want me, or I didn't want you. But I won't do it again. Not for anything. I promise you that."

He kissed me then, gently, carefully, as if afraid I would break. When he pulled back, he let out a snicker.

"What?" I asked.

"I want you," he whispered, pressing his forehead to mine. "More than I can say. I want to tear the clothing from you and pleasure you in every way imaginable."

I tensed up, expecting some quiet, kindly rejection. "Why do you say that like it's a bad thing?"

"Because before I can let you near me, I need a long, hot bath."

CHAPTER FORTY-THREE

THALANIR GOT HIS WISH.

I instructed the guards to escort him to a bathing chamber, reminding them that their lord and lady were in full support of his release.

"He's your guest now," I warned. "And no prisoner of war. If anything happens to him, I will not be pleased. Do you understand?"

The guards nodded aggressively, fear in their eyes—and for the first time, I felt what it was to be a High Fae holding extraordinary power in my palm, in my very *presence*.

With a kiss, Thalanir and I said a temporary goodbye, then I watched a guard lead him away as the rest of us went to meet with Lord and Lady Dewlyn in the dining hall.

They fed us a feast of pheasant, steak, wild turkey, and every side dish Castelle had to offer.

I felt suddenly guilty for all the times I had criticized Castelle's lord in my younger years for his reputation as a slovenly drunk. I realized now that the truth had always been far more intricately woven. He was flawed, just as so many of us were. Imperfect, yet generous. Judgmental, yet fair.

Lord Dewlyn was, in fact, almost everything a leader should be.

And, above all, he and his wife both had the human capacity for empathy—the very trait I had exploited when I had persuaded them to release Thalanir. The spell hadn't altered either of them, but simply opened their minds to my emotions —to my love for him—and the second they had felt it, they had no choice but to comply.

"Word has it Corym's army is advancing rapidly," Lord Dewlyn told us as we ate. "Scouts spotted them last night at a large encampment in Belleau."

"We saw them as well," Mithraan said, throwing a grave look in Lyrinn's direction. "We need to get to Tíria and speak to the High King. It's time to muster what forces are left in Tíria and ready ourselves to defend our border."

"We will travel north after we've eaten," Lyrinn promised, "if the lord and lady give us their leave."

"Of course," Lady Dewlyn said, taking her husband's hand. "We do hope there are no hard feelings about your Valdfae." She threw me a suggestive smile. "Your Thalanir is such a handsome thing. I can understand why you were so eager to have him back."

I laughed. "As handsome as he is, that's not what makes me want him by my side so badly—though I'll admit it doesn't hurt. I appreciate the fact that you treated him decently."

"Of course," Lord Dewlyn said. "Neither my lady nor I wishes to inflame the conflict between our people. If anything, our interest in holding him here lay only in the potential for persuading both sides to come to a swift conclusion to this foolish war."

"The war, I'm afraid," Mithraan said, "will grow bloodier before it's resolved, unless we uncover a secret weapon that stops the mortal army in their tracks. Their numbers are vast—

and if they're under Prince Corym's influence, there's no telling what damage they might inflict."

At that, my left hand pulsed with a strange, nagging pain, and I looked down to see the dragon wrapped around my finger flaring to life.

"I'm...going to check on Thalanir," I said, pushing my chair away from the table.

Rising to my feet with a bow of my head, I took my leave.

I found Thalanir in a large bathing chamber in the palace's east wing.

He was already half dressed when I opened the door, and I stood staring at him as I had so often—at his extraordinary chest and finely sculpted abdomen, the braided muscles of his arms tensing as he fastened the belt at his waist.

"I—came to see if you needed anything," I told him, doing my best to sound casually disinterested, rather than desire-filled. "Before we leave."

It wasn't easy to conceal my disappointment when he simply said, "Thank you, no."

Part of me had hoped he would lunge toward me and kiss me hard, press me to the wall, tear my clothing off as he'd threatened—or rather *promised*—earlier.

But his face bore the look of the serious Valdfae I had come to know, rather than the lover with whom I'd shared far too few moments of sensual intimacy.

He was all business, resolve engraved on his every feature. I supposed he, too, was nervous about the coming battle.

He pulled on a clean shirt—one gifted to him by Lord

Dewlyn's people—and was about to tuck it in when he pulled his chin up and met my eyes, his body freezing momentarily.

"Lahnan."

"Yes?"

With a chuckle, he shook his head. "Nothing at all. Except—"

I assumed he was going to continue preparing himself, but instead, he strode toward me, took my face in his hands, and kissed me. When his tongue found mine, my insides rolled with pleasure even as my legs seemed to give out under me. For a moment, I lost the sensation of where I was in the universe—forgot there was a floor beneath my feet.

My head swam, my knees turned to liquid, and my core ached for him.

When Thalanir pulled back, it took me a moment to open my eyes and blow out a breath. "You saw my mind," I said. "You knew how much I wanted that. And here, I've been so careful to keep my thoughts to myself."

It was half accusation, half admiration.

"No, actually," he replied. "I saw my own mind. And if you could see my thoughts—how many hours I've spent since I last saw you fantasizing about what it would feel like to slip my tongue between your legs just one more time—you would probably slap me."

"I sincerely doubt a slap would be my first reaction," I laughed, my hands finding his chest, the hard throb of his heart rising up to meet my palms. "And for the record, I will gladly part my legs for you every day for the next thousand years. But for now, it seems we're heading north. Perhaps I'll get a chance to show you my home when we pass."

"Dúnbar," he said, his lips delicious as the word eased out of him. "You know, it wouldn't be the first time I've seen that town."

I raised an eyebrow, surprised. "Oh, you've been? I must have missed you."

With a chuckle, he replied, "It's been many long years, of course. There are other ways out of Tíria—paths through the mountains leading to various harbors on the east and west coasts. But the Onyx Stair was once my favorite route. It was used by my people for centuries before we were cut off by the mist mortals called the Breath of the Fae—and before so many of our kind were turned into Grimpers."

I couldn't help the shudder that assaulted me when he uttered the word. Those beasts of shadow and bone had tormented my dreams when I was younger, though I had never seen one. They were the stuff of nightmares, creatures so malevolent that even the Fae themselves feared them.

Fae like me.

"It was a Grimper that killed our father," I said quietly. "Our adoptive father, I suppose I should say—given that Kazimir is our blood-father."

"If Martel raised you and you loved him, then he deserves the title," Thalanir half-whispered, his voice a caress on my mind. "Such an honor is earned, not simply bestowed. High King Kazimir has been no father to you, whatever your lineage. He was little more than an unfeeling donor of his seed."

I sighed. "So strange to think he's out there somewhere. I wonder if he even knows about the conflict in our lands. I wonder if he cares."

I was about to ask whether Thalanir had felt Kazimir's presence in our futures, but I wasn't entirely sure I wanted to know.

The last thing I needed was another reason to worry about the days to come.

"I suspect he is aware of the war," Thalanir said. "The Kazimir I've encountered seems to know about the goings-on in most corners of Kalemnar. He was always wildly oblivious to much of what occurred in his own realm of Aetherion, however. He didn't realize, for instance, how much those in the North despised him, and how little respect the Order of Priestesses had for him."

Kazimir had never seemed like someone I wished to know. But in light of what had occurred with our mother, I couldn't help but feel a little sad at the thought that I may never meet him.

"Lyrinn didn't like him much, from what I can gather," I said with a wince. "Though I think maybe she came to understand him a little over her time in his palace. Perhaps he really is just broken, like so many of us. You said once that High Fae are complicated, and High Kings even more so. I'm beginning to see how right you are—to feel it in my blood."

"Being broken," Thalanir replied, "strikes each of us differently. Some hide the cracks and fractures away under thick shields, while others wield our wounds like jagged weapons, inflicting pain on the world in hopes of healing themselves."

I could feel his sorrow as he uttered those words.

He had always been the kind to hide his pain, to bear it as best he could. But it was time now for him to shed the last of it —to free himself of it.

"Tell me what happened," I said. "That night in the Dragon Court. I—I want to hear it from you."

I didn't need to explain myself. He understood exactly who and what I was talking about.

He exhaled. "How much do you know?"

"I know you killed Gallia to protect your people. To protect the future of Tíria."

He nodded once. "Not only to protect Tíria, but all of Kalemnar. I was fighting for nature itself. The power that had grown inside her was vicious, and over the course of months, it had taken her mind. She was no longer the Fae I had once known. She had grown into a stranger, consumed by something parasitic and cruel. She developed an obsession with the wings on her finger—the mark," he said, taking my left hand and stroking his thumb over the dragon permanently engraved into my skin. "She thought it meant she was entitled to claim the Dragon Court." He sucked in his cheeks for a moment before continuing, "They say something similar happened to your mother—a corruption of the blood."

"Yes," I replied quietly. "Perhaps it was the same illness that infected Gallia. They say it was our mother's desire for power that took her down. It robbed her of kindness—of empathy. She had grown into a predator who killed for sport, rather than a reasoned Fae."

Thalanir nodded. "When Gallia came of age and her powers began to grow, something inside her slowly drove her to madness. When she and I were still close, I began to feel it acutely. I felt the struggle, the battle she fought daily, and I was there when she began to lose that fight. I watched her change into someone I didn't know—someone who seduced Fae left and right, offering herself to them in exchange for secrets, for training—for anything that could lead her toward the power she craved. Rowland wasn't the only Fae who took advantage of her weakness—and he wasn't the worst of them. I only wish I'd been there when she decided to murder the Spell-Master and seek out the charmed flute."

"That's when she..." I began, but I couldn't bring myself to mention the Fae children she'd slaughtered in their beds.

"Yes," Thalanir said, bowing his head. "If only I had seen it coming. If only I had stopped her sooner."

"It wasn't your fault. You cared about her—you couldn't have seen it, even if you'd tried. I can't begin to imagine loving someone and watching them turn like that—watching them wilt and fade, then come back as something else entirely."

He seemed so devastated when he looked into my eyes, and I could feel a thousand years of torment in him all at once.

"You are *good*, Thalanir," I said, slipping my palms onto his stubbled cheeks. "You're kind. You are the best, most noble man I've ever known. You need to let it go, once and for all. Turn a new page in the book that's been your life all these years. Start a new chapter...with me."

With a smile that just barely managed to reach his eyes, he slipped his hands onto my waist.

"You are here," he said. "You, your sister, and many others are living, breathing. Because of what I..." He stopped, and I watched the tears form in his beautiful eyes—perhaps the first tears he'd shed in centuries. "Because of what I did to her. That's my consolation. That is proof that what I did was right."

"I'm so sorry," I said, wrapping my arms around him to hold him tight as he freed his tears, allowing them to fall at long last.

They weren't tears of sadness or pain, but relief—and I could its release with each breath he expelled. For hundreds of years, he had never once allowed himself to express what he had just conveyed to me. He had never once allowed himself to see the good in what he had done.

He had only ever punished himself for it.

Finally, he pulled back, clearing his throat.

"You are a Násuire," he said. "You have the flame in your soul. Your fate is bound to the Dragon Court—yours and Lyrinn's. To say I'm afraid of what might happen when we go north is an understatement—but I promise you, I will never, ever hurt you, whatever vision of the future may torment me." He swept a hand through my hair, pushing it away from my forehead and kissing me gently there. "I would sooner plunge my blade into my own heart than harm you, Lahnan."

I shook my head, tears in my own eyes now. "No. I won't accept that," I said. "You have to promise me, if I go mad—if I ever so much as *think* about killing innocents—that you will end me."

A quiet cough met my ears and I swung around, a hand instinctively raised against any threat. But after a moment, I realized it was Lark, who had just flitted into the room.

"Forgive me, Princess," he said softly. "I didn't mean to listen to your private conversation, but…"

"Lark," I replied, wiping away a tear as I laughed. "You *always* mean to listen."

He cocked his head to the side as he hovered in the air, his wings flapping wildly behind him. "Fine, then. I'm here to make you an offer."

"Which is?"

"If the madness ever takes you—if you should ever be over-come by a lust for power as *she* was, and as your mother was…"

"Yes?"

"I will kill you myself. I know I'm capable of it, and though it would pain me, I would do it…for you."

I glanced at Thalanir, whose face was impassive, and nodded.

"Thank you for offering to murder me, Lark."

"You're welcome." At that, he raised an eyebrow comically, and I almost—*almost*—thought I detected a smile. "Now, I'm afraid it's time to head north," he said. "Much as I'm sure you would both like to get some well-deserved rest."

"We'll rest when we reach the Dragon Court," I said. "If only for a few hours. We have a war to stop in its tracks, after all. We just have to figure out how."

"Very good," Lark replied, spinning around to fly out the door, calling over his shoulder, "Then if you'll come with me…"

Silently, I took Thalanir's hand and led him out of the bathing chamber and down the corridor after the sprite.

The road ahead would be long and difficult. But together, if Thalanir and I managed to stay alive long enough to see the mortal army defeated...

We might just find a little happiness.

CHAPTER FORTY-FOUR

THE VOYAGE NORTH was a quick one, with our party rejuvenated and Mithraan's eagle untiring as always.

Before we left Castelle, Lyrinn and Mithraan voted to skip over Dúnbar and head straight for Fairholme to warn the Fae there about the coming army. As much as I wanted to revisit our old home, I agreed in the end that it would be for the best.

"We could warn Dúnbar's residents about troop movements," Mithraan had assured me. "But it's unlikely mortals will listen to Fae, or care what our kind have to say. As I understand it, many humans still see Prince Corym as their great future leader rather than a tyrant in the making."

I wondered how our old acquaintances would look at Lyrinn and me—if they would regard us with the same scrutiny as they offered other Fae. Or if they would recognize us and embrace the two young women who had lived among them as mortals for so long.

Given what had happened to our adoptive father before we'd both disappeared, though, something told me our old acquaintances would look at us both with an untrusting eye.

I rode on the silver eagle's back once again, with Lark

perched before me. As we soared over the Onyx Rise and came upon Tíria for the first time, my breath caught in my throat.

This land, which had apparently been dead and grim for centuries, flourished now, its green landscape more vivid and beautiful than any I had ever seen.

Fairholme was Mithraan's domain, his home—and the castle was beautiful. Stone towers rose up at each corner of the elegant, enormous structure, their flags proudly displaying the sigil of the silver eagle.

I held on tight as Mithraan, Thalanir, and Lyrinn descended for a soft landing in the castle's primary courtyard, and two excited Fae jogged out to greet us.

When Mithraan had shifted into his Fae form, they embraced him and Lyrinn fondly, like family members who hadn't seen one another in some time.

One of them—with jet-black hair and a suspicious look on every feature—eyed me skeptically.

"Khiral," Lyrinn said, taking me by the hand and leading me over like a nervous child, "this is my sister, Leta."

His redheaded companion, who had been introduced as Alaric, stepped forward and hugged me tight. But Khiral, still reserved, nodded his head and muttered, "Welcome to Fairholme," before signaling us all to enter the castle.

"He's nervous because you look like Mother," Lyrinn whispered as we walked. "But don't worry—he'll come out of his shell soon enough."

I wasn't so sure about that. In Khiral, I could feel more than simple nerves. There was something deeper, almost a loathing in his heart when he looked at me.

Inside, Mithraan filled his old friends in on Corym's troop movements. "The army of thousands will be here in two days at the most," he cautioned, "and they have plenty of Fae with them. Whether those Fae are simple traitors or have been swayed by Corym's mind-bending influence is unclear."

"They're bastards either way," Khiral said under his breath. "I hate to break it to you, but we don't have the numbers to defeat them, Mith. We have a few hundred, at the most. Corym will have gathered Valdfae and Summoners. It will be hard to compete."

"That's why we're headed to the Dragon Court," Lyrinn interjected. "We will be asking the High King for aid. He has an army of his own, though it probably won't match Corym's numbers."

"The High King hasn't stepped into Fairholme in centuries," Khiral griped. "You really think he'll send Fae to die in the name of protecting Fairholme?"

"If Lyrinn and I ask him, he will," I said, stepping forward confidently.

Khiral eyed me up and down, and then his eyes landed on my left hand. "You're a Násuire," he said, and with that, I understood where his hostility came from.

My cheeks heated. "I am," I replied. "What of it?"

"Your kind is volatile. I have never yet heard of a Násuire who didn't eventually break, their mind corrupted. How do we know you won't turn into a psychopath like your moth—"

"Watch it," Lark growled, drawing his small sword and flitting toward Khiral. "Leta is not her mother. She's nothing like her, in fact."

"A sprite?" Khiral said, chuckling. "In Fairholme. I never thought I'd see the day." With a wave of his hand, he scoffed, "Put your weapon away. I won't fight you."

"No? Say another word against Leta, and I will see to it that you do."

"Lark!" I snapped. "Thank you—but it's all right." Turning Khiral's way, I added, "I will not let you down. I promise."

"I'll believe it when I see it." Khiral stepped toward me. "You know what happened in the Broken Lands, don't you? You know what she tried to do?"

"I know enough. But as Lark said, I am not my mother. I have no wish to rise to power, and I never will. I only want peace, and for this beautiful land to remain as lovely as it is now."

I felt Thalanir's warmth as he stepped up close to me.

"I can attest to that," he said, a quiet threat in his voice. "She is strong, Khiral—stronger than you know. And she has a purpose in the North—one that I have felt in my bones, though I don't yet know what it is. There are some who believe she and Lyrinn are the keys to winning this war and defeating Caedmon's men once and for all. I have faith in Leta, and so should you."

Khiral raised his hands in mock apology. "Far be it from me to doubt the word of a newly Changed High Fae with no wings and the mark of the Násuire on her hand. I suppose I should just hope for the best and be done with it, should I?"

"She will have her wings soon enough, you ass," Lyrinn shot. "Besides, wings aren't what make a Fae. No one around here had them for a millenium, and you all survived just fine."

Khiral went to speak again, but this time, Alaric shushed him. "Let her show her strength," he said gently. "Just as her sister did. You underestimated Lyrinn once, too, you dolt—or have you forgotten what a judgmental prick you can be?"

"Fine," Khiral finally submitted. "Go, then. Speak to your grandfather and do what you can, or every male and female Fae in this castle will end up charred beyond recognition when a Flame-Summoner comes and burns us where we stand."

"We'll be back with the High King's army," Mithraan told them, glancing around at the rest of us. "I had hoped to stay in

Fairholme for a few hours—but I'm afraid we don't have that luxury. To the Dragon Court it is."

We flew over beautiful, lush green lands dotted with wildflowers for what felt like hours before I spotted a series of snow-capped mountains in the distance, with one peak rising higher than the rest. At its base was an immense castle of pure black. Crafted of onyx, just like the Rise itself, its towers rose higher than any I'd ever seen, and at its base was what looked like a large city of gray stone.

"The Dragon Court," Thalanir's voice called out over the chill wind that I'd only just realized was assaulting us. "Your grandfather's home—and the place where your mother was born."

"What happened to my grandmother?" I asked over the cutting wind. "I never hear about her."

"She died many years ago, at the beginning of the siege of Tíria. It's one reason your grandfather has been so reclusive all these years. He will be pleased to meet you and Lyrinn, to put it mildly. Lyrinn bears some resemblance to your grandmother, actually."

When we were close, he and Lyrinn banked and swooped downward, and Mithraan's eagle did the same, heading for the palace grounds when we drew near.

We landed in the large inner courtyard just beyond the main gates. Two Fae guards in silver armor awaited us, a dragon emblazoned on each of their chests. The sigil so resembled the mark on my left hand that I was starting to think I had been summoned here by some power deep in my blood.

"High King Rynfael welcomes you all," one of the guards

said with a bow of his head. "We're to escort you to the throne room to meet with him."

My stomach churned with anxiety as it hit me for the first time that I was meeting a Fae High King. A creature powerful beyond my comprehension.

To make matters worse, I didn't know anything about him, other than that he was my grandfather.

What was he like? Was he friendly? Warm? Cold?

Terrifying?

"Don't worry," Thalanir whispered, leaning in close and taking my hand. "Rynfael may appear daunting at first, but he is kind. Whatever Khiral may say, the High King cares about his people, and he will do what it takes to protect them."

I gripped the pack that was slung over my shoulder, feeling for the hilt of the Blade of Dracrigh and grateful when I found its distinct outline under my fingers.

I would ask Rynfael what its purpose was—why he had forged it, and why it had ended up in my hands. I could only hope he wouldn't expect me to train as some sort of knife-throwing maniac in the next day or two before sending me into battle.

When we arrived at the throne room, the doors flew open in greeting and our party of five, including Lark, marched or flew inside.

The High King was seated on a silver throne at the room's far end, and as we approached, he rose to his feet to greet us, stepping down from the dais. He wore an outfit of violet and black, a crown of silver and gold filigree atop his head.

Though he was almost exactly Thalanir's age, he looked as I had always pictured an ancient Fae. Gray hair and a finely trimmed beard to match, skin lightly lined with experience and emotion. Still, he looked young in his way, his eyes bright and intelligent. He was handsome, his jaw chiseled, his cheekbones high.

When we were close, Thalanir and Mithraan stopped and bowed, and Lyrinn and I curtseyed awkwardly. I had worn a long skirt, and was grateful that I had its fabric to grasp in my nervous fingers.

"Your Grace," Mithraan said. "I would like to present—"

Rynfael put up a hand to stop him, moving first to Lyrinn and assessing her, then turning to me. "You don't need to identify my own kin to me," the High King said. His tone was cold, his expression almost hostile.

He looked down at my left hand. Then, taking hold of it, pulled it up to examine the dragon engraved on my skin.

"You're uncannily like your mother," he said, looking into my eyes. "Yet utterly different. Perhaps you are her opposite—a chance to set the world right."

"I can only hope I won't disappoint you, your Grace," I said, my voice quivering.

"We'll see," he huffed, eyeing my bag. "Did you bring it?"

I was about to ask what he meant when I remembered the hilt.

I nodded.

"Do you and your sister have the pendants?"

I glanced over at Lyrinn, wondering if she had any idea what we were talking about. She gave me a look that conveyed, *Whatever this is...I'm in.*

"Yes, Grandfather," I said, nodding again.

At that, Rynfael smiled. "*Grandfather,*" he echoed with a sigh. "Do you know how I've longed to hear that word?"

He pulled me close and embraced me, his arms wrapping around me so tightly that I could scarcely breathe. Even after so many years spent on the throne, he was *strong.*

It was strange, to think he was the same age as Thalanir, or perhaps even younger, yet he felt so...different. Maybe it was because he had married and had a child.

Thalanir, on the other hand, had spent his life denying himself the pleasure of love—of happiness. He had forced lone-liness upon himself, and it seemed to have preserved him and forced him to remain as he had been so long ago—inhabiting the body of one who frozen in time.

Rynfael let me go and moved back to Lyrinn, hugging her tight before stepping back.

"My granddaughters could not have found themselves worthier mates," he said to Mithraan, then stepped over to Thalanir and cupped a hand onto his shoulder. "Thank you, my friend," he said, his former coldness entirely gone now. "For saving my life so long ago. For granting the world the gift of these two."

Thalanir nodded wordlessly, and the look that passed between them was so deep and meaningful that I found it hard to hold back my tears.

"Lyrinn, Leta," Rynfael said. "We have a task ahead of us—but it will need to wait until morning. For now, you all must rest for the battle ahead. My guards will show you to your quarters. They'll bring you all the food and drink you could wish for, and tomorrow, when our task is complete, I will lead my army south to Fairholme."

"Your Grace," Thalanir said. "Lead? You mean—"

Rynfael nodded. "I have gathered a force of Tírians, and I will be accompanying them into battle."

"What?" Mithraan interjected. "No, your Grace, you can't—"

Once again, Rynfael held up a hand to stop him from speak-ing, and this time, he chuckled. "Lord Mithraan, I have been imprisoned in my home for a thousand years," he said, exhaling a huffing breath. "All I have wanted is to do battle one last time.

Please, don't try to dissuade me. You have your fate, and I have mine."

Mithraan nodded once, shooting a sideways glance at Thalanir, who shrugged as if to say, "Who are we to stop him?"

"And you," Rynfael said, stepping over to where Lark was hovering next to Mithraan. "I see you have brought your sword."

"I have—and I will gladly use it to protect this realm."

"I know you will, my friend. And I thank you for it."

Backing away and clapping his hands together once, Rynfael called, "Guards, take them to their rooms. And Grand-daughters…"

Lyrinn and I stood at attention.

"I have business to attend to and an army to muster. But I will see the two of you first thing in the morning, down in the smithy. Bring the hilt—and the pendants. It's time to forge the Blade of Dracrigh at long last."

CHAPTER FORTY-FIVE

THE MOMENT our bedchamber's lock clicked into place, I threw myself into Thalanir's arms, my lips crashing into his.

The High King had not explicitly stated that we were to stay in the same room. But his servant had escorted us here together —and for that, I was grateful.

It had been far too long since we'd made love.

So much had happened since that first night together. So much pain and emotional turmoil for us both, and I was desperate to renew our bond, to start again.

Thalanir picked me up, a feral rumble rising in his throat, and carried me over to a nearby table of thick, dark wood. Next to it, he set me down and spun me around, turning my back toward him.

"Bend over for me, and spread your legs," he commanded, an erotic dominance in his voice.

I obeyed, leaning over the table, my fingers curling over its surface, nails digging at the varnish.

Tearing my skirt upward, Thalanir fell to his knees behind me, burying his face between my legs, his mouth frenzied as it met my flesh. I couldn't help myself—I let out a cry of delighted surprise as his tongue worked me in hungry brushstrokes, my core shamelessly throbbing for more.

Instead of taking his time and lingering there, he let out a famished roar, leapt to his feet and with one hard thrust, sheathed himself inside me. His hands reached around, tearing the blouse from my chest. He cupped my breasts, my nipples hardening to meet his coarse fingers, my hands reaching helplessly for the far end of the table. My legs spread still farther apart, my body begging for him to take me fast—hard.

"Gods, I have craved this," he breathed against the back of my neck. "Dreamed of it—of feeling myself deep inside you one more time."

He drove himself into me in hard, punishing thrusts, his thickness splitting me open all over again, and my eyes rimmed with tears at how good it felt—how *complete* I felt.

"Does it please you, my Lady?" he snarled, and his animalistic tone only drove me closer to madness.

"Like nothing else," I murmured. "It's the greatest feeling in the world."

He pulled out, his swollen head teasing my opening, and, his hands moving to my hips, said, "Tell me more."

"You're going to make me beg for it?" I asked over my shoulder, laughing.

"Tell me how much you want it. I want to hear your words."

My cheeks heated with a mixture of embarrassment and desire, but after struggling for a moment to gather myself, I managed to say, "I want it more than...*anything*."

Not exactly poetry—and definitely not the most erotic language in the history of dirty talk.

"Try again," he replied, pressing himself in an inch or so— just enough to make me moan—then tormenting me by withdrawing. "Tell me more. Tell me how it feels for you. I want to hear it from those rose-colored, perfect lips of yours. The lips that suck my cock so expertly."

"You..." I breathed, distracted by the image he'd just conjured in my mind. "You make me so wet, Thalanir. So...so tight that I ache—I *throb*...for you to be deep inside me—so that I can feel all of you and...and..." I smiled, confidence taking me at last. My voice steadied when I said, "I crave the moment when my body milks you dry. The instant when you explode inside me, and you are fully mine."

At that, Thalanir let out an approving moan, his fingers digging into my flesh. "Gods. I didn't expect *that.*"

He thrust deep again, and this time, I cried out then clapped a hand over my mouth to stifle the sound.

"More," he said, drawing out again. "Tell me more."

I pulled free of his grip and turned around, squatting down before him wrapping both hands around his substantial shaft. He stared down at me, smiling, his eyes flaring bright, and when I took him in my mouth, he let out a groan so loud and deep that it shook the table behind me.

"I love," I said, stroking my tongue over him, "how you feel in my mouth. How your cock pulses with pleasure when you're close—how you throb against my tongue, my lips. I love the taste of you. I love drinking you down when you finally..."

"Lahnan," he chastised. "You're going to make me come if you keep it up. Then again, I *did* ask for it."

I stood up again, turned around and pressed my bare breasts to the table, parting my legs. "Show me," I commanded.

This time, when he sheathed himself, it was slow—careful. He drew himself out almost entirely, then broke me all over again with another thrust.

He reached an arm around me and flicked a finger over my most sensitive place, reveling in the feeling when I clenched

around him in response, tightening all the more with the pleasure of it.

He stroked me until I erupted with a cry of ecstasy, eyes
rolling back in my head. When he felt me convulse around his
length, he sped up his thrusts again, driving into me with
exquisite ferocity before finally unleashing inside me.

I collapsed onto the table, and he on top of me, hot liquid
dripping down my thighs.

"Nothing," he moaned, "in this world or any other...will
ever be as delicious as you, Leta Martel."

"Nor you...Thal."

He laughed against my back. "*Thal.* You've never called me
that."

"No," I chuckled against the hard wood. "But I like how it
feels in my mouth. Thal. *Thaaal*...It reminds me of the feel of
you on my lips, my tongue."

He rose up, turned me around, and fell to his knees once
again before me, his fingers finding my opening. "Say it again,"
he commanded.

"Thal," I repeated, and he slipped a finger inside me.

"Thal." Another.

I threw my head back as he devoured me again, his hand
working me slowly, carefully, and I knew now that he was
reading my body, my nerves, my emotions—waiting for me to
show him again how I reveled under his magnificent touch.

We were bound, he and I, by something that could never be
broken again. The truth—and forgiveness—had freed us both
at last.

When night had descended on the Dragon Court and Thalanir had fallen into a deep, peaceful sleep, I slipped out of bed and into a dressing gown that had been hanging on the wardrobe.

For a moment I watched Thalanir, outlined as he was in the moonlight, his chest rising and falling with an inner peace I'd never seen in him. When I'd satisfied myself that I shouldn't wake him, I left the bedroom, clicking the door quietly shut behind me, and headed down to find the palace gardens.

I had seen those same gardens in my last vision. I was about to take a peaceful walk through the very place where Gallia had died. But I wasn't seeking the location out to mourn, or to revisit the memory.

All I wanted now was to revel in the beauty of this place, this land, so different from the rest of Kalemnar.

There was power in the air, and magic. The flowers grew brighter, taller. The air tasted fresh on my tongue, almost sweet.

Were it not for the war nipping at the border, I told myself I could be very happy here.

"It's hard to believe this is our birthright."

Lyrinn's voice came from somewhere behind me, and I turned and smiled as she stepped closer, wrapping her arms around herself.

"I've known for some time who we were," she said, "but I finally feel at home. Still, I'll admit—I'm still getting used to being referred to as 'Highness.'"

I laughed. "I take it you couldn't sleep either?"

She shook her head and took in a deep breath. The night air was cold, but neither of us felt it like we would have in the days before we both Changed. It was almost like we were made for this land.

"Our grandfather is quite reserved, isn't he?" Lyrinn observed. "But kind. You know, I was always afraid to meet him.

Especially after my experience with Kazimir. I thought maybe all High Kings were assholes."

"I take it the two of them are quite different?" I asked with a chuckle.

"Very," she nodded, gesturing to me to sit down on a nearby stone bench. "Kazimir is like a wall of rage, and everyone—even his closest ally—is a potential enemy to him. I think his trust was broken all those years ago when he realized the truth about our mother. Then again, I don't think he was ever particularly kind-hearted."

Seating myself and looking up at the purple-black sky above, I replied, "I suppose he's been through things we can't imagine. Trust is fragile, and easily broken." With a sigh, I turned to my sister. "I didn't trust Thalanir enough. In so many ways, he always seemed—*felt*—too good to be true, and I kept telling myself he was nothing more than a dream. I think my mind was eager to make him into a nightmare just to prove myself right."

Lyrinn nodded. "I did the same with Mithraan, though I will admit that he never made himself out to be perfect, either. He was a royal pain in my ass, truth be told. It was like he was testing me—assessing me to see if I would love him in spite of his flaws. And sure enough, I did. I *do*."

"As for Grandfather," I said, "I suppose he's wary, too...after what happened with our mother. It must have broken his heart to have her leave him like that—desert him and never look back."

"Maybe it *was* our mother," Lyrinn said, her gaze distant. "Or perhaps he's wary for another reason entirely."

"What reason could that be?"

"Perhaps he knows what's coming when Corym's army reaches the top of the Onyx Rise." She shuddered. "Whatever the case, our fate is approaching, whether any of us likes it or not." Looking me in the eye, she asked, "What's the hilt that our grandfather mentioned?"

"The mysterious hilt." I snickered when I said, "The truth is...I don't know. Only that our grandfather crafted it long ago, and tomorrow, he intends to forge the blade. They say it will stop the war in its tracks, but I'm not so sure. Still, there's something you should know about it."

"Oh?"

"It was given to me by someone you know. Erildir. He acquired it after our mother's death."

The color seemed to seep out of Lyrinn's face then, her jaw clenching.

"Normally, I would tell you not to trust that snake," she said. "Erildir is not my favorite person, as you've probably gathered. But if our grandfather made it—if he wants to forge the blade—then it must serve some important purpose."

"You know, it's partly thanks to Erildir that I managed to escape the Sisterhood when they held me captive."

"The Sisterhood?" Lyrinn raised an eyebrow and said, "Some day, when all this is over, I'm going to sit you down and ask you to explain everything that's happened since the last time I saw you."

"I will. I promise."

We went silent a moment, quiet fear working its way through both of us.

"I used to dream of being a princess," I finally said, lightness forced into my voice. "Do you remember when we were little girls, how I used to make crowns out of twigs? I was so certain I would marry a handsome prince one day. And then..."

"Then, when you had the chance to do exactly that, you ran away as fast as your legs would carry you," Lyrinn laughed. "As did I."

"To think how I worshiped Corym from afar all those years,

staring longingly at his portrait in Dúnbar. What a little fool I was."

Lyrinn reached over and took my hand. "Not a fool. A dreamer. There's a fine line between the two...but it's a line nonetheless."

With my eyes fixed on the stars, I asked, "Do you think we'll survive all this? Do you think we can really end the war quickly?"

Lyrinn contemplated the question for a moment, then said, "Corym pretends to be a deep thinker and a great warrior. But he's not. He's impulsive and foolish. He's moved too quickly, amassing his army and coming north like a raging storm before he's so much as trained them. Most of the mortals in his charge don't know how to fight, let alone take on Fae—and for them, it's a suicide mission."

"He's using untrained fighters?" I asked. "But I thought—"

"No doubt he told you in Domignon that he had a massive army, trained and ready. But he lied." Rage filled her when she continued, "His sole intention is to destroy Tíria, not to win a war with any real strategy. He hopes simply to tear us apart, starting with Fairholme. Mithraan and I insulted him gravely by falling in love—as did you and Thalanir. His pride is injured, and he's risking the lives of thousands of mortals and many Fae to avenge himself." She squeezed my hand when she added, "You and I must be wary, Leta. He will have his sights set on us both—and there's no telling what he'll do to punish us."

I nodded. "Sometimes I wish Thalanir had killed him when he had the chance, days ago now. But the fact that he didn't proves his goodness. Most people would have taken full advantage of a situation like that one. Thal didn't want to cause a permanent rift between mortals and Fae, and assassinating Corym would have been a guarantee of it. He understood the consequences. Corym doesn't."

"I've heard the prince is doing a fine job of precipitating the rift himself, anyhow," Lyrinn sighed.

"What do you mean by that?"

She winced, then said, "Word has it many of the fires set around Kalemnar—villages and towns being burned, people slaughtered in their beds—were orchestrated by the Crimson Cloaks."

"I thought the Crimson Cloaks were rebel militias—independent of Corym and the king. I thought—"

"Nope." Lyrinn shook her head. "We're meant to think so. But the Cloaks are part of Corym's command. They've been sent out to every corner of Kalemnar to sow chaos and create conflict —to feed into a fear of Fae and a loyalty to the prince. Which, ironically enough, means he has more Fae on his side than we thought. Powerful ones. Fairholme will not be an easy fight, whatever our grandfather might plan to unleash."

Genuine fear raced through my blood then, and in response, my sister wrapped her arms around me, her cheek resting for a moment on my head.

"Together," she said, "we can do anything. Remember that. We will not let the bastards win." She let me go and pulled herself to her feet. "Now, come on—let's get some sleep. Dawn will be here sooner than we imagine, and we have a blade to forge."

CHAPTER FORTY-SIX

WHEN DAWN CAME, Lyrinn and I met by the palace's large smithy.

It was an extraordinary space designed for crafting everything from steel arrows to broadswords and axes, and its scent brought back memories of our father—of his forge, his leather apron, his worn-down tools.

As we stood in the broad doorway, Lyrinn put an arm around me, holding me close—something she would never have considered in our earlier years. My sister had never been one for affection. But I couldn't deny how much I appreciated it now.

"Do you feel it?" she asked.

I knew just what she was talking about. A force in the air, a tension—a sensation that the war was drawing nearer with each passing moment.

I nodded. "They're close to Tíria now," I said. "Closer than we'd imagined."

"The Fae among their numbers are driving their forces," Lyrinn said. "Moving them with unnatural swiftness. We have to get back to Fairholme before all hell breaks loose. I fear last night was the last time we'll sleep here before the battle."

"I suspect you're right," I replied, and the thought of it instilled a fear in me like none I'd ever felt.

I had just begun my life with Thalanir, one that should have been devoid of weight and worry. The last thing I wanted was to have our time together cut short for the sake of fighting off Corym's ego-driven army.

The prince's relentless need to prove himself most powerful in the land was going to disrupt the lives of every man, woman, and child in Kalemnar.

"What do you suppose the Blade of Dracrigh will do?" I asked Lyrinn. It was probably a stupid question. It was a dagger, after all, much like the one Thalanir had used to kill Gallia.

"What all blades do," Lyrinn said, raising her shoulders. "It will cut."

"It will do far more than cut," a low voice added, and we turned to see High King Rynfael making his way toward the smithy's entrance from the grounds beyond. He moved easily, his gait smooth like Thalanir's, though there was a slight hunch to his shoulders that betrayed his age a little.

Our grandfather exuded power and grace, and watching him now, I understood how he had once been an extraordinary force in the world.

It was his daughter's betrayal, I thought, that had cast that weight upon his shoulders. Fleeing to Aetherion with Kazimir as she had, and taking a piece of Rynfael's soul with her.

"What do you mean, far more?" Lyrinn asked him, eyeing the hilt I was holding in my hand.

"The Blade of Dracrigh is intended for many purposes," Rynfael replied. "One of which is to open doors that have long been sealed. You will open one today, beyond which lies the true weapon you will wield…" I expected him to aim the words at Lyrinn, but instead, he turned my way. *"Leta."*

"*Another* weapon?" I frowned. "Is everyone forgetting I'm untrained? Shouldn't Lyrinn be the one..."

Rynfael shot me a look that told me to stop talking before I said something foolish. "You know a good deal about your predecessor—the one who possessed your Essence long ago."

I nodded. "Gallia."

"She wished to take control of our dragons in those days—and she failed, thanks to your noble mate's actions."

My cheeks flushed and I mustered the merest smile. I wasn't sure what Gallia's failure had to do with any of this. Nor was I certain I liked her name being conjured. All I wanted now was to forget her—to forget what had haunted Thalanir's mind for so long.

"Did you ever see her wings?" Rynfael asked.

"Wings?" I replied with a raise of my brows. "I didn't think she had wings."

"That's because she didn't. But you will." The High King nodded once and said, "Take off your pendants, both of you."

Lyrinn and I each slipped the dragon pendants over our heads and handed them over, and Rynfael pulled them off their chains then stepped over to a nearby anvil.

"You saw your father forging steel in your younger days, did you not?" he asked.

"We did," Lyrinn replied. "Many times."

"My methods are a little different from mortal ones," Rynfael admitted, clasping the two pendants tight in his fist. "I avoid using a forge when I can. I'm not one for sweating profusely."

When he opened his hand, the jewelry had melted into liquid silver, his palm glowing orange just as my flesh did when rage overtook me.

Startled, I looked into his eyes to see if the same anger dwelled there, but he looked perfectly calm. Kingly. Noble.

"Learn to control the rage that sometimes eats at your mind, Leta, and you'll find that anything is possible," he said with a wink. With that, he stepped over to a glowing iron mould in the shape of a needle-sharp blade, which was filled with molten metal, and let the silver drip in slowly.

"The pendants are spell-crafted from Fae Silver," he told us, watching the two metals combine, swirling together as one. "And they're now melding with Elven Steel. Of course, it's the *hilt* that gives the blade its true power." Turning our way, he added, "Now, I need one hair from each of your heads."

Lyrinn and I weren't about to protest, so we did as he asked, handing him a silver and a red hair, which he laid in the mould with the newly blended metal.

"Now to cool it," our Grandfather said.

Passing a hand over the mould, Rynfael summoned the newly forged weapon, which rose in the air to hover before him. He flicked his fingers toward a nearby anvil, where he took hold of a mallet and, grabbing the floating blade from the air, he quickly shaped it into the sharpest dagger I had ever seen, its tip impossibly fine.

When the blade's red glow faded, it gleamed the purest silver.

I let out a gasp of awe. Lyrinn and I were staring at a creation the likes of which our father could scarcely have imagined.

"The hilt," the High King said, and, pulling it from the place where it was tucked into my leather belt, I handed the ornate piece to him.

With little effort, he slipped the two pieces together, murmuring a few words in an ancient tongue as he did so.

"The blade knows only one owner," he said, handing the dagger to me. "Try it out."

"Try it?" My eyes went wide with nervousness. "On what?"

Rynfael nodded toward the nearby anvil. It was impossibly thick and incredibly dense, and I looked at my grandfather as though he'd lost his mind. "You'll find the weapon slices quite easily," he insisted.

I stepped over to the anvil, sliding the blade downward, my mind filled with skepticism. But the second the silver metal met the hard block of iron, it slipped through as easily as a sword through half-melted butter. The anvil split in two, its sections falling with a terrifying thud to the ground.

"Gods," I said as I leapt backwards. "I heard the blade could cut portals to other realms—but I wasn't sure I should believe it."

"You should indeed," the High King replied. "But before we start opening new worlds, you have another task." He stepped over to a nearby table and grabbed an ornate leather sheath, handing it to me.

"This will protect you and the blade both," he said as I unbuckled my belt and carefully slipped the sheath on, tucking the blade safely inside.

"Now," Rynfael added, "take my hands, both of you. We have one more task ahead of us before I lead my army to Fairholme. The blade is now our greatest weapon—and you'll soon see why."

"We cannot defeat an entire army with one blade," I protested.

"Perhaps it's time you found out its true purpose, then."

Lyrinn and I exchanged a dubious look as we took his hands. I couldn't conceive of what our grandfather had planned for us, but excitement crept through me to imagine the possibilities. Whatever it was, however dangerous, Rynfael seemed to have faith in me. He was so confident, so certain this was my fate, that I couldn't help but assume a *little* of his confidence.

For a moment, I felt like a little girl again from the days

when I had so often held onto my father's hand as he guided me into some unknown. Along dark forest paths or across raging creeks, he had always made me feel safe, protected.

Rynfael had that same quality—the ability to make everyone around him feel simultaneously invincible and dependent on him.

"Are you ready?" our grandfather asked, squeezing our hands reassuringly.

With one more look, Lyrinn and I answered in unison. "Ready."

"Close your eyes, then. Off we go."

CHAPTER FORTY-SEVEN

I wasn't sure what Rynfael was about to do to us.

But even with every possible scenario spinning wildly through my mind, this was probably the last one I could have imagined.

Power surged through me as Rynfael held onto my hand— and then, I was falling. Wind swept at my hair, my skin. The air, which had felt warm in the smithy, was frigid now, and I shivered as it bit at my flesh.

"We've arrived," the High King said, and I cracked my eyes open only to see that we were standing...on a mountain.

No. Not simply *on* a mountain. We were near its peak, facing a wall of black stone, the summit a short distance above us.

Turning around, I could see the Dragon Court in the valley far below, all of Tíria stretching off to the south.

Around us, snow fell in large flakes that tumbled lazily to earth.

I pivoted to face the cliff wall, then glanced over at Lyrinn, who wore the same expression as I did.

Why are we here?

"I have waited many years to find my family," the High King

said, letting our hands go. "And though our time together may be brief, I need to tell you both that I am proud of who you have both become."

His emotion was palpable on the air—grief blended with the greatest joy, and I felt it, too. After all these years, we had a grandfather—and he was a good man. A good *Fae*.

"Why do I get the impression something momentous is about to occur?" Lyrinn asked, her tone guarded. "Why have you brought us here?"

"Do you feel it?" Rynfael asked, raising a hand. "What lies beyond the onyx wall?"

Lyrinn nodded, sudden fear in her eyes.

For a moment, I was confused. What was she feeling? What didn't I know?

And then, it came to me.

A presence—one so powerful that I trembled to sense its proximity.

Something was alive inside the mountain. Something huge and strong...and above all, hostile.

"What are we doing here, Grandfather?" I asked, and once again, I felt like a vulnerable little girl, too frightened to move for fear that something terrible might occur.

"The greatest weapon in all the realms lies beyond this wall of stone," Rynfael replied gently. "One the likes of which has not been wielded in thousands of years. It is to you, Leta, to open the door and release it."

"Door?" I asked. "But there *is* no door."

Rynfael shot me a look, his eyes flaring.

Instantly, I understood. "You want me to slice into the mountain."

"There are two possible outcomes to Prince Corym's attack on Fairholme. He wins and burns Tíria to the ground, after all

our efforts to rebuild. Or we end his onslaught quickly, deci-
sively. Today."

Today.

I had thought we would have a couple of days in the Dragon
Court. Time to rest, to gather our thoughts. Time spent with my
mate.

"But—" I breathed.

"Leta," Rynfael said. "You are a Násuire—one whose
Essence has passed through many lives, and has now been
gifted to you. Many of those who came before you were flawed.
Some were too weak to bear the power that comes with such an
Essence as yours. But like your sister, *you* are strong. Your blood
is both Lightblood and Tírian from the lines of two High Kings.
Every moment you spent in the wilderness making your way
toward home, was leading you to this end. Your destiny lies
beyond this wall, Granddaughter. Now, it is time for you to go
and meet it."

Seeing the look of panic in my eyes, Lyrinn stepped over and
took my face in her hands. "I'm with you," she whispered. "I
won't leave your side, no matter what."

I nodded once, strengthened by that promise, then
extracted the blade from its sheath.

Grasping it in my shaking hand, I held it up to the onyx
wall, hesitating for only a second before leaning down, slicing
upward, then across, and down again.

The black stone that I had cut into flashed white and then
vanished, opening a doorway large enough for all three of us to
walk through.

Without a word, we stepped into the mountainside.

I expected to encounter pure darkness. A tunnel of black,
perhaps, leading into the mountain's depths. But instead, we
found ourselves in a large, rounded cavern, two points of yellow
light coming at us from somewhere in the depths.

I slipped forward, fearful but curious to see what it was that had called me to this place. What force lay in this mountain—why was I here?

When my eyes adjusted and I could finally make out the silver silhouette against gleaming black stone, I gasped, nearly dropping the blade.

"A...dragon," Lyrinn breathed from beside me. "My gods, it's a real, living dragon."

The two points of light I'd seen were two flaring nostrils, flaming quietly as the dragon lifted its enormous muzzle to sniff at the air. Its large eyes were focused on the three of us, cold and hostile, and it pushed itself upwards, filling the cavern with its massive body, wings pressed to its sides.

Rynfael flicked a hand in the air and the space around us illuminated so that for the first time, I saw the beast clearly.

He was beautiful, his scales a silver as polished as the Blade of Dracrigh—though as my eyes ran down his form, I could see that one large scale on his belly appeared tarnished as if the flesh had died, the dragon's natural armor damaged.

"His name is Kelduin," the High King said. "He is the last of the dragons of our realm. The others were freed after the incident with your predecessor, Leta—to prevent anyone else from trying to claim them. But Kelduin chose to stay in this den, where he's been resting quietly for many years."

"Why?" I asked, sensing pain in the creature. "Why would he choose this darkness over freedom?"

"Dragons thrive in darkness—they often choose to live underground, where it's safe. As for why he didn't choose freedom, he suffers from an old injury, as you can see. A Summoner hurled a spell at him years ago—one imbued with Dark Magic. It managed to poison the flesh between his scales, and the damaged armor that you see was the result."

"Can't someone heal him?"

"Not without removing the scale, unfortunately," Rynfael said with a sad shake of his head. "And there is only one weapon in this world powerful enough to slice clean through dragon scale." He raised his eyebrows, nodding toward the Blade of Dracrigh.

"He has food here in the mountain," Rynfael added, "though truth be told, he has spent most of his years in hibernation. It's time to free him and unleash his might. And that task falls to you, Leta. The blade was forged for this very moment—a moment I saw in my mind's eye many centuries ago."

Feeling the exquisite silver and gold hilt in my hand, I took a step toward the great beast, who raised his head warily, his nostrils flaring with threatening puffs of orange flame.

"I don't understand," I said, turning back to Rynfael. "What exactly am I supposed to do with the dagger?"

Rynfael smiled slightly. "Ask him."

I looked at Lyrinn, who appeared as baffled as I felt.

When I turned back toward the dragon, his eyes flared with a terrifying threat.

"Grandfather—you can't be serious," Lyrinn said. "He'll kill her."

As if to prove her point, Kelduin shot out a burst of searing flame, which hit the ground at my feet and flared brightly before fizzling away.

A warning shot.

Lyrinn stepped forward and reached for my arm. "Leta—come away from him. This is folly. There *has* to be another way. We'll fly to Fairholme and fight without the dragon. Perhaps there will be enough of us to win."

"Wait," I said softly, holding up a hand and taking a step toward Kelduin.

The dragon let out a moan that sounded not like a warning, but a plea. I thought of what Thalanir had done not so long ago, when he had instantly tamed the gelding named Surly into letting us ride him with no bit or saddle.

Thalanir had felt the horse's need, his emotions, his thoughts, even. He had connected to him in a way that only a Valdfae could.

"Gallia was a Valdfae," I murmured, digging into my memories, seeking guidance. "She must have had some sort of connection to nature—to animals. And we share an Essence, so maybe..."

"Leta..." Lyrinn said again, but I shook my head.

"It's all right," I said. "Just give me a moment. Please."

I closed my eyes and reached a hand out toward Kelduin, my voice gentle when I said, "Tell me. How do I help you?"

A throb set itself in my left hand, and I opened my eyes and looked down to see the dragon mark flaring red-orange. In an instant, I understood his need—and I understood why no one else had been able to help him.

I stepped forward, my hand still outstretched.

"I won't hurt you," I told Kelduin. "You know I won't."

Flames erupted from his nostrils, his eyes flashing bright again. His enormous pupils narrowed as he focused on my face, my mind. But still, I advanced, my free hand in front of me, the blade clasped in the other hand.

I didn't breathe, didn't make a sound as I approached...and didn't stop until I had laid a hand on his chest to feel one of the glinting silver scales. It was cold under my touch, and smooth, and as I pressed my palm into him, I could feel Kelduin's pain. A throb, deep in his body—one that had hindered him for many long years.

I moved my hand slowly until it landed on the tarnished scale of green, which raged hot under my palm.

"This is it," I said. "This is what's hurting you."

Kelduin groaned under my touch, but still did nothing to stop me.

I grasped the blade in my right hand and, without hesitation, sliced around the infected scale, then pulled it away from the dragon's body. It was as large as a shield, and as heavy, and it dropped to the ground with a clatter.

In its place on his belly, the flesh was red and angry, and I held my hand up, drawing light from the cavern.

A ball of bright white erupted between my palm and the dragon's wound, spinning in the air between us. I watched as his flesh lightened, healing slowly under the spell.

After a time, he raised his head and let out a cry not of threat this time, but of triumph.

When I was confident that he was healed, I slipped over to his head and stroked his cheek. "That feels better," I said, "doesn't it?"

"How did you know what to do?" Lyrinn asked, stunned. "How the hell did you get a dragon to let you cut away at his flesh?"

"He told me about the poison the Fae had inflicted on his bloodstream," I said. "There was a chronic throb in his nerve, like a toothache—which shot into his wing whenever he tried to lift it. It's no wonder he never wished to leave. He was imprisoned here because he couldn't fly."

"Well done, Granddaughter," Rynfael said. "It seems you understand the blade, after all your protests."

At that, I smiled, then sheathed the dagger at my side. "I still think it's mad to hand me a weapon in the first place."

"Yet you have done what no one else could for hundreds of years. And now, you have at your disposal a creature who will do anything to thank you."

In that moment, I finally understood it. The power that Gallia had tried in vain to wield—the Gift bestowed to her by her Essence. It was not a spell or a weapon, exactly. It was a deep connection to creatures of flame. The dragons she had wished to use to conquer a kingdom.

I felt that same desire for power now as it coursed violently through my veins. I wanted—needed—to connect to Kelduin. To become one with his mind.

But I didn't want to use him to fight my enemies. I didn't want to rage and conquer.

All I wanted was to *stop* a war.

The dragon raised his head, and silently, I asked him, *Can you fly now? Are you willing to do battle with us?*

As if in response, he pushed himself up onto his feet and began to walk, then to run, toward the door I had carved in the mountainside.

"It's not big enough!" I cried out, but with a flick of Rynfael's hand, the doorway expanded. The dragon shot through, leaping into the sky, his wings spreading wide.

Lyrinn stared after him in wonder. "When we were girls back in Dúnbar," she said, "did you ever imagine we'd see anything like this?"

"No," I replied. "Then again, I never thought we'd turn out to be Fae. I figured I'd marry a semi-wealthy man, live in his large house, and eat all his bonbons on a daily basis."

"I figured I'd live in a cabin in the woods with many books and a raccoon for a companion," Lyrinn laughed. "Fate is a strange creature."

"Indeed it is."

Our grandfather led us outside, where the dragon was soaring in happy circles in the air, his mind still connected to my own.

"Won't he fly off?" Lyrinn asked.

I shook my head. "He has offered to help us," I replied. "I've already promised him that when his job is done, I'll free him to find his own kind."

"And once he's gone, the Dragon Court will no longer be," Rynfael added with a sigh. "One day soon, it will require a new name."

"Not just yet," I said. "Not until Corym is stopped, and Kelduin is free."

With a wistful smile, our grandfather said, "When he's free, then. Let's hope it happens sooner rather than later. Now—it's time we went back. We have a battle to fight."

CHAPTER FORTY-EIGHT

TAKING hold of our hands once again, High King Rynfael brought Lyrinn and me back to the palace.

This time, we traveled to the dining hall, where we found Mithraan and Thalanir standing by a large window, watching Kelduin soar through the skies.

Thalanir turned to me, a worried look in his eyes.

"This is what the blade was for?" Mithraan asked coldly, eyeing the hilt at my side. "To release a creature of fire powerful enough to destroy entire cities?"

"It is one of its purposes," Rynfael retorted, a calming note in his tone as he turned to address Thalanir. "Valdfae, you have seen a peaceful future. Do you suppose such peace will be possible without a little help along the way?"

"Help," he replied, "or risk? It seems to me like a fine line. I have seen a possible future for Leta and me—but truth be told, I'd hoped we would not rely on a dragon to get us there."

"It's all right," I told him, stepping forward to take his hand in mine. "I...I think I understand now. I know who I am—what I'm meant to do. I even understand a little why I have no wings." I shot a look at the dragon, still soaring in spiraling rings above the palace. In a courtyard far below, scores of Fae soldiers stood around watching him in wonder, pointing and gesturing as if they, too, knew just how important this moment was. "I'm no warrior," I said. "I don't fight with swords or bows. But Kelduin is my weapon...and *those* are my wings."

"Leta," Thalanir said, a plea in his voice. "He could take your mind from you—his power could eat away at you in ways you can't even imagine. I've seen it before—seen what that sort of force can do to even the strongest Fae. Please—reconsider this madness. He's a wild beast."

"A wild beast my sister saved from years of torment," Lyrinn replied, moving toward him. "She felt his need—his pain. She understood him as no one else ever has. Our grandfather is right—if you have seen a bright future for you both, then you must know this was meant to be."

"My friend," the High King said, taking a few steps toward Thalanir and clapping a hand onto his shoulder. "You saved my life long ago. I owe you everything. I promise you, I would not lead Leta astray. She was born for this—and she deserves it. Let her show you her strength. Let her prove to the world, and to herself, who and what she really is."

Those words seemed enough to appease Thalanir, whose tense form relaxed at last.

"It seems I'm outvoted," he said, mustering a crooked smirk. "Who am I to go against the wishes of a High King, Lyrinn Martel, and my true mate, all at once?"

My true mate.

Hearing those words spoken aloud filled me with sparking embers, heating my every inch and strengthening my resolve.

"I won't let Kelduin take my mind," I promised. "He and I have a bond—a way of communicating silently. If he pushes me too far, I'll bring him back. I promise you that."

More than once in recent memory, I'd been overcome by the

desire to burn the world around me—to kill those who had wronged me. But if I wanted a future with Thalanir—one of happiness and light—I had no choice but to keep the dragon at bay.

Thalanir kissed my forehead. "You have a way with wild things. Perhaps we'll make a Valdfae of you yet, Lahnan."

"Except for the sell-blade bit," I laughed. "I could never do what you do. I'm not sure I have the constitution for it."

I thought then of the Fae and mortal guards I killed in Tarroc...how I had sliced them open like it was nothing.

Perhaps I was more cold-blooded than I knew.

I shook off the thought. "What news of the mortal army?"

"It's not good," Mithraan said, looking to the High King. "They're approaching Dúnbar—moving on the wind, thanks to a spell. They will reach Fairholme within a matter of hours."

"Then we must leave," the High King said. "Leta, Lyrinn... you must ready yourselves."

"But I..." I began, looking down at my clothing. I was wearing a pair of leather trousers, an off-white linen shirt and leather boots, and Lyrinn was dressed similarly.

Hardly the gear one wore when charging into battle.

"Go to your chambers, my Granddaughters," Rynfael said. "There, you'll each find some light armor awaiting you. It won't protect you from spells, but it will help against mortal blades and arrows."

"Thank you, Grandfather." I stepped forward, taking his hand and kissing his cheek.

"You will all do me proud today," he replied with a smile. "I know it."

"We'll try."

"Come, Leta," Thalanir said. "Let's get you ready to thwart a war."

It didn't take long to get back to our bedchamber and find the tunic of mail that my grandfather had sent for me.

"Do you suppose I'll need it?" I asked, picking it up and inspecting the fine, twisting strands of silver.

"That depends," Thalanir replied. "Are you intending to ride the dragon, or fight on the ground?"

"I'll ride."

He looked worried by the revelation, though not entirely surprised.

"Thal," I said, grabbing his hands, pulling myself close to him, and kissing his rough chin, "I will be safer on Kelduin's back than anywhere imaginable. I have seen his mind. He is willing to fight for me. For *us*. I told you—his wings are my own, at least for now."

"You're certain about this."

I nodded. "You don't need to worry about me. I won't let the power go to my head. We'll fight, and gods willing, we'll win. And then, I will free him forever...and you and I will go on with our lives."

"If we live to see tomorrow's dawn."

I peered into his eyes and saw the fire dancing there— flames of worry, of anger that after all we'd been through, our lives could end today.

"What does your mind tell you? And your heart?" I asked. "What future do you see for us now?"

He closed his eyes, a reluctant smile slipping over his lips. "A beautiful one," he admitted.

"Then trust in it. The Blade of Dracrigh was never intended as a weapon of war, but a tool meant to *shorten* the war—to reduce the casualties and end the conflict quickly. I used it to free Kelduin, and in the moment when I did it, I began to understand the power I was given when Erildir handed me that hilt."

"Then who am I to cast doubt?" Thalanir asked, kissing me deeply before stepping back. "Fine, I'll stop worrying. Put on your mail, Lahnan. Let me see you in all your glory."

Dropping my belt and sheath onto the bed, I picked up the glinting silver tunic. I pulled the tunic over my head, then strapped the belt back on.

"You see?" I said, twirling around. "I'm totally safe."

"You've become quite the optimist," Thalanir chuckled, kissing me again before taking my hand and stroking his thumb over the dragon marking. "Let me say just one more thing, and then I promise I'll stop. A small warning, that's all."

"What warning would that be?"

His face went stern, serious—that of the Valdfae I knew and loved. "A dragon is not a fighter, Leta. Not a warrior. A dragon is a war *ender*. An apocalypse with wings. Take care when you're on his back—those who cause catastrophes are seldom loved by their people."

"Then I will be careful, my love," I said, pulling him close to kiss him. "There will be no apocalypse today."

Not if I can help it.

We gathered outside the Dragon Court's main gates, on the road leading south toward Fairholme. Rynfael stood at the head of his small but impressive army of Fae as they moved into formation, and Lark joined us, dressed in full battle armor.

"You look very handsome," I told him.

"I don't care about my appearance," he replied with a sneer.

"I'm just planning to stay away from that dragon of yours. I have a fear of creatures whose nostrils are larger than my entire body."

I glanced up into the sky to see Kelduin banking this way and that, flying in joyous figure eights. "He's not so bad. But I *would* advise you not to piss him off."

Lark let out a grunt and took off toward Mithraan and Lyrinn.

"Fae of the Dragon Court!" Rynfael called out, and the assembled members of his military immediately sprang into disciplined rows of silver-clad fighters. "Listen, now. We will make haste down to Fairholme. Once we're on the move, I will cast a spell of swiftness, and those of you who cannot fly will nevertheless reach the southern tip of this realm within the hour. There, you will find the battle already raging. It is to you to drive back the mortal forces."

There were silent nods from the leaders, and then Rynfael added, "You should know that word has it the High King of mortals will not be in attendance for today's...festivities."

I glanced at Thalanir, who looked as surprised as I was.

"Caedmon is ill, and has returned to Domignon. It is unlikely he will survive to see the end of the day. Some say he's been poisoned."

The words were stunning. I wondered when my grandfather had learned the news, and why he hadn't divulged it sooner.

Who could have poisoned Caedmon?

Even as I considered the question, the answer that came to me was "Too many people to count." The king had enemies everywhere, mortal and Fae alike.

But if he died, Corym would become king.

The thought of it inspired a swell of nausea in my belly.

"Leta," Rynfael said, turning to me. "It's time."

I gave Thalanir one last look, nodded, and, focusing my eyes on the sky, called Kelduin to me.

The dragon shot down from the clouds and came in for a hard landing at the courtyard's far end, his wings folding to his sides. Smoke huffed from his nostrils as I made my way over, grateful when he pressed his head to the ground to let me climb on.

"Thank you, my friend," I told him. "Help me today, and I will keep my promise to you and set you free."

Kelduin let out a growl of consent, then, when I had taken hold of his spiky mane, he took off into the sky with a speed that elicited a joyful cry from my lips.

I looked down at the courtyard, where Mithraan's, Lyrinn's, and Thalanir's wings appeared like beacons set against dark stone. They too took off into the air, flying south behind us. Lark was perched on Lyrinn's shoulder, his stance that of a fighter ready to do battle for the good of the world.

High King Rynfael stayed on the ground with his Fae, and I watched as they began to move as fast as galloping horses along the long, broad road.

In an hour or less, we would reach our destination.

Whether Fairholme would still be standing when we arrived was another question entirely.

CHAPTER FORTY-NINE

EVEN FROM A GREAT DISTANCE, I could see what looked like smoke rising over the land near the Onyx Rise just south of Fairholme.

"What's happened?" I asked, leaning forward. "Is the castle burning?"

"Someone has summoned a rolling mist," Thalanir called out over the wind. "Dense fog, so the army can approach without being seen."

"If it's the Breath of the Fae," Lyrinn said, "the army won't get far."

"Unfortunately, no. It's merely a distraction." Thalanir pointed toward the castle, where I could see that the fog rolled up to just before its gates, then ceased. "A mere smokescreen."

"We must rid Fairholme of it," Mithraan called out. "We need to see our enemies if we're to defeat them. Thal, you know what to do."

Silently, I asked Kelduin to pause in mid-flight and he obeyed, his enormous wings beating slowly at the air. Lyrinn and Lark stayed close by, watching with their breath tight in their chests as Thalanir, almost at Fairholme now, cast his eyes down toward the fog, a hand outstretched.

Almost instantly, the mist began rolling backward, revealing a massive army of mortals and Fae standing just beyond Fairholme's gates. Some of the mortals had swords or spears in hand, others were readying their bows to loose a sea of arrows.

Even from a distance, I could see hands trembling in fear as the mortal soldiers stared up at the line of Fae lined up along the castle's parapet, their fierce eyes cast downward as they awaited orders from Mithraan, Lord of Fairholme.

The Fae among the enemies' numbers challenged our side with cold stares, their eyes bright and filled with malice. None of them was a High Fae, from what I could tell. Not a single pair of wings blessed any of their backs.

Still, I knew how dangerous they were.

Before Mithraan had a chance to issue a single order, a cry rang out from somewhere on the ground.

A simple, quick command.

"Fire!"

It was Corym's voice—the desperate cry of a desperate leader hoping to keep the advantage.

The long row of mortal archers unleashed a sea of flaming arrows toward Fairholme, which collided a moment later with the castle's thick stone walls.

The fire had been called up by Flame-Wielders, and they were cursed—so hot that the stone itself caught fire, burning as if it were little more than timber.

Fairholme's Fae scrambled to douse the flames before the castle's entire façade risked crashing to the ground.

A cry rang out from somewhere in the distance, and I turned to see that far below Lyrinn and me, Rynfael's army was moving south as one, gliding with extraordinary swiftness over the shallow hills just north of Fairholme.

It would only be a matter of minutes now before they collided with Corym's forces and a bloody battle erupted.

"Lyrinn!" I called out over the wind.

"I see them!" my sister cried back.

"Kelduin and I need to drive as many mortals back as we can, thin their numbers before the battle begins—or it's going to be a bloodbath."

Lyrinn nodded. "Do it!" she shouted. "I'll help Mithraan and the others." Turning to the sprite, she said, "Lark—come with me!"

Watching them go, I urged Kelduin to shoot down toward the mortal army, and he obeyed without hesitation. Only when I had flown fully over Fairholme did I see that Corym's front line was entirely made up of Fae dressed in crimson, marching fearlessly forward as the castle burned.

Whether they were blindly loyal or under the prince's influential mind-bending spell, I couldn't tell. But most of them kept their sights locked on the castle, ignoring the dragon above them entirely.

It was the humans among their number who stopped marching, pointing and staring fearfully at Kelduin. But after a few seconds, some force took hold of their minds again, forcing them forward.

Corym is bending them, I thought. There was no longer a question in my mind that he had taken hold of their minds.

But where the hell *was* he?

With furious cries, fighting erupted between Mithraan's forces and the front-line Fae. Spells shot back and forth between the castle wall and the Immortals, raging through the air in bolts of flame, lightning, ice, or any other projectile the casters could dream up.

I tried not to think of the danger Thalanir was in. It was up to me to end this. I had freed Kelduin from his mountain prison for one reason—and if I failed, Fairholme would fall. The war would drag on, and all of Kalemnar would suffer for it.

Kelduin, I called to the dragon's mind. *We need to drive as many of the mortals back to the Onyx Stair as we can. We need to inspire fear in them—enough to send them racing toward their homes and abandon the battle. Do you hear me?*

But the dragon didn't respond.

I felt a wall rising between us as Kelduin thrust my wants and needs away in favor of his own. The dragon hurtled through the air toward the mortal forces, determined and enraged.

Flames rose from his nostrils in plumes of red-orange as the dragon readied himself for an attack.

They are the enemy, his voice finally rumbled in my mind. *We should kill them, and rid the world of their ilk.*

"No!" I shouted. "We're not here to commit mass murder!"

They are evil-doers, his deep, gravelly voice echoed. *Intent on destroying our realm. There is no reason to let them live.*

I was about to cry out that they were only weak mortal soldiers taken over by the cruel, manipulative mind of a Gifted prince.

But as I opened my mouth to speak, my sight was overtaken by a familiar, blinding flash, and a vision came to me.

Not of the past this time, but of the near-future.

I saw a vast field of black, littered with the charred, inhuman remains of an entire army. A thousand bodies or more lay on the ground, burned beyond recognition. The scent of cooked meat permeated the air to the point where I tasted it on my tongue—and it was a horror.

You see? Kelduin's voice continued. *We can end them, you and I—we will stop mortal-kind in its tracks. And then, all of Kalemnar will be ours, Princess.*

Princess.

Against my wishes—against my very nature—my mind reeled with the fantasy. The very notion that I could take over the realms, Fae and mortal alike, from the back of this beautiful beast.

We could burn anyone who stood in our way—take down entire cities of dissenters.

I could...be Queen.

"Lahnan." From some distant place, Thalanir's voice came to me. "Remember who you are. Remember your strength."

I fought against the vision—against the ambition gripping my neck in a stranglehold. But the desire to conquer, to kill—they were almost too great to resist.

No.

I promised I wouldn't let malice take me over.

I am not breaking my word for anything. We will not hurt these mortals—not unless we must.

But still, I could feel the dragon below me struggling against my mind, surging toward the army, the fire and rage building inside him.

With a shaking hand, I reached for the dagger sheathed at my waist—the Blade of Dracrigh—and, drawing it, pressed it to Kelduin's neck. I knew how easily this blade could slice through his scale into his flesh...and I knew the consequences for us both if I did so.

Feeling the threat of steel against his scale, the dragon cried out and banked sharply right, pulling us away from the army and back toward the North.

"Kelduin," I said aloud, my voice trembling, "I do not wish to hurt you. I want to *free* you. But if you try again to consume my mind—if you try to draw me into an act of cruelty—I *will* kill you. I don't care if I die along with you—I will not allow cruelty to take control of me."

Why not? he asked, confusion flowing through his veins, his violent, feral instincts doing battle with reason. *Why would you choose death over eternal reign?*

"Because," I told him, "those men below us—they don't deserve death. They're being manipulated by someone malicious—someone who doesn't value their lives for one second. If they had a choice, they would be home in front of their hearths with their families, not here."

At that, I felt Kelduin's mind began to calm, almost as though he were able to process and understand what I'd said. The flames threatening to shoot from his muzzle calmed and faded, and he spoke to my mind once again.

Then I will do as you ask, Highness, he said. *I will drive the humans back to their homes. Because it is your wish.*

With my hand trembling ferociously now, I re-sheathed the blade. "Thank you," I said.

I had just asked a dragon to go against his nature, his most primal instincts...and he had obeyed. Were it not for the fact that I was so close to vomiting, I might have allowed myself a small moment of triumph.

We banked southward again and shot southward.

Much of Coryn's army was now clashing with Rynfael's, mortal and Fae alike locked in vicious combat. I could see my grandfather far below, doing battle alongside other High Fae. Colorful, deadly spells flew from his fingers, making quick work of his enemies.

But hundreds of terrified men still marched on Fairholme— and it was those men I intended to stop.

To save.

"Drive as many back as you can," I commanded to Kelduin. "But don't kill them!"

The dragon shot down toward a line of mortals who were not yet engaged in battle—young, blank-faced men who looked neither excited nor terrified. The dragon stopped them in their tracks, hurling bolt after bolt of flame at the earth at their feet. Fire rose up like a massive wall, keeping them from marching further toward Fairholme and death.

Watching them, I reached out with my mind, trying to sense the men's emotions.

But I felt...nothing.

It was as though they had been robbed of the capacity for fear, for joy—for any emotion whatsoever. They stared ahead at the wall of fire, all thoughts stripped from their souls.

Corym had them locked in a mindless state. They were nothing but fodder, served up to the Fae on a silver platter.

"Fly down lower," I said, and when Kelduin obeyed, I stared down at the men, willing them to look up at me.

Come on, I thought. *Break free of the foolish prince's mind.*

A set of eyes on a pale face moved up to stare at the dragon, his face slowly registering the wonder of the sight. He grabbed at the soldier next to him, thrusting a hand in the air to point up toward Kelduin.

"Mortals of Kalemnar!" I cried. "Return to your homes. Flee down the Onyx Stair, and don't look back. Tell any who are marching toward Tíria to do the same, and I promise—I will spare you."

And then another soldier looked up, and another, and like a spreading contagion, their minds drew away from Corym's influence and forced them into the reality they were now facing.

For a few seconds, the soldiers looked petrified with fear, their eyes locked on Kelduin's gleaming silver form as his enormous wings carved at the air.

One or two mortals looked like they might advance on Fairholme despite the wall of fire before them, obedient to their heartless master and still thoroughly caught up in his mind control.

But when Kelduin shot another warning ball of flame at

their feet, they cried out, dropped their weapons to the ground, turned, and fled for their lives.

Soon, the entire unit of soldiers was following suit, springing toward the Onyx Stair and Dúnbar beyond.

"Well done, my friend," I said, stroking my hand over the dragon's neck.

When I was satisfied that we'd saved as many human lives as we could, we turned back toward Fairholme, only to see newly lit flames rising from the castle, engulfing the entire south wing in a terrifying conflagration.

My breath caught as a projectile came hurtling toward us. It took me a moment to realize it was Thalanir, flying up to shout a warning.

"It's Corym!" he cried as a huge ball of flame shot through the air toward Fairholme in the distance. "He's siphoned powers from his Flame-Wielders. It seems he's not happy about your secret weapon here." With that, he nodded toward Kelduin.

I looked down, searching the ground below for the prince.

It didn't take long to see that he'd positioned himself on top of a large boulder just east of the castle. He was glaring up at us with a hatred on his features so vivid that I could read it like words on a page, even from this distance.

"Kelduin," I said, leaning forward. "I won't ask you to take mercy on that one. We need to stop him by any means necessary. Understand?"

Instantly, the dragon shot downward, hurling an angry ball of fire at the prince.

The moment he looked into the dragon's enraged eyes, Corym leapt off the boulder, cowering behind it like a frightened child.

I was about to issue the final command to take Corym down when something shot through the air from somewhere to our left, and Kelduin had to veer hard to the right in order to avoid it. As the projectile passed, I saw that it was a large, thick bolt, seemingly crafted of crystal.

It had unquestionably come from the hands and mind of a Fae.

"There's a Summoner below, Lahnan," Thalanir called out. "Watch your back—I'm going to try and stop her."

With that, he disappeared in search of the assailant.

I looked down to spot the Fae he was talking about—a red-haired female, dressed all in gray, her eyes glowing orange. She was motioning with her hands, eyes locked on Kelduin as she prepared herself for the next assault.

"Fly as high as you can!" I cried, and the dragon surged toward the clouds just as another bolt of summoned glass came at us, and another, and...

The blow that collided with Kelduin's belly felt as if it had struck my own body and I doubled over, my stomach twisting with agony.

The last projectile had found its mark.

The dragon shrieked as the summoned weapon lodged in his flesh, sinking into the one place on his body devoid of scale. It was the only truly vulnerable spot on him—and the Summoner had managed a direct hit.

"No..." I breathed as the dragon cried out in pain, his wings folding reflexively into his sides.

"Fly, Kelduin! Please...you *must* fly!"

I could feel his panic as he tried to stay airborne. He shot his wings out, fighting to soar away, to distance himself from the Summoner and vanquish the pain tearing at his mind. But the wound had hit a nerve, and taken away his ability to extend his right wing.

With an agonized cry, he began to tumble toward the earth.

His body spiraled, spinning helplessly through the air as we barreled downward as one. I held on for my life, my knuckles bone-white as they grasped frantically at the spikes on the dragon's neck.

But the protrusions were smooth as polished silver, and when a violent roll overtook Kelduin, I lost my grip, slipping from his neck.

I twisted and turned in the air, my hands reaching for something—*anything*.

But I was falling through space, and there was nothing around me but the sky...and nothing below me but Fairholme.

I was alone, and death was coming for me like a razor-sharp arrow shot squarely at my chest.

CHAPTER FIFTY

THE WORDS CIRCLED my mind over and over again.

I will not die like this.

I was a High Fae. Granddaughter of Rynfael. Daughter of Kazimir.

This is not my fate.

As those words came to me, I felt myself slowing, my mind taking control of gravity itself.

Somewhere far below, my grandfather's army was still doing battle for their lives. My sister, too, was fighting for the future of the realms, as were my mate and Mithraan—and Lark.

I refused to let them down by dying a ridiculous, needless death.

Sealing my eyes shut, I called on the elusive power I had never attempted to summon—the one power I had never felt worthy of.

Perhaps, after all, Kelduin's wings were *not* my own.

"I am a High Fae," I murmured. "I am a creature of flame and fury—and I will not die today. *Not. Like. This.*"

And then, as if a rope had twisted itself around my torso

and yanked me upwards, I shot toward the clouds, light as air and quick as wind.

I was flying.

I could see the wings that spread behind me, cutting through the air. They were not like Thalanir's or Lyrinn's, delicately forged of light and beauty. Instead, they were pure flame, streaking through the sky and leaving sparking embers in their wake. Streams of red-orange flickered in my periphery, painting the air with each stroke.

I truly was a creature of fire now, bound to the dragon—and because of him, I had found my wings.

Kelduin had spread his wings at the last moment before crashing hard to the ground far below me. But he was still alive, still whole, and I shot down to meet him as he pushed himself to his feet, shooting angry bolts of flame at any member of Corym's forces who dared come near.

Where Corym was, I couldn't say.

When my feet touched down, I leapt toward the dragon, wrapping my flame-wings around myself like a shield as I examined his wound. The glass arrow had already disintegrated, the Summoner's spell broken. It seemed Thalanir had gotten to her—and with any luck, she would not be casting any more spells.

But in the arrow's place was a large gash in the dragon's raw flesh—right at the center of his scar tissue.

Once again, I held my hands over his chest, asking the light to come to me, to heal him quickly. And once again, a ball of the purest white appeared between us. The wound sealed up, the flesh whole again.

I stepped over and laid a hand on his face.

"You've done what I asked of you," I told him. "Their numbers are thinned—and we can defeat them now. I know it."

Princess, I can still fight, he protested.

I shook my head. "They'll kill you if you remain here. Fly away. Find your family, as I've found mine. Be free at last."

With a groan and a shake of his enormous head, he spread his wings. But as he was about to take off, a shot of flame blasted from his nostrils toward someone behind me.

I spun around to see fire colliding with earth, which rose up in an angry explosion of stone and grit.

And then, I saw him.

Corym was standing twenty or so feet away from me, encircled by a slew of bodies from both sides of the battle. He held Lyrinn tight to his body, an arm around her chest, a blade at her throat.

She didn't look fearful—but something was keeping her from fighting him off.

Kelduin took off into the air, but instead of leaving he hovered over me, readying himself to fire at Corym again.

"Let her go," I snarled at the prince, unfurling my wings so they spread out behind me.

"I always knew you were a devil of some kind," he growled back at me, his eyes moving up to the dragon then back to mine. "You and this bitch of a sister of yours. Entitled creatures, both of you. You do realize you will lose this battle, don't you? You can't win, even with that monster of yours at your beck and call."

I glanced around. Both sides were fighting still, spells shooting through the air. In the distance, I saw Mithraan doing battle with a Crimson Cloak—a Fae with dark hair and bright eyes who was rapidly proving no match for the High Lord.

Thalanir and my grandfather were nowhere to be seen, but from the looks of it, our side was most certainly winning.

"You have few Fae left," I pointed out. "We have many. Your remaining mortal soldiers will all die if you insist on continuing this madness. Call them off and return to Domignon while you still can, Corym. If you hurt my sister, I promise you—you will not survive the day."

Despite his attempts to hide it, I could feel his fear when he shook his head, the tip of his blade digging into Lyrinn's throat. "I wouldn't dream of hurting her, Leta. I *need* her—or you. Either of you will still do as my wife. I don't care that you've each given your wretched bodies over to those ridiculous Fae. I *earned* you. You're mine. I'll take both of you, if I must—I'll imprison you in Domignon's dungeons, and you whores will give me heirs more powerful than any Fae High Lord who's ever lived. My father promised me as much when I was younger—it is what I've fought for all my life. I deserve it, damn it!"

I deserve it.

The sentiment was laughable.

For hundreds of years, even after he'd saved a realm from destruction, Thalanir had wandered the wilds of Kalemnar and Aetherion, telling himself he deserved nothing. And meanwhile, this pretender to the throne—this absolute *ass*—felt entitled not only to me, but to my sister?

"Do you know what's on this blade, Leta?" Corym asked, threatening to jab it deeper into Lyrinn's neck, to draw blood.

A shot of fear hit me when I saw the malice in his eyes.

"No," I confessed. "I don't."

"The poison of a Red Asp. A creature cursed with the Old Magic—a poison so potent that it cannot be cured by any healer. It can kill even the most powerful Fae within a minute, and believe me when I tell you I will happily kill your sister, if I must."

My hand gripped the hilt of the Blade of Dracrigh. I was no knife-thrower. I never had been. But I had to do *something*.

Thalanir, Lark—where are you?

"Please, let her go," I said, trying to mask my rage with the look of innocence I'd inflicted on Corym so often. "I'll do whatever it takes."

"I doubt that very much." The prince laughed. "But I'll tell you what—I'll give you a choice. I dislike both of you intensely. Still, I'll allow one of you to live, to be my wife. The other will die. You two can choose—but make it quick."

Lyrinn's eyes widened and I thought I spotted the slightest shake of her head.

Don't do it, Leta.

Do not do it.

"Kill me," I said, stepping forward and lowering the blade. "Let my sister go, and take me instead."

In the air, Kelduin let out a tormented cry, but I raised a hand. "Fly away," I told him, twisting around and drawing my face up to look at him. "Go. This won't end well, no matter what happens."

With another roar, he banked and flew off, disappearing into the distance.

"There," I said, turning to Corym and sheathing the blade. "There's no risk in releasing Lyrinn. Let her go, and you can take me."

But Corym *didn't* let her go.

Instead, the look of panic in his eyes only seemed to grow, his knuckles white as he grasped his blade.

"I don't believe you," he snarled. "You two are liars! I—"

"Prince Corym, son of Caedmon!"

The deep voice echoed against Fairholme's singed stone façade, spinning on the air like an angry wind.

Corym twisted his head around to see our grandfather striding toward him. Behind him, the battle was still raging in small pockets where spells flew through the air or men attacked Fae with futile strikes, gleaming swords in their hands.

"You will let my granddaughter go at once, Highness," Rynfael commanded.

"So that you can kill me?" Corym asked with a snicker. "I know what you are, Fae. I know how deceitful your kind is, High King of Immortals or not. You are dishonorable bastards, all of you."

"You have no right to discuss matters of honor," Rynfael said, glancing first at Lyrinn then at me. "Still, I will not kill you, Corym. My life is full after many long years of emptiness—and I do not want it to end with your murder. Come. Let her go, and take me instead. Think of the glory that comes with overpowering a High King."

He stood before Corym, his hands in the air as proof that he would not cast a spell—would not try to destroy the prince.

"Grandfather!" I shouted. "You don't know what he—"

I froze when a voice came to my mind then, deep and soothing. Rynfael's voice—one that had come to be a part of me in the short time since we had first met.

He is a proud, foolish boy, and I am a very fortunate Fae. This is the only way to save your sister—to save you. Lyrinn will make a fine queen. Help her when she needs it—it can be a lonely, difficult life.

"No!" I cried.

In a blur of frenzied movement, Corym shoved Lyrinn from him and hurled the poisoned blade at Rynfael's chest. It sank in deep, and the High King fell to his knees, landing hard on the ground.

Enraged, I shot a bolt of white light at the prince, but he had already leapt away, hiding once again like the coward that he was.

I raced over to my grandfather, crying out in despair as I collapsed next to him. In an instant, Lyrinn was next to me, tears cascading down her cheeks.

I held my hands over Rynfael's chest, calling to the light to heal him—begging for it. But he reached up weakly and took my wrists, pulling my hands away.

"There is no healing me," he said. "But you already know that."

"Why?" I asked. "Why did you let him..."

He smiled up at me. "I told you both already," he said, his voice thin and weak. "It's time the Dragon Court had a new name—and a new ruler. I am so tired, my girls, and I wish to see your grandmother again. I would have left the world years ago, were it not for the fact that I was waiting for you. Now that I've seen you, I am...so happy."

With those words, his head sank down, and his eyes closed.

I leapt to my feet, spinning around in search of the cowardly bastard of a prince.

"My Lady!"

The voice was Lark's. He was bloodied but in one piece, at least, when his eyes veered down to the High King's body. "What..."

Thalanir flew down a moment later, crying out as he crashed down and took the High King's head in his hands. Mithraan joined us after an instant, his head bowed as he stood to one side.

"We must heal him!" Lark shouted. "Someone must—"

But Mithraan shook his head. "Rynfael was always capable of healing himself, even against the most dire poisons," he said, his voice fractured. "He's the only Fae I've ever known who could do so. If he had wanted to...he would have."

In the distance, cries of pain and rage still filled the air. The battle was still going, though its din was fading slowly. Corym's army had no leader, and his men would soon realize they were risking their lives for a coward.

Lyrinn called out, "Where is the prince? He can't have gone far."

My head jerked up, a vision overtaking my mind.

"He's retreated," I said. "He's headed down the Onyx Stair to Dúnbar."

Something in the air changed in that moment, as if Corym's remaining forces had heard my words. The Fae who had been under the prince's command stopped fighting and backed away —and soon after, the mortals followed their lead.

As they slowly registered that their leader had fled, they followed, running for the Onyx Stair and away from Fairholme, leaving their weapons behind.

I stood up, my wings of flame spreading behind me. Thalanir stared at me, his eyes filled with wonder and worry combined.

"Leta," he said. "You can't..."

"I can," I replied. "And I will." With a look at Lyrinn, I added, "Are you coming with me, Sister?"

"Of course I am."

She took my hand and we shot into the air, hurtling toward the Rise.

CHAPTER FIFTY-ONE

As we soared down the Rise, I could see Corym's army fleeing into the distance. Many of them were already well beyond the town's gates, running with all their remaining strength.

They had torn Dúnbar apart in their haste, leaving broken windows and shattered façades in their wake, and my rage grew as I stared down at the near ruin of what had once been my hometown.

"Corym will slaughter his men if he ever tracks them down," Lyrinn said. "He'll call them deserters and hang the lot of them."

"He'll never get a chance," I replied, rage boiling in my veins. "I won't allow it."

Without looking, I knew my flesh was glowing orange, the fire stoking itself within me. I knew how terrifying I must have looked when I set down in the town's main square.

But not a single mortal in the gathered crowd turned toward Lyrinn or me. Every set of human eyes was focused on something at the square's center—something far more interesting, apparently, than a couple of Fae.

When we had concealed our wings and pushed our way

through the crowd, I spotted Corym, surrounded by angry townsfolk and cowering on the cobbles like a frightened child.

Why is he afraid of mortals? I wondered, pulling my eyes up to take in the gathered crowd.

"What's happening?" I whispered to Lyrinn, who shook her head.

"I'm your prince!" Corym cried. "Your leader! You can't do this to me!"

In response, a woman in a gray apron hurled a rock at him, hitting him squarely in the back.

Corym rose to her feet and rounded on her, ire in his eyes. I could feel him trying and failing to take her mind—to bend her to his will.

"How are they fighting off his spell?" I asked under my breath. "Why are they..."

Lyrinn nodded toward a figure tucked between two shops— a male in a black robe, his hood pulled down over his features. "I suspect the answer lies with him."

When the figure stepped out from his hiding spot and lowered his hood, I understood.

I had never known Erildir well—not as Lyrinn had. I had never been witness to his power. But I could feel it now, pulsing on the air as he adeptly turned the small force of mortals against their prince using the same mind-bending spell that Corym had employed so many times to subdue enemy and ally alike.

As it turned out, the prince was no match for a Spell-Master intent on proving his loyalty to the Fae who wielded the Blade of Dracrigh.

"We know what you did!" a man cried out, leaping forward and kicking Corym in the stomach. "Burning our mortal towns and blaming the Fae for it! You think we're fools?"

Corym lunged at him, his eyes glowing with the sort of

emotion I had only ever seen in the irises of Fae. But just as he was about to reach the man, something stopped him in his tracks and his body went rigid. He doubled over in pain, falling to the ground.

I looked over at Erildir, but his eyes weren't on Corym.

Instead, they were locked on Lyrinn.

It was my sister who had brought the prince to his knees.

"I want him dead," she muttered between clenched teeth. "I want him to suffer for what he's done to so many."

Corym looked drunk now—dirty, disheveled, stumbling around as he tried to push himself to his feet again. Every citizen of Dúnbar watched in amusement, not an ounce of fear or sympathy in their eyes even as he shrieked at them.

"My father is dying, and I will soon be king! You *must obey me!*"

"Why, exactly, is your father dying?" Erildir's smooth voice cut through the cacophony around us. He stepped toward the prince, taking him by the collar of his tunic and yanking him close. "Tell them why—and be honest, now."

Corym shook his head. "He..." he stammered. "He fell ill on the Kingsroad. That's all."

"Your Poison-Master would beg to differ," Erildir said, flicking a hand into the air. "Wouldn't he?"

"No! I—"

But it was too late.

Every mortal in Dúnbar now knew Corym was using this makeshift, false war—this unruly battle of his—to try and assume control over all of Kalemnar. He had tried to draw the realms' eyes away from his dying father while he stole the throne from under him.

I had no love for Caedmon. But his son was worse—and I wanted Corym dead now, more than ever.

But before he died, I wanted him *humiliated.*

Slowly, I stepped toward him.

"What are you doing?" Lyrinn hissed.

"Giving Corym what he wants," I told her.

"I know you," a man called Julius—an old friend of my father's—called when I had stepped up to the prince. "You're Leta Martel. And Lyrinn...goodness me, you girls have changed."

I smiled at him, nodding. "I *am* Leta Martel," I replied, pulling my eyes back to Corym. "And when I was a girl, I wanted to marry a prince. I still do."

His eyes red with emotion and exhaustion, Corym reached a hand out for me, and I took it.

"Leta," he moaned. "We can make this work, you and I. I know we can. Tell them—tell them you love me!"

I could feel him digging into my mind, pushing his way inside it. Trying once again to control me, to steer my emotions and my thoughts to suit his needs.

Just once, I allowed it. I threw open the doors to my mind, and when I welcomed him inside, he offered up a smile of such relief that I almost embraced him.

For the first time in weeks, I saw before me the Corym I had known in the palace, the one I once thought I loved. He was handsome, kind, charming.

For a moment, I felt myself giving into his false charm.

"Do you still want me, your Highness?" I asked softly, laying a hand on his scarred cheek.

"Of course," he said, laughing as he wiped a tear away. He glanced around at the hostile crowd as if to say, *You see? I'm not so bad.* "I've always wanted you, Leta. I...I...*love* you. You just forgot—that's all."

Murmurs rose up around us from confused townspeople.

"Leta," Lyrinn warned from behind me. "Don't listen to his lies."

"It's all right, Sister," I replied over my shoulder. "He's right. I've been so confused—I've been lost. I thought I was meant to be with an Immortal, so I fled from Corym. But I was a fool. I see now how strong he is. How mighty. *He* is the one I am meant to marry. He's the *only* one for me."

For a moment, Corym looked skeptical. But when he tried to delve still deeper into my mind, I allowed him in, welcoming him with open arms.

Yes, I thought. *Come and see my plans—come and see the beauty of the future unfolding before us both.*

I showed him my thoughts, my dreams. Children laughing and playing on vast, exquisite palace grounds. Fae and humans living together in harmony. My smiling, happy face, fiery wings spread behind me.

I knew without asking that Corym could feel the truth in the vision—he knew he was seeing everything I wanted, assembled in that brief moment.

"Yes, I see it," he whispered, and all around us, townspeople exchanged baffled looks. "I want it, too, my darling Leta."

I smiled, casting my eyes to the sky above Dúnbar's rooftops just as Kelduin rose up, his wings beating slowly, his piercing eyes focused squarely on the prince. Smoke rose from his nostrils, a look of rage on his terrifying features.

"Do you really want it?" I asked, pulling Corym close. "Because the thing is..." I kissed his cheek, then whispered into his ear, "Those visions of the future—the dreams of a perfect life that you just saw?"

"Yes?" he replied, shaking with relief.

"You're not in any of them. That is not your palace—those are *not* your children..." I shoved him hard and he stumbled backwards, shock in his eyes. I snarled, nodding once to my ally in the sky. "And you are no king."

The dragon shot a bolt of pure white flame at the prince, so searing hot that he didn't even have time to cry out in pain.

In an instant, what remained of Corym was falling to the ground in a pile of black ash.

When the townspeople cheered, I thought at first that it was because they were still under Erildir's spell, taken in by his brand of deceit.

But the Sidhfae, as it turned out, was nowhere to be seen.

Behind me, I heard Lyrinn expel a breath—one of relief, of shock, of every emotion conceivable.

"You had me going," she said, grabbing hold of my arm and turning me to face her.

"I needed you to think he'd taken me in," I told her. "I needed you to believe he'd turned me—so that he would believe it, too."

Together, Kelduin and I had murdered a prince.

The feeling sank into me like a stone. Guilt swirled inside me, alongside a deep fear of what I may have just become.

Fear that I had enjoyed it just a little too much.

But when a set of powerful arms wrapped themselves around me from behind, every ounce of that fear disintegrated in the blink of an eye.

I exhaled, Thalanir's scent enveloping me, calming me—reminding me of who I was.

"It's done, Lahnan," he whispered. "It's over. You have done the impossible—and your grandfather would be proud."

"Thank you." I nodded, and with tears in my eyes, looked up once more at Kelduin, who was still hovering above the town, his wings beating at the air.

I told you that you were free, I told him. *Yet you stayed. Why?*

~Because he needed to die—and though fire courses through your blood, Princess, you are no killer. You could have used the Blade

of Dracrigh to take his life, but you had used it once—to save me. I didn't wish to mar it with the blood of a traitor.

"Go," I mouthed with a half-smile, raising a hand to bid him farewell. "And thank you."

I could have asked him to stay with me. I could have remained the Fae who controlled a dragon—who inspired fear in all others. But I had never wanted such a fate.

After seeking attention all my life...all I wanted now was peace and quiet.

Kelduin had given me my wings, and for that, I would always be grateful.

For ending Corym's life, the Five Realms of Kalemnar would be grateful, too—and it was with mixed feelings that I turned back to the citizens of Dúnbar, took my sister by the hand, and, with my voice breaking, cried out.

"The High King of Tíria is dead! Long live Queen Lyrinn!"

EPILOGUE

High King Rynfael's funeral was held in the Dragon Court the day after the Battle of Fairholme.

It was, unsurprisingly, a solemn affair—though Lyrinn and I managed a few smiles through our tears as the Fae who had known our grandfather recounted tales of exploits in his younger years.

Rynfael, it seemed, had always been kind and good. Through heartbreak, he had shielded his people when the Mist had descended on his realm—and he had provided food and shelter to those who had lost loved ones to the Grimpers. When the Mist had fallen, he had helped to rebuild the beautiful land that had been forsaken for so long.

After the funeral, I used the Blade of Dracrigh one last time to open a portal for Erildir to return to his distant home.

"I—we," I told him cautiously, "appreciate what you did for Dúnbar's mortals and all of Kalemnar."

Thanks to him, word had spread quickly of Corym's subterfuge and lies, which meant mortals' acceptance of the Fae in their midst had come more easily than we ever could have hoped.

With a quick apology to Lyrinn, Erildir had disappeared through the portal, and I had sealed it shut behind him with another swipe of the blade—which was now locked in a vault deep inside the Dragon Court's Keep.

It was Lyrinn's coronation, a fortnight after the High King's death, that drew the greatest number of Fae to the North. Many had already heard her name after what she'd done in the Broken Lands—though she insisted quietly that it was Lark who deserved the credit for saving the world from the Elar's presence.

"I would never accept so much attention," Lark had told her with a wince. "There's a reason I thrive on invisibility, my Queen."

The coronation was a grand affair, held in the city square below the palace. Every resident of the Dragon Court was in attendance, as well as Tírian High Fae from every corner of the realm.

King Caedmon had succumbed to the poison Corym's servant had administered, and with no heir, Kalemnar's mortal realms were without a leader. The lords and ladies of the realms had signed a letter that stated their intention to recognize Queen Lyrinn as their sovereign—a High Fae who had lived as a mortal most of her life.

Who better, the letter had asked, *to bring all the realms together for the first time in over a thousand years?*

Dressed in elegant outfits of white and silver at the coronation, Lyrinn and Mithraan were more beautiful than any two Fae I had ever seen, their wings on full display as Alaric and Khiral placed the silver crowns atop their heads.

There was little doubt in my mind they would make a splendid queen and king—they were fair and kind, and above all, determined to unite mortals and Fae for the first time in many centuries.

After the ceremony had ended, when I found myself standing aside and watching the guests leave with joy filling their hearts, Lyrinn approached me.

I smiled, gesturing with raised eyebrows to her delicate silver crown.

"It's ridiculous, I know," she said.

"No, it's not. It suits you in a way I would never have imagined in a thousand years," I assured her. "I mean it. I may once have been the little girl who fancied myself a princess—but you were always more noble. More..." I searched my mind for the proper turn of phrase. "More *good*."

"Gooder."

"I don't think that's a word."

"I'm the Queen," Lyrinn snickered, raising her chin haughtily. "I hereby decree that it is."

I chuckled, then let out a sigh. "I should probably tell you that I'm going to ask Thalanir to come with me on a trip. Lark wants to go home, and I thought perhaps we should escort him."

Lyrinn's eyes widened with surprise. "Really? To Aetherion? Are you sure you want to do that?"

I hesitated for a moment, then said, "I'm sure."

"You do realize—" she began, but stopped herself when she saw my face. "Yes. Of course you do."

Nodding, I replied, "I know Kazimir is there. It's precisely why I want to go." I glanced over at Thalanir, decked out as he was in an elegant uniform of blue and silver. "Our grandfather is gone, after we only ever had a brief taste of him. Our mother...

gone. Martel, too. We have only one parent left, and I'd like to know him a little."

"He's not much of a parent," Lyrinn cautioned. "Is there such a thing as an anti-parent? Because if so, that's Kazimir."

I drew in a breath. "I know. I don't expect warmth or hugs. But I want to meet him, regardless. Word has it he's called the Priestesses of the Order back to Aetherion to punish them—as well as any Lightbloods disloyal enough to have teamed up with Corym. Whether or not he's a good father, he's making an effort to lead his realm in the right direction. I suppose I just... want to find out where we came from. Does that make me sound utterly mad?"

"Yes," Lyrinn replied. "But I understand."

As she spoke, Thalanir stepped up beside me, slipping an arm around my waist and kissing the top of my head. I soaked in the sensation, letting out a deep breath as I sank into him.

My mate. My everything.

Never had I felt so safe, so protected...and so strong, all at the same time.

"What are you two discussing so secretly over here?" Thalanir asked.

"Whether or not it's folly for me to meet my blood-father," I told him. "And we both agree that it is, but I'm planning to do it anyhow." Twisting to look him in the eye, I said, "If you'll come with me."

I could see the concern in Thal's expression, but he managed to subdue it and nod. "I would follow you to the edge of the world, Lahnan. You know that."

"Good. Then we'll leave by ship in the morning." Turning back to Lyrinn, I said, "I only have one thing to ask of our new queen."

"What's that?"

"If we're not back in two moons' time..."

"Yes?"

"Feel free to go to war against our jackass of a father."

The End

ALSO BY K. A. RILEY

If you're enjoying K. A. Riley's books, please consider leaving a review on Amazon or Goodreads to let your fellow book-lovers know about it.

Dystopian Books:

The Cure Chronicles:

The Cure

Awaken

Ascend

Fallen

Reign

Resistance Trilogy:

Recruitment

Render

Rebellion

Emergents Trilogy:

Survival

Sacrifice

Synthesis

Transcendent Trilogy:

Travelers

Transfigured

Terminus

Academy of the Apocalypse Series:

Emergents Academy

Cult of the Devoted

Army of the Unsettled

The Ravenmaster Chronicles:

Arise

Banished

Crusade

Apocalypchix | Lock Down | Final Exam

Thrall | Broken | Queen

<u>Fantasy Books</u>

Seeker's Series:

Seeker's World

Seeker's Quest

Seeker's Fate

Seeker's Promise

Seeker's Hunt

Seeker's Prophecy (Coming Soon!)

To be informed of future releases, and for occasional chances to win free swag, books, and other goodies, please sign up here:

https://karileywrites.org/#subscribe

Follow K. A. Riley on TikTok: @karileywrites

K.A. Riley's Bookbub Author Page

K.A. Riley on Amazon.com

K.A. Riley on Goodreads.com

COMING SOON: THE AMNESTY GAMES

They're getting played to death.

Every year, one hundred of the most dangerous convicted criminals from the impoverished Ward are given a chance to earn their freedom and to live a life of luxury in Nova Heights, the walled-in city of glass and steel estates built into the side of a mountain.

All that's standing between the Hopefuls and a full pardon are the Amnesty Games, a seven-day barrage of challenges, puzzles, mazes, traps, obstacles, contests, and competitions.

The games are wild, dangerous, and beamed by satellite onto every crumbling surface of the Ward where they are enjoyed by thousands of rowdy fans.

This electrifying global phenomenon makes World Cup football hooliganism look like a church picnic.

In an added twist, at the Usurper Stage of the Amnesty Games, some of the Hopefuls are digitally "taken over" by selected Warders, who get to compete as avatars for the chance to win medicine, food, and water rations for themselves and for their families.

As trained warriors and defenders of Nova Heights, seventeen-year-old Alora and her team of Hawkers are assigned to *oppose* the Hopefuls in their quest for amnesty. Alora is confident in herself, in her team, and in the importance of the games for the ongoing stability of the elite members of Nova Heights.

But what happens when buried secrets are revealed and the two sides stop playing the game by the same rules?

Pre-order on Amazon until the release date: ***Amnesty Games***

COMING SOON: THRALL

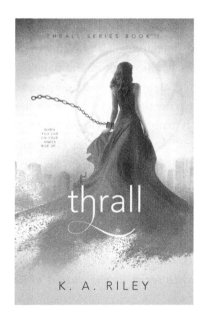

In the realm of Kravan, children of lower-class citizens are raised in a prison-like structure called "The Institution" from birth until adulthood. Known as the Thralled, their powers reveal themselves around the time of their eighteenth birthday.

Every year, the Thralled who are tested and deemed harmless are chosen to leave the Institution and join the outside world as servants to the ruling class. Epics—those who are considered threats for their destructive powers—are sent away. Though none of the Thralled know for sure, they have long suspected that the Epics are killed by the Elite.

Rell has spent her entire life in the Institution, longing for the day she will be chosen to leave. She's always been certain her powers would be minimal just as her mother's were, and that she would be assigned to a life of simply servitude. However, as she nears her eighteenth birthday, she begins to fear the worst. The powers that have begun churning inside her are anything but harmless, and if the truth comes to light, she faces a grim fate at the hands of the ruling class.

When a handsome and wealthy young man visits the Institution and invites her to work in the palace's kitchens, she's ecstatic...but when a mysterious fellow worker offers her an opportunity to attend the annual Elites' Ball and to see their world for what it truly is, she begins to learn an ugly truth about the divisions between the ruling class and the Tethered.

After a life spent in near-isolation, Rell must now learn to distinguish friend from foe, and to decide if her new allies are who they claim to be...

or if they will turn out to be her greatest enemies.

Thrall is based on the fairy tale Cinderella, the first in a new Dystopian Romance series by the author of Recruitment and The Cure.

Pre-order on Amazon until its 2023 release: ***Thrall***

ABOUT THE AUTHOR

As a writer of Adult and New Adult fantasy and dystopian fiction, K. A. Riley is dedicated to creating worlds just different enough from our own to be entertaining, intriguing, and a little frightening all at once.

For Riley, writing isn't a job or even a hobby. It's a playground where readers can scamper around, giggling, gasping, and freaking out to their hearts' content until one of the bigger kids comes along and pushes them off the swings, thus injuring their knee, their pride, and destroying what could otherwise have been a very promising metaphor.

* * *

Stay in touch with K. A. Riley

Website: https://karileywrites.org/

K.A. Riley's Bookbub Author Page

K.A. Riley on Amazon.com

K.A. Riley on Goodreads.com

on TikTok: @karileywrites

To be informed of future releases, and for occasional chances to win free swag, books, and other goodies, please sign up here:

https://karileywrites.org/#subscribe

Printed in Great Britain
by Amazon

38413164R00239